## About the Author

Pauline Lawless is from Dublin and now lives in Belgium and spends winters in Florida. She is the bestselling author of six previous novels: *Because We're Worth It, If The Shoes Fit, A Year Like No Other, Behind Every Cloud, Birthday Girls,* and *Meet and Delete.*

For more information on these books visit her author page on Amazon *www.amazon.com/paulinelawless* and *www.amazon.co.uk/paulinelawless*

# all at sea

## pauline lawless

POOLBEG

Published 2017
by Poolbeg Press Ltd.
123 Grange Hill, Baldoyle,
Dublin 13, Ireland
Email: poolbeg@poolbeg.com

1

A catalogue record for this book is available from the British Library.

ISBN 978-1-78199-242-5

Printed and bound by
CPI Group (UK) Ltd, Croydon, CR0 4YY

www.poolbeg.com

*To all my loyal readers. Thank you for sticking with me for the past ten years.*

# Chapter 1

Fiona McElroy was dressed in a royal-blue, silk-jersey evening dress as she sat at her dressing-table, fingering her jewellery. She lifted the glittering diamond-and-sapphire necklace and bracelet and then the simple silver collar and cuff, unable to decide which set to wear.

"Honey, could you spare me a minute?" she called to her husband, Gavin, who was also getting ready.

"Sure," he replied, coming into the dressing room.

Although they'd been married for two years, she still felt a frisson of excitement every time she saw him. Tonight, he looked sexier than ever in his tux and dress shirt. Their eyes met in the mirror and she smiled at him as he kissed the top of her head.

"I can't decide which jewellery to wear. What do you think?"

"Hmm . . . I guess the sapphire-and-diamond set would be more suitable with that dress and I know it would please my mother if you wore it."

1

"You're right, as usual," she said with a grimace. "I still can't get used to wearing jewels like these. They're not really me. But I suppose, since it was a wedding present from your mother, I should wear it."

"That's my girl! You know how she is," he said, putting the necklace around her neck. "The more bling the better and it does match the blue of your eyes exactly."

Fiona saw it was true. The sapphires did emphasise the deep blue of her eyes.

"You look beautiful tonight," he said huskily as he fastened the necklace for her.

She rose to face him and pulled him close, inhaling the familiar aftershave he wore.

"I love you," she whispered as she reached up to kiss him.

"Even though I have a mother who insists we dress up in this ridiculous formal gear just for a dinner party?" he asked, scowling. Gavin was much more a jeans and open-necked-shirt guy. "How I hate wearing these monkey suits!"

Fiona laughed. "Bunny is Bunny. I sometimes think she fancies herself as Lady Grantham from *Downton Abbey*."

"You said it. I wouldn't be surprised if she'd hired Carson for the night." Gavin sighed. "Now you can do something for me." He handed her his bow tie.

She fastened the tie for him, then, picking up her evening bag, took one last look in the mirror. "I hope I pass your mother's scrutiny tonight."

"You look ravishing, regardless of what my mother may think. To be honest, I'd much rather be taking that dress off you and carrying you to bed right now."

"It'll have to wait," she said with a laugh. "That must be the taxi at the door. Let's go. Bunny will never forgive us if we're late."

"I suppose," he said with a resigned air. "But later, I promise."

As they drove to Ballsbridge Fiona thought how amazing it was that she and Gavin had found each other at all, since they had mixed in very different social circles. She came from a modest background and had grown up in Santry on the north side of Dublin. Gavin, by contrast, came from a privileged wealthy family and had grown up on the south side. The rivalry between Northsiders and Southsiders was as old as Dublin itself and jokes ridiculing each other were commonplace.

Fiona had excelled at school and won a university scholarship, without which her parents could not have afforded to pay for a university education. She had opted for a degree in Physical Education at Limerick University because her passion was sports and she adored children and wanted to teach. She had graduated with first-class honours and then been offered a teaching position in one of the best girls' schools in Dublin, on the south side. She'd found she loved the job. She'd also worked two nights a week as a trainer at the local gym, in exchange for free membership. She had shared a house with three of her teaching colleagues in nearby Donnybrook. All her hard work had paid off and six months later, when she met the man of her dreams, her world was complete.

Gavin, on the other hand, had been born with a silver spoon in his mouth. His father, Richard, had founded Security Solutions in the days before anyone worried about security. A brilliant businessman, it was now the largest security company in Ireland with offices in all the major cities and towns. Gavin was a director of the company and poised to take over the business when his father retired. *If* his workaholic father ever retired.

He had led a charmed life and coasted through his school years, due to the fact that he was an all-rounder at sports and a brilliant rugby player. Thanks to his handsome blond looks and his rugby prowess, he had no problem attracting girls but he'd lost count of all the women he'd dated as none of them had ever lasted very long. Until Fiona. For Gavin, it was love at first sight.

"What do you think could be the big surprise Bunny says she has in store for us?" Fiona asked him as they neared his parents' house.

"God only knows! But, knowing my mother, it's bound to be something dramatic."

Fiona laughed. "Do you think it's anything to do with Christmas?"

Bunny had invited them to spend Christmas in Ballsbridge. Since Fiona's parents were spending it in Florida with her older sister, she had been quite happy to accept.

"We'll know soon enough," Gavin replied as the taxi pulled up at the McElroy mansion.

Fiona remembered how terrified she'd been the first time Gavin had taken her to meet his parents. She'd been awestruck by the lavish house which was situated on the most prestigious tree-lined avenue in Dublin. She'd also found his very glamorous mother intimidating. Bunny was in her fifties but could have passed for forty. She had been a model in her day and was still beautiful and incredibly stylish. She wore her hair in a honey-blonde bob and her silky-smooth skin had a year-round golden glow. Always perfectly groomed, with make-up expertly applied, she was the quintessential high-maintenance woman.

Bunny had hit the jackpot when she'd met and married the wealthy Richard, who had been happy to indulge her taste for designer clothes and jewellery. Although many people had thought it was his money that had attracted her, nothing was further from the truth. Bunny loved her husband deeply and their marriage was still strong thirty-three years on. Richard was a gentle, kind man but despite Bunny's high-handed ways it soon became obvious to Fiona that *he* was very much the boss and Bunny knew just where to draw the line.

Gavin's mother had several suitable – as in 'well-connected' girls in mind as potential brides for Gavin and he'd faced a lot of opposition from her when he announced that he had asked Fiona to marry him. It was Richard who had put his foot down and welcomed her into the family with open arms. Bunny had no choice but to follow suit. As it turned out, she now accepted that Fiona was indeed the perfect wife for her son.

Gavin liked the simple life, to the chagrin of his mother who enjoyed being a leading light on the Dublin social scene. He took after his father and shunned what he considered her artificial lifestyle. His mother's histrionics had regularly embarrassed him growing up and he often found it difficult to keep his cool with her fanciful ideas like this very formal dinner party tonight. He would have been much happier to be having a simple family dinner around the kitchen table.

Fiona always made a special effort when she had to meet her mother-in-law but resisted all Bunny's efforts to be drawn into her social circle with their various charity lunches and dinners. Gavin supported Fiona in this, despite his mother's many entreaties. They were happy living a normal life and had no interest in all that Dublin razzmatazz or being photographed for the social magazines, unlike Bunny who lapped it up.

"Darlings, welcome!" Bunny greeted them as they entered the drawing room. She kissed them both and stood back to scrutinise Fiona from head to toe. "You look lovely, my dear," she said. "I'm happy to see you're wearing the sapphires I gave you. They lift the simplicity of your dress."

Fiona caught the amused look Gavin gave her.

"You look beautiful, honey," said Richard as he kissed his daughter-in-law. "I think your dress is perfect." He threw his wife a warning glance.

"Yes, of course. Simplicity always looks good on the young," Bunny back-tracked.

She herself was wearing a long silver gown embellished with crystals which sparkled as she moved. Diamonds added to the dazzle. Bunny could never be accused of simplicity.

"I've asked Sarah to come early too but that's no guarantee she will," she said in an exasperated voice. She and her youngest daughter did not always see eye to eye.

Sarah was nineteen years old and a student at Trinity College though 'student' was a bit of a misnomer. She was more a party-girl there as she partied much more than studied. Fiona and Gavin had tried talking to her but it was a waste of time. Her sole ambition was to have a good time and then marry a rich man who would keep her in the style to which she had become accustomed – just as her older sister Jess had done. In the meantime, Sarah spent her time shopping, partying and mixing with the right social set. She took after her mother more than Bunny was prepared to admit.

6

There was no Carson to attend them but as always Bunny had her usual firm of caterers booked for the evening and a young waiter poured them some champagne.

"*Hmmm* . . . Cristal? What's the special occasion?" Gavin asked as he took a sip.

"I'll tell you when Sarah gets here," Bunny replied, looking at her Patek Philippe watch in annoyance.

Gavin, at thirty-one, was the eldest of her three children and very much his father's son. He'd been an easy-going, gentle child who'd lived for sports and had never given them a day's worry. Jessica, who was twenty-nine now, had also been an ideal child. As beautiful as her mother, she became a highly successful model like her. To Bunny's delight she had married an English aristocrat and now lived in a beautiful home in Kensington, London.

Bunny had considered she had the perfect family – two beautiful blond children and a loving husband – but then, when Jess was ten, along came Sarah. Bunny didn't know what had hit her. No model child this. Sarah turned out to be exceedingly naughty and high-spirited. At the age of two she had learned how to throw tantrums and stamp her foot to get her own way. She was an exceptionally beautiful child who could look and behave like an angel whenever she chose.

Despite her behaviour, they all adored her with the exception of Jess who felt displaced by this intruder. She felt Sarah had stolen her brother and parents' affections. As she got older Sarah grew tired of being compared to the perfect Jess so the two had never really become friends and bickered with each other constantly. Bunny had hoped that Sarah would also become a model – she certainly had the looks and figure for it – but her younger daughter obstinately refused to consider it. From the age of fourteen she was getting offers from model agencies but had turned them all down.

"That's like too much bloody hard work," she'd remarked, pleased to see her mother squirm at her bad language.

Instead, on leaving school, she'd opted to go to Trinity because all her friends were going there and she'd heard the social life was brilliant. She enrolled to study art history although she had absolutely no interest in it whatsoever. The older she got, the more she and her mother were at loggerheads with each other. They were too alike.

Twenty minutes late, Sarah walked into the party accompanied by a good-looking boy who Gavin had not met before. Sarah changed boyfriends more often than most people changed their bed-linen. It was not surprising that she attracted them like bees to a honey-pot. She was very beautiful with deep-brown eyes that were ringed with long curling dark lashes which she used to great effect. They seemed at odds with her long white-blonde hair which was her natural colour – not dyed – or even highlighted. It hung like a silk curtain half-way down her back.

She was almost a clone of Bunny – tall and shapely with tanned legs that seemed to go on forever which she made sure people noticed by wearing very short skirts or short shorts. Tonight she was wearing a long red-satin dress which clung to her curves, with a slit almost up to her crotch. It was low-cut in front and at the back with lots of tanned skin on show. It was very glamorous and would not have looked out of place on the Oscars Red Carpet.

"You're here," Bunny greeted her coldly. "Late, as usual. And do you have to show quite so much flesh?"

"Mummy, for goodness sake! Come into the twenty-first century. Where's the champagne?"

Bunny beckoned to the waiter to pour it and let out a long sigh. Her daughter was incorrigible. Of course, it was partly her own fault. She and Richard had spoilt her dreadfully.

Sarah introduced her date. "This is Tarquin Spencer-Churchill. Tarki is at Trinity too. He's from London."

They all shook hands and the change in Bunny's attitude was immediate as she took the young man's arm, quizzing him about his family, in the hope that he was related to Princess Diana. Wouldn't that be something! Gavin raised his eyebrows and made a face at Fiona. It was all she could do not to laugh out loud. Bunny was so transparent.

"Give over, Mummy," Sarah said in annoyance as she drained her glass in one go. She signalled to the waiter to refill it. "Now what's this surprise you have for us?"

"Okay, everyone," said Bunny. "Dad and I have decided that as we're all spending Christmas together we should do something special and glamorous . . . so . . ." she paused dramatically as they looked at her expectantly, "we're taking you all to Florida and then on a Caribbean cruise for Christmas and the New Year! *Voilà!*" And she threw her hands in the air in a grand gesture.

They all looked at her open-mouthed.

"Are you serious?" Gavin asked.

"Deadly," replied Bunny.

"We're not going on that huge ship *Harmony of the Seas*, are we?" Fiona asked nervously. The two most terrifying films Fiona had ever seen were *Titanic* and *The*

*Poseidon Adventure*. They'd both scared the hell out of her. "I've read all about it – it's the largest ship in the world the size of four football pitches and it caters for almost 7000 passengers." She shuddered. "It doesn't bear thinking of what would happen if it were to sink with that many on board."

"Fiona, do I look like the kind of person who would travel on a ship with 7000 passengers?" Bunny demanded, her voice sharp.

"Definitely not! Much too low-class for Mummy." Sarah sniggered, swishing her long blonde hair back.

Bunny glared at her. "We'll be sailing with one of the most upmarket cruise-lines on the market. It's French and the food is superb. We travelled to French Polynesia with them five years ago, and it was wonderful. Wasn't it, Richard?" She appealed to her husband for confirmation.

He didn't disappoint. "Yes, indeed, dear."

"There will be less than seven hundred passengers on board so you need have no fear, Fiona. It will be a wonderful experience for us all."

Fiona knew better than to say more. One didn't argue with Bunny once her mind was made up. It was a fait accompli and it looked like they would be spending Christmas sunning themselves in the Caribbean.

Gavin wasn't too happy about it. "I can't be away from the office that long," he complained to his father.

"Nonsense! You know how we Irish are," Richard replied. "There'll be no business done from the week before Christmas until after the 6<sup>th</sup> of January – except for drinking and socialising. Anyway, you've been working far too hard – you've earned a break and it will be nice to have the family together for two weeks."

Gavin didn't think that spending two weeks on a ship with his mother and sister would be much of a break. "Do you think it's a good idea for us to be cooped up together for two weeks?" he asked apprehensively.

"We won't be cooped up," his father assured him. "You can all do your own thing and there'll be other passengers on the ship to mingle with."

"Will Jess be joining us?" Gavin asked.

"Of course not," Bunny answered. "She and Philip go skiing in Gstaad every Christmas with Philip's family."

While Gavin was not sure that spending two weeks with the family was such a great idea, Sarah was even less so.

"Cruising is for old people," she whined. "I don't want to be locked up with a load of old fogies and miss all the fun here with my friends."

"Actually, Sarah, cruising has changed," Tarquin intervened in his modulated English accent. "I went on a cruise with my parents two years ago and it was jolly good fun."

"Really?" She sounded doubtful.

"Yes. And Dublin can be awfully dull because most of our crowd go home for Christmas anyway."

Bunny had an idea. "Would you consider joining us, Tarquin?" she asked him sweetly, giving him her full thousand-watt mega-smile. "As our guest, of course. It would be great for Sarah to have a friend along."

"That's very kind of you, Mrs McElroy. Are you sure you want me to?"

"Would you really come, Tarki?" Sarah asked breathlessly. "It would be sheer hell there with all those old people." She ignored the way her mother glowered at this.

"I'd love to come. We go to our country house every

year for Christmas but it's all hunting and shooting which I hate. This will be a lot more fun than mingling with the old dears in my family. Most of them are deaf and I spend half my time shouting at them."

"From all that shooting no doubt." Bunny beamed at him.

"That's settled then," Richard said. "Let's drink a toast to a wonderful Christmas in the sunny Caribbean!"

They all raised their glasses and once more Sarah drained hers in one go. Bunny frowned at her again.

Oh boy, this is going to be some Christmas, Fiona thought.

"Dear me, look at the time," Bunny exclaimed, glancing at her watch. "If you'll excuse us. Our other guests are due any minute" She smiled at Tarquin. "So happy you'll be joining us, dear boy."

"I'll look forward to it."

"He may regret accepting," Gavin muttered to Fiona under his breath. "God, this will be a weird Christmas!"

"But an awfully jolly one," she whispered, mimicking Tarquin.

He laughed aloud. "It will be different. I grant you that."


The evening continued, with Bunny regaling her friends with her plans for the cruise. Much to her annoyance, Sarah and Tarquin made a quick getaway after the main course. It had been quite a coup for Bunny when Jess had married Philip whose family were close friends of the Royal Family. And now her youngest daughter was dating a Spencer-Churchill no less! Bunny basked in the envious looks of her friends.

Gavin and Fiona couldn't wait to make their getaway. They did so after dessert.

"Phew! I'm not sure I'll survive two weeks of that," Gavin remarked as they waited in the foyer for their taxi.

"Don't worry – as your dad said, there will be enough space on the ship to escape and besides we'll be meeting lots of other people."

She had never been on a cruise before and now that she knew they were not sailing on the 7000 monster she began to feel quite excited about the whole thing.

Gavin was a lot more apprehensive. He had a bad feeling about this trip.

# Chapter 2

Across the country in Galway, another family were planning to take the same cruise. Ann Kenny was excited about spending Christmas without having to cook and entertain. She was the eldest of seven siblings who descended with their families in droves every Christmas to spend the holiday with them, as she was the only one still living in Galway. Their excuse was that they wanted to spend Christmas with their mother who lived in the gate lodge of the Kennys' large Georgian house. The reality was that they enjoyed the hospitality afforded to them by their sister and her family. The previous Christmas, Ann had been absolutely exhausted by the time the last of them had left on New Year's Day.

Her husband, Tony, had started out as a small auctioneer in Galway and through his business acumen had succeeded in becoming the largest property developer in the west of Ireland. He subsequently expanded to the rest of the country and was now quite wealthy. Just recently he had closed a very lucrative deal in Dublin and decided it was time they enjoyed Christmas without his wife's family taking over their house yet again. Let Ann's brothers and sisters organise their own Christmas for a change. He knew his children – Jack who was twenty-one and Emily nineteen – would be pleased to have a Christmas without numerous aunts, uncles and cousins swarming around the house.

Ann had always hankered to go on a cruise after seeing the *The Loveboat* so when Tony spotted the offer online for a Christmas Caribbean cruise he went ahead and booked it.

But when he told his wife what he'd done she was appalled.

"What about my family? If we go we'll disappoint them!" she wailed.

"Tough shit! It's about time they catered for themselves for a change." Tony was a self-made man and proud of it but he was also forceful and aggressive, even with his wife.

Ann shook her head. "They come here every year. How can I possibly tell them we don't want them this year? They'll have a fit."

"Frankly, my dear, I don't *give* a damn how you tell them. Just do it!"

Ann knew he wouldn't budge. Whenever he used that *Gone with the Wind* expression he meant business. He was as determined as Rhett Butler any day. She put her hands to her face, trying to take it in.

"I thought you've always wanted to go on a cruise?" he asked.

"I have," she replied, "but not at Christmas. I don't know how I'll break the news to my family."

"You'll find a way," he said with a sigh. His wife's

timidity and lack of backbone got on his nerves. The fact that his bullying over twenty-two years was what cowed her was lost on him.

He told the children that night over dinner.

"Isn't cruising only for old people?" Jack asked.

"No, that was in the old days. Things have changed. Look at this website." Tony handed over his iPad. "They cater for young people now. There's a gym and disco and lots of activities, plus a cinema and shows. We'll have a great time."

Jack wasn't convinced. He was in his final year of engineering at Galway University but although he had passed his exams every year he had little interest in it. He was much more interested in music and dedicated to the rock band he had formed with some friends four years previously. More than anything he wanted to make music his career.

Emily was in her second year of law at the same university and had gained top marks in her first-year exam. She had a bright future ahead of her. She was a shy girl whereas Jack was outgoing and extrovert, and Ann often wondered how she could have produced two such differing offspring.

"I thought it would be nice to spend a week in Florida after the cruise. What do you think?" Tony asked.

That sealed it for Jack. "Brilliant!"

"That means we'll be there to celebrate your forty-fifth birthday!" Ann cried.

Tony glared at her. The last thing he wanted to do was even think that he would be turning forty-five. He dreaded getting older and didn't think it was a cause for celebration. However, Ann and her family had a thing about birthdays.

She'd thrown him a surprise party for his fortieth and he'd gone ape-shit. He'd warned her that he absolutely did not want a party this year. She could celebrate if she wanted to – he would be drowning his sorrows. He had hoped that by being in Florida his birthday might pass by unnoticed. Not by Ann obviously.

Emily was happy to go along with whatever her parents wanted.

"But what about your family at Christmas?" she asked her mother, a worried frown on her face.

"I guess they won't be too happy," Ann replied anxiously, "but your father has made his decision so that's that."

Her family were furious with her for cancelling Christmas as they put it.

"I'm not cancelling Christmas – I'm just not hosting it this year," Ann told her sister-in-law, Marie, in Dublin. "I've done it for over twenty years and I think it's time someone else took a turn."

"But we don't have a house as big as yours!" Marie whined.

"You'll manage. Between the three of you there you can put everyone up."

"But what about your mother?" Marie demanded. "Where will she stay?"

"That's up to you guys to decide between you. I invited her to come on the cruise with us but she declined."

"Well, I must say I think you're being very selfish. This is all Tony's doing. I know it."

"No, I –"

"He thinks because he has money that he can bully us

like he bullies you," Marie said spitefully and banged down the phone.

When Ann recounted this conversation to Tony over dinner that evening he was furious. She left out the bit about bullying of course.

"How dare she say you're selfish after all the years we've had them here?" he fumed. "She's the selfish one!"

"Yes, she never lifts a finger to help with the cooking or anything," Emily chimed in. "She doesn't even look after her own children. She expects me to do it even when I'm helping Mum in the kitchen."

"All Marie does is sit on her fat backside and knock back our wine," Jack added his bit.

"Ah now, no need for that," Ann admonished him. "Let's not be nasty."

"I still feel she's out of line. Calling you selfish, indeed!" insisted Tony. "I've a good mind to call her and tell her so."

"No, leave it, please," she begged, not wanting to cause a row. "Let's forget about her and just concentrate on our holiday."

"You're much too soft, Ann. I really wish you'd be more assertive. You let them walk all over you," said Tony irritably.

It had always been a bone of contention between them.

The cruise was two weeks away and back in Dublin Fiona asked Bunny what she would need to wear for the trip. She had some nice bikinis and cover-ups from Penneys but her mother-in-law blanched when she mentioned this.

"They may be fine for Brittas Bay, my dear, but not for cruising. You absolutely must buy some decent cruise-wear. I'm taking Sarah in to Brown Thomas next Saturday. Why don't you join us?"

Fiona thought that one bikini looked much like another and figured that a toned body was more important than what you put on it. She mentioned this to Gavin that evening as they watched TV together.

"I agree with you but you know my mother. Just go along but don't let her pressurise you into buying something you don't want. Trust me – if you stand up to her she'll back down." He pulled her close and kissed her cheek. "Why not treat yourself? You hardly ever go shopping for clothes. Splash out! Just put it on my card in Brown Thomas."

So it was that Fiona found herself in BTs with her mother and sister-in-law the following Saturday, trawling through the fabulously expensive cruise-wear department. Bunny had a personal shopper to whom she gave orders to pick out suitable swimwear and lounge-wear for herself and the two girls. Fiona nearly fainted when she saw the price-tags. One bikini and matching cover-up cost almost as much as she earned in a week.

"My God, I can't believe these prices! They're scandalous!" she exclaimed.

"For God's sake, don't be such a pleb," said Sarah, throwing her eyes to heaven. "Gavin can afford it."

"That's not the point." Fiona stood her ground and refused to buy more than one bikini and one beach dress, both of which were on sale.

Sarah never batted an eyelid as she chose six bikinis and cover-ups to match, all at full price.

"If I was married to Tarki, I wouldn't think twice about what I spend. His family are filthy rich. Own half of London."

"Is it that serious between you?" asked Fiona.

20

"Not yet but you have to admit he *is* a great catch. I'd be a fool to let him go, don't you think?"

"But do you love him?" Fiona looked at her searchingly.

"What's love got to do with it?" asked Sarah.

She spied another beach dress that the shopper had brought into the dressing room. She grabbed it.

"You don't have to be in love to marry someone," she remarked casually as she slipped it on.

Fiona looked at her in disbelief. Was she serious?

"Sarah's right in a way," Bunny intervened. "It's more important that you have a lot in common and that you're friends first and foremost."

"Yes, look at all the people who marry for love and then get divorced. Anyway, you have to admit I'd have a great life with Tarki," Sarah said blithely.

"You certainly would." Bunny smiled at her daughter.

Fiona shook her head in dismay. She honestly did not understand Sarah. How could she be even remotely related to her Gavin, who was exactly the opposite, thank God.

They decided to break for lunch before they hit the dress and shoe departments.

"I think we've all earned a nice glass of wine," Bunny announced.

"I'm sorry but I've arranged to meet a friend for lunch," Fiona lied, unable to escape quickly enough. She was beginning to understand Gavin's apprehension about spending two full weeks in their company. Now she too was worried that it could be a disaster.

Gavin had told her to buy some sexy dresses for evenings so she high-tailed it up Grafton Street to Coast on Stephen's Green where she bought three lovely dresses for a fraction of the price that Sarah would probably pay for one.

That same afternoon Ann and Emily were also shopping for the trip. Ann, who was now forty-seven years old, was not overly concerned about keeping up with trends though she did like to look good. Her daughter had even less interest in clothes which Ann knew was unusual for a young girl these days. Most of Emily's friends spent all their money on clothes and make-up whereas her pocket money went on books. It took all of her mother's persuasion to get her to go shopping at all.

First they picked up some swimwear, shorts and tops in Penneys along with some nice sandals. They also visited Wallis and Miss Selfridge where Ann found some nice dresses for evening and insisted that Emily choose some too. Ann decided that with mixing and matching she would have enough for the trip. She didn't think people would take too much notice if she wore the same thing twice.

Although they were wealthy Ann didn't have the prejudices or expensive taste of the McElroys. As a result she and Emily spent €450 in total on their cruise wardrobe compared to the €8,500 Bunny and Sarah had managed to rack up.

Since they would be staying on in Florida for a week, Ann planned to do some shopping there. She'd heard the outlet shops in Orlando were fantastic and was looking forward to visiting them. Now that she'd got used to the idea of this holiday she was getting quite excited about it.

Thrilled with her purchases, Fiona modelled them for Gavin that evening as he sat up in bed, enjoying the show.

"You certainly filled my brief of sexy," he stated, pulling her into bed with him. He slipped the new dress off her and started making love to her, banishing all thoughts of her in-laws from her mind. She relaxed. Once Gavin was by her side everything would be okay.

Fiona was a little emotional the following day as she saw her parents off at the airport for their trip to Orlando to visit Ciara, her older sister. It would be the first Christmas in all her twenty-six years that she would not be with them for the holiday but she was delighted that they were getting this opportunity. They had never been in the US and were dying to see Ciara, who was expecting her first baby in January.

That night as they lay in bed she told Gavin what she was feeling.

"I was thinking, sweetheart," he said. "We arrive back in Fort Lauderdale on the 5th of January. Neither of us are due back to work until the 9th. Why not pop up to Orlando for a couple of days and surprise them? We can fly home from there."

"Are you serious? Could we do that?" Fiona asked excitedly.

"I don't see why not."

She pulled him close and kissed him and this time she initiated the love-making. They had been trying for a baby for five months now and every time they made love Fiona hoped this would be it.

"I love you very much," she whispered drowsily when they had finished.

"And I love you," he said, stroking her back gently as she drifted off to sleep.

Gavin had been immediately attracted to her the first

time he saw her in the gym. She was different to other girls. She was so natural and he saw that her eyes, which were a deep blue, had an honesty he'd never encountered before. Her face was devoid of make-up yet she was by far the most beautiful girl in the room. All the models and society girls he'd dated with their fake tans, fake boobs, fake hair-extensions and fake God-knows-what-else paled by comparison. He was instantly smitten.

She had a great body, very toned and fit, and he loved how she moved, graceful as a ballerina yet strong. He couldn't take his eyes off her.

One night he was having a pint in Kiely's with his old rugby mates when he spotted her across the bar. She must have felt his eyes on her because she looked up and smiled. His heart almost stopped. She had the smile of an angel. He smiled back and decided to approach her. He made his way nervously across the bar as she watched him. He didn't know what to say.

"Hi, I'm Fiona," she smiled, sensing his diffidence.

"Yes, I know. I'm Gavin."

"Yes, I know."

And they both laughed. And that was that!

He still couldn't believe his luck that she was now his wife.

# Chapter 3

Over seafood tapas on Howth Pier in Dublin's northside, Cassie Jordan was confiding her worries to her best friend, Julie.

"I honestly don't know what's wrong with Declan lately. He's hardly ever home and when he is he seems preoccupied. We haven't had sex in two months." She was picking at her thumbnail the way she always did when she was worried.

"You're not serious?" exclaimed Julie, shocked.

"You don't think he could be having another affair?" Cassie voiced her fear aloud for the first time.

Julie's heart sank but it came as no surprise to her. Declan was the epitome of tall, dark and handsome and a charmer to boot. Small wonder that women found him irresistible and Cassie was no exception. Declan had left school and home at sixteen but had not let that deter him. Highly ambitious and ruthless, he had used his wits and charm to propel himself up the career ladder and finally landed a good position in banking. He appeared to have it all except for the one thing he craved, which was class. And class was something Cassie had by the bucketful.

The daughter of a diplomat, she had spent her childhood travelling the world with her parents, living in various embassies. Sadly, her mother had died in an accident when she was just sixteen and she and her father, Mark, had become extremely close.

Cassie was beautiful and had a cosmopolitan style and elegance that Declan had never come across in other women. She was also a talented artist and fluent in six languages which impressed him greatly. She was everything he had ever dreamed of, so he set about wooing her and within six months of their meeting he proposed. He wanted to get married right away. As she was only twenty years old and in her second year at the National College of Art and Design, her father did his best to persuade her to wait, at least until she graduated. But Cassie was head over heels in love and anxious to do as Declan wished. Reluctantly her father agreed to the marriage on condition that she complete her degree. Cassie happily agreed.

Declan loved and admired his fiancée but unfortunately that did not cure him of his philandering. Two months before the wedding he cheated on her. Cassie found out by accident and was devastated. Being young and inexperienced, she had no idea how to handle it. It was at times like this that she needed her mother. She dared not tell her father as she knew he would hit the roof. He was unhappy enough as it was that she was marrying Declan. She was so embarrassed that she told no one except her best friend, Julie, who advised her to finish with him.

She finally confronted Declan who threw himself at her

feet and sobbed – swearing he loved her and begging her forgiveness. After many tears and despite her misgivings, she forgave him. She was still madly in love with him and didn't want to lose him.

Their wedding was an intimate affair held at her father's mansion on Lake Geneva and the honeymoon was spent in Mauritius. Her father gave her a lovely house on Howth Hill as a wedding present and Cassie was blissfully happy with her new husband and her new life. Declan was a loving husband and she knew she had been right to marry him. Her father's connections had helped Declan land a lucrative job as a hedge-fund manager in the Financial Centre and their future looked bright.

Two years later Cassie finished her degree and her first art exhibition was a huge success. She'd also started designing jewellery and her pieces were selling like hot cakes. She felt it was time to start a family but Declan was completely against it. He said she was too young and they had plenty of time for kids. She was disappointed but went along with him and agreed to wait.

Their life seemed perfect and then, four years into their marriage, Cassie got a phone call from a woman who claimed she and Declan had had an affair. When Cassie confronted him he at first denied even knowing the woman but when Cassie started to call her back he admitted that they'd had a fling. This time she threatened to leave him but again he wooed her back with tears and promises that it wouldn't happen again.

That was twice that Cassie knew of but Julie suspected it was many more times than that. Julie had tried to warn her but she didn't want to listen. She was still in love with her handsome, charming husband and could not imagine a life without him. Now it looked like Julie would be picking up the pieces once again.

Cassie's fears were justified as Declan was indeed having an affair. Her name was Alix and he'd met her nine months previously. It happened on a flight to Zurich. Deirdre, his friend John's wife, was one of the first-class cabin crew on the flight. She got Declan upgraded from business class where she introduced him to her colleague. Alix was a redhead with green catlike eyes and a voluptuous body who sashayed up and down the cabin, her hips swaying provocatively, aware of his eyes on her. Declan fancied her like crazy and she made it obvious that she found him attractive too. He invited the two women to join him for dinner later that evening and during it Alix covertly slipped him her phone number and mentioned that she was staying on in the city for a few days. It was a blatant invitation and he couldn't resist it. They all left the restaurant together and he put the two women in a taxi and said goodnight. His hotel was close by so he said he'd walk. Ten minutes later he texted Alix with the name of his hotel. Twenty minutes later they were in bed together.

She was insatiable and a wonderful lover and it was the best sex he'd ever experienced. He was due to fly back to Dublin late the following afternoon but decided to stay on. He called Cassie to say that the business was taking longer than expected and he'd have to stay a few more days. He and Alix spent three days and nights together, getting out of bed only to eat.

Since that time he had been seeing her at least twice a week, often flying to spend nights with her when she overnighted in foreign cities. He'd intended it to be a short fling but the sex kept drawing him back. She was the most exciting woman he'd ever met.

However, it had started out as a sexual liaison which had satisfied them both but recently Alix was looking for more. She'd started dropping hints of a more permanent relationship which was not on his agenda at all. It made him very nervous. Only last week she had told him she loved him and suggested that he leave Cassie and move in with her. The very thought horrified him. He thought of Alix solely as a sex partner. It was Cassie he loved and he had no intention of destroying his marriage for the sake of casual sex.

He often wondered what it was that made him cheat on her time after time as there had been many one-night stands. He suspected he was addicted to sex for he found the excitement and danger irresistible. He wished it were otherwise but that's how it was. He just couldn't help himself. He knew he should never have let this affair with Alix go so far. He had to finish it once and for all.

Deirdre and John, neither of whom knew anything about Declan's affair, had invited Cassie and him for Christmas and they had happily accepted the invitation. On hearing this, Alix had wangled an invitation for herself by telling Deirdre that she would be all alone for the holiday. When John casually mentioned to Declan that Alix would be joining them he went into a tailspin. There was no way he could let Alix near Cassie. God knows what she might say, especially with a few glasses of wine inside her. It didn't bear thinking about. He didn't know what to do. He had to avoid their meeting at all costs.

"I'm thinking of escaping to the sun over Christmas,"

he confided to his colleague, Tom, over a pint after work. "Where would you recommend?"

"My wife was rabbiting on last week about a special offer on a Caribbean cruise. I think she was hoping I'd cancel my parents who are coming to us for Christmas but there's no way I could do that."

"Do you know what company it's with?" Declan asked, thinking a cruise would be perfect. Alix couldn't reach him there.

"I'll call her," said Tom, taking out his phone.

One minute later Declan had the information he needed.

Cassie was surprised when Declan arrived home carrying a bunch of roses and a bottle of champagne.

"What's going on?" she asked, puzzled.

"I'm sorry. I know I've been a bastard lately, preoccupied by problems at work, but now I'm going to make it up to you. I'm taking you on a Caribbean cruise for Christmas."

"*Whaaat?*" Cassie almost dropped the flowers. "But we've already said we'd go to John and Deirdre's."

"Oh, they won't mind. They'll understand."

Cassie didn't know what to make of this. "You never said there'd been problems at work."

"I didn't want to worry you, love. A holiday is just what we both need right now and a cruise will be romantic – like a second honeymoon." He took her in his arms and kissed her. "Let's take this champagne up to bed and we can eat later," he murmured, nuzzling her neck.

He took his time making love to her, paying more attention to her pleasure than his own. She was taken aback. It had been a long time since he'd done that and it surprised her. She was relieved that it was problems at work that had affected him and not something to do with their marriage.

"Just think, two glorious weeks together far away from here," he sighed happily as they finished the champagne.

Cassie agreed with him. He was right. A holiday was just what they needed. Hopefully it would get their marriage back on track.

Two evenings later Declan was on his way to see Alix. He knew it would be his last visit. He dreaded having to break the news to her that he would be going away for Christmas. He didn't know how she'd react but had a fair idea what to expect. Tears and tantrums! He arrived at her apartment armed with a bottle of champagne and wine and a huge bouquet of roses. She was wearing nothing but a flimsy slip dress which clung to her voluptuous body. She never wore underwear anyway. He found himself getting aroused as she moved around the room putting the roses in water.

"Let's take this champagne to bed," he suggested, his voice husky with desire.

Her reply was to drop her dress and, taking the bottle, she led the way into the bedroom.

He grabbed two glasses and followed, barely able to contain himself. The champagne was forgotten as they tumbled on the bed, she as hungry for him as he was for her. She was an amazing and inventive lover and knew how to pleasure him. By the time she straddled him he was about to explode, but with her expertise she brought him to orgasm at just the moment she climaxed too. He lay back panting on the bed as she rolled off him onto her side.

"You like?" she asked, running her finger down his chest.

"I like very much," he replied, caressing her breast.

He opened the champagne and they lay back, savouring the post-sex state of satiation. Then Alix got up and filled the jacuzzi bath. Surrounded by candles they finished the champagne, enjoying the warm jets of water playing on their bodies. When the bottle was empty they had sex again and he thought ruefully that he really was going to miss this big-time.

Dressed again and back in the living room, Alix read the label on the bottle of wine he'd brought. "You *are* spoiling me tonight." She looked at him, eyebrows raised, as she put the French-cheese board on the coffee table.

There was a fire in the grate and she had candles lit all around the room. It was really very romantic. He felt sad knowing it was going to end.

When they had finished the cheese and wine he took her hand in his.

"I think you have something to tell me," she said, leaning in to him.

He looked at her, wondering if she knew what was coming.

But before he could say anything, she spoke. "You've decided to leave your wife for me, haven't you?" she said, her eyes glittering.

His courage failed him and he decided to soften the blow. "Well, no, that's not it," he told her, trying to sound as sorrowful as possible. "There's been a family emergency so I won't be able to see you till after the New Year."

"What do you mean?" she asked, perplexed. "You'll be in Deirdre's for Christmas, won't you? We'll see each other there."

"I'm afraid not. I've had to cancel."

As he had anticipated she went ballistic. She jumped up and came at him, her fists flailing.

"You come here letting me think we're going to be together and this is what you have to tell me?" she said.

"I never said we were going to be together. I can't leave my wife," he said lamely.

"*Get out, you bastard! Get out!*" she yelled, hurling the flowers at him.

He didn't wait for more and, grabbing his briefcase, left as fast as his feet would carry him. The last he heard was what must have been the empty wine bottle shattering against the door behind him.

The following day Alix called Deirdre.

"All set for Christmas?" she asked, after exchanging niceties.

"Sure," Deirdre replied. "By the way we'll only be seven. Declan and Cassie won't be here."

"Why not? What's the problem?"

Deirdre laughed. "No problem. Declan is taking her on a cruise instead. Lucky thing!"

Alix was dumbstruck. *That bastard!* "Really? Where are they going?" she managed to ask, trying to keep her voice calm.

"They're flying to Miami and going on a Caribbean cruise for Christmas. Cassie is very excited about it."

"I'll bet. Sounds great. What cruise-line are they going with?"

"Not sure. It's a French line, I think. Hang on – Declan gave me the details – I'll check my iPad . . . Yes, here it is. They fly to Orlando on the 21st and then sail on the 22nd.

The ship is called *Liberté*."

"How lovely!" Alix tried to keep her voice from trembling. "No wonder Cassie is thrilled."

"Yes. Declan said it will be like a second honeymoon for them."

Alix said goodbye as calmly as she could and hung up.

"*The bastard! Second honeymoon! Family emergency indeed!*" Alix yelled, flinging the phone at the wall. She was seething with fury.

# Chapter 4

It was the week they were due to leave and Gavin and Fiona were having Sunday lunch with his parents and Sarah when the door opened and his sister, Jess, walked in.

Bunny's hands fluttered to her face. "Jessica! What on earth?"

Bunny always called her by her full name when she was angry or, as in this case, shocked.

"What are you doing here?" she cried, rising to greet her daughter.

"Hello, Mummy, Daddy. I've come home. I've left Philip."

"*Whaaat?*" Bunny went pale and fell back down on her chair.

Richard stood and went to his daughter who collapsed into his arms. She promptly burst into tears.

"What happened?" Richard asked as the others looked on in shock.

"I found him in bed with the housekeeper," said Jess, choking on her tears.

"Oh dear, is that all?" Bunny asked, staying seated. "That's surely not enough reason to leave him?"

"*Not a reason to leave him?*" Jess shrieked, pulling herself out of her father's arms. "You may have ignored Daddy's little peccadillos, Mummy, but I assure you I am not you and will not put up with my husband's infidelities." She glared at her mother.

Richard had the grace to look abashed as the colour rose high in Bunny's cheeks. She was embarrassed and angry with Jess for bringing this up in front of Gavin and Sarah, not to mention Fiona.

Gavin tried his best to diffuse the situation. "C'mon, Jess, let me pour you a glass of wine and we'll discuss this calmly. I can see you're very upset."

"Thanks, Gav. It's been a nightmare."

"I'm sure it's all a big mistake," Bunny declared. "Are you not exaggerating a little, Jessica?"

"I found him in bed with the housekeeper. They were both naked and having sex. What's to exaggerate?" She started to cry again.

"Okay, love, we get the picture," said Richard, not wanting to hear all the gory details.

"I tell you, if I'd had a gun I'd have shot the bastard – and her too!" Jess cried defiantly.

"Of course you wouldn't," said Bunny soothingly. "Men do this all the time. It's in their nature."

"Mother!" Gavin looked at her, horrified at her words. Did she really believe this?

"So what are you going to do, Jess?" Sarah asked. She was equally shocked. She'd always envied her older sister's perfect life.

"I'll divorce him, of course," Jess replied, jutting her

chin out, "and take him to the cleaners for every penny."

"Now don't be rash, Jessica." Bunny waved her hand dismissively. "I understand you're feeling humiliated and hurt right now but I'm sure Philip is dreadfully sorry. Divorce is a major decision. You need time to think this through carefully."

Bunny was thinking of all the backlash that would come if Jess were to go through with her threat. Philip was a member of the English aristocracy and their wedding had been *the* social event of the year in Dublin. It had even been covered by *Hello* magazine for a large amount of money. She couldn't bear to think of the fallout and publicity should there be a divorce.

"So, what are your immediate plans, Jess?" Gavin asked.

"I thought I'd spend Christmas here with you guys. I need to get away from all the nosy-parkers in London, not to mention the media."

Her family looked in dismay at one another.

"Actually, we're not staying here for Christmas. We're all flying to Florida and taking a Caribbean cruise until the New Year," said Bunny, dismayed that her plans might be upset.

"Can I come too?" Jess asked. "It might help me get over this. Please, Mummy?"

"I'll see what I can do," Bunny replied. "You could share with Sarah."

"No way!" her two daughters cried simultaneously.

Bunny sighed. The thought of the two of them squabbling for two weeks was not an attractive proposition. She was beginning to think that this cruise had not been such a good idea after all.

However, Jessica was family and they had to stick together, come what may. The following day she made the arrangements for her older daughter to join them.

Two days later Jess's husband, Philip, arrived on the doorstep, suitably embarrassed. Jess absolutely refused to speak to him and locked herself in her bedroom. Bunny tried desperately to persuade her to see him, to no avail. Jess had always been the most strong-willed and assertive of her children.

Bunny passed the message on to him. "She will not talk to you. I'm so sorry."

He put his head in his hands and cried like a baby. "I really love her, you know."

Sarah was there at the time. She and Jess had their moments and, despite their rivalry and continuous arguing, in this she had her sister's back.

"Maybe you should have thought of that before you screwed the help," she declared, glaring at Philip. "You may as well go home. She definitely won't see you and she's coming to the Caribbean with us for Christmas. You betrayed her and she can't forgive you. So fuck off! Go spend Christmas with the housekeeper!"

Richard was shocked at his youngest daughter's language but proud of her for standing by her sister. These young women today! They were certainly more defiant than in his day. Bunny had her moments but he could handle her. He knew she loved him and, when push came to shove, she knew when to back down. He certainly wouldn't fancy coming up against this new breed of young women.

The last few days before the holiday flew by in a flurry with

Christmas drinks parties and lunches as they said goodbye to everyone. Despite Bunny's best endeavours Philip had returned to London without speaking to his wife. She hadn't realised her daughter could be quite so determined or vindictive. Meanwhile Jess was trying to come to terms with the break-up of her marriage. It wasn't easy but catching up with all her old friends in Dublin helped a little.

Fiona's period was overdue. Her breasts had become very sensitive and she'd felt nauseous a few mornings for no good reason. She wondered if she could possibly be pregnant. She hugged the secret to herself, wanting to be sure before she raised Gavin's hopes.

Two days before they were due to fly to Orlando, having missed a second period, Fiona bought two pregnancy tests. She was so nervous she could barely read it – her hand was shaking that much. To her immense joy, it was positive. She did it again and, no, she wasn't dreaming. It was true – definitely positive! After she had calmed down she decided that she would wait until Christmas Day to tell Gavin. She couldn't think of a nicer Christmas present to give him.

Gavin and Fiona were busy packing for the cruise.

"I don't suppose I could forget to take this monkey suit?" he asked, holding up the dreaded tuxedo.

"I'm afraid not. There are two formal nights. I'm taking two evening dresses."

"Oh Lord, what have we got ourselves into?" he moaned.

"It will be fine," she assured him.

Fiona was excited about their trip now.

They were flying Aer Lingus to Orlando the following day and taking a limousine to Fort Lauderdale where they would overnight. The ship would sail from there the following afternoon.

Meanwhile the Kennys were spending the night in the Maldron Hotel at Dublin Airport. They had driven up earlier in the day with Ann's mother who would stay with her other daughter in Blackrock while they were away. Ann had thought that perhaps one of her brothers would offer to put them up for the night but their wives were so annoyed about her abandoning them this Christmas that no invite was forthcoming.

"Well, that's the last time they're coming to us for Christmas," Tony insisted, furious with his in-laws.

They had dinner in the hotel and there was a festive air about it. The place was packed with people having Christmas drinks and parties and everyone was in great form.

"Are you flying out somewhere for Christmas?" the wine waiter asked them as he poured the wine.

"Yes, we're flying to Florida tomorrow and then taking a cruise in the Caribbean," Tony told him.

"Oh wow! You lucky things. I'm green with envy."

They all smiled happily at him.

"It's like a fairy tale!" Ann sighed with contentment as they got ready for bed that night.

"Better than having your family descend upon us for ten days," Tony noted, still disgusted with them.

Gavin and Fiona were surprised to find that Bunny had booked them all to fly Aer Lingus business-class to Orlando. Gavin offered to travel economy and to pay for the flights but despite his entreaties Bunny wouldn't hear of it so business class it was.

Sarah and Jess had no such qualms. They couldn't imagine travelling any other way. Bunny wondered for the umpteenth time how her children were so different. Gavin was caring and down-to-earth whereas the two girls were spoilt and extravagant. She supposed she was partly to blame. She was the one who had spoilt them.

Bunny had accepted that she had been foolish to think Fiona wasn't good enough for her son. She and Gavin were perfect for each other. His life would have been a misery married to any of the girls she had picked out for him. High-maintenance girls like Sarah and Jess. He had made a good choice.

The following morning, they all met up in the business-class lounge where they relaxed over a Bucks Fizz before boarding. Fiona refused the drink, saying that it was too early for her. She wasn't much of a drinker anyway. She had only flown business-class once before on her honeymoon to South Africa which had been Bunny's wedding present to them. Business class had been an amazing experience so she was looking forward to it again today. After turning left into the business-class cabin, they were offered a glass of champagne which she also declined. Once in the air they tucked into a delicious breakfast as they winged their way across the Atlantic.

Sarah was fairly merry as she accepted all the drinks offered by the cabin crew.

"It's not a good idea to drink too much on a long-haul flight. It's dehydrating," Bunny advised her but the advice fell on deaf ears.

Jess was unusually quiet and slept for most of the flight. They were met by a limousine at Orlando Airport and a little over two hours later arrived in style at the Ritz-Carlton in Fort Lauderdale. After checking in they just had time for a quick shower before meeting up in the bar for drinks.

Gavin and Fiona were first down and then Bunny and Richard arrived.

"How is your room?" Bunny asked. "I hope everything is satisfactory?"

"Everything's wonderful," Fiona replied as the waiter arrived with a bottle of champagne. She accepted a glass so as not to let the cat out of the bag but didn't intend to have more than a sip.

"That's good. We try to stay in a Ritz-Carlton whenever possible. It's without doubt the most superior chain in the world."

Gavin caught his father's eye and grinned. Richard threw his eyes to heaven.

Jess was next down and gladly took the glass of champagne handed to her.

"Well, have you cooled down over Philip's little dalliance?" Bunny asked her quietly, hoping that she might have come to her senses. They'd been so busy the last two days that she hadn't had a chance to talk to Jess about it.

"There's nothing to cool down about, Mummy. He betrayed me. I plan to divorce him. Where's Sarah?" She looked around, hoping to change the subject.

"She should be here," Bunny replied, looking at her watch with a frown. "That girl is really bothersome. She can never be on time for anything. I hope we haven't made a big mistake including her in this trip."

"Leave her be. She'll be down when she's ready,"

advised Richard, beginning to wonder whether they should be embarking on this trip at all. They were still on terra firma and already there were problems. He sighed. He could handle Bunny on her own but with Sarah and Jess added to the mix – well, that was another story. At least Gavin and Fiona were here to help.

When Sarah still hadn't arrived after thirty minutes, Bunny said she was going up to get her.

"No, no, let me go," Gavin said, jumping up quickly. "What room is she in?"

He had to knock three times on his sister's door before she answered, clad only in a towel. It was obvious from her dishevelled hair that she had been in bed.

"For God's sake, get your ass downstairs. Mother's having a seizure. You should have been there thirty minutes ago."

"Oh sorry," she mumbled. "We fell asleep."

Gavin could see a naked Tarquin jump out of bed behind her. "Well, better be downstairs in five," he ordered, "or she'll be up herself to drag you down."

"Okay, okay," Sarah grumbled.

Tarquin was already running into the shower. He was obviously more scared of Bunny than her daughter was.

"They'll be down right away," Gavin reported back to his mother.

"*Huh!*" was all Bunny could say.

Ten minutes later Sarah arrived down, her face sulky, Tarquin in her wake.

"So terribly sorry, Mrs McElroy. It was all my fault," Tarquin apologised, his voice contrite. "I was tired and fell asleep. Sarah kept banging on my door but I didn't hear her."

Tarquin was squirming as he told the lie, looking at Sarah nervously. It was obvious to Gavin that Sarah had instructed and schooled him in what to say.

Bunny was suitably mollified. "I understand, Tarquin. And please call me Bunny." She smiled at him and ordered another bottle of champagne.

She and Richard were planning an early night and had decided to eat in the hotel.

"I think I'll order room service," said Jess. "I don't feel like going out."

Bunny looked at her in alarm. This was not like Jess. She'd always been game for everything.

"We'd like to go to a good steak restaurant," Gavin said. "I checked on Trip Advisor and there's a Longhorn very close to here."

"We'll come too," Sarah chimed in. "Then we're going clubbing – right, Tarki?"

He looked nervously at her mother, expecting a problem.

"Just make sure you are down here on time tomorrow morning. We leave for the ship at ten-thirty," Bunny told them sternly. "I'm relying on you, Tarquin, to make sure Sarah is ready."

"Of course, Mrs . . . er . . . Bunny," he replied.

She beamed at him once more. What a nice well-mannered boy, she thought.

"Why don't you come with us?" Fiona asked Jess gently. "It won't be a late night." She'd noticed how red-rimmed Jess's eyes were and guessed she was crying quite a lot. She also had dark circles under them which suggested she was having problems sleeping. Fiona could tell Jess was hurting, much more than she was letting on.

"No, I'm not hungry," Jess replied listlessly.

While Gavin was leaving their keys at reception Fiona took Jess aside.

"Jess, I know you're having a hard time. If you need to talk, remember I'm here to listen." She looked kindly at her sister-in-law.

"Thanks, Fiona. I'll remember that. Mummy and Sarah are not exactly the best of confidantes." To her embarrassment, she felt her eyes well up.

"Well, I'm here for you," Fiona assured her, giving her a hug.

They all said goodnight and on the way to the restaurant Gavin asked what they'd been talking about.

"I told Jess that I'm here for her if she needs to talk. I think she's hurting much more than anyone realises," Fiona confided.

"She'll get over it. She's strong, like Bunny."

Fiona was not so sure.

# Chapter 5

Both Gavin and Fiona would have preferred to be on their own at the restaurant but could hardly have said so. The meal was wonderful but was spoiled because Sarah was drinking far too fast and became quite drunk, laughing uproariously at the slightest thing.

"Hey, steady on there," Gavin admonished when Sarah wanted to order a third bottle of wine. She had consumed more than a whole bottle by herself at that point.

"Oh God, you're as bad as Mummy," Sarah fumed. "Come on, Tarki, let's go have some fun."

Tarquin looked at Gavin helplessly and shrugged his shoulders before following her out of the restaurant.

"Well, I never!" Fiona exclaimed. "They didn't even offer to pay their share of the bill."

"That's Sarah, running true to form," Gavin said with a sigh.

Sarah had ruined their night. Fiona hoped that she wouldn't ruin the cruise also. She was *so* looking forward to it. But it would be a challenge.

Just as they got up to leave, the Kenny family entered the restaurant and sat down at the next table.

Gavin overheard them talking.

"Is that an Irish accent I hear?" he couldn't resist asking.

"Yes, indeed," Tony Kenny replied. "From Galway. And you?"

"Dublin. Are you here on holiday?"

"Yes and no. We're taking a cruise tomorrow."

"What do you know? So are we," Fiona told them, smiling.

"What ship are you sailing on?" Ann asked.

"*Liberté*," Gavin told him. "It's a French cruise-line."

"How amazing! That's the ship we're taking too!" Ann cried in delight.

"What a coincidence!" Fiona laughed. "I hope we'll see you on board."

They parted company, all of them thinking what a small world it was turning out to be.


The Kennys were staying in a small hotel not far from the McElroys'.

After they'd eaten Tony and Ann were ready for bed but Jack wanted to go to a bar he'd spotted where there was a rock band playing.

"Go ahead – but why don't you take Emily with you?" Ann suggested, worried that Jack might get into trouble on his own. Emily was sensible and would make sure he'd get back to the hotel okay.

Her Jack had always been a wild child, more interested in rock music than his studies. He was a dare-devil who, despite her fears, had bought a motor-bike with money he'd earned in Germany during summer holidays. She spent many sleepless nights listening for the sound of it which told her that he was home safe. He was also a charmer and that, combined with his dark good looks, attracted girls like bees to a honey-pot. She knew that he had left many broken hearts in his wake.

"Don't be too late," Tony ordered. "Tomorrow is a big day."

"Don't worry, Dad," Emily assured her father. "I'll make sure we're not late."

Tarquin and Sarah had found a bar with live music. He sat helplessly as she worked her way through yet another bottle of wine.

"Don't you think you've had enough?" he asked.

Sarah glared at him. "God, don't tell me Mummy and Gavin are getting to you too? I'm on my holidays. Can I not drink if I feel like it?"

Just then the hottest guy she'd ever seen entered the bar. Her heart skipped a beat as their eyes met and he held her gaze. He was accompanied by a pretty girl. He had longish jet-black hair, olive skin and eyes that were so brown they were almost black. He wore a leather jacket with the collar pulled up. He was the image of her childhood crush, the tennis player Rafa Nadal. Seriously sexy! She guessed he was a Latino. He was hot!

She wished there was some way they could meet but he was with a girl unfortunately. She emptied the little that was left in the bottle into her glass.

"Sarah, I insist we leave now," Tarquin declared, standing up.

She didn't want to but she could see that he was angry.

Throwing back what was left in her glass, she followed him out.

Tarquin was worried about how things would go on the cruise where the drinks were free. He hoped it wouldn't be a total disaster. He was seeing a different Sarah to the one he'd been dating in Dublin.

The Jordans had been on the same flight as the McElroys from Dublin but they were in economy and had opted to spend the night in Orlando.

Although Cassie had been to Orlando before, she had never been to Epcot. After checking into their hotel, they took the shuttle-bus there and stayed on for dinner and the firework display. It was the best firework display she'd ever seen. Declan had been very attentive and loving all day and it felt like old times to her. Back at the hotel, although they were tired after the long day, he wanted to make love. He was a changed man. Cassie determined that when they got back home she would make sure he didn't work such long hours and they would take more romantic breaks.

Her last thought as she drifted off to sleep was that this holiday was a lifesaver. It had brought them closer and tomorrow they would fly to Fort Lauderdale to take their cruise. Their relationship had improved in just one day. Things were looking up.

Tarquin was as good as his word and somehow managed to have Sarah down in the lobby for ten-thirty the following morning. She looked the worst for wear and was clearly hungover.

"I could use a drink," she said, about to head for the bar but the look from Bunny stopped her in her tracks.

"By the way, we met an Irish family in the restaurant last night," Gavin told them. "They're from Galway and would you believe it? They're going on the same cruise as us."

"I hope they're not the kind of Irish who'll be drunk all the time," Bunny sniffed.

"Mother, stop that! They seem like very nice people," Gavin scolded her.

"Now, now, Bunny, we mustn't pre-judge people," Richard firmly rebuked his wife.

Bunny and Sarah had so much luggage that they needed two limousines to convey them to the port. The traffic was horrendous and they soon realised why. *Harmony of the Seas* was getting ready to sail and it looked like a million people were offloading luggage and embarking.

"Oh my God!" Fiona exclaimed. "It's even bigger than the photographs suggested."

They all gazed in awe at the humongous ship.

"My worst nightmare," Bunny shuddered. "Can you imagine all those people together?"

"I don't know, I think it's fantastic," Sarah commented.

"They do have amazing facilities such as a 100ft water slide and surf machine," Fiona informed them. "They also have a zip-line and climbing walls."

"Just what I need," Bunny remarked sarcastically.

"Is that the ship with the Bionic Bar? You know, the one where robots mix your drinks?" Sarah asked Fiona.

"Yeah, that's the one."

"Wow! That would be awesome. I'd love that."

"I bet you would," Jess remarked, throwing her eyes to heaven.

Sarah ignored her. "Could you not have booked us on that one?" she demanded of her mother.

"Over my dead body," Bunny replied.

"How could you seriously want to travel on that monstrosity, Sarah? It's crass," Jess berated her.

"They're trying to appeal to young adventurous travellers and it seems to be working," Fiona intervened, wishing to avert a row.

"That sure rules Mummy out," Sarah sniggered, earning a scathing look from Bunny which shut her up instantly. Her parents were paying for this holiday and she knew she was walking a fine line. If she crossed it Bunny would be perfectly capable of sending her packing. Best to stay quiet until they had sailed.

A little further on they spotted their ship, the *Liberté*. It looked like a minnow in comparison to the other one. It also looked less frenzied and the people boarding it were way more elegant and classy. There were not many people offloading luggage and, as Bunny and Richard had booked a suite, they and their guests flew through the embarkation process. In less than ten minutes they were walking up the gangway.

Gavin took Fiona's hand and smiled at her obvious excitement. It was contagious and he now found himself excited about the trip too.

They were welcomed aboard as their photo was taken and then were handed glasses of champagne.

Sarah, who had been sulking, brightened up as she took two glasses off the tray.

"Things are looking up," she declared as she downed one.

"Here's to a wonderful cruise and a Happy Christmas!" Bunny raised her glass to them.

"How nice to have all the family together this year,"

Richard said. "That makes it extra-special. Here's to a very Happy Christmas, everyone!"

Gavin raised his glass along with everyone else but Fiona could sense his anxiety. She hoped it was misplaced and that it would be a happy Christmas.

Bunny and Richard were shown straight to their suite. The others had to wait as their cabins were not yet ready. The first thing Sarah did was to go to Guest Relations to get another key to her cabin for Tarquin. If her mother thought they would sleep in separate cabins she was mistaken.

Smoking was absolutely forbidden on the ship except for two designated areas. One was in a corner of the swimming-pool deck and the other on Deck 15 behind the outdoor Montmartre bar. Sarah headed for the second one with Tarquin tagging along behind her. There were two handsome sophisticated men sitting there and they all started chatting. They looked to be in their thirties. She wasn't surprised to hear they were from Rome. She'd always thought Italians had such style.

"I'm Sarah and this is Tarki," she said, flashing a smile.

"I'm Carlo," the taller of the two guys said. He was wearing a cream linen suit with a pink shirt which was perfect with his dark colouring. He looked Sarah up and down slowly and gave a low whistle. It was obvious he liked what he saw.

Tarquin squirmed at Carlo's brazen manner.

"And I'm Enzo," the other guy introduced himself.

"Care to join us for a cocktail?" Carlo asked, gazing at Sarah.

Tarquin disliked these two men and was not keen to accept but before he could say so Sarah had answered.

"We'd love to."

The men led the way to the Montmartre bar where two beautiful girls were seated.

"Hello, who's this?" the darker one asked, looking at Sarah suspiciously.

Carlo introduced them. Sofia and Paola were stunning and very chic and were both models.

They paid Tarquin a lot of attention, saying how much they loved his English accent. He felt very uncomfortable and after one drink excused himself. Sarah refused to leave with him. She was having too good a time and was flattered by Carlo's interest in her.

Gavin and Fiona were doing a tour of the ship, checking out all the facilities. It was more luxurious than Fiona could ever have imagined. There was a central atrium with glass lifts going up the fifteen floors. A huge Christmas tree decorated in white and silver dominated the central space. It was stunning and Fiona decided she would use this colour scheme herself the following year. Two magnificent staircases led to the next floor with garlands wound around the banisters. The whole ship was very festive with a real Christmassy feel.

At the Guest Relations desk they picked up maps of the ship.

"Heavens, I'll never find my way around!" Fiona cried as she looked at it.

They strolled through the casino, spotting the various bars along the way before making their way to the pool deck which was on Deck 12. The pool had sunbeds and curtained cabanas all around it and there were also two hot-tubs and a bandstand and dance-floor.

"How fabulous!" exclaimed Fiona breathlessly.

They strolled through the Buffet and they couldn't believe their eyes at the amount of delicious food on display.

"Uh-oh, I see a few pounds coming on," she giggled.

"More like a few stone, I'd say," Gavin noted with a grimace.

Fiona was relieved to see a well-equipped gym and running track on the top deck. "Well, at least we can utilise these to work off all that food."

They strolled to the back of the ship to the Montmartre bar where they spied Sarah sipping cocktails with a very noisy group of people.

"Italians, I bet," Gavin murmured under his breath.

"Come and have one of these delicious cocktails!" Sarah called out to them.

"No, thanks. It's a bit early for us," Gavin replied.

"Trust Sarah to find fellow party-goers within an hour," observed Fiona.

As they took the elevator down to their cabin, Gavin remarked, "Luckily drinks are all-in, otherwise Sarah would cost Dad an arm and a leg in the bars."

"She *is* drinking an awful lot," Fiona agreed.

"I feel a bit guilty because I haven't paid her much attention since we got married," Gavin admitted. "And with Jess away in London she's had no one to look out for her."

"You have no reason to feel guilty, darling. She's nineteen. She's a big girl. You're not responsible for her and I doubt you could stop her anyway."

Gavin bit his lip but said nothing. He'd always looked out for his sisters. It was what brothers did. He knew they were both spoilt but he felt a responsibility for them, often keeping the peace between them and Bunny. He knew Fiona thought he was much too soft with them and she was probably right but it was hard to change the habit of a lifetime. Now they were both having problems, they needed him more than ever.

Their cabin was very compact and more than adequate for their needs. With so much going on around the ship they didn't expect to spend much time in it anyway. They had a veranda and a big King-size bed which was all they needed.

"I can't believe we're actually here," Fiona said excitedly as she looked around.

"We are, indeed, and we're going to have a wonderful time," Gavin said, pulling her close. "How about we try out this bed?"

She giggled as he pulled her down on it. He slid her dress from her shoulder and cupped her breast. Suddenly she propped herself up on one elbow and looked at him very seriously. He stopped what he was doing.

"What is it?" he asked, perplexed.

"I love you so much," she said, looking deep into his eyes.

"I know that. Now *show* me how much." He slipped her dress down further as she too undressed him.

Afterwards he nuzzled her neck and murmured, "You make me so happy."

She kissed him, smiling. He had no idea how much happier she was about to make him.

They found a newsletter in the cabin, outlining all the facilities and activities on board and they read it as they lay in bed, Gavin's arm around her.

"Wow! There's so much to do," she exclaimed. "Besides

the gym and running track there are all kinds of exercise classes: stretching, Pilates and yoga. There are also dance classes and Zumba, not to mention a casino, cinema and theatre with live shows every night. And on top of that there's wine-tasting, cookery demonstrations, computer classes. Boy, I'm exhausted just reading about it!"

Gavin laughed at her. "I think we can rule out the casino. You know I hate gambling."

"Me too. I'd like to spend some time at the pool though, enjoying the sun." This cruise was looking more exciting by the minute.

Luckily they were up and dressed when their cabin steward knocked on the door to introduce himself. Like all the crew they had met so far, he was friendly and smiling as he told them his priority was to make their cruise an enjoyable and memorable one. They were impressed.

They went up to the Buffet for lunch. The food was amazing and they walked around the various stations, marvelling at the selection available. There was so much choice that they had a tough time deciding. Fiona was drawn to the fantastic array of salads while Gavin couldn't resist the delicious-looking ribeye steak.

The restaurant was very busy so they had to share a table with another couple who were elderly.

The woman, when she heard them speak, exclaimed, "Oh my Gawd! You're Irish. How cute! We're Irish too."

"Really?" Gavin remarked, surprised. They certainly sounded American. "What part of Ireland are you from?"

"I'm not sure. My great-grandfather was from the South, I think. And Bill's family are from Northern Ireland somewhere."

"Oh, I see," Gavin replied, not seeing at all. He didn't know it then but almost every American he would meet over the next two weeks would claim to be Irish too.

They were a nice friendly couple but Gavin and Fiona lost count of how many times they went back to the Buffet, returning with full plates every time. It was unbelievable.

"I gain fourteen pounds every time I cruise," the woman, who was very overweight, admitted cheerfully as she returned with a plate of cakes and pastries.

Fiona and Gavin weren't in the least surprised.

"But that's one of the joys of cruising, isn't it?" she smiled at them.

Not for us, Gavin and Fiona thought simultaneously.

"The ice-cream bar here is fantastic," the woman informed them, "and it's open all day."

"Sounds good. Would you like an ice-cream, Fee?" Gavin asked.

"Sure. Could you bring me a sugar-free one, please?"

The woman looked at her, aghast. "No, honey, you can't possibly go for sugar-free. You gotta try the chocolate chip and strawberry and caramel. That's my favourite combination."

"Thank you, I will," Fiona replied, afraid to catch Gavin's eye in case she laughed.

# Chapter 6

The Kennys embarked later than the McElroys. Like them they were relieved not to be sailing on the *Harmony of the Seas*.

"That is plenty big enough for me," Ann laughed as they spotted the *Liberté*.

Jack took photos of her with his phone as she walked up the gangway beaming with excitement.

As they stepped on board a very attractive girl offered them champagne, smiling at Jack as she handed it to him.

"Thank you . . . Iveta," he said, reading her name tag. She blushed prettily.

Another beautiful girl welcomed them on board. She wore a dark-blue naval-type suit which emphasised her fabulous figure.

"Welcome aboard the *Liberté*. My name is Maja and I'm your Assistant Cruise Director. We hope you have a wonderful cruise with us."

She caught Jack looking her over and stared back at him

brazenly. "If I can do anything for you – anything at all – please don't hesitate to let me know."

"I will indeed," he replied as she held his gaze.

Jack whistled under his breath. On the way to their cabins he spied more beautiful girls at every corner who all responded to his smile and good looks. Wow! He hadn't been expecting to find such gorgeous girls here. This cruise was going to be more interesting than he'd anticipated.

The Jordans were the last to board. Cassie was surprised by the expensive décor that greeted them everywhere. It was luxurious but done in a very elegant and subtle way.

"Trust the French. They're the masters of chic and sophistication," she observed admiringly. She had cruised with her parents in the Mediterranean a few times when she was younger but nothing she had seen then came close to the opulence of the *Liberté*.

Declan was also suitably impressed.

"It's perfect, just perfect," Cassie exclaimed as she looked around their cabin and then went out to check the veranda.

Declan came up behind her and put his arms around her waist. "This is going to be a brilliant trip, honey," he said as he kissed the back of her neck. "Our second honeymoon."

Cassie turned to face him. "I hope so. I can't believe we're actually here and we have two whole weeks to enjoy it. This is the best Christmas present ever. What a great idea of yours!" She smiled and kissed him.

All three families were in their cabins when the alarm calling them to the obligatory Emergency Drill rang out. Taking their life-jackets they put them on and headed to their pre-ordained Assembly Stations. Everyone was in good humour and chatting energetically. Fiona was amazed to hear that some of their fellow passengers spent six months of the year cruising and were staying on board to continue with a back-to-back cruise. They even met one man who told them that since he retired he did nothing else but cruise.

"I think cruising is a great way to holiday but six months of the year?" Fiona whispered to Gavin as they made their way back to their cabin with their life-jackets.

"And that guy who cruises all year round? Seriously? I couldn't bear it." Gavin shook his head. "Some people lead strange lives."

"Yeah, but he told me that he's all alone and has no family and he finds cruising staves off the loneliness. So who can blame him? I guess not everyone is as lucky as we are."

Bunny and Richard's Assembly Station was actually in the Members' bar which was reserved for those occupying suites. Again, there was an air of anticipation about it that made for a party atmosphere. They were sitting with two couples who also had their families on board.

"We love them all dearly but it's nice to have this place to escape to once in a while," one of the ladies confided.

The others all agreed.

The Kennys felt an excited buzz among the passengers at their Assembly Station with everyone looking forward to a great two weeks cruising. They met some Germans who had sailed with this cruise-line many times before – and they assured them they were in for a treat.

"Gosh, I hope we won't need to put these on again after today," Emily commented nervously as she tackled her life-jacket.

"Wouldn't that be exciting?" Jack teased her. Seeing his father's glare, he added, "I'm only joking, Em. Of course we won't."

"This is so much fun," Ann remarked as they made their way back to the cabins. Her family had to agree with her. It was certainly different to anything they'd ever done before. They couldn't wait for the ship to sail.

Like the others, Declan and Cassie enjoyed the great atmosphere and sense of anticipation at their Assembly Station. Cassie noted that there were more young people on board than she'd expected. Cruising was obviously not just for retired people any more.

They met a lovely young couple from Paris who were very impressed with Cassie's fluency in their language. They were even more surprised when they heard her speaking Italian and German fluently to some other passengers.

"My goodness, your wife is a wonderful linguist," the French girl, Marie, said to Declan. "You must be very proud of her."

"I sure am," Declan admitted, smiling as he put his arm around Cassie's shoulders. "Very proud indeed." And it was true. She was so accomplished and beautiful. He was a lucky man indeed. He would show her just how much he appreciated her over the next two weeks.

Declan felt himself relaxing. It had been a great idea to come on this cruise, away from the pressures of work and the dreaded Alix. He planned to relax and thoroughly enjoy himself on this holiday. It was just what the doctor ordered.

The ship was due to sail at 4 p.m. and Gavin and Fiona

went up on deck to see the cast-off. His parents and Jess were there before them.

"Are you settling in okay?" Richard enquired.

"Just great. It's really wonderful," Fiona told him. "We're so looking forward to this trip."

"Is your cabin comfortable?" Bunny asked. She had offered to book a suite for them but Gavin had adamantly refused to accept.

"Perfect, just perfect," Fiona replied, grinning at Gavin.

"I'm just looking forward to chilling out and relaxing," Jess admitted.

"Have you seen Sarah?" asked Richard. "We thought she might join us here."

"We saw her earlier. She seems to have made some new friends already." Gavin omitted to say that they had been drinking and were probably still at the bar. Bunny didn't need any more ammunition against her.

As the horn sounded their departure, Gavin put his arm around his wife's shoulders and they stood at the rail and watched as the ship pulled away from the Florida coast.

"Isn't this wonderful?" Fiona said, cuddling into him. "This is like a second honeymoon."

"It can't be as good as the first."

"It may be even better. Who knows what will happen?" She put her hand on her tummy. She could hardly believe that there was a new life growing inside her. She was finding it difficult to keep the secret to herself.

The Kennys also went on deck to watch the sail-away. There were some pretty young girls standing beside them and Jack had caught their attention. They were giggling and throwing sideways glances at him. He started chatting to them and found out they were the professional dancers from the shows. They watched together as the ship sailed out into the Atlantic.

"We're going for a drink in the Disco bar now," Galina, the prettiest one, told him shyly. "Would you like to join us?"

"Yeah, sure. That would be great," he replied, smiling at her. She was gorgeous.

The Jordans enjoyed the cast-off from their veranda. Declan had ordered champagne cocktails from room service and they sat in the sun, watching the coast of Florida slip away.

When they had finished, they walked to the deck above the pool where the traditional sail-away party was in full swing. They watched the dancers from the railing above and Sarah's white-blonde head caught Declan's attention. She had a beautiful face and fabulous legs. She looked young and innocent but her body and the way she moved were at odds with that. He could only imagine what she would be like in bed. He sighed. Unfortunately, he'd never get to find out.

Once they were out on the sea the McElroys headed down to the pool deck too. They spotted Sarah dancing with wild abandon to the music. Gavin noticed she was with the Italians she'd been with earlier. Tarquin was nowhere to be seen.

"Oh dear, I have a feeling that Sarah is going to cause problems on this trip," Bunny fretted as she watched her daughter dancing wildly.

"How about I go order us some cocktails?" Gavin suggested.

"Good idea!" his father agreed. "How about Mai Tai's?"

"I'll need more than Mai Tai's to keep my cool with that girl," Bunny remarked, shaking her head.

Gavin went off to order as Richard tried to mollify his wife.

Sarah spotted them and left the dance-floor to join them.

"I'm having a super time," she cried gaily. "I've met some cool friends. This trip won't be as boring as I feared." She was wearing a pair of very short Daisy Dukes and no bra beneath a skimpy crop top. She had obviously been drinking.

"Could you not wear a little more clothing?" Bunny asked as she saw the men in the vicinity ogling her half-naked daughter.

"Oh, Mummy – ever the frump!"

"Stop it, Sarah. Show some respect!" cried Jess, glaring at her.

"You're nearly as bad!" Sarah made a face at her sister.

"Where's Tarquin?" Richard asked, trying to diffuse the situation.

"He's around somewhere." Sarah waved her hand in the air dismissively. "I sent him back to the cabins with our life-jackets."

Just then Gavin arrived back with Tarquin in tow. Tarquin seemed a little upset.

"I've been looking for you everywhere, Sarah," he complained, biting his lip.

"Oh, Tarki, don't be such a twerp. I told you there was going to be a sail-away party. I'm with our new friends. Come on over. We're meeting them for dinner."

"I'd rather hoped we'd all have dinner together as it's our first night," Bunny said.

"Mummy, *puhleeese*! I promised these guys we'd meet them. You're not going to spoil everything by insisting, are you?"

Bunny shrugged helplessly and Fiona felt a little sorry for her mother-in-law.

"You will come to our suite for drinks before dinner, won't you?" Bunny asked.

"Do we have to?" Sarah asked.

"Yes, you do," Gavin insisted, glaring at her.

She dared not go against him. "Okay, we'll be there," she acquiesced.

Sarah was still smarting from the fact that her mother had cancelled the suite she'd originally booked for her in exchange for two cabins – one for Tarquin and one for her. Was her mother stupid? Surely she realised they would be sleeping together and now they were both stuck sleeping in a small cabin without even a veranda instead of a luxurious suite. She'd make her mother sorry for doing that. At least she didn't have to share with Jess. That would have been the pits. Jess had become a real pain since she'd started mixing with those snobby Royals in London. In fact, Sarah thought that her sister was morphing into Bunny.

Just then a waitress arrived with the cocktails.

"Yummy, Mai Tai's, my favourite!" cried Sarah, reaching for one of them.

"Oh sure, have mine," Gavin said sarcastically. "I'll order another. What will you have, Tarquin?"

"A Mai Tai would be fine, thanks."

Gavin ordered two more. Sarah had drained hers even before the waitress returned. "I'm going back to my friends. C'mon, Tarki!"

"Eh . . . no . . . I'll stay and wait for my drink."

"Whatever!" She flicked back her long hair. "See you all later."

"Six o'clock, Sarah, and don't be late," her mother warned, "and please wear some clothes. That would be nice."

Sarah threw her eyes to heaven and flounced off, leaving Bunny fuming. Not only was she behaving disgracefully but she was treating Tarquin abominably.

"I'm not sure it's a good idea to have alcohol on tap all day," Jess said quietly to her father as they watched the party continue.

"I agree. It's nice to have a cocktail or two before dinner and wine with your meals," her father replied, "but if you were to drink all day the cruise could pass in a blur of alcohol."

"Seemingly that won't bother Sarah. She's obviously been drinking since we came on board and it's not even five-thirty yet," Jess remarked with a grimace. She wondered what her sister would be like by midnight with unlimited drinks available.

"I don't like those guys she's dancing with," Richard remarked. "They're much too old for her."

"They seem very slick and self-assured," Jess observed as she watched them.

Bunny, who had overheard, joined in. "I don't know what we'll do with her. She's drinking far too much." She had a worried frown on her face.

"I agree. We can't let this continue," Richard agreed.

The drinks had arrived and Tarquin was sipping his and looking very uncomfortable. "Maybe it's just the thrill of the first day," he suggested. "I did try to dissuade her but, well . . . you know Sarah," he finished lamely.

"We do indeed and we don't hold you responsible, Tarquin," Bunny assured him.

"Maybe you could go down and keep an eye on her," Richard suggested.

Tarquin was relieved to get away. He was beginning to think he'd made a dreadful mistake coming on this cruise.

"I had great hopes for them," Bunny said sadly, "but I'm afraid it's not to be. He's not able to handle Sarah at all."

"Is anyone?" Gavin asked. "Maybe I could have a talk with her?"

"Would you, son?" Richard asked.

"Not that it will do a damn bit of good," Bunny remarked bitterly.

Fiona thought that what Sarah needed was a strong hand. She was completely spoilt and treated her parents with no respect. She tried to imagine what her parents would have done if she'd ever behaved like Sarah. She shuddered to think.

Back in their cabin, she mentioned this to Gavin and his reply shocked her.

"You know, she's no different to all her friends. Spoilt, selfish, vain little darlings all of them. They think the world revolves around them. I should know. I've dated enough of them."

"You never!"

"Unfortunately. That was our social circle when I was younger but then I met you and realised that not all women are like that."

"Aaah, that's nice!" She reached up and kissed him.

"I mean it," he said seriously as he kissed her back.

At 6 p.m. the McElroys congregated in the suite and for

once Sarah was on time. Fiona suspected that Tarquin had something to do with that. He was being extremely courteous while Sarah was very subdued.

The suite was incredible with a wraparound veranda. There was a big living room with a dining area and views of the ocean through floor-to-ceiling windows. It was breathtaking and as luxurious as any five-star hotel suite.

"It's lovely, isn't it?" Bunny was pleased by how impressed they obviously were.

"It's amazing!" Fiona exclaimed. "I've never seen anything like it."

"Jolly nice," said Tarquin and let out a low whistle.

Sarah stayed mum – even more miffed now that she could see what she was missing.

"I wish you could have booked a suite for me," Jess complained enviously.

"Consider yourself lucky that I was able to book a cabin for you at all," Bunny rebuked her sharply. "Ah, here's Raphael – he's our private butler. He's a gem." A smiling man entered with a tray of canapés.

"What can I get you to drink, Madame?" he asked, bowing slightly.

"Are Bellinis okay for everyone?" Bunny asked.

Fiona asked for a juice, explaining that the motion of the ship was affecting her. Everyone else agreed to Bellinis except Sarah who wanted a Harvey Wallbanger.

"For goodness sake, Sarah, why can't you be like everyone else?" asked Jess irritably.

"Because I'm not like everyone else," Sarah declared, with her signature flick of the hair. "I *am* different."

Bunny threw her eyes to heaven and Fiona didn't blame her.

At seven Sarah and Tarquin left to join her new friends for dinner in the speciality French restaurant, Maxim's. It had a supplement of $25 per person which Sarah knew would piss her mother off big-time. Tarquin was beginning to piss her off too. He seemed to be more on her parents' side than hers and it was obvious he didn't like her new friends.

# Chapter 7

After an hour, the McElroys headed to the mezzanine of the main restaurant which was called Tour Eiffel. They had opted for open dining so that they would not be seated with the same people every night – in case they turned out to be dreadful bores, as Bunny had discovered on previous cruises.

"Would you mind joining some other people?" the maître d' asked. "We don't have a table for five at the moment."

"That's fine," Bunny replied. "We don't mind sharing, do we?" She looked at the others who nodded agreement.

The hostess showed them to a table where there were already four people seated.

It was the Kenny family.

"Well, hello again!" Gavin greeted them. "What a coincidence!" He turned to his parents. "These are the Irish people we met in Fort Lauderdale."

There were introductions all round and Bunny felt a bit guilty at having suggested they might be drunks. These were obviously civilised people.

71

"Where are you from?" Bunny asked.

"Galway," Tony replied in his lovely soft lilting accent.

"I've always loved Galway," Richard declared. "We used to go there on holidays when I was a kid."

"I never knew that," exclaimed Bunny, surprised.

Ann felt dowdy beside Bunny who was glamorous and sophisticated and would have put Sharon Stone or Kim Cattrall to shame. She was very slim and was wearing a beautiful, obviously very expensive dress. Her hair was sleek with blonde highlights and her skin was glowing with not a wrinkle in sight. Ann was sure she must have had Botox. Bunny had to be quite a bit older than herself but she certainly didn't look it.

Jess was also beautiful. She'd inherited her mother's cheekbones and figure and startling green eyes, but there was a sadness behind them. She didn't seem like a happy young woman.

"Isn't this just great?" Ann remarked, smiling. "It's always been my dream to come on a cruise and now we're here I almost have to pinch myself to believe it's real."

The others laughed at her enthusiasm.

"Mum is so high we almost have to tie her down," Jack confided, patting his mother's hand.

As Bunny listened to them she thought how nice it must be to feel that excited about something. Nothing excited her any more. She'd been everywhere, done everything. Her palate was jaded. She was slightly envious of Ann's enthusiasm. She had to be in her early forties but she looked older. She was make-up free except for a dash of lipstick. She noticed Ann had a few grey hairs amongst the brown and there were tiny lines around her eyes and mouth. It was a shame. She was pretty and with some effort could have done so much more with herself.

Bunny and her friends were all high-maintenance women with stylists, personal trainers and shoppers on hand. She guessed Ann would consider all the time that she and her friends spent on their looks a waste of time. She was certainly a refreshing change. Bunny liked her.

Tony was another story altogether. He was dark and good-looking with a toned muscular physique and he was groomed to perfection. His looks obviously mattered a great deal to him and Bunny disliked his self-confident macho attitude. Typical of a self-made man, she thought. She should know – she'd met enough of them. She knew this type of ultra-male man was attractive to many women but she wasn't one of them.

She couldn't help noticing how very patronising he was to Ann, who constantly looked at him for his approval. He was seated beside Jess and had turned his full attention on her while ignoring his wife. Jess appeared to be enjoying it and Bunny hoped Ann wouldn't notice. Bunny had an instinct for these things. He was a charmer for sure but he was not a nice man.

The daughter, Emily, seemed to be a sweet unaffected girl who took after her mother. As for the son, Jack – he had inherited his father's dark looks and charm and oozed sex-appeal. Luckily Sarah was not with them. There was no doubt but that she'd have gone for him in a big way. Bunny sighed. She had enough problems on her plate at the moment.

The waiter came, introduced himself as Pierre and handed out the menus. They were incredulous at the size of them.

"It's almost a full novel!" Ann cried to much laughter.

There was so much choice they barely knew where to begin. There were six courses to choose from.

"God! I'll be as big as a house if I'm to have six courses every night," Fiona cried.

"Don't worry, you need only have one starter instead of three," Gavin suggested.

"But I want them all!" she wailed.

"You're on holiday. Have them all!" said Richard.

"You can always do an extra half-hour in the gym tomorrow," Bunny suggested.

Fiona gave in and was happy she did. No doubt about it, it would be a challenge not to gain weight over the next two weeks. Luckily, she wouldn't be drinking, she thought as she belatedly remembered she was pregnant!

They all agreed the food was out of this world. The ambience was great and the conversation flowed with the wine. Jack, who played rugby, was thrilled to hear that Gavin had played for Leinster and, together with Richard, they discussed rugby while the women chatted away.

Tony concentrated on Jess.

"Are you still at school?" Bunny asked Emily who was very quiet.

"No, I'm in second year at college in Galway," she replied.

"Goodness, I thought you were only about sixteen." Bunny was embarrassed.

"Me too," Jess agreed. This girl looked so much younger than Sarah.

"No, I'm nineteen," Emily told her. "Don't worry. Everyone thinks I'm younger. I'm used to it." She smiled shyly.

"It's a change," Fiona chimed in. "Most of my sixteen-year-old students look nineteen and older. What are you studying?"

"Law."

"Wow, that's not easy," Fiona observed.

"She got the highest marks of her class in her first-year exams," Ann stated proudly.

"*Mu-um!*" Emily cried, blushing.

"Clever girl," Fiona complimented her admiringly.

Gosh, Bunny thought, what have I been doing wrong? Sarah barely scraped through her re-sits in September and Jess was now contemplating divorce. She envied Ann. Emily was obviously a model daughter.

The McElroys and Kennys had hit it off well and after dinner went for a nightcap together. Jack and Emily were going to meet Galina and her friends in the Saint Tropez Disco.

"You're welcome to join us," Jack said to Jess.

She was flattered but declined to go with them. It had been quite a while since she'd been to a disco. Seeing all those young things prancing around would not be good for her ego. Soon enough she'd be a single woman again and she did not relish having to rejoin the dating pool. Besides, she was enjoying Tony's attention. Philip had sapped her confidence with his betrayal and it felt good that a man as attractive as Tony would find her desirable, as he obviously did.

They went to the Martini bar and Tony sat down next to her rather than beside his wife. Bunny caught the nervous look Ann threw at him.

The waiter came to take their order for drinks.

"I'll have a Martini – stirred not shaken," Tony instructed.

Jess burst out laughing and he laughed with her and put his hand casually up on the seat behind her.

"Didn't James Bond say shaken not stirred?" Ann asked, perplexed.

"That's the joke," Tony replied irritably.

"You know, you remind me of James Bond," Jess said, looking at him, her head to one side. "Sean Connery – the sexiest one."

Oh dear, Bunny thought, I'll have to keep an eye on him. It was obvious he fancied Jess and she was lapping it up.

Tony monopolised Jess for the rest of the evening, much to Bunny's dismay. Ann wasn't too happy about it either but she tried not to show it.

The Saint Tropez Disco was packed. The Captain was there with many of his officers and Jack wondered who the hell was steering the ship. Emily could see that her brother was very popular with all the female dancers. No surprise there! They were a fun group and she enjoyed herself. Galina, who was Russian, asked them to come to the *Strictly Come Dancing* activity the next day when she would be teaching the samba. Jack and Emily promised they would be there.

When they got back to their cabin Gavin and Fiona were excited to find a newsletter detailing all the activities on offer for the following day. Fiona took a pen and circled all the things she wanted to do. The pages were littered with circles.

"I don't know where you'll find the time to eat," Gavin commented.

"That won't be any harm," she said with a laugh.

"Now come on and let's test this bed again," he ordered, pulling her down on it.

"Life doesn't get any better than this," she murmured as he took her in his arms.

Ann and Tony also found the newsletter in their cabin. Ann read all the available activities aloud to Tony. He threw his eyes to heaven as she underlined all the things she'd like to attend. All he wanted to do was relax by the pool. It was a holiday for God's sake, not an activity boot camp.

"The McElroys are a really nice family, aren't they?" Ann commented.

"Absolutely. I'm very pleased we met them," Tony agreed.

"That daughter of theirs, Jess, is a bit strange though, isn't she?"

"How do you mean strange? I thought she was gorgeous. Very classy."

"What were you two talking about anyway?"

"Oh, this and that. She was telling me about her life in London. It was fascinating to hear about it. Very upper-class. How the other half lives."

"Bunny tells me that she's just left her husband."

"I know. She told me."

Ann bit her lip. She could tell that he was hugely impressed with Jess. He always was with those he thought were above him socially and Jess was obviously at the top of the social ladder. It didn't hurt that she was stunningly beautiful.

"I wonder where that younger daughter of theirs is? I felt some tension there when they mentioned her."

"Yeah, I gather from Jess she's very wild. They don't get on. Not every family is as lucky as we are with our offspring," Tony observed.

"Amen to that," said Ann as she undressed for bed.

Sarah and her friends were the last ones in the restaurant.

Tarquin had not enjoyed himself at all. He did not like these people that Sarah had picked up. They were cocky and arrogant and were drinking far too much. They were also very loud. Coming on this cruise had been a big mistake. He was seeing a side of Sarah that he did not like very much. The way she treated her mother was unacceptable. The thought of introducing her to his parents made him blanch. That would certainly never happen now. How had he ever thought otherwise? He'd had a miserable night and had stopped drinking wine halfway through the meal.

Now Tarquin had had enough. Enough of these shallow people, enough of the drinking and enough of Sarah. He wanted nothing more than to go to bed. "Don't you think it's time we retired?" he asked Sarah.

"Come on, don't be a party-pooper. The night's still young. We're going to the disco!" she cried, her voice slurred.

"No. I'm off to bed. I'm awfully tired."

"Oh, come on! I'm having fun." She pulled at his arm.

"You go if you want. Count me out."

"Oh, all right," she grumbled sulkily. "Let's go to bed."

When she stood up she stumbled and Tarquin realised she was really very drunk. He had to practically carry her to her cabin where she collapsed on to the bed. He looked at her in disgust. There was no way he was going to share a bed with her. He left her there and went to his own cabin.

God, how did I get myself into this? he asked himself. How could I have been so stupid? He buried his face in his hands and wondered how he could ever have thought she might be The One. She was a nightmare.

It had been a very international group at Declan and Cassie's table that first evening. They had arranged to dine with Marie and Michel – the French couple they'd met earlier  and also at the table were an Argentinian and Italian couple and two American guys. The conversation was interesting as they exchanged information on their differing lives and cultures. Cassie couldn't believe how great the food was. Better than some Michelin-star restaurants she'd been to. She would really have to watch it if she didn't want to balloon over the next two weeks.

After dinner she went with Marie to the gift shops while Declan and Michel went to the Louvre bar for a nightcap. That was when Declan's world came crashing down around his ears. As he sat chatting, he heard a voice behind him.

"Hello, Declan! Fancy meeting you here!"

He turned his head and standing there was Alix and she was smiling. He almost dropped his drink and for a moment thought he might be hallucinating, but no, it was Alix, in the flesh. He went as white as a sheet as he stood up.

She hugged him.

"Surprise, surprise!" she whispered in his ear.

Surprise was putting it mildly. He was in shock. He didn't know what to say.

"What are you doing here?" was all he could think of.

"I decided I needed a break and *voilà!* Here I am."

Declan realised that Michel was looking at them strangely. "Oh, excuse me, let me introduce you. Michel, meet Alix Lynch. Someone I know from Ireland."

They shook hands and just at that moment Cassie arrived back with Michel's wife. Declan wished the ground would open up and swallow him or preferably Alix.

When he made no effort to introduce them, Cassie spoke up.

"Hello. I'm Cassie and this is Marie."

"Hi, I'm Alix. I work with your friend Deirdre."

They shook hands.

"Oh yes, Deirdre has often spoken of you. You were going to her for Christmas too, weren't you?"

"I was but I really needed to get away – escape actually – so I flew to Fort Lauderdale and this cruise happened to be the first one available."

"What a coincidence!" Cassie laughed. "Are you alone?"

"Yes, all alone." She said it with a pretty pout.

Declan stood transfixed. Cassie broke into his reverie.

"Darling, can you order a drink for Alix?" She indicated the chair next to Declan. "Please join us, Alix. What would you like?"

"A glass of champagne would be lovely." Alix smiled sweetly at Declan.

"Allow me," said Michel, beckoning the waiter.

"What happened to make you need to escape – and at Christmas too," Marie asked.

"It's a sad story but not unusual. The man I love dumped me unexpectedly and I just had to get away." Tears welled in Alix's eyes, making them glitter like emeralds. She looked up from under her long lashes at Declan.

He clenched his fists. What was she playing at?

"We were going to move in together," Alix continued,

"and I thought he was The One and then – *wham* – he left me high and dry." She sniffed as a single tear rolled down her cheek.

Her performance was worthy of an Oscar, Declan thought. What on earth could he do?

"You poor thing," said Cassie, her voice full of sympathy.

"Men can be so cruel," Marie added.

"Yes, he was terribly cruel." Alix sniffed once more.

"Do you want to talk about it?" Cassie asked gently. "Sometimes it helps to share a problem."

"Not tonight. Maybe some other time," Alix replied, looking directly at Declan.

He said not a word as the others sympathised with her.

"Are you open-dining in the restaurant?" Cassie asked.

"No. Unfortunately I booked so late that only the fixed early-seating dining was available. I would have preferred open dining."

"That's what we have," Cassie replied. "What a shame. You could have joined us for dinner every night."

Declan heaved a sigh of relief. At least he wouldn't have to suffer that.

"You're too kind," Alix smiled wanly at Cassie. "Now tell me, what are your plans while on board? There's so much to do."

Cassie filled her in on all the activities she had planned. "I'm going to Pilates in the morning if you'd like to come with me."

"I'm not really into fitness," Alix confessed with a grimace. "What do you do, Declan, while your wife is off dancing and exercising?" She turned to him with parted lips and eyebrows raised.

"I keep busy," he replied nervously.

Declan didn't know how he got through the next hour but somehow he did. He couldn't wait to get away.

Cassie and Alix exchanged cabin numbers as they said goodnight.

"Isn't that amazing – Alix being here?" remarked Cassie as they walked back to their cabin.

Not amazing, bloody terrifying, Declan thought. Just what did the bitch plan to do? He was very afraid and was quite sure he should be. When they reached their cabin they found chocolates and rose petals on the bed.

"It does feel like a honeymoon," Cassie laughed.

Declan couldn't have laughed to save his life. He felt he was living a waking nightmare.

# Chapter 8

Fiona slept like a baby, lulled by the gentle movement of the ship.

"This must be what babies feel when they're being rocked," she murmured as they lay in bed the following morning. "It's lovely. No wonder it puts them to sleep."

They would be at sea all day – a 'sea-day' the newsletter called it – en route to Andros in the Bahamas where they would dock the following morning. Meanwhile they had a full day of activities planned on board. First off, they hit the gym for an hour before returning to the cabin for a shower. Gavin called his parents' suite to see if they wanted to meet up for breakfast.

"No, we're having breakfast here with Jess but we'd like to meet up with you all for lunch. One o'clock in the Tour Eiffel restaurant. Does that suit you?"

"Sure. We'll be there."

Gavin and Fiona then headed to the Buffet for breakfast. Again the selection of food on offer was mind-boggling but they decided to restrain themselves and keep it simple – juice, poached eggs on toast and coffee. Their eyes were out on sticks when they saw the loaded plates some people were carrying.

"Have you noticed?" Gavin whispered as they found a table. "The fatter they are the more they're eating."

She giggled. "I guess for some people this is the highlight of a cruise."

"Sad!" was his reply.

"I couldn't agree more."

There was no sign of Sarah. No doubt sleeping off a hangover!

The morning passed in a flurry of activity for Fiona. When she left him to go to Pilates, Gavin retired to the pool which was buzzing as it was a beautiful sunny day.

To his surprise, Tarquin was there but no sign of Sarah.

"Good morning, Tarquin. All alone?"

"Yes, I guess Sarah's still sleeping."

"Is everything okay?"

"Not really. She was terribly drunk last night. I slept in my own room." He sounded very despondent. "I don't know what's got into her. She was never like this in college."

"How long have you two been seeing each other?"

"Only this term. About two months."

Gavin felt sorry for the guy. "Well, there's eight years between Sarah and me. She came along when my parents had given up hope of having another child. As a result they've spoilt her terribly. Now she expects to get her own way all the time."

"It's not just that. Her drinking is out of control."

"I know. My parents are worried about that too. In fact, I promised them I'd have a word with her today."

"I don't think these new friends of hers are helping." Tarquin frowned. "I don't trust them."

Gavin realised that he really liked this young guy and felt sorry for him. It was true what he said – Sarah was being more outrageous than ever.

Fiona was right. Sarah needed a good shaking-down. He vowed to talk to her later.

"The parents would like us all to meet for lunch at one in the Tour Eiffel restaurant. That okay with you?"

"Absolutely. And thank you, old chap."

"Less of the 'old', please." Gavin laughed.

"Sorry." Tarquin blushed with embarrassment. "I didn't mean that. Too many years listening to my father, I'm afraid."

There was great coming and going as people went to the various activities. The Pilates started at ten and Alix took her chance, knowing Cassie would be occupied. She scoured the ship looking for Declan and found him sunning himself on the top deck.

"We need to talk," she stated, "privately. Come to my cabin. It's 365. Easy to remember. Days in the year."

She left and he had no choice but to do as she said.

He knocked nervously on her door, making sure nobody else was in the corridor. She let him in and he faced her, apprehensive of her plans.

"What do you want to talk about?" he asked.

"Are you serious? You lie to me, telling me you have a family emergency, and then I find out that you've taken off with your wife on a cruise."

"I can explain," he stuttered.

She stood with her arms akimbo, her face like thunder. "This better be good."

Declan was trying to think fast on his feet of something – anything – that would calm her down.

"I had no choice. Cassie booked it unknown to me. What could I do?." He was perspiring profusely, praying that she'd buy this.

She uncrossed her arms and looked at him dubiously. "Why did she do that?"

"I think she suspects that I'm seeing someone."

"Maybe it's time you told her about us then." She smiled slyly.

He had to play along. "Yes, I plan on telling her after this cruise," he lied.

Alix was overjoyed.

"Does this mean that you'll divorce her and marry me?"

Declan had no choice but to play along. "Yes, my sweet, but you can't breathe a word of this to anyone. There's no knowing what Cassie might do. I have to wait until we get back home. In the meantime, we have to be careful."

Alix put her arms around his neck. "Don't worry, honey. I promise it will be our little secret."

She smiled seductively at him. "I've missed you and I know you've missed me too," she pouted, letting her beach-dress drop to the ground.

She stood before him naked. Despite himself he found himself becoming aroused. Her voluptuous body always had that effect on him.

"We shouldn't be doing this!" he cried, dropping to the sofa, his head in his hands.

"Come on, Declan, you're not really in a position to refuse, are you? You don't want me spilling the beans to

Cassie, do you? What would she say if I told her you were the lover I was trying to escape?"

This was blackmail but he had to play it carefully. "What do you want?" he asked, trying to keep the desperation from his voice.

"To continue as lovers," she informed him, straddling him where he sat. "For the moment . . ."

Despite himself, he had a full erection.

"That's my boy," she said as she felt it press against her. She pulled his head down between her large breasts.

He took a nipple in his mouth and moaned and the next thing he knew they were having crazy sex.

"You need it, don't you?" she smiled at him when he'd exploded inside her. "You can't live without me."

He was angry with himself for his weakness but he never could resist the temptation of sex. Besides, he knew he had to keep her sweet.

"This is what I propose," Alix announced, her voice brooking no argument. "For the moment, we'll get together whenever we can. Any time Cassie is busy, you call me. I don't want to upset her but I do need to see you. Our time will come. I know we are meant to be together."

"I have to go," he said, looking at his watch in a panic when he saw the time.

"Keep me happy and I'll keep my mouth shut. See you later, lover boy," she purred, kissing him deeply.

He refrained from wiping his mouth as he made his getaway. The palms of his hands were wet with sweat. What a hole he'd dug for himself! How would he get out of this?

Fiona found the Pilates session easier than what she was used to. Next to her was a pretty girl who was also in her late twenties. When the girl asked a question of the instructor Fiona was surprised to hear the Irish accent.

"You're Irish?" she asked as they picked up their mats at the end of the class.

"Yes," Cassie smiled. "From Dublin."

"Me too," Fiona laughed. "Well, that's a good one. We met another Irish family at dinner last night."

"We just can't escape each other, can we?" Cassie laughed with her and held out her hand as she introduced herself.

"Fiona." She took an instant liking to Cassie who had a warm handshake and was very attractive. "Have you time for a smoothie in the Spa bar? I'm parched."

"Sure," Cassie replied, smiling.

"Great."

"You were so good at those Pilates exercises. I'm afraid I'm not nearly as fit as you," Cassie confessed as they walked to the Spa.

"I should hope not. I'm a PE teacher by day and I work part-time in a gym too."

"That figures," Cassie grinned. "I don't feel so bad now."

They ordered their smoothies and bonded even more when they found out they were both from the Northside of Dublin.

"Though I live on the Southside now," Fiona admitted.

"Traitor!" Cassie teased and they both giggled as Fiona pretended to swat her.

They were so at ease with each other that the time flew by and Fiona jumped up when she looked at her watch and saw how late it was.

"Oh my God, I told my husband I'd meet him after the

class. I'd better run. How about we meet up later?"

"I'd like that. I'm going to the cookery demonstration after lunch."

"Great! Me too. I'll meet you there."

Cassie looked after her, thinking what a nice person she was. She had a feeling they would become good friends.

When Fiona got back to the cabin Gavin told her about his meeting with Tarquin. "He really is a fine young man," he said.

"I think so too but I don't think he's right for Sarah. He's much too gentle."

After that they went for a swim in the pool which was fun as the gentle rocking of the boat caused small surf-like waves. They then got into the hot-tub which was heavenly and so relaxing. They would have stayed longer but they had to go and change for lunch.

Ann was keen to go to the jewellery-making class that morning but was nervous about going alone so Emily agreed to accompany her. They sat beside a very nice American called Nina and by the time the class was over she and Ann had become friends. Nina confided that her husband Paul spent all his time in the Casino but that it didn't bother her. She did her own thing and had a full agenda planned for the day. She invited Ann to join her and Ann was more than happy to do so as they both wanted to do the same things.

Jack went to the pool where there were non-stop games, music and dancing, organised by Maja and her Activity Team. Emily joined him there after the jewellery class. She was relieved that her mother had found someone who shared her interests and could accompany her to the various activities. It let her off the hook a bit.

Tony was anxious to get a tan and wanted to find somewhere away from all the noise where he could chill out and lie in the sun. He scoured the decks and at the very back of the ship he found a very secluded veranda that held only four sun-beds. There was no one else there. What a find! It was not overlooked at all and he realised he could even sunbathe nude here without anyone seeing him.

He had settled down to relax when he heard footsteps on the stairs. He looked around in irritation at this interloper and was pleasantly surprised to find it was Jess. Thank God he hadn't stripped off!

"So you found this place too!" she said with a laugh. "Great minds think alike. You don't mind if I join you?"

"Of course not, you're very welcome," he said as she dropped her sarong to reveal a tiny white bikini. His eyes were out on sticks as he took in her beautiful firm body and full breasts, their very prominent nipples pushing against the flimsy material. It was enough to arouse a saint.

"How did you know about this place?" he asked her.

"I sussed it out the minute we came on board yesterday. I need somewhere away from the hordes to chill out."

"Me too," he confessed. "I think we're two of a kind, you and me."

She smiled, her perfect white teeth shining. She saw the way he was looking at her and knew she was turning him on.

As she stretched out on the sun-bed he turned over on his stomach so she wouldn't see his erection. He felt like a teenager unable to control his emotions. It was exciting.

She lay with her eyes closed as he watched her surreptitiously. She was the most beautiful creature he had ever seen. Everything about her was perfect. That face, that hair, and that magnificent body. When she opened her eyes and smiled at him, he felt like he was drowning in an emerald sea.

He enjoyed chatting to her although for periods they didn't talk as she lay, eyes closed, soaking up the sun. But they were comfortable silences and they allowed him to drink in her beauty.

Jess told him about her life and what had happened with Philip.

"Your husband is a fool. Going out for hamburger when he had the best steak at home," Tony declared.

Jess gave a rueful smile.

"I couldn't imagine any man cheating on you," he added. He meant it. She was not only beautiful but strong like her mother. He admired gutsy women like that. How he wished Ann was more was like them.

"What about *your* marriage?" Jess asked, sitting up to face him.

"What can I say? When we married I was just starting out but as I became more successful we grew apart. I'm ambitious, Ann is not. She'd prefer to have me in a mundane nine-to-five job, living a dull, ordinary life like so many of her friends' husbands. That's not me."

"I can see that. I have to say it's nice to meet a real man for a change." She flashed another dazzling smile at him and he felt flattered. "Especially after all the wimps I mixed with in London," she added with a grimace. "All of them feeling entitled, living off Daddy's money. They have no ambition, no interest in anything other than being seen in the best places with the best people."

"Was your husband like that?"

"No, he wasn't, but most of his friends were."

"Will you go back to him?"

"No way!" she said vehemently. "How could I ever forgive him?"

He believed her and admired her for being so determined. What a fool that man must be.

They were both reluctant to leave their secluded spot to go and have lunch with their families.

"I just wish we could skip lunch and stay here," she murmured.

"Me too," he agreed.

"But I guess we can't," she said, standing up and stretching. "Duty calls."

"Will you be back here after lunch?" he asked hopefully.

"I guess so." Why not? Jess thought. This was fun. She had been aware of his erection and it gave her a sense of power. It was obvious how much he admired her. "Yeah, sure. Will you be here?"

Wild horses wouldn't have kept him away but he wouldn't let her know that. He tried to play it cool. "I guess so."

"I hope no one finds our hideaway. Let's leave our towels and some stuff on all four beds here so they get the message."

"Good idea. Let's keep it our secret."

"Fine. Not a word to the others." She reached over and put her finger to his lips. Her touch was electric. He could feel the chemistry between them. Tony felt alive again.

Jess felt a little flirtation was just what she needed right now. It made her feel good. Of course, there was Ann to consider so it could only be a flirtation. As she watched him dress she admired his fine physique. *Hmmm* . . . He *was* attractive and quite sexy.

"Where's Sarah?" Bunny asked as they met in the restaurant for lunch.

They all looked at Tarquin who blushed deeply. "Er . . . she's still sleeping," he admitted, embarrassed.

"I don't believe it!" Bunny exploded.

"She's feeling rather unwell," he explained.

"She'll be feeling more unwell by the time I'm through with her," Bunny snapped, her face flushed with anger. "Richard, that's it! We have to do something with that girl. I've a good mind to send her home from Andros tomorrow."

"Hang on, Mother," Gavin appealed to her as he tried to diffuse the situation. "I'm planning on having a talk with her after lunch. Let's wait till then."

"Can't we just forget about Sarah for now," Jess pleaded, "and enjoy our lunch?"

Jess was still remembering how Tony had looked at her and did not want talk of Sarah to spoil it.

"I suppose," said Richard. "She's not going anywhere anyhow."

They ordered lunch and tried to put the problem of Sarah out of their minds.

Bunny noticed that Jess's mood had changed. That dead-eye look was gone. She even caught her smiling to herself. She wondered if she'd come to her senses and decided to go back to Philip. She certainly hoped so.

Ann was already seated in the Buffet with a woman she introduced as Nina when Tony arrived. Nina was from Long Island and was the type of sassy, smart-talking New

93

Yorker that Tony abhorred. She and Ann talked pretty much non-stop all through the meal. Ann found Nina very entertaining but Tony tuned out and allowed himself to think of Jess. He couldn't wait to see her again.

When Nina went back for yet another plate of food, Ann whispered to him. "Is something wrong? You're being very quiet."

"I didn't get a chance to get a word in edgeways, did I?" he snapped. "Where did you meet that dreadful woman?"

"Shush, she's coming back," Ann whispered.

He couldn't wait to make his escape. He was relieved when Ann and Nina left to go to some cookery thing. He hurried to his secret hideaway, hoping Jess would be waiting for him.

She was stretched out on the sun-bed, eyes closed. She smiled up at him lazily. "How was your lunch?"

"Boring as hell," he replied, settling down on his bed. "Ann foisted a dreadful American woman on me who yapped non-stop all through lunch. I thought it would never end."

"Poor baby," she cooed, reaching out to rub his arm. Her touch was again electric and once again he had to turn over on his stomach so she wouldn't see his erection.

She recounted the problems they were having with Sarah.

"I honestly don't know why the parents brought her along at all. She's just trouble. They don't need it." Suddenly she sat up. "Could I ask a favour? Would you mind putting some oil on my back?"

"Of course."

She lay on her stomach and opened her bikini top while he oiled her back. He had never felt skin so soft. It was like velvet.

"*Mmmm . . .*" she moaned as he stroked her. "That feels good." Her voice was low and sexy and in that moment he wanted her more than he had ever wanted any woman.

"Don't forget the sides," she instructed him.

He obeyed and, as he stroked the oil on, he could feel the sides of her large soft breasts which drove him crazy with desire. He lay back down on his bed, trying to contain his excitement. Her skin was a lovely shade of pale gold and he watched her as she appeared to snooze a little.

She'd enjoyed teasing him. It felt good to see how much he wanted her. It boosted her confidence. *Take that, Philip, you lousy bastard,* she thought. *Some men find me desirable.* When Tony had been rubbing the oil on her sides and touched her breasts she'd become quite turned on. It was a nice feeling. He was hers for the taking, she knew. For a brief moment she was tempted to do something about it but then thought better of it. It was out of the question. His wife and kids were on this ship too and they were friends with her parents. No way. She quite liked the idea of a little fling but it would have to be with an unattached man – but where to find one?

# Chapter 9

While Jess had been toying with Tony, Bunny and Richard were being pampered in the Spa. The others were taking part in the golf-putting competition organised by the activities committee. It was great fun and, to Gavin's embarrassment, Fiona, who had never had a putter in her hand before, won the competition.

"Maybe you should take up golf," he suggested.

"I will someday but not just yet," Fiona replied. With work and a baby to look after there would be little time for golf.

"Time I had that talk with my little sis," Gavin announced when Fiona had accepted her prize which was a voucher for the gift boutiques.

"Would you like to join me for an ice cream?" she asked Tarquin as Gavin hurried away.

They went to the Palais de Glace, the speciality ice-cream parlour.

She found Tarquin to be charming. Once you ignored

his plummy accent he was really a lovely sweet guy. He was definitely not the right match for Sarah. Talking to him she soon realised that he was thoroughly pissed off with her too. She didn't blame him. Sarah was acting like a spoilt brat.

Fiona left him to go to the cookery demonstration in the state-of-the-art culinary centre. Cassie was already there and had kept a seat for her. Ann was there too, sitting with a woman who passed some funny comments throughout the demonstration which didn't go down well with the French chef. However, most of the audience enjoyed her and laughed at her witticisms.

Fiona and Cassie found the demonstration very informative and intended to try the recipes when they got home. It was most interesting and they were happy to sample the wonderful food afterwards. When it was over they went for a coffee to Le Café. They learnt a bit more about each other over coffee and Fiona was surprised to hear that Cassie was an artist. When she admired the necklace Cassie was wearing she was amazed to hear that she had designed it herself.

"Wow! It's beautiful. You're very artistic. I'd love to have one like it. Where can I buy your jewellery?"

Cassie was just telling her when Alix walked in and she waved her over. She introduced her to Fiona and invited Alix to join them.

"Another Irish passenger? I don't believe it!" Fiona laughed.

"What have you guys been up to?" Alix asked.

"We've just been to the cookery demonstration. It was very interesting."

Alix was furious. So Declan had been free and hadn't contacted her. She wondered why. She'd make him sorry for that.

"And now what?" Alix asked.

"I'm going to the Art Gallery. There's a talk on modern art which I want to hear," said Cassie.

"My, aren't you the busy bee," Alix remarked.

Cassie missed the sarcastic tone of her voice but Fiona didn't.

Cassie looked at her watch. "Oh my gosh, I'd better go. It starts in five minutes."

She jumped up and agreed to meet Fiona at the Captain's Welcome Cocktail Party later that evening.

"I'd like you to meet Declan," she said to Fiona. "See you there too, Alix. Bye, must run."

Alix looked after her, a gloating expression in her green eyes. Cassie was so perfect. Her looks, her life, she had everything. Yet she, Alix, was about to take it all away from her.

Fiona saw the expression on Alix's face as she watched Cassie leave and was shocked. Something weird was going on here but she couldn't imagine what. She'd have to keep an eye on this one. She didn't want her new friend hurt.

Meanwhile Gavin was searching for his sister. She wasn't in her cabin or at the pool and he trawled the bars looking for her. He found her in the Montmartre bar drinking what looked to be a mojito. She was with those darned new friends of hers.

"Sarah, could I have a word?"

"Sure, grab a seat," she replied, patting the seat beside her.

"*In private*," he hissed between clenched teeth.

Sarah knew better than to argue. She'd always worshipped her big brother but at that moment she was a little afraid of him. They moved over to the rails.

"What is it?" she asked nervously.

"I don't think you need to ask. Your behaviour on this cruise has so far been outrageous. You're drinking far too much and we're all very concerned about that."

"So-oh? I'm on holidays, aren't I?"

"We all are but we're not drinking ourselves stupid."

"I'm having fun with my friends," she pouted.

"Cop on, Sarah! These people are not real friends and what about Tarquin? You're treating him dreadfully. He's really pissed off. If you don't stop this wild behaviour Mother might very well pack you off home."

"She'd never do that. We're on a ship."

"Don't underestimate her," Gavin warned her. "She said as much to me. We're in Andros tomorrow. There's an airport there. If I were in your shoes I wouldn't risk it."

Sarah look alarmed.

"I'm trying to help you, Sarah. Now say goodbye to your friends. You can come to the Trivia with us or lie in the sun but no more drinking during the day. Okay?"

She nodded. "Okay, I'll sunbathe. I need to work on my tan."

He left her, hoping she would heed his warning.

Alix headed straight for the top deck where she found Declan tanning himself in his usual spot. It was a secluded spot by the rail bordering the jogging track. There were people jogging past him and, as she watched him, she could see his eyes following the girls. She marched up to him.

"Why didn't you call me when Cassie went to her cookery thingamajig?" she demanded.

"I tried but you weren't in your cabin."

She looked closely at him to see if he was telling the truth.

"You could have called my mobile."

"I had no signal," he told her.

She didn't quite believe him but she let it go.

"Well, she's gone to some art thing now so we have an hour or so. C'mon, let's go."

Declan groaned inwardly. This was so dangerous. If anyone saw him he was a dead man. He had no choice however and, after watching all those young dancers jogging past, he was feeling quite horny so he followed her to her cabin. He was beginning to dislike Alix as a person but the sex was great as usual and she appeared to have calmed down somewhat.

I'm doing this for Cassie, he told himself. I don't want her hurt.

Ann wondered where Tony was. She walked around the ship searching for him but couldn't find him. Nina, her new friend, wanted her to go to a lesson on eye make-up that was being held in the beauty shop. She had no interest in it but, when she couldn't find her husband, she decided she might as well go. It was very boring. She hoped Tony remembered that they were due to play Trivia at four-thirty.

Jack and Emily had gone to the *Strictly Come Dancing* session in the Disco. They were surprised to see so many people there. Galina waved at them as she prepared to give a lesson on the samba. It was fun but Emily found it impossible. The steps were so difficult she just couldn't remember them all. Jack, on the other hand, grasped them straight away.

At the end, Maja – the Assistant Cruise Director who was the judge – had to pick six people to go into the final. Emily, naturally, was one of the first to be eliminated but Jack made it through to the final six.

Each of them then had to dance with one of the professional dancers and the audience would choose the winner.

Galina grabbed Jack's hand and whispered to him as the music started for the final dance. "You're a natural. You were by far the best."

He felt very flattered.

At that moment, Sarah arrived into the room. She'd forgotten about the dance class. She would have liked to join in. It was then she saw him. Her heart skipped a beat, quite literally, as she watched him dance. It was the Latino guy from the bar in Fort Lauderdale. The one she'd thought was so hot.

He was dancing with a very pretty blonde and they were burning up the dance-floor. There was better chemistry between them than the other couples and all eyes were on them. He was tremendously attractive and Sarah felt excited as she watched him. She wondered what it would be like to have sex with him. From the way he moved his body she guessed it would be fantastic. He was wearing tight black jeans and a red shirt, over which he wore a black waistcoat. He looked like a matador. All that was missing was a red cape.

It was time to vote and, as each of the six couples were brought forward, the audience had to applaud. He and his partner were last up and the applause for them went through the roof. They were deemed the outright winners. As he smiled his thanks and looked around the room, his black eyes met hers and her heart did a somersault. It only lasted a moment but there had been a connection that felt like an electric shock running down her spine. She desperately wanted to meet him but it was obvious he was with the blonde as he kept his arm around her shoulders while people crowded around them.

"Damn!" Sarah said crossly under her breath. He was always with another girl. She had to think of something to make him notice her. The thought excited her.

Tony lay beside Jess, soaking up the sun, and realised how fortunate it was that he'd met her. He'd been waiting for a woman like this all his life. There was no denying that his marriage to Ann was dead in all but name. Maybe he was being given a second chance. They'd have to be careful of course but sparks were definitely flying between them. He knew that she was attracted to him too and she'd told him that her marriage was over. Why not? He felt like a teenager in love for the first time.

Jess had no idea that Tony was thinking like that. She was having fun and he made her feel sexy again. She felt desirable and it certainly added spice to the afternoon. She would have liked to stay having her ego cosseted but she'd promised Gavin that she'd go to the Trivia with himself and Fiona.

She stood up stretching and Tony drank in her fantastic body which was now turning a golden brown all over. She was completely uninhibited as she stood before him in that ridiculous revealing bikini and he loved that.

"I'm sorry, sweetie, but I have to leave you," she said, as she tied on her sarong. "I promised Gavin I'd go to the Trivia with them."

"Oh my God!" said Tony, jumping up and looking at his watch. "Is that the time? I told Ann I'd go to that too."

"Great. I'll see you there."

"It's been wonderful talking to you . . . honestly," he said, his voice husky.

"It's been fun," she said, blowing him a kiss. "*Au revoir, chérie!*"

Tony's heart was bursting with excitement. "Till the next time." His eyes followed her as she left.

Jess was sitting with Gavin, Fiona and Tarquin, waiting for the Trivia to start when she saw Tony come in with Ann. His white shirt and shorts showed up his newly acquired tan and she felt a frisson of excitement on seeing him.

Gavin saw them at the same moment. "Ann, Tony, over here! We need two more for our team. Will you join us?"

"Delighted to," Tony replied, taking a seat beside Jess. His leg pressed up against her bare one and he could feel the heat of her skin. He didn't think he could concentrate for one minute on the questions being asked with her so close beside him.

Thanks mainly to Tarquin and Fiona the *Irish East/West* team, as they called themselves, got twenty-three of the twenty-five questions correct and came in second place. Tarquin had really enjoyed it and surprised them with his general knowledge. After the Trivia they all went to the Buffet for afternoon tea.

After that Tarquin went in search of Sarah. He eventually found her lying at the pool.

"The Captain's Welcome Cocktail Party is in thirty minutes," he said. "Do you want to go?"

"Oh, I'd forgotten all about that. Of course I want to go. I'll go and get ready right away."

A cocktail party was just what she needed. She hoped her matador would be there. Just in case, she dressed in her sexiest bandage dress. She knew her mother would think it was far too short and too tight. Too bad.

Twenty minutes later they entered the Notre Dame Club where the Captain and his officers greeted them at the door. Sarah enjoyed the attention of the young officers who buzzed around her. What was it about men in uniform? she asked herself.

There were waiters swanning around with trays of cocktails. Sarah took one off every tray that was proffered, trying a different cocktail each time as Tarquin looked on in despair.

"I don't see the parents here," she observed, looking around. "It's not like Mummy to miss *this* party. She would love hob-nobbing with the Captain and his officers."

It was then she spotted her matador. He was chatting to a girl dressed in a uniform. Sarah saw it was Maja. She saw him bend down and whisper something which made the girl laugh. She felt insanely jealous as she watched them. At least the blonde dancer was nowhere to be seen. That was something.

Tarquin lost count of the cocktails Sarah guzzled as she flirted with the young officers. He saw that Bunny and Richard had arrived and left her to go over to chat to them.

"Bunny, you look lovely this evening," he greeted her and he meant it. She could have passed for Jess's older sister.

"Thank you, my dear boy," she replied, giving him her most charming smile. "And where is that errant daughter of mine?" she asked, frowning as she looked around for Sarah.

"She's over there talking to some of the ship's officers."

"Typical."

Ann and Tony had arrived at the party with Emily. As soon as they'd greeted the Captain and his officers Ann's new friend, Nina, swooped down on them.

"I'm out of here," Tony muttered to his wife when he saw the obnoxious American approaching at speed. He had spotted Jess across the room. "I'm going to say hello to the McElroys. Coming, Emily?"

He walked off and she followed.

"Good evening, everyone," Tony greeted them. "I must say, ladies, you outshine all of the other women here tonight." He bowed, smiling extra brightly at Jess.

"Why, thank you, Tony," Bunny replied, flattered. "I must go to the Spa more often. I'm quite enjoying all these compliments."

"Tarquin, you haven't met my daughter, Emily, have you?" said Tony.

"No. Nice to meet you, Emily," Tarquin said, shaking her hand.

"Where's Ann?" Fiona asked.

"She's been hi-jacked by a dreadful American woman she met earlier."

"Oh yes, I saw them at the cookery demonstration," Fiona told him. "They seemed to be getting on well together."

He grimaced. "Ann picks up these lost sheep everywhere we go. She attracts them like a magnet."

"Poor dear," Bunny sympathised. "She's too nice. I'll have to take her in hand."

"I really wish you would," said Tony with feeling.

Just then Cassie and Declan arrived and Fiona introduced them all round.

"Gosh, I didn't expect to meet so many Irish people on this cruise," Cassie confessed after Fiona had introduced them.

"We Irish like to stick together," said Gavin.

"I guess we understand each other," Cassie replied, smiling.

"Yeah, we all love the craic," Fiona agreed.

Like Fiona before him, Gavin took to Cassie immediately. He thought she was lovely – so natural, warm and friendly.

Bunny, who could spot good breeding from a mile away, was anxious to know all about Cassie.

"I'm from Howth where we still live but Dad was a diplomat so I've lived pretty much everywhere," she told Bunny.

"How interesting!" Bunny was suitably impressed. "And what's your father's name? Perhaps I know him."

Fiona and Gavin exchanged glances and grinned. Bunny was in high interrogation mode.

"Mark Smithson," Cassie replied.

Bunny put her hands to her face. "*I don't believe it!* Richard and I know your father well. A lovely man." She was beaming from ear to ear.

"Yes, indeed, we met him a few times in Rome when he was ambassador there," said Richard. "What a coincidence!"

They were very impressed with Fiona's new friend. Such a lovely girl.

Cassie smiled at Fiona who gave her the thumbs-up.

Fiona had told her a little about Bunny and she had obviously passed scrutiny.

Bunny was so taken with Cassie that she decided to hold a cocktail party in the suite the following evening and invited all of them to attend. It was Christmas Eve after all and it would be nice to have all the Irish together – and Tarquin of course. Declan was delighted to accept. He was more than happy with the way things were going. People like the McElroys impressed him greatly.

Bunny, however, was not so taken with him. She could see he was charming and handsome but it was obvious he was not in the same league as his wife. She had seen through him immediately.

"All front, no substance," she said later to Richard. "That poor girl deserves so much better. I'm sure her father is appalled at her choice of husband."

Fiona did not like Declan much either. He was one of those people who keep looking over their shoulder when they're talking to you as if they're looking for someone more interesting to come along. She detested people who did that. Like Bunny, she secretly thought Cassie was way too good for him. Her instinct told her he was not to be trusted.

Bunny was not too happy either with the way Tony was monopolising Jess again. From the look on his face he was obviously very smitten with her. Not that she blamed him. Jess was looking gorgeous and was doing nothing to discourage him. Oh dear!

They were all having a good time, enjoying the cocktails and canapés, when Cassie spied Alix approaching.

"Oh, here's Alix. I asked her to join us," she said, turning to Declan.

Fiona saw Declan go very pale as his eyes shifted to the

glamorous redhead who was sashaying towards them.

"Another Irish person? I don't believe it! We're being overrun," Tarquin cried, to much laughter.

"Yes, we're the Irish Mafia, didn't you know?" Richard teased him. "Better not let your parents know that."

"Don't mind him, he's joking," Bunny assured Tarquin, afraid the poor boy might have taken Richard seriously.

Tarquin blushed. "Of course. I was joking too."

Emily was happy to see that she wasn't the only one who blushed frequently. It endeared Tarquin to her.

A bell rang and silence was called for as the Captain took to the stage to welcome them. He was Greek and hilariously funny and they were all in stitches, laughing at his anecdotes.

Fiona was very aware of the tension between Alix and Declan. Something was definitely wrong there. She wondered what it was.

Again, Jess enjoyed being the object of Tony's attention. From time to time his hand brushed against hers and Jess knew he was doing it intentionally. She wondered why Ann was not with him. Maybe what he had told her about their marriage was true. *Mmmm* . . . interesting.

Bunny also invited Alix to the cocktail party the following evening. On hearing this Declan almost had a panic attack. How was this happening? Was Alix going to blight this whole cruise? He broke out in a sweat.

Alix smiled at him triumphantly.

Sarah gave her family a wide berth at the party. She wanted to keep out of her mother's way as much as possible. She searched for her Italian friends but they were nowhere to be found which was unusual. They were not the type to miss

109

a party. She had arranged to meet them for dinner in La Brasserie, another speciality restaurant.

As the party was winding down Tarquin went back to her.

"Are you coming to dinner?" he asked.

"I suppose. We're eating in La Brasserie tonight with Carlo and the others."

"No, Sarah. I do not want to dine with them tonight. I don't like those people. They're shallow and loud and drink far too much."

"They're my friends and they're fun. You eat where you like. I'm going to La Brasserie with them." She stamped her foot.

"Fine. I will," he said coldly as he turned on his heel and left her.

She stared after him, not believing that he had walked out on her like that. Well, fuck him, she thought. He can't tell me what to do.

Tony saw that Ann's friend had left her, so reluctantly he had to leave Jess and go back to her. He took Emily with him.

"I'm sorry – Nina was alone so I had to stay with her," Ann apologised.

"Does she not have a husband to keep her company?"

"She does but he spends all his time in the Casino. I hope the McElroys didn't think that I was being rude?"

"No. I explained the situation to them."

Ann looked relieved.

Tarquin was passing by, his face like thunder, when he saw them and stopped abruptly.

"Are you okay?" Ann asked him, concerned.

Tarquin blushed. "Yes. Just had a tiff with my girlfriend

Sarah," he admitted. "She wants to dine with some new friends she met but I can't stand them, so I told her she could go without me."

"You're welcome to join us for dinner," said Ann.

"Thank you but I wouldn't want to intrude."

"Don't be silly," Tony said. "We'd be happy to have you join us. In fact, we insist."

"That's very kind of you," said Tarquin, blushing again.

He left then but agreed to meet them for dinner at seven-thirty.

"Sarah is the younger McElroy girl, isn't she? Just what is going on with her?" Ann asked when he was gone. "He's such a nice boy even if he does speak with a hot potato in his mouth."

"I gather she's a spoilt bitch," said Tony. "Not at all like her sister, Jess."

# Chapter 10

"I've invited my friend, Nina, to join us too," Ann announced as they made their way to the restaurant for dinner.

"You've what?" Tony snapped, not able to believe his ears.

Ann looked at him nervously, twisting her ring in agitation. "Well, I didn't exactly invite her. She invited herself," she confessed.

Jack saw that Tony was about to explode. "Dad, calm down. It's done. There's nothing we can do about it now."

Tony threw his wife a furious look and with a scowl marched ahead of her to the restaurant where Tarquin was waiting for them.

Nina and her husband Paul were there too.

They were an odd couple, Nina and Paul. He was older than his wife, much older, and whereas Nina talked a lot her husband hardly said a word. Tony guessed that he had tuned out years ago. The mystery was why he hadn't physically removed himself too. God knows, I would have, Tony thought to himself.

"This is our fourth cruise this year," Nina told them.

"Four?" Ann exclaimed. She loved cruising but four in one year?

"Paul knows I like to meet people and, as he spends his days in the Casino, cruising is perfect for us. Right, honey?" She patted her husband's hand.

"*Hmm*," was his reply.

Just then another American woman joined them at the table and this woman was even more talkative than Nina. Tony thought he'd died and gone to hell.

When the newest arrival, whose name was Liz, heard that it was Nina's fourth cruise of the year she announced, "That's nothing. This is my eighth cruise since last January."

Now Ann was totally shocked. That was really over the top. Even Nina seemed disbelieving.

"My husband died last year and we used to cruise a lot together. I saw no reason to stop just because he was gone." She looked at them, almost daring them to disagree.

The others were appalled at the woman's insensitivity.

"We'd been all over the world," she announced proudly. "We'd been to forty-seven countries."

"Have you visited Ireland?" Ann asked.

"Yes, we've been to Dublin and Glasgow."

"Er . . . Glasgow is in Scotland," Jack informed her.

"Maybe, but they're close, aren't they?" she replied, unaware of her faux-pas.

Tarquin caught Jack's eye and saw that he was trying to suppress his laughter.

"Did you spend long in Dublin?" Emily asked her.

"Oh, just about six hours. Lovely city."

"That's not really visiting a country, is it?" Jack couldn't resist it.

Ann shot him a look that stopped him saying more.

Tony completely ignored the woman but it didn't seem to bother her. The more the meal went on the more the others tuned out to Liz's monologue. Even Nina was silenced. At one point Paul almost nodded off, much to Jack's amusement.

Tony had spotted Jess at another table. She was facing him and so he could watch her without it being too obvious. She spotted him once and gave him a smile which lifted his heart. It was the only thing that made the meal tolerable. She was looking radiant. He was relieved when the meal was over.

Tarquin was the first to leave.

Liz wanted to exchange cabin numbers with Ann and Nina and Ann was about to scribble hers down when Nina cut in.

"We'd rather not, if you don't mind. I'm sure we'll see you around the ship."

Ann looked at her admiringly, wishing she had the courage to deal with obnoxious people like that.

Liz was a bit miffed but Nina held firm.

"I hope we can have dinner together again," Liz said as she left.

"Over my dead body," Jack mumbled under his breath, garnering a frown from his mother.

"Mine too," Tony mouthed to Jack behind her back.

"Interesting people," Ann remarked when Nina and Paul had left.

"Interesting people? You think?" Tony demanded. "That Liz is the most obnoxious woman I've ever come across. Nina is very talkative too and, as for her husband, I didn't hear him say a word," Tony remarked sarcastically.

Ann looked abashed. "Liz certainly had some interesting stories of her travels," she added nervously.

"Seriously Mum, she's dreadful!" Jack snorted.

"At least she stopped Nina from talking," Emily chimed in.

"Thank God for that," said Tony.

"Now, guys, let's be charitable. I like Nina. She's very friendly," Ann insisted.

"She's that all right," Tony remarked to sniggers from his kids.

Sarah's night was not going as well as she'd planned. When she arrived at La Brasserie the two Italian girls raised their eyebrows when they heard that Tarki would not be joining her. She could almost feel the freeze emanating from them.

"I was surprised you weren't at the Captain's party," she said to Carlo. He shrugged nonchalantly.

"We had some business to attend to," Enzo told her.

At this, the two girls exchanged glances. It was obvious there was an undercurrent in the air. The girls spoke Italian for practically the rest of the meal and Sarah felt completely left out. Carlo was flirting with her as usual and Paola, who'd had quite a lot to drink, suddenly stood up and threw her glass of white wine at him. Carlo grabbed her arm and let out a tirade at her in Italian. At this Paola stormed off and Sofia quickly followed.

"What was that all about?" Sarah asked.

"Paola is a jealous woman," Carlo remarked, shrugging his shoulders.

Sarah and the two men left the restaurant and went up

to Deck 15 for a smoke. They were the only guests out there and Sarah, who'd had a lot to drink, basked in their sole attention.

She asked them if they had plans for the following day, hoping that she could join them, but they were both evasive.

"I apologize for Paola's behavior," Carlo said as he took a packet of white powder out of his pocket.

He then set up three lines of what Sarah guessed was cocaine. He rolled up a Euro note and handed it to her.

She had never done this before and didn't want to appear gauche. "After you," she said, watching how he did it.

"This is good quality stuff," Carlo told her as he handed the note to her.

"Where did you get it?" she asked.

"From Bruno, the barman in the Montmartre bar."

She snorted and was quite unprepared for the wonderful feeling that swept over her. She felt she was floating. It was mind-blowing.

"So, *bambina*, how do you like that?" Carlo asked. He suspected it was a first for her.

"It's wonderful," she enthused.

Carlo ran his hand softly down her back. She closed her eyes, enjoying the sensuous feeling. Then he slipped the strap of her dress down and kissed her shoulder. She felt desire bubble up inside her and moaned with pleasure.

It was Enzo who broke the spell. "I think it's time we went to bed," he said, standing up.

Carlo glared at him but took the hand Enzo extended to him. Sarah felt deflated and Carlo sensed her disappointment. They both walked her to her cabin.

"I am sorry, *cara mia*. Right girl, wrong place, wrong

117

time," Carlo whispered as he kissed her goodnight at her door. "Here, this might compensate." He pressed the packet of cocaine into her hand. "Sweet dreams, *mio tesoro*." With that he was gone.

As she drifted off to sleep she wondered what he'd meant by wrong place, wrong time, but she was too sleepy to try and work it out.

When Tarquin got back to his cabin after dinner he sat with his head in his hands. The Kennys were lovely people but he felt he could not intrude on their family holiday like a lost puppy. Things were obviously over between himself and Sarah and he felt guilty that her parents, who had been so welcoming, had spent so much money for his fare. But he realised that this cruise had been a dreadful mistake and he felt he had no choice but to leave the ship the following day and fly back to London. He hoped Bunny and Richard would understand. He was sure Gavin would. He decided to call him and explain things. There was no reply so he left a message. Gavin called back thirty minutes later.

"Tarquin, Gavin here. Is everything okay?"

"I need to talk to you. I've decided to leave the ship tomorrow in Andros."

"What?" Gavin almost dropped the phone. "Hang on a minute. Are you serious?"

Tarquin heard him mumble on the other end and guessed he was telling Fiona the problem.

"Oh no!" he heard her cry.

"Listen, we have to talk," Gavin said. "Meet me in the Louvre bar in five."

When he got there both Gavin and Fina were waiting for him.

Fiona took his hand as he sat down. "You don't really want to go, do you?" she asked anxiously.

"I'm afraid that Sarah and I are done and I feel it would be awkward for me to continue," Tarquin explained hesitantly.

"Look, Sarah is a brat and she's brought this on herself," exclaimed Gavin furiously. "We've grown very fond of you as have Bunny and Richard. I know they'd hate to see you leave as much as we would."

"Please, Tarquin," Fiona joined in, "please reconsider. We'd like you to stay."

"Yes, you have us and the rest of the family," Gavin continued, "and the Kennys love your company too. C'mon, let's have a drink and sleep on it and we'll talk again in the morning."

They had a drink and then two more and by the end of it they had persuaded him not to make any rash decisions.

"We're meeting my parents for breakfast at eight tomorrow morning. Why don't you join us? You can talk to them then."

Tarquin agreed to do that.

At seven-thirty the following morning Tarquin's phone rang. Jumping out of the shower he reached for it. It was Bunny.

"Tarquin, what's this I hear about you leaving the ship? Richard and I are terribly upset about it. Gavin says you're meeting him for breakfast but we want you to come to the suite for breakfast. It's more private. Gavin will join us later. Come as soon as you're ready."

Tarquin smiled to himself. This was the equivalent of a Royal Command! The ship had stopped moving so when he was dressed he looked out the window and saw they were anchored in the most beautiful turquoise water he'd ever seen. There were fifty shades of blue and green between the ship and the beaches. Of course, it was a barrier reef which was what made the diving and snorkelling here so fantastic.

He was surprised to see Sarah's friends walking down the ramp into a tender – the small boats that would take them ashore. Carlo and Enzo were carrying suitcases and the two girls had rucksacks. It looked like they were leaving the ship. He would be happy if they were but couldn't help but wonder why they would mid-cruise.

There were no other passengers disembarking yet. The tours were not starting till eight-thirty. But they wouldn't be carrying suitcases if they were just going on a tour.

Very strange indeed

Bunny seemed agitated when he arrived at the suite.

"Gavin told us about your conversation and we couldn't be more sorry," she began, pacing up and down. "Sarah has behaved abominably and we can't say we blame you for wanting to leave, but Richard and I would really like you to reconsider, regardless of your relationship with her."

She looked to Richard for confirmation.

He nodded. "Absolutely, old chap. We accept that you and Sarah are finished but please don't let that affect your decision."

Bunny took over again. "We've become very fond of you, as have Gavin and Fiona –"

"Not to mention the Kennys," Richard chimed in.

"So could you not continue as *our* friends?" Bunny looked at him hopefully. "You need have nothing more to do with Sarah if you don't want to. In fact, you could

120

probably avoid her the whole time if you so wish."

"That's really very kind of you," Tarquin stammered. "I have no problem being just friends with Sarah but I thought it would be an imposition on you if –"

"Nonsense!" said Richard.

Bunny looked at him earnestly. "Please say you'll stay on. It would upset us terribly if you left."

Tarquin raised his hands. "What can I say? You're so kind. I feel you're like family to me. Yes, I'll stay, if that's what you want."

Bunny beamed and then hugged him. Richard did the same, thinking how persuasive his wife could be.

Tarquin became quite emotional. These people were wonderful, treating him like one of their own.

Gavin and Fiona arrived just then with Jess and they were also thrilled to hear he was staying on.

"That's settled then," Gavin said delightedly. "You can join us today. We've rented a boat with Marie and Michel to take us bone-fishing and snorkelling. It will be good fun."

"Will Sarah be going?" Tarquin asked.

"Lord no. We did invite her but she refused to come."

"Can you honestly see Sarah fishing?" demanded Bunny, her voice incredulous.

"Not my cup of tea either," said Jess. "I'm going to chill out somewhere on a gorgeous beach."

"The chill-out queen, that's our Jess," Richard remarked, laughing.

Bunny rang for Raphael and ordered champagne and orange juice to be served with breakfast to celebrate Tarquin's decision.

They had breakfast on the veranda looking out over the glorious aquamarine sea.

"It's almost impossible to believe that it's Christmas Eve," Richard observed as he toasted them.

"Just think what I'd be doing if I was back in Ireland," mused Bunny.

"Running around like a blue-arsed fly," Richard laughed.

"You said it! Not any more. This is how I always want to spend Christmas in the future."

Ann also woke at seven-thirty to the shrill ringing of the phone.

"Who the hell is calling at this hour?" Tony growled.

It was Nina. "Hello, Ann. Poor Paul is not feeling too well today and can't come on the historical tour excursion we've booked and I was wondering if you'd like to come in his place?"

Ann took one look at Tony's face and said she'd call Nina back.

"What does that woman want?"

Ann told him. Jack and Emily had booked to spend the day snorkelling, paddle-boarding and kayaking.

"Go if you want," Tony said, happy to have a quiet day to himself.

"You don't mind?" she asked timidly.

"No, no, as long as *I* don't have to tolerate that woman. You go if you want. It should be interesting."

Ann was delighted and called Nina back immediately to tell her she'd be delighted to join her.

Tony wondered what Jess had planned for the day. He was longing to see her again.

Declan and Cassie had booked an excursion to visit a Batik

factory that she had heard about. She was interested in their traditional designs which were famous. Then after lunch they would be taken to the Barrier Reef to snorkel. Declan was looking forward to a peaceful day without the stress of Alix hanging over him.

He was humming to himself as he shaved when Cassie called out to him.

"By the way I've invited Alix to join us today!"

Declan nicked himself and let his razor fall with a clatter. "Damn!" he cried as he tried to stem the bleeding.

"What's wrong?" Cassie put her head round the bathroom door.

"I've just cut myself." He swore again.

"Did you hear what I said about Alix?"

"Yes, I did."

"You don't mind, do you? She's all alone and I felt sorry for her."

"No," he lied. "But I would have preferred a romantic day alone with you."

"Sorry, I didn't think. That's a nice thing to say." She reached up and kissed him, laughing when she got some shaving cream on her face.

When she'd gone back to continue dressing, he gripped the edge of the sink. Was this nightmare never going to end? He couldn't take much more of it. How on earth had he got himself into this mess? He had to take big deep breaths to steady himself before he could continue shaving. He had a strange premonition that things were not going to end well.

# Chapter 11

As Tony was having breakfast with Ann, Jess entered the Buffet. She sat at a table on her own with a coffee and, when Ann rushed off to meet Nina, Tony made his way over to her.

"How can you look so beautiful at this hour of the morning?" he asked.

She smiled, flattered by his compliment. "Where's Ann gone?"

"She's going on a tour for the day with that awful Nina woman."

"You're not going with her?"

"No way," he replied, looking appalled at the idea.

"And what about Jack and Emily?"

"They're going off soon, doing some kind of water-sports thing."

"And you?" She looked at him, her head to one side.

"I was hoping a beautiful woman I know would be free to sneak off with me to a secluded beach somewhere." He looked at her hopefully.

"Are you sure I wouldn't be in the way? Because that's exactly what I'd planned to do myself." She grinned at him.

His heart lifted. "Are you really free? You haven't booked any tours?"

"God no. The others are going on a fishing trip. What I really would like to do is find a secluded talcum-powder beach and feel that beautiful turquoise water caress my naked skin." She closed her eyes as she spoke.

The image she'd conjured up was driving Tony crazy. "What are we waiting for?" he whispered, barely able to conceal his excitement or arousal.

She debated whether she should go or not because, after all, he was a married man. But then why had his wife gone off and left him alone for the day? She was beginning to believe that, as he'd told her, it was a marriage in name only. She knew many couples like that who stayed together out of convenience. Both she and Tony wanted to spend the day at a secluded beach. Where was the harm in going together? They both liked to do the same things and it would be fun. She said yes. They agreed to meet at nine once the others had disembarked.

Sarah woke much later with a massive hangover and tried to recall what had happened the night before. It was all a bit of a blur. Then she spied the packet of cocaine sitting on the coffee table and it all came back to her. She was dying for a coffee and a cigarette so after a quick shower she made her way to the Buffet. There she picked up a large coffee then took it outside to have a cigarette. She'd hoped to see Carlo and Enzio there but there was no sign of them. She wondered if they were up yet.

She saw that they were anchored in the middle of a

beautiful sea. The ship was almost empty and she went and sat by the pool for a while but she was restless. She was dying for a drink but thought she'd better not. It was only eleven-thirty. When there was no sign of the Italians she went to Le Café where she ordered a latte and helped herself to a big slice of chocolate cake. This was her go-to whenever she was upset. She followed this with a triple chocolate gelato and felt better after that.

She supposed she should get off the ship as everyone else seemed to have done so she took the tender to the island but there was not much to see in the town. She did buy herself a ring and bracelet in a duty-free shop and then after a glass of white wine made her way back to the ship. There was still no sign of the Italians. She went to her cabin and snorted a line of the coke which lifted her spirits somewhat. This stuff was great.

She went on Deck 15 for a smoke and saw that Bruno was behind the bar alone. She asked him if he could get her some coke and he readily agreed, happy to have a new customer. He wanted US dollars for it. While she was getting the money for him in her cabin she noticed a leaflet that offered spa treatments at a discount when the ship was in port. Great! Why should she be miserable when everyone else was off enjoying themselves? After collecting the coke, she headed to the spa and spent a very pleasurable three hours being pampered.

Cassie was having a lovely day but not so Declan. He was sick with apprehension that Alix would say something to his wife.

Cassie didn't know what to make of her. She was a little strange. Over lunch she had tried to draw the other woman out about her failed romance but Alix was very evasive and wouldn't say anything.

Declan meanwhile was rigid with fear that Alix might blurt out the truth. He had to find a way to stop her. His heart couldn't take much more.

Cassie noticed how uptight he was and couldn't figure out why. There was a tension in the air that she found uncomfortable. This second honeymoon had been going so well but suddenly it was going wrong. She guessed it had been a mistake inviting Alix along but she'd felt sorry for her, all on her own. Declan was probably annoyed about that. She'd have to talk to him later when they were alone. Things had been going so well. She didn't want to do anything to spoil it.

In contrast Tony and Jess were having a fantastic day. She had brought the makings of a picnic from the Buffet and they'd bought wine in a shop in the town. They also rented snorkelling equipment there. At the harbour they found water-taxis offering trips to a secluded cove nearby that could only be reached by boat. The man promised to be back for them at four when Tony told him he'd make it worth his while.

There were only a dozen people on the beach and luckily none were from the *Liberté*. It was paradise. Jess threw off her dress to reveal a teeny black bikini which barely covered her assets. Tony couldn't keep his eyes off her and wanted her so badly it hurt. She ran down into the water, calling at him to follow. She dived in and surfaced with her long blonde hair streaming out behind her. She was laughing and Tony thought she was the most beautiful thing he'd ever seen. She was a strong swimmer and he had a job keeping abreast of her as she swam out to sea.

"Isn't this sheer bliss?" she asked as she turned on her back and floated, looking up at the clear blue sky.

"It's heavenly," he replied and indeed he felt like he had died and gone to heaven.

They floated together, basking in the heat of the sun and the warm azure water lapping their bodies.

After their swim they stretched out on their towels and dried off in the sun.

"Do you think anyone would notice if I took off my top?" Jess asked, looking around.

The nearest people to them were fifty yards away and they were lying down sunning themselves and not looking their way.

"I don't think so," Tony replied, hoping and praying that she would.

"You don't mind? You won't be embarrassed?" she asked. "I hate having a white stripe across my chest."

"I certainly don't mind. As far as I'm concerned you can take it all off," he said with a grin.

"Uh-oh, that's a step too far," she laughed, undoing her top.

Tony couldn't help himself. He stared at her voluptuous body, desire in his eyes. Her breasts were very full and the nipples erect. He longed to reach out and caress them but had to restrain himself. He watched as she oiled her body, wishing it was his hands doing it. He turned on his stomach, not wanting her to see his erection again.

But Jess had seen the desire in his eyes. If only he wasn't married, she thought to herself, she would happily have encouraged him. He was damn sexy and they had a great rapport together.

After thirty minutes she sat up and took the sun oil out of her bag.

"Do you mind doing my back again?" She smiled at him as she handed him the bottle. "It's so good to have someone to do this for me."

He refrained from saying that it was a pleasure to be able to touch her. His hands caressed her skin as he stroked the oil all over her back. He'd never imagined skin could feel this soft and silky and as his erection threatened to burst through his swimsuit, he thought he'd explode. Jess closed her eyes and enjoyed the sensual touch of his hands. As he stroked the oil on her side, his hand again touched her breast and she moaned softly. He knew that she was enjoying it and it gave him hope that she felt as turned on as he did.

When it was time for their picnic Jess put her bikini top back on and set out the food while Tony opened the wine. They chatted as they ate and sipped the wine and Jess was amazed that she felt so at ease with him. They were as comfortable as old friends although they barely knew each other a couple of days.

After their picnic they soaked up the sun once more but to his disappointment she kept her bikini on. Then they went snorkelling and it was amazing experience. Tony had never seen any colours as beautiful as those on the myriads of fish they saw. It was magical. He was sad when the water-taxi arrived, as promised, to take them back to the town. He wanted this day to go on forever.

As they left their paradise Tony realised he was falling in love with Jess.

"This is the best Christmas Eve I've ever had in my life," he told her as they sat close in the small boat.

"It was cool, wasn't it?" she replied, smiling.

When Bunny and Richard arrived back to take the tender to the ship they saw that there were police boarding it with them. Declan, Cassie and Alix were on the same tender and they all wondered what the problem was. When they got back to the ship, rumours were swirling that there had been some burglaries on board.

Raphael was waiting for them at the door to their suite.

"Madame, can you please check your valuables in the safe? I'm afraid there's been a problem."

Bunny rushed to the safe and opened it. "Oh my God! It's empty!" she cried.

Richard went to double-check. "I don't believe it."

"I'll call Security, Madame."

They arrived pronto.

"Good afternoon, I'm CSO Allen," the Chief Security Officer introduced himself, "and this is my deputy, Officer Martin. Could you tell us what's missing, sir?"

"Well, some dollars and my wife's jewellery," Richard informed him.

"Don't worry, they're not my real jewels," Bunny hastened to add. "They're paste copies. I never travel with the real thing."

"Thank goodness for that," the CSO replied, relieved. "Some people have had real jewellery stolen."

"Have you any idea who did it?"

"Not at the moment but we believe the robberies occurred during the Captain's Cocktail Party yesterday evening. All of the suites have been targeted and many of the veranda cabins. It looks like they were professionals, I'm afraid."

"Oh dear. Please let us know if you find out anything," said Richard.

"Just hold on while I check with my son and his wife," Bunny said to the officers.

She rang Gavin right away and gave him the news. He went to the safe and discovered that they had also been burgled but luckily Fiona had taken Bunny's advice and had copies made of her jewellery too. Thank God for that. They too had lost some dollars and an iPad, but it could have been so much worse. The CSO and his deputy went straight to their cabin to take details. Fiona then called Cassie who discovered their safe had been tampered with too.

"Luckily, I only have my own jewellery line with me and I keep it in a bag under the bed," she told Fiona. "They didn't find it, not that it would be as valuable as some passengers' diamonds and such."

Jess had heard the news and called her mother. Luckily, the thieves hadn't touched her own cabin.

"Yes, they hit us but didn't get more than a few hundred dollars, apart from my paste jewels," Bunny told her. "You haven't forgotten drinks at six-thirty, have you? I've invited the Irish Mafia, as Tarquin calls them now."

Jess caught her breath. "Who? The Kennys and Jordans?" she asked her mother.

"Yes, who else?" said Bunny laughing.

Jess smiled. That meant she would be seeing Tony sooner than either of them had expected. This was turning into one hell of a Christmas.

Bunny called the Kennys to make sure Tony had told Ann about the party. She knew men could be useless about things like that sometimes. He hadn't. Ann told her they had escaped the burglars which was just as well as Tony had a lot of dollars in his safe.

"Please bring Jack and Emily to the party too," Bunny added, in the hope that they might be a good influence on Sarah.

The deadline for embarkation came and went while the police investigated the crime. They had a good idea who the culprits were but still had to trace them.

Bunny tried contacting Sarah but there was no reply. She went in search of her and found her sitting alone at the bar of the Montmartre where she was waiting forlornly, hoping to see Carlo and Enzo.

It was Bruno who saw Bunny first, striding towards them. Her face was like thunder.

"Mummy!" Sarah cried out in alarm when she saw her.

Bruno was quaking in his boots, scared that this dragon of a woman had heard that he had sold her daughter drugs and was coming for him. But she ignored him and pounced on Sarah.

"I want a word with you, Miss, in private," she said, glaring at Bruno who did a quick disappearing act.

Sarah quaked under her mother's glare. She looked around for her father, hoping that he would diffuse the situation but he was nowhere to be seen.

"You've tested my patience one last time, Sarah. I have been checking the flights from St Thomas and there's one back to Heathrow the day after tomorrow. I think the best thing for all of us would be to send you home."

Sarah was panic-stricken. "Please, Mummy, please don't do that!" She started to cry.

"You should have thought of that before behaving so

disgracefully. The way you've treated Tarquin, your drinking, your total disrespect for everyone . . ."

Sarah was crying harder now. "I'm sorry," she sniffled, "I truly am."

Bunny didn't let up. "I have no intention of letting you spoil this holiday for the rest of us which is exactly what you have been doing."

"Please, Mummy, I promise I'll change. Please let me stay."

Bunny sighed. "Well, I'm willing to give you a second chance. But I swear if you don't change your behaviour at once you'll be on your way home."

Sarah grabbed her hand. "Thank you. I will, I promise."

"Yes, and I also want you to apologize to Tarquin. Do you know he considered flying home today?"

Sarah looked away, shamefaced. "Oh no! I'm sorry. I'll do whatever you say."

"Very well. We've invited the other Irish for drinks this evening. Be there at six-thirty sharp and please be sober and not dressed like a stripper. Now get out of my sight and remember what I said about Tarquin."

Bunny was turning to go when she saw CSO Allen and his deputy approaching.

"Mrs McElroy, we'd like a word with your daughter Sarah."

Bunny was shocked. "Why? What's this in connection with?"

"The burglaries."

"Burglaries?" Sarah asked, shocked.

"Yes, I believe you were friendly with the Italians who left the ship this morning."

"They've left the ship?" Sarah looked dazed.

"Yes, and we're trying to trace the two brothers and their girlfriends."

134

"Brothers?" Sarah cried, incredulous.

"Sarah, could you please stop doing an imitation of a parrot," Bunny ordered her daughter sharply.

"Mummy, what are they talking about?"

Bunny saw in her eyes the vulnerable child that Sarah really was and softened. For all her bluff and bluster she was still her child. Putting her arms around her daughter, Bunny went into mother-hen mode to protect her chick.

"I'm sorry, gentlemen, but my daughter is in shock. She obviously knows nothing about these people she befriended. She's been taken in by them too. Now if you don't mind, it's Christmas Eve and we have friends coming for drinks . . ." she looked at her watch, "in twenty minutes. Sarah and I will be happy to help you with your investigation in any way we can." She laughed. "We're not exactly a flight risk." Taking Sarah by the hand she walked away. Neither of the men had the nerve to stop her.

She walked Sarah to her cabin.

"Now go and get dressed and be at the suite by six-thirty," she ordered. "We'll have a nice evening."

"I feel such a fool, Mummy," Sarah sniffled again.

"I know, I know, dear. We all make bad judgments about people sometimes."

Ann had enjoyed the tour of the island very much and over lunch Nina had revealed her early life story which was really very sad. Her father had been a Polish Jew and ten years old at the time Hitler was unleashing his terror. His mother, knowing what was coming, had paid a friend to take him to the US with her. Three days later his whole family were arrested and sent to Auschwitz.

In the US, the friend's brother had sexually abused the

poor frightened boy and at fourteen he had run away to New York. He worked day and night for years, saving every penny. Eventually he went back to try and find his family but discovered they had all perished in the concentration camp.

He returned to New York where through his hard work he built a business and amassed his fortune. In his forties he met and married Nina's mother, a Polish Jew with a similar history to his, but she died when Nina was only seven years old. He then dedicated his life to raising his daughter to be proud of her Polish Jewish heritage. They adored each other but he died when Nina was seventeen. All alone in the world, she married the first man who showed her a little affection.

"The affection did not last long but that is a whole other story," she confided. "I divorced him after ten horrific years and that was when I met Paul. He was very kind to me and has always been more of a father-figure to me." She smiled. "I did not marry him for his money as people supposed because my father left me a wealthy woman but I needed to belong to someone and Paul filled the bill. He needed me and that meant a lot to me. I've never loved anyone other than my father and in my own way I love Paul, although he's only a shadow of his former self now."

Ann had tears in her eyes listening to Nina's story. She'd had such a lonely life. That was the reason she so wanted to be liked. She could see past the smart-assed attitude and constant talking to the lonely soul within. She vowed to be a good friend to her.

Tony and the kids were already on board when she got back with Nina and she saw they were all nice and tanned.

They had afternoon tea together and she listened to Jack and Emily telling about their day.

As they gabbled on about all they'd seen, she noticed that Tony was very quiet. She asked about his day and he said it was grand but didn't elaborate. She wondered why he was being so secretive. But he was smiling and looked happy so she guessed he hadn't minded her going off on the tour.

When they got to their cabin there were three messages waiting on the machine from Nina.

*'Really enjoyed your company today. We'll meet you at the restaurant at 8 p.m. Looking forward to it.'*

"Can that bloody woman not leave us alone?" Tony said irritably as he heard her messages. "I do not intend to spend every evening listening to her rabbit on."

Ann could see he was very angry. It made her nervous.

"I can't very well say, 'I'm sorry but we don't want to sit with you', can I?" she replied, worried about his reaction.

"Well, *I* will if she continues pushing herself on us like this."

She looked at him aghast. "You wouldn't!"

"I most certainly would," he avowed resolutely.

"She's really terribly lonely. She's had a sad life."

"That's nothing to do with me," he growled.

Ann was very worried as she stepped into the shower. Tony could be very determined when he wanted to be. She hoped he wouldn't carry out his threat. How embarrassing that would be!

She was surprised when Bunny called to remind them they were invited for drinks at six-thirty. Tony had forgotten to mention it. She was pleased Emily and Jack were invited too. Ann was dying to see what a suite looked like.

# Chapter 12

Bunny looked around the suite with satisfaction. All was ready for her cocktail party and the suite looked very festive indeed. Raphael had organised a Christmas tree which sparkled in the corner as well as some elegant decorations. Bunny had set out the presents for the family under the tree and the children would put theirs under it when they arrived.

Sarah was the first one in on the dot of six twenty-five and felt tears come to her eyes when her father wrapped her in a big bear-hug. Bunny was gratified to see that her daughter was wearing a very demure dress, probably the most modest one in her wardrobe, and she was sober. She noted that she was more subdued than usual. She hoped this meant that she'd learnt her lesson and would behave from now on.

Jess arrived next. She looked stunning in a very short red skater dress which showed off her long tanned legs to perfection. When Sarah saw the presents she was carrying she realised with a start that she hadn't bought any presents yet. She'd have to do it later. The boutiques and gift-shops on board would be open late.

Gavin and Fiona came in shortly afterwards, arms full of gifts. They were accompanied by Tarquin.

"You look different," Gavin remarked as he kissed his sister.

"That's because she's actually dressed for a change," Jess remarked snidely.

To everyone's amazement Sarah didn't answer with a smart remark.

"Hi." She greeted Tarquin with a kiss on the cheek, which surprised him.

He thought she looked very pretty in that dress.

"Are you okay?" he asked her warmly. "I heard about your friends. I'm really sorry."

She was touched by his concern. "Thank you. You were right about them all along, it seems." She smiled at him. "I'm sorry I was such a bitch."

"That's okay. We all have our moments."

"Friends?" she asked, holding out her hand.

He took it and then kissed her on the cheek. "Of course," he replied.

Bunny saw this exchange and was pleased. She asked Sarah to take care of the door as Raphael was busy mixing drinks.

Tony, Ann and Emily were next to arrive and Sarah was unusually gracious as she introduced herself and showed them in. Three minutes later there was another knock on the door. Sarah opened it and stood there dumbfounded when she saw him. *Oh my God! Is it possible it's my matador?*

Sarah shook her head to clear it but no, there he was, in the flesh.

"Hello, what are you doing here?" she asked, shocked.

"Actually, I was invited," he replied coolly.

Sarah was so shocked that she just stood there.

"Now if you don't mind I'd like to come in," said Jack.

She realised she was blocking the doorway. "Oh, I'm really sorry. I'm Sarah. Come in."

He brushed past her, not bothering to introduce himself. He'd seen her around of course. She'd been hard to miss. She was the best-looking girl on the ship and she knew it but he knew her type – rich spoilt little darlings who thought they could have anything and anyone they wanted and then they broke your heart. Definitely not his type.

Sarah stood by watching, stunned, as all of her family greeted him warmly.

"Jack, so good you could make it. You know everyone," her mother greeted him.

It seemed he did. He even kissed Jess on the cheek. The last straw came when he greeted Tarki with a slap on the shoulder as if they were old buddies.

The Jordans arrived next with Alix.

When Sarah got a chance, she took Tarki aside.

"How do you know Jack?" she hissed.

"We had dinner together last night and I believe your parents and Gavin had dinner with him the first night."

She couldn't believe it! And all this time she'd been wasting her time with those crooks. She was frazzled. She needed to steady herself so she went into the bathroom and spread out a line of coke. It might calm her down. She made sure she left no evidence of anything or her mother would disown her completely. Checking her nose, she went back to the party, hoping to do a number on Jack. God, he was hot!

Someone else was thinking the same thing about her.

141

Declan was surprised and delighted to find out that the white-haired blonde he'd admired dancing at the pool was actually Bunny's daughter. She was simply gorgeous. It was obvious she and Jess had inherited Bunny's beauty but there was an underlying sexiness about Sarah that attracted him. She was a right little Lolita, very aware of her sexuality and power to seduce. He would love to have engaged her in conversion but with Alix's eagle eye on him he didn't have a chance in hell of doing that.

The party was in full swing as Richard played Christmas tunes on the piano. When he started playing 'O Holy Night' he called Jess up. She shyly joined him and when her pure voice soared everyone was moved. Tony was spellbound as he gazed at her. She was mesmerising.

Jess had finished singing to rapturous applause when there was a knock on the door. It was CSO Allen. Bunny listened to him and then returned to tell everyone that they'd been in touch with Interpol and it was indeed the Italians who had committed the crimes. They were professional thieves who were being sought by the police in many countries. They had aliases of course. They had taken a ferry to Nassau but there the trail had run cold. However, the airport there was being watched along with the ferries and should there be any further developments, they would be the first to know.

Just then the sail-away blast rang out and they all went out on the veranda to watch the ship leave Andros.

"I hope they find the bastards," Richard whispered to Bunny. Not just because of the money they'd taken but for how they'd treated his daughter.

Alix had to leave the party early as she had to go to the first seating of dinner. As she was thanking her hosts, Bunny clapped her hands for attention.

"I was thinking, everyone," she announced, "that as we're all far away from home tomorrow on Christmas Day, it would be nice if we Irish Mafia – and Tarquin of course . . ." she waited for the laughter to die down, "could all have Christmas Dinner together tomorrow night. If you're all agreed, I'll reserve a table for all fourteen of us." She turned to Alix. "And I'll arrange that you can join us too."

"Thank you so much, Bunny," Alix purred, throwing a glance at Declan. "That would be wonderful."

Fiona saw the look of panic that passed over Declan's face. What was he afraid of? She decided that tomorrow she would seek Alix out and try and find out what was going on.

Declan relaxed once Alix had left. This was his chance to talk to Sarah. He went out to the veranda where she was standing alone at the railing.

Despite her best efforts, Jack had ignored Sarah all the time during the party although she noticed him paying lots of attention to Jess which made her extremely jealous. They were seated at a small table and seemed to be getting along great.

She stood looking forlorn as Declan approached her.

He started to chat her up which she thought was funny. He was so old. But she played along with him, hoping to attract Jack's attention. It didn't work. Jack didn't even look their way.

Tony was also wildly jealous as he watched Jess talking to his son and laughing at something he was saying. He longed to go to her but he was caught inside with Ann, chatting to

Richard and Bunny. He could see no way to get up and leave. It would have been beyond rude, even for him.

"Would your parents mind awfully if we leave to go to the sail-away party at the pool?" Sarah heard Jack ask Jess as soon as the ship had left the port.

"I'm sure they wouldn't," she replied, seeing them in the suite, deep in conversation with Ann and Tony.

Jess approached and asked them.

"Go ahead," said Bunny. "I'm sure Sarah would love to go too." She wanted Sarah to be with people her own age for a change.

"You coming, Jess?" Jack asked.

"Sure," she said, "why not?"

Before they left, Bunny took Sarah aside. "Don't forget what I said earlier," she warned her daughter. "Do *not* get drunk tonight. I expect to see you change your ways or you'll be flying home from St Thomas."

"I will. I promise," said Sarah. She knew she was skating on thin ice. Her mother did not make threats she did not intend to carry out. She would have to be on her best behaviour.

Tony was upset to see her leave with Jack. He would have given anything to have gone with her.

Declan would like to have gone too. That Sarah was one hot babe – but he had no choice but to join Cassie who was sitting on the far veranda with Fiona and Gavin.

"Great children you have there," Bunny commented to the Kennys when the youngsters had left.

"They're good kids," Tony agreed, "though Jack is a bit of a rebel." He was still smarting from seeing him laughing with Jess.

"He's a good boy," Ann chimed in. "When I see the trouble some of our friend's kids get into, I realise we've been very lucky."

Bunny sighed. "Don't tell me!"

"What time are you going to dinner tonight?" Richard asked. "Maybe you'd like to have dinner with us here?"

"Thank you, but unfortunately we've arranged to have dinner with another couple tonight," Ann told them.

"*We* did not arrange to have dinner with them. *We* had no choice in the matter," Tony snorted, disgruntled.

"What do you mean?" Richard asked, puzzled.

Ann frowned at Tony but he paid no attention to her.

"Well, Ann met this dreadful woman at something on Monday and since then she's practically hi-jacked us."

"Hi-jacked you?" Bunny exclaimed. "Whatever do you mean?"

Tony continued to ignore Ann's discomfort. "Well, she attached herself to Ann at the Captain's party and asked to join us for dinner last night. Then she insisted Ann accompany her on a tour today"

"She didn't insist," Ann interrupted him. "I wanted to go and you said you didn't mind." She was close to tears.

Tony ignored her. "Then before we came here this evening we got a message saying she'd meet us at the restaurant tonight at eight. No 'please', no 'Are you free?'." He was really on a roll now.

"You're not serious?" Bunny exclaimed. "How rude! And you say she's dreadful?"

"Worse than dreadful," Tony said viciously. "She talks non-stop and –"

Ann interrupted him again. "She can't help it, it's just her way. She's really very nice and I can't very well say to her that we don't want to sit with her, can I?"

"She sounds rather awful, I must say," Richard commented.

"She does indeed," Bunny agreed. "You shouldn't let her intrude like that."

"That's what I think too," said Tony, feeling justified. "It's becoming an issue between us, to be honest," he admitted, looking at his wife.

Ann looked miserable. "What can I do?" she wailed.

Bunny felt sorry for her. "Why don't we join you tonight? The four young ones can go to another table and then we'll be nine," she suggested. "There are no seats for eleven so she'll have to go somewhere else."

"That's a great idea," said Tony enthusiastically, "because my wife is just not able to say no to this woman."

Ann smiled wanly. "She's really nice but Tony doesn't see that. I would hate to hurt her feelings."


The pool party was in full swing but Sarah felt put out. Jack knew everybody – at least all the females there – and she had to look on as they all vied for his attention. Maja was leading the dancing and she blew a kiss to Jack when she saw him. Then the singer in the band did the same while the blonde dancer with whom he'd won the samba competition grabbed him to dance.

"How does he know all these people?" Sarah asked Emily, mystified.

"Oh, Jack gets around," she grinned. "If there's an attractive woman within a mile, Jack will get to know her. Women are constantly throwing themselves at him."

Sarah was miffed. Jack didn't even ask her to dance so she sat watching glumly as he danced with one girl after another. He even asked Jess if she could jive and Sarah was madly jealous as he swung her sister around – her skater dress flying up, revealing far too much of her fabulous legs. Sarah was furious and blamed her mother for making her wear such a demure dress tonight. If she'd been in her Hervé Leger dress Jack would have taken notice all right. She was dying for a drink but knew she couldn't risk it with Bunny's eagle eye on her, waiting for her to cock up.

At seven-forty their parents and the others joined them and Bunny announced that they would all be dining together.

"Sarah, you and Tarquin can sit with Jack and Emily. Jess, you sit with us."

Sarah was happy that she'd have no competition from her sister for Jack's attention. Now was her chance!

They all made their way to the restaurant where they found Nina waiting.

"Hello, Nina. I'm afraid we've invited our Irish friends to dine with us tonight," Ann explained apologetically, indicating Bunny, Richard and the others.

"That's no problem. Any friend of yours is a friend of mine," Nina replied, smiling.

Ann looked at Bunny helplessly.

"You don't understand, Nina. I'm afraid this won't work," Tony tried patiently to explain. "There are nine of us. There is not enough space for us all. We're one too many."

Nina stayed put.

By this stage the maître d' was tearing his hair out as the queue behind them grew longer. The hostess showed the four young people to their table as the drama continued in the foyer.

"Nina, there are nine of us and with you and Paul that would be eleven." Tony tried again to get through to the stupid woman. "The biggest tables only seat ten."

"Not a problem," Nina said in her New York twang. "Paul's not feeling well tonight so it's just me." She beamed at them, oblivious to the undertones and unable to take the hint that she wasn't wanted.

Ann looked helplessly at Bunny who shrugged her shoulders and murmured, "I guess we lose this round," as they followed the hostess to their table.

Tony's face was like thunder.

"Don't stress," Jess whispered to him as she took the seat beside him. "Deep breaths."

He smiled at her. She was like balm to his frazzled nerves.

Declan was disappointed that Sarah was sitting at another table. He'd like to have continued chatting her up.

"What was that all about?" Sarah asked the other three young people, not understanding the fuss about the table with Nina.

"That woman has practically hi-jacked my mother since she met her," said Jack.

"Mum likes her but Dad can't stand her," Emily told her.

"I can vouch for that," Tarquin chimed in.

Sarah didn't care about the stupid woman. She only had eyes for Jack and she had him more or less to herself for the next hour and a half. If she used all her charm, he would surely find her irresistible.

Meanwhile, back at the adults' table Nina was in full flow.

"I see exactly what you mean by hi-jack, Tony," Bunny murmured. "Don't worry. I'll sort her out damn quick."

The conversation that followed was worthy of a scene in a film as Bunny proceeded to put Nina in her place. She kept up a stream of conversation herself so that the other woman couldn't get a word in. When she did start to say anything, Bunny talked over her. Tony watched in fascination. Nina finally got the message and shut up but Ann felt terrible for her. She knew Nina was hurt and that she couldn't even understand why Bunny was doing this. Ann was surprised at Bunny but even more furious at Tony. This was all his fault.

Even before dessert Nina stood up, saying that she had to go and check on her husband. As she was leaving, Bunny said, "Nice meeting you, Nina. Unfortunately, we probably won't meet again as Ann and I are both on family holidays and would prefer to dine with our children." She smiled sweetly all the time she spoke.

Tony felt like applauding her as Nina left.

"That, Bunny, was a masterclass," he exclaimed admiringly.

"I think she got the message."

"You see, Ann," Tony turned to his wife, "that is how you assert yourself. You really should be more like Bunny. You're much too much of a pushover."

Bunny heard the annoyance in his voice and felt bad for Ann.

"You don't understand!" cried Ann. "She's a very kind woman who's just terribly lonely. You don't know what a hard life she's had." She had tears in her eyes as she stood up. "Now if you'll excuse me I'm going to her to see how she is." She practically ran from the room.

Bunny felt sorry for what she'd done. She had misunderstood the situation. She realised now that this was a problem between Ann and Tony and that he was in fact a bully. This marriage was in trouble and Tony's obvious interest in Jess wasn't going to help.

# Chapter 13

Ann found Nina sitting alone on the top deck behind the Montmartre bar. She was nursing a whisky.

"Will you join me in one?" she asked Ann as the barman appeared.

"Yes, thank you. Nina, I'm really sorry for what happened at dinner."

"It wasn't your fault nor even your friend Bunny's. I know it was your husband who orchestrated it. I don't know why he hates me. Do you?"

"I don't think he hates you but he's behaving very strangely lately. I have no idea why."

The barman returned and Ann gratefully took the whisky.

"He bullies you a lot, doesn't he?" Nina remarked.

Ann sighed. "I suppose so. He always has done. It's habit now, I suppose."

"You shouldn't let him. You're worth much more than that. You're a lovely warm woman and he should appreciate that."

"He says I'm too timid. That I should stand up for myself more."

"I agree and I think you need to start by standing up to *him*. That would surprise him."

"It certainly would."

"So let's start *'Operation Standing Up To Tony'*. From now on it's goodbye 'Timid Ann' and hello 'Assertive Ann'. Okay?"

Ann laughed as Nina raised her glass and she raised hers too.

"You're a good friend, Nina." Impulsively she put down her glass and hugged the other woman.

"Thank you for that," Nina replied with a tear in her eye. "I don't have many friends."

She was very fond of Ann who was so kind and sweet and she hated to see the way her husband was mistreating her. It brought back bad memories of her first husband.

When dinner was over the four young people headed to the Disco. Bunny was pleased to see that Sarah was behaving herself. She could tell that Sarah liked Jack a lot, and Emily was a very sensible girl. It was looking good. They were much more suitable friends for her wayward daughter than those awful Italians had been.

Sarah still had to do her Christmas shopping but as it was Christmas Eve the boutiques would be open till midnight. She'd slip away later. Right now she needed to stick with Jack and continue her charm offensive.

Once inside the Disco Jack disappeared, flitting around greeting everyone.

"I don't know how he does it," Tarquin remarked. "Women are drawn to him like to a magnet."

"It's been like that since he was a little boy," Emily admitted. "You've no idea how popular I was at school and now in college as well – with girls who use me to get to Jack!" She laughed.

Sarah felt bereft. Jack barely seemed to know she existed. She'd never had that happen to her before. It was upsetting. She drank steadily and then decided to go and buy her Christmas presents. Then she'd change into her sexiest dress. That would grab his attention.

While deciding what to wear she snorted a line of coke, sighing as the lovely feeling hit her. She felt on top of the world as she chose the black backless mini-dress that was semi-transparent and showed quite a bit of side-boob. If that didn't get Jack's attention, nothing would.

Meanwhile the adults went to the Louvre bar for a nightcap and Declan was on edge, terrified that Alix would turn up at any moment. He just couldn't take any more. Cassie noticed how tense he was and vowed to tackle him about it later. Something was up with him and she aimed to find out what.

To his relief there was no sign of Alix and he started to relax and enjoy himself. He liked the McElroys a lot. They were obviously very up-market. He was at his most charming to Richard who he planned to cultivate with a view to doing business with him when they returned home.

In Declan's eyes the Kennys were not quite in the same class. Ann was a nonentity and her husband typically nouveau-riche. It bugged him that Tony was having such success with Jess as he watched her laugh at something the Galway man said. She was classy and though not as overtly sexy as her younger sister he suspected she was smouldering beneath it all. He wondered what it would be like to be in bed with her. He felt his erection beginning at the thought of it. Sadly, he'd probably never get to find out. He was jealous of Tony, certain that he would have Jess – if he hadn't already. Declan had a nose for sensing when people were sexually attracted and he was pretty sure these two were. Lucky sod!

Tony wondered where Ann had got to but didn't go looking for her. He was sitting close to Jess, talking quietly to her, and that was all he wanted. He could tell their relationship was deepening but he was aware of Bunny's eagle eye on them so he tried to play it cool.

When he got back to his cabin Ann was in bed.

"Why didn't you come up to the bar?" he asked her.

"I didn't want to."

He got into bed and smelt the whisky on her breath. That was a surprise. He'd never known Ann to drink whisky in her life. What had got into her? He didn't ask as she seemed to want to sleep.

When the Jordans got back to their cabin, Cassie asked Declan what was bugging him.

"Nothing. Why?" he asked as he undressed.

"I know there's something wrong and I'd like you to tell me what it is."

"Why should there be something wrong?"

Cassie became infuriated. This was Declan at his evasive best. Answering her question with another one. Whenever he was guilty of something he resorted to this tactic. He'd even joked about it once and told her he did this to avoid answering when he didn't want to.

"*Stop it, Declan!*" she shouted at him. "Just answer my question honestly. What the hell is wrong with you?"

"What makes – " he started to say but stopped when he saw her face. He was on thin ice here. "I'm sorry, I apologise. I'm just tired. I haven't been sleeping well on board." He sat down on the bed. "Come here . . ." He reached for her.

She sat on the bed beside him.

"I promise I'll make it up to you," he said. "We'll have a nice Christmas Day tomorrow. You'll see." He put his arms around her and rested his head on her shoulder.

"I don't know, I don't understand you. The first day you were like the old Declan I knew but since then you've been acting strangely. It scares me. I love you very much but sometimes you're like a stranger to me."

"I'm sorry. Come to bed and let me make it up to you."

She undressed and climbed in beside him, relieved. They started to make love but to his mortification he couldn't get it up.

"I'm sorry, sweetheart, I guess I'm more tired than I thought."

Inside he was raging. This had never happened to him before. That bitch Alix was the cause of this. His nerves were shattered. He'd have to do something.

Back in the Disco Jack took a break from dancing and sat beside Tarquin. "Hey, man, tell me what's going on with you and Sarah? Are you not together any more?"

"No. We barely knew each other really before this cruise and she treated me pretty badly once we got here. In fact, I was going to fly home from Andros but her parents and Gavin persuaded me to stay on. Not as Sarah's boyfriend – just as a friend of the family."

Jack was shocked. "So it's definitely over between you?"

"Yes. Why are you asking? Do *you* fancy her?"

"No way, not my type," Jack stated firmly. "I hate these spoilt little rich girls who think they can have anything and anyone they want. I've met quite a few, believe me."

"You sound bitter. Why is that?"

"When I was seventeen I had my heart broken by a girl like Sarah. My first and only love. But she was only toying with me. Once bitten, twice shy."

"I don't know if Sarah is like that. She *is* beautiful."

"She sure is but there's more to beauty than good looks." Jack pulled a face.

"I guess you're right." Tarquin high-fived him.

Jack suddenly looked more serious. "No, the reason I asked is that I know Emily is getting fond of you and I wouldn't want to see her hurt – if you were to go back with Sarah, for instance."

"That won't ever happen, trust me," Tarquin insisted. "And I would never hurt Emily. I'm fond of her too," he added, blushing.

"That's okay so." Jack laughed and punched Tarquin on the shoulder. "We understand each other. Just doing my brotherly duty. Looking out for my kid sister."

At that moment Sarah arrived back and made her way confidently across the floor to Jack and Tarquin. She felt on top of the world as she saw all the men in the room ogle her. Tarquin saw what she was wearing and blushed with embarrassment.

"Jack, wanna dance?" Sarah held out her hand to him.

"No, thanks," he answered coolly. "I'd be afraid what's left of your dress might fall off and leave you naked."

She recoiled as if he'd slapped her.

"Why did you change? I think the other dress was much nicer." He got up and moved away.

Sarah slumped in the chair he'd vacated. Just what did she have to do to get Jack interested?

Tarquin broke in on her thoughts.

"Sarah, Jack is right. That dress really is too much," he said. "If Bunny —"

"Fuck Bunny!" she cried, tears in her eyes. Then she jumped up and dashed out of the Disco, leaving Tarquin looking after her, a puzzled frown on his face.

"What was that all about?" he said aloud to no one in particular.

Sarah got back to her cabin and lay on the bed, sobbing. She couldn't understand why Jack was being so horrible. She would not give up.

She thought of her favourite heroine Scarlett O'Hara. Sarah had always felt a terrific affinity and connection to her. She took the small bottle of champagne from the mini-bar and stood looking at her reflection in the mirror.

Toasting herself with determination in her eyes, she raised her glass. "Tomorrow is another day!"

Back in the Disco, Tarquin sat talking to Emily. He found her to be very sweet and highly intelligent and as different to Sarah as chalk from cheese.

Jack spent most of his time on the dance-floor with Galina and the other dancers.

"He's a jolly good dancer," Tarquin noted, watching Jack enviously. "I'm afraid I have two left feet."

"Me too," Emily admitted, blushing. "But I really enjoyed

157

the samba lesson yesterday. You should come tomorrow afternoon. It's great fun."

"You think they could teach even me?" he teased.

She laughed. "If they could teach me, believe me you'd be a piece of cake."

"Okay. It's a deal." Emily was so calming after Sarah and he found her company very relaxing.

Jack was pleased that Emily and Tarquin were hitting it off so well. He really liked him. The poor guy had obviously got a rum deal with Sarah. Emily was much more his type.

Christmas Day dawned bright and sunny. It would be pretty much like other sea-days on board with the usual activities taking place. This evening however would be very special as it was a Formal Night. Everyone would wear their most glamorous gear – the men in their dress suits and the women in their finest gowns and jewels. It would start with a champagne cocktail reception followed by a gourmet dinner. There was also a special Christmas show in the Theatre which they were all looking forward to.

"Happy Christmas, darling. What a beautiful way to spend Christmas Day," Bunny exclaimed as she joined Richard on the veranda. The sun was already hot in the blue sky and the beautiful Caribbean water glistened like a jewel.

"I've been thinking how nice it is that we have all three children with us this year," he said. "It's been quite a while since we spent it together as a family."

"Yes – but, although it's wonderful to have Jess here, I'd be happier if she was still with Philip, even if it meant she'd be in Gstaad," Bunny fretted.

"My dear, they're adults now and we have to allow

them to make their own way," Richard chided her. "Though I have to admit she doesn't seem to be missing him a whole lot."

"No. That's what worries me," Bunny admitted, frowning. "I have a feeling that there might be something going on between her and Tony."

"Surely not. He's must be almost twenty years older than her and besides he's married."

"When did that ever stop a man?" she remarked adroitly.

He had the grace to blush.

They had breakfast on the veranda and then called their friends and family in Ireland to wish them a Happy Christmas. Bunny was gratified to hear how envious they all were when they heard what she was doing.


"I really think you should make the effort – today of all days," Ann rebuked Tony as she dressed.

"Why? I haven't been to Mass in years. I don't believe in any of that shit any more. Why be a hypocrite?"

"You could go for the children's sake," Ann said, frowning.

"Bullshit! Jack hasn't been to Mass since he left school and Emily only goes to please you."

"What will everybody think?"

"That's all you care about, isn't it? What will people think? Well, I don't give a damn what they think. I don't believe a thing the Catholic Church says any more and I'm not going to pretend I do for appearances' sake."

Ann wrung her hands. Here they were fighting even on Christmas Day. What was happening to them? Tony had definitely changed. He was acting like he didn't love her any more.

"I obviously can't make you go." Ann gave up. "I'm going to call my family now and wish them a Happy Christmas."

"Good luck with that," he snorted. "You'll probably only get grief from them. I'm off to breakfast." He stormed out.

Ann waited till he was gone to let her tears fall. This was meant to be the trip of a lifetime but now she wished she'd stayed home. She'd have been happier slaving for her family like she'd done every year. Maybe then she wouldn't have noticed her marriage unravelling.

# Chapter 14

Declan was dressing to go for a jog when Cassie woke up. She expected him to say something about the night before but he acted as though nothing had happened. She was certain he was hiding something. She waited till he'd left the cabin and then called her father to wish him a Happy Christmas. His voice lifted when he heard her voice.

"Are you having a wonderful time?" he asked her.

"Yes. The ship is beautiful and I've met some very nice friends, the McElroys. You may remember Bunny. She says she met you in the Embassy in Rome a few times."

"Ah yes, indeed I do. A lovely lady." He hesitated. "Is everything okay, love? You don't sound too happy."

Cassie felt tears come to her eyes and a lump to her throat. Her father knew her so well. "I'm fine, Dad," she replied, trying to keep her voice from wobbling but she knew he wasn't fooled.

"I hope so, love. I want you to call me as soon as you get home. We need to talk."

"I will, Daddy. I love you."

"Chin up, darling. I love you too."

Cassie was feeling very emotional. Try as he might, her marriage was one thing her father couldn't fix. This she had to do all by herself. But how?

Calming herself down, she called her best friend Julie who picked up on the first ring.

"Hi, girl, Happy Christmas! I was hoping you'd call."

It was so good to hear Julie's voice that tears threatened Cassie once more. "How's it going there? How's the second honeymoon?"

Cassie couldn't answer.

"Cassie, are you there?"

"Yes, I'm here," Cassie managed to say.

"Are you okay?"

"Yes, I'm fine," she said but her voice faltered.

"Cass, what is it? What's happening?"

Cassie took a few deep breaths and then told her friend how Declan was behaving. Julie groaned.

"What are you going to do?"

"What can I do?" Cassie replied. "Put a good face on it for the rest of this trip anyway. Then we'll see. I wish he would talk to me. I just don't know what's gone wrong between us."

Tony and Jess had breakfast together.

"Where's everyone?" she asked.

"The kids are still sleeping, I presume, and Ann has gone to Mass."

"She doesn't still go? Even Bunny doesn't go any more," Jess said.

"I know," Tony scowled. "The worst of it is that she

expects me to go too. We had a bit of a row about it."

"Poor baby," she said, rubbing his hand. Remembering where she was, she quickly withdrew it.

He softened and laughed with her. She had that effect on him. She had a knack of taking away his bad humour.

"Will I see you in our secret hideaway today?" she asked.

"Try and keep me away," he answered her with feeling.

Ann went back to the cabin after attending Mass with Emily. Tony was gone from the room with no message as to where he might be. She honestly did not know why he was behaving like this. She wished she could talk to someone about it but there was no one except Nina.

As she was deciding what to do she got a call from her friend who asked her if she'd like to go to a lecture on Fabergé. She was pleased to hear from her and, although she had no idea who Fabergé was, she happily agreed to join her.

Declan spent his morning jog thinking of ways to keep Alix from destroying his life. Cassie was getting suspicious – he was sure of it. He'd have to find a way. When Cassie left for her Pilates class he went to Alix's cabin.

"Here comes my Christmas present," she purred as she opened the door to him. She was wearing a very saucy black-leather basque and thong, with black stockings and high heels. Her breasts were spilling out of the basque and she was wielding a whip. "And I have a nice present for you too, my sweet."

He had to admit she looked incredibly sexy and despite himself he found himself getting excited. He'd been apprehensive that he might not be able to perform but she was as good as any professional and before long he was hot and ready. What a relief!

"I can stay an extra hour today," he said. "Cassie is going to a lecture after her Pilates. That's my Christmas present."

What followed was worthy of a porn film and he wallowed in it. She was incredible. If only she'd been happy to keep it on a sexual basis they could have gone on having fantastic sex for years to come.

After their Pilates class, Fiona and Cassie went to Le Café where they both splurged on large cappuccinos with slices of chocolate cake.

"It's Christmas Day. We don't need to feel guilty," Fiona laughed.

Cassie gave a half-smile.

"What's up, Cass? You don't seem in very good form today."

To Cassie's embarrassment, she felt the tears well up again. "I'm sorry. I don't know what's wrong with me. I'm feeling very emotional today."

"I understand." Fiona reached for her hand. "It's probably because it's Christmas Day and you're away from home. I feel a little like that too."

"No, it's much more than that," Cassie replied, taking out a handkerchief and wiping her eyes.

"What is it, Cass?" Fiona asked gently. "You know you can trust me."

"I know." She took a deep breath. "It's Declan. I don't know what's going on with him but something is."

Fiona feared the worst.

"This was meant to be like a second honeymoon but it's all gone astray," Cassie continued. "He's been behaving very erratically lately. He's tense and edgy."

"I noticed that," Fiona admitted.

"He won't tell me why. He won't confide in me. I don't know what to do." She looked distraught. "Our marriage is in trouble."

Fiona didn't know what to say. Should she mention her suspicions about Alix? That might only make things worse. She vowed to have a talk with that woman later and try and get to the bottom of it. She was convinced that Alix was involved.

"Try not to worry about it today. It won't do any good."

"Thanks, Fiona. You're right."

"Now let's get to that Fabergé lecture or we won't get a seat."

"Well, were we assertive this morning?" Nina greeted Ann with a smile.

"Yes, but it caused a row unfortunately. However, I did not cry in front of him so that's a start."

"Good girl!" Nina applauded her.

The talk was very interesting and Ann was fascinated with the beautiful bejewelled enamelled eggs that had been made for the last Russian Czars. Fiona was there with Cassie and waved over at her.

Ann waved happily back.

Fiona was surprised to see that Ann was sitting with Nina.

"Obviously she's still friends with her," she whispered to Cassie.

"Actually, I think Tony is the one who has the problem

165

with Nina, not Ann," Cassie responded. "She seems very fond of her."

"Let's do lunch," Nina suggested when it was over. "Paul is still not feeling great. Then we can go to the ice-sculpting demo afterwards."

Ann was happy to see that Bunny's put-down of the night before hadn't affected Nina in the least. Tony's face if she turned up to lunch with Nina didn't bear thinking about – but then she thought, why shouldn't I have lunch with my friend if I want to? Tony would probably find fault with her for something or other anyway. Timid Ann was gone so Assertive Ann took her courage in her hands.

"Great idea, Nina. I'd like that."

Tony spent another idyllic morning on the veranda with Jess and again nobody intruded on them. He was falling in love with her and he had hopes that she was feeling the same way. He hated having to leave her but she had a family lunch and he supposed he had better put in an appearance with his. Jess made him feel young again and he realised that he had outgrown Ann. They had nothing in common any more, now that the children were grown up. He was at a crisis in his life and he had no idea where it was heading but he hoped it would include Jess.

When he got to their cabin Ann was there changing.

"By the way, Nina asked me to have lunch with her," she informed him. "And then we're going to the ice-sculpting demo."

He couldn't believe his ears. "I do not believe that she didn't get the message last night! Is she stupid or what?"

"Don't call her that," Ann said angrily. "She's my friend

and I want to have lunch with her. You're welcome to join us though I'm sure you don't want to. So I'm off. Enjoy your lunch."

Tony was dumbstruck. What was that all about? Ann had never gone against his wishes before. He went to the Buffet and ate his lunch alone.

Ann and Nina had a lovely lunch in the Brasserie restaurant.

"My treat," Nina insisted.

They even shared a bottle of wine.

The McElroys met at twelve in the suite for pre-lunch drinks and to exchange presents. Bunny had invited Tarquin but he kindly declined, saying he was taking Emily to lunch. Bunny assured him that she and Richard understood. Sarah arrived bang on time which surprised her mother. Jess arrived shortly afterwards and she was glowing. Richard raised his eyebrows. She certainly didn't look like a woman who was missing her husband. Maybe there was something in what Bunny said. She always had great instinct for these things. He'd have to keep an eye on that Tony guy. Gavin and Fiona arrived shortly afterwards and he noticed Fiona was also glowing. This cruise was certainly having the desired effect on the women in the family.

Bunny asked Raphael to pour the champagne as Richard prepared to hand out the presents, as he had always done. Fiona was beside herself with excitement.

First up was Bunny and she couldn't believe her eyes when she opened Richard's present. It was a beautiful diamond necklace with matching earrings that she had admired in the diamond boutique.

"Well, darling, I didn't want you to have no jewellery to wear tonight since those thieves made off with your other stuff," Richard explained.

Fiona's gift from Gavin was also jewellery. The lovely set that she'd admired on Cassie from her own design line. She looked at Gavin enquiringly.

"Like Dad, I felt bad when your jewels were stolen, even though they were paste copies," he explained. "So I persuaded Cassie to sell one of her designs. She told me you'd liked this one."

"I love it. How thoughtful. It's beautiful, thank you, darling." She kissed him.

Richard continued to distribute the presents.

Sarah had bought perfume or aftershave for everyone.

"Very original," Jess remarked.

"It's your favourite – Angel," Sarah said, pretending to be annoyed, but she was smiling.

"Oh! Well, that was thoughtful. Thank you, Sis." She hugged Sarah.

Fiona's present to Gavin was the last to be handed out. Gavin looked at it, frowning, wondering what it could be. It looked liked a small pen. "For golf, maybe?" he asked her, puzzled.

"Go on, open it," she ordered him.

He did and still looked perplexed as he unwrapped the small tube. He hadn't a clue what it was. It looked like a thermometer.

"Clear Blue," he said. "What is that?"

"Read what it says!" Jess cried, realising what it was.

"Positive," Gavin said and then the penny dropped.

He looked at Fiona and saw that she was crying.

"You're not . . . we're not . . . pregnant?" He moved to her.

"Yes," she said, standing up, "we are." He wrapped her in his arms and lifted her off her feet.

"I don't believe it. That's fantastic," he cried, his voice breaking with emotion. All hell broke loose then as his family gathered round them, congratulating them.

"You dark horse," said Jess, "pretending you were suffering from sea-sickness!"

"So that's why you wouldn't drink," said Sarah accusingly as she realised she was about to be an aunt.

Gavin looked at his mother and father. They were beaming.

"I thought I was never going to be a grandmother. Congratulations! We're so happy." Bunny hugged them both.

"More champagne!" Sarah called out and this time nobody reprimanded her. "I bags be godmother," she said.

"No, I'm the oldest aunt," Jess insisted.

"We'll do like the Royals and have multiple godparents," Bunny said, settling the issue. "When is the baby due?"

"The end of June," Fiona told them.

"To the next generation of McElroys!" Richard raised his glass. "What a wonderful Christmas present!"

Jess was in a really good mood when she got back to rejoin Tony in their hideaway.

"We've just had the best news," she told him excitedly. "Gavin and Fiona are going to have a baby. I'm going to be an aunt."

He heard the longing in her voice.

"You sound like you're happy but sad too," he observed, taking her hand.

She shook her head. "You only know me a few days but you know me better than anyone," she said wistfully.

"What is it?" he asked gently.

"I suppose I always thought I would be the first to give my parents a grandchild. Obviously, it's not to be." She brushed away a tear.

"Did you want a baby?" he asked softly.

"Oh yes, but it didn't happen. I went for tests and there's no problem with me but Philip refused to go." She shrugged her shoulders. "One of those things. Says a lot about my marriage."

"Oh Jess, I'm sorry. But you're young. It's not too late."

"No. But I need to find the right man first."

He wanted to cry 'I'm the right man!' but he didn't want to scare her away. He was becoming obsessed with this beautiful woman.

# Chapter 15

Most passengers congregated around the pool after lunch, happy to relax and soak up the sun, reminding themselves it was the 25<sup>th</sup> December and probably freezing back home.

Fiona relaxed on a sun-lounger, delighted with the way her news had been received. Gavin was at a talk by the golf pro with Richard and she planned to read a little. However, there was too much distraction at the pool so she settled for people-watching.

She saw Sarah arrive and join Tarquin and Emily at the other end from where she was. She looked fabulous in her sexy white bikini. Fiona noticed the men – even the old ones – admiring her nubile sister-in-law. She wondered where Jess was. She did nothing else but lie in the sun. She must be on another deck somewhere.

Then she spotted Ann. She was sitting alone in the shade. She was staring into the distance with a worried look on her face. No sign of Tony. Things were definitely strained there, Fiona thought. Well, she had enough to worry about with Cassie and Declan besides worrying about the Kennys.

Sara was very disappointed to find Jack was not at the pool to appreciate her new white bikini. She wondered where he was and where Jess was too, for that matter. She was very aware of the lustful glances she was getting from both the male passengers and staff. It made her feel good. She had a fun afternoon and joined in the pool games organised by the activities team, aware that all eyes were on her. If only Jack had been there to see her.

Jack *had* seen her. He was standing on the top-deck veranda and, as he watched her jump and splash around the pool, he grudgingly admitted that she was very hot-looking. He felt the start of an erection as he watched her and cursed himself. In other circumstances he would have moved in on her – she certainly seemed up for it – but something inside his head told him that she was trouble. Big trouble. He decided not to go to the pool. He was afraid that Sarah might prove too tempting – prancing around in that ridiculously tiny bikini.

He had spent the last hour watching the dancers rehearse for the show that night. They were amazing and he enjoyed being allowed behind the scenes. He'd promised Galina to be at the *Strictly* dance class later.

Fiona was considering going in search of Alix when she saw her arrive at the pool. She was dressed in a revealing leopard-skin bikini and was sipping a cocktail. She was walking around the pool, looking for a free sun-lounger. As luck would have it, the bed beside Fiona had just been vacated. She called out to the other girl.

"Hi Alix, there's a bed free here beside me if you'd like to join me."

"Gee, thanks, Fiona. It's pretty busy here," Alix said, plonking down beside her.

Fiona could see it wasn't her first cocktail of the day.

"Hi, how are you? We haven't really had time to get to know each other," said Fiona, smiling.

Alix was flattered. She knew that Fiona was a friend of Cassie's and was pleased she wanted to be her friend too. She liked Fiona who she thought was very down-to-earth, unlike the stuck-up Cassie.

After a little small talk, Fiona said, "I think you're so brave to come on a cruise alone. I wouldn't have the courage to do that."

"It's not easy, especially when there are so many couples on board."

"Could you not have persuaded your ex to come with you? Maybe you'd have got back together again under these romantic conditions."

Alix laughed uproariously.

"What's so funny?" Fiona asked her.

"You have no idea!" Alix continued laughing.

Fiona called for another drink for Alix and a Coke for herself.

"Tell me about him?" she asked Alix innocently. "Is he Irish?"

"Yep."

"Is he good-looking?"

"Extremely and *soooo* sexy. What a stud! He can go all night and all morning. Best sex I've had ever." She licked her lips thinking about it. Her drink had arrived and she took a big slug of it.

"You must miss that."

"I don't have to. He can't keep away from me." Alix smiled to herself.

"What do you mean?" Fiona was puzzled.

"Don't say a word to anyone," Alix said, lowering her voice, "but when a colleague told me he would be on this cruise I booked myself on it too."

"Seriously? He's on this ship? But I've never seen you with him."

"Don't be silly. How could you? His wife is with him. But he makes time for me – in private – if you know what I mean." She winked.

"Oh, he's married?" Fiona's heart sank. There was now no doubt that the stud in question was Declan. She knew it wasn't Gavin and was certain it wasn't Richard either and that left only Tony or Declan. It could hardly be Tony as he seemed more interested in Jess.

"Yes, he's married but he won't be for long!" Alix declared triumphantly.

"Are there kids involved?"

"No, he has no kids."

Now Fiona knew for sure it wasn't Tony. That left Declan.

"Aren't you worried about his wife?"

"Why should I be? She's been spoilt rotten all her life. Rich little Daddy's girl who always gets what she wants. Well, now I'm going to take it all away from her!"

"You've been having an affair with Declan, haven't you?" Fiona asked, trying to keep the disgust from her voice.

Alix looked startled, then moved in close to her. "Yes, but please don't tell Cassie. Declan has promised to tell her once they get home."

Fiona didn't want to hear any more. She wanted to get

away from this awful woman as quickly as possible.

"Oh dear, look at the time! I've arranged to meet Gavin. Have to run." Fiona scrambled to her feet and picked up her belongings. "Bye-bye."

"See you later – it's been lovely talking to you!" Alix called after her as she fled.

Fiona went back to her cabin and lay on the bed, thinking. What should she do? Should she tell Cassie? What a bastard! No wonder he was edgy and tense. He was probably terrified of what Alix would do. And to think that they were still having sex here on board. It was sickening. She needed to talk to Gavin. He'd know what to do.

She didn't have long to wait. He arrived into the cabin five minutes later.

"What is it, sweetheart?" he asked when he saw her face. He went pale. "It's not the baby "

"No, no, nothing like that," she assured him and told her about her conversation with Alix.

"Unbelievable," he said.

"But what should I do?" she wailed. "Should I tell Cassie?"

"Lord, what a conundrum," he said, rubbing his chin. "That's a tough one." He sat thinking for a while. "If it was me, would you want Cassie to tell you?"

"Don't even hint at that!" she cried tearfully.

"I don't mean 'us' literally! I mean, would *you* as a wife want to know?"

She pondered this. "I suppose. I think what he's doing is despicable and Cassie suspects something. I don't know. I'll have to think about it."

"Do that. Maybe today being Christmas Day would not be the best time anyway."

"True."

"What a cad! I never liked him."

"Yes, I'll leave it till the Christmas festivities are over. Maybe even till the end of the cruise. But I *will* tell her."

"That's the best plan of action."

"What a mess!"

"By the way, Bunny has reserved a table for all of us at dinner tonight. It should be fun."

"Yes, except that we'll have to look at Alix and her stud all night," groaned Fiona. "It will make my blood boil."

Sarah was in great form heading to the *Strictly* class, having snorted a line before leaving her cabin. The dance lesson was on the salsa that afternoon. She was delighted she had worn her red off-the-shoulder crop top and a multi-coloured flouncy short skirt. She couldn't have dressed more suitably for the salsa if she'd tried. She knew she looked good. Tarquin and Emily were there also and Jack sauntered in at the last minute.

The male dancer who was teaching the salsa with Galina divided them into couples. Tarquin clung onto Emily's hand tightly not wishing to inflict himself on any other girl. Emily found it touching.

Sarah nearly died when the dancer put her hand in Jack's. "I think you two look good together," he announced mischievously.

Jack looked Sarah up and down slowly, which unnerved her. "All you're missing is a flower in your hair," he remarked.

She didn't know if it was a compliment or if he was teasing her.

"C'mon, let's see what you can do," he ordered.

Sarah was nervous at first but she was a good dancer

and a quick learner and she soon relaxed. The music was infectious and dancing with Jack was bliss. All eyes were on them as they twirled and shook their hips. They were electric together. When they had the routine down pat, the competition proper started. When they finished she was panting and perspiring and so was Jack.

"Not bad," he said nonchalantly which infuriated her.

He could at least have said something nice. Why was he treating her like this? She was beginning to think he was a prick and big-headed to boot.

"I'm so honoured you think I'm not bad," she replied sarcastically.

As expected, Sarah was chosen as one of the six finalists. As Jack had already won the samba the first day he wasn't eligible.

The professional dancers came to partner the finalists. The head dancer took her hand and smiled at her.

"Just a sec," said Jack. He ran to a floral arrangement that was sitting on a table. He took out a flower then brought it to her and put it behind her ear. She blushed as the crowd went wild cheering. Then the music started and she was lost in it as she gyrated and twirled around her partner. Sarah won the competition hands-down. She felt flushed and elated when she was announced the winner. That was the best fun she'd ever had. She gave Jack a disdainful look as she passed him by.

"Not bad, eh?" she threw at him over her shoulder.

As he watched her saunter away he was aware of her effect on the men around. She sure knew how to attract them and, boy, could she move! The problem was she knew it. He had to admit she was also damn sassy.

Sarah had caught the attention of two good-looking

athletic boys who lost no time in approaching her after the dance. Jack watched, annoyed, as she joined them for a drink. They told Sarah that they were college footballers and were effusive in their praise of her dancing. They were both vying for her attention and Sarah lapped it up. She saw that Jack had noticed. Take that, Jack Kenny, she said to herself. There are other fish in the sea besides you.

The ship became transformed that evening as the lights were turned down in the atrium and hundreds of candles under glass made for a magical romantic ambience. The jewels the ladies wore were stiff competition for the sparkling Christmas tree. Everything glowed and the passengers, dressed in their best finery, could have been actors in a glamorous Hollywood movie.

The cocktail party started at five-thirty and as Bunny arrived on Richard's arm she thought how elegant everything was. Old world elegance! That was until she saw Alix who was wearing a flimsy white lace gown which was see-through in places. It was very low cut with a slit to the thigh. Trashy beyond words!

There were two photographers stationed to the side of the atrium taking portrait photos that everybody wanted to have. Richard wanted one of his three girls together and, when Bunny stood flanked by Sarah and Jess, people stopped to admire the stunning trio. Fiona and Gavin were next, followed by Declan and Cassie. Declan tried to relax and smile but it was difficult with Alix looking on.

She was next and, as the photographer set up, she pouted. "I feel stupid standing here on my own dressed up to the nines. Can I borrow a man, please? C'mon, Declan, do me a favour! Stand in with me."

Declan gritted his teeth but when Cassie pushed him forward he had no choice but to do it. If not Alix might have caused a scene. She'd already had quite a bit to drink and he was nervous about the evening ahead. He looked like he had rigor mortis in the photo but Alix didn't seem to notice as she posed with one leg out. She leaned in to him, smiling seductively at him for the camera.

Fiona looked at Gavin in alarm. He raised his eyebrows and she could see he was worried too. They both looked towards Cassie but she was engrossed in conversation with Bunny and wasn't watching. Fiona prayed the evening would go off without incident.

There was a string quartet playing carols and many passengers sang along with them. The cocktails were coming fast and furious and Tarquin was pleased to see that Sarah was drinking less and not grabbing two every time as she usually did. Bunny noticed it too and hoped it meant Sarah had taken her words to heart. For the hundredth time she thanked God that those dreadful Italians were gone.

The Captain came over to her while she was talking to Cassie. He bowed and kissed their hands. "The two most beautiful ladies here tonight," he said as he bowed.

"You are a charmer," Bunny laughed. "I bet you say that to all the ladies."

"Believe me, this time I mean it," he said, his hand on his heart.

He was very attractive and Cassie blushed. He smiled at her and she blushed even more. Bunny could sense the chemistry between them. This man obviously knew class when he saw it.

"I apologise, ladies, for the trauma you have suffered. Believe me, we are doing everything to find those thieves."

"Any news of them?" Bunny asked.

"Not yet. But we'll get them. I promise you." He noticed Cassie's necklace.

"That is very beautiful," he remarked, pointing to it. "May I ask where you got it?"

"You want to buy one for your wife?" Bunny asked.

"Sadly, I have no wife. What woman would want to live with a ship's captain?" He gave a small grimace. "For the moment I am married to the sea. Maybe one day. No, not for a wife, but maybe I could buy one like it for my sister."

"Actually, I'm a jewellery designer and this is one of my own pieces. I designed this myself," said Cassie. "If you like I could give it to you for her."

He looked surprised. "Beautiful and talented," he murmured. "No, I couldn't deprive you of it but if you give me your business card I shall order one from you."

"I don't have –"

"She doesn't have one on her but she can let you have one later," Bunny butted in.

"I shall invite you to dine at my table tomorrow night and you can give it to me then," he said.

Cassie blushed a deep red as Bunny smiled.

"And you too, Mrs McElroy, of course."

"Thank you, Captain. We'd be delighted," Bunny replied graciously.

"You will have the invitations in your cabin tomorrow morning."

Bunny could see other passengers scrutinising them. The Captain never spent longer than two minutes talking to anyone. People were curious. She was elated.

"You've made quite a conquest," she said delightedly to Cassie after he had left. "He's a very attractive man and so interesting."

"Yes, indeed, but I love my husband," Cassie replied, smiling.

Declan had watched this social intercourse with anger as he stood talking to Alix. He wanted desperately to go and join Cassie and the Captain but he knew Alix would go ballistic if he left her. She was knocking back cocktails by the new time.

"Don't you think you should go easy on that stuff?" he suggested, trying to control his temper.

"You're not my husband yet. I can drink what I like."

Uh-ho, he thought nervously. He sensed danger ahead. After the cocktail party they all headed to the Moulin Rouge Theatre to see the live show where more cocktails and canapés were on offer. Declan wondered if the Captain wanted to get them all drunk.

The show was fantastic and they were amazed at the excellence of it. The musicians, singers and dancers were all of the highest calibre and the staging was spectacular. They all agreed it was as good as any West End show.

By the time the show ended everyone was happy and more than a little tipsy as they arrived at the restaurant for Christmas Dinner.

Ann had told Nina earlier that Bunny had arranged for the Irish group to have dinner together that night.

"I'm sorry but I'm afraid there will be fourteen of us and Bunny had to make special arrangements as the tables normally seat only ten," Ann explained. "I hope you don't mind."

"Of course not. As it's Christmas night I've planned to have dinner with Paul in our suite. He's still not a hundred per cent, I'm afraid."

Ann was relieved. She hoped Tony would be in a good mood that night.

# Chapter 16

The head chef had pulled out all the stops and the menu for Christmas night was simply fabulous. There were seven courses with a wide range of choices.

There was caviar, foie gras, lobster, scallops and prawns for starters. This was followed by champagne sorbet to cleanse the palate, followed by lobster bisque or various soups. For the main course the choice was between sea-bass, rack of lamb, fillet steak, venison, prime rib and of course turkey and ham with all the trimmings.

"This really *is* a novel," Fiona laughed as they all perused the menu, trying to decide what to have.

"I want everything," Gavin groaned.

"Me too," Tony agreed. "What a choice!"

Finally they were done and the head waiter took their orders.

When it came to Ann's turn she ordered turkey and ham.

"How can you order that with so many other fabulous things on the menu?" Tony asked irritably.

"I like it," she replied, "and it's what I always have on Christmas Day."

"For God's sake, for once can't you do something different?"

He had raised his voice and everyone felt sorry for Ann who looked humiliated.

Even Jess looked away, embarrassed.

"*Dad!*" Jack's voice broke in sharply. "Just stop it. If Mum wants turkey she can have it." He turned to the waiter. "Actually, I'm gonna have turkey too."

Tony glared at him.

"You know something? Ann is right," said Bunny, smiling at Ann. "It's Christmas dinner after all. Let's stick with tradition. I'll have the turkey too." She was still feeling bad about the way she'd treated Nina and she wanted to take Tony down a peg or two.

"Me too," Emily chimed in, followed by Fiona and Gavin who had realised what was happening and thought Tony was way out of line.

Ann smiled at them all gratefully as Tony shrugged, conceding that she'd won this round.

"See what you've started?" he hissed under his breath to Ann when he got a chance.

Sarah had taken a seat as far away from Jack as possible. She didn't need his sarcasm ruining her night.

Jack was sitting opposite Jess and Tony and was surprised to see the camaraderie between them. It was as if they'd been friends forever. He had never seen his father in such good humour and he seemed to hang on Jess's every word. He appeared to be mesmerised by her. It made Jack feel uncomfortable. He certainly hoped his mother didn't notice.

The food was as good as it sounded and was accompanied by the appropriate wines.

Declan had been keeping a sharp eye on Alix who was still drinking like there was no tomorrow. By the time it came to order dessert, she was completely drunk.

"I think maybe she should go out for some air," Cassie suggested to him in a whisper.

"Good idea," he agreed with alacrity – anything to get her away from the table. "I'll take her." He leaned over and whispered in Alix's ear.

"Really?" she said, grinning and giving him her arm. He had to hold on to her to stop her from falling as they left the restaurant.

"I told Fiona today that you couldn't get enough of me," she mumbled, slurring her words as they made their way up in the glass lift. "You're proving it now, aren't you?" She leaned in to kiss him but he pulled back.

Declan hoped he had misheard. Surely she hadn't said anything to Fiona – Cassie's friend? Oh God! He couldn't wait to question her once he got her inside her cabin.

Inside, she made for the veranda. "Let's have sex under the stars," she suggested, swaying as she opened the glass door.

He followed her outside.

"Did you tell Fiona about us?" he demanded. He was terrified of what her reply would be.

"Sure. Why not?"

He lost it then. "*Why not?*" he yelled at her. "*What the hell do you mean? Are you out of your mind?*"

She looked shocked as she stood there swaying drunkenly. "*You crazy bitch!*"

At that she launched herself at him, clawing at his face.

185

He pushed her off and she fell, hitting her head against the sharp edge of the metal table. Then she slumped to the ground like a rag doll.

He looked at the blood pouring from the huge gash in her head and was frozen to the spot. Her head was at a strange angle and she was motionless. She didn't appear to be breathing.

He bent down and checked for a pulse but couldn't find one.

She was dead.

He felt faint. It had all happened so fast.

He tried to think clearly. He couldn't risk being found here with her dead body. It was an accident but who would believe him? He'd be finished. He panicked. He had to get rid of her. It was his only hope.

Lifting her inert body with difficulty, he managed to get it up on the rail and pushed, watching it drop to the dark water below. He watched her float for a few minutes, her white dress billowing around her, before she sank beneath the water.

Checking there was no one in the corridor, he left her cabin and went to his own. There he washed his hands and checked his clothes for any signs of blood. He was clean. Reaching for a whiskey in the mini-bar he found his hands were shaking so much he could barely lift it to his mouth. He gulped it down in one go to steady himself.

His breathing finally slowed to normal and he sat on the bed to gather his thoughts. Knowing that the others would be wondering where he was, he realised he had to pull himself together and go back to join the party.

Shakily he made his way back.

"You were gone a long time. Is she okay?" Cassie asked,

a worried frown on her face.

"Yes. She was plastered so I took her up on deck for some fresh air. Then I persuaded her to go to bed and saw her to her cabin."

"Good. That's the best thing for her."

Declan was very quiet after that and seemed lost in his own thoughts. Fiona wondered about the change in him. He'd been gone for quite a while. She suspected he'd been having sex with his mistress – drunk as she was. He was despicable.

When the meal was over they all decided to call it a day, except for the young ones who were heading to the Disco. They were just leaving the table when they heard three blasts of the ship's klaxon. They looked at each other nervously. They knew the emergency signal was seven short blasts and one long one so it wasn't that. Then an announcement came over the tannoy.

It was the Captain.

*"Ladies and Gentlemen, I am sorry to have to you inform you that we have had a report of a man overboard. We will be turning around to do a search. You could help by going on deck and alerting any crew member should you see anything in the water. If anyone in your party is missing, please let us know. Your help is very much appreciated."*

They looked at each other in horror.

Fiona noticed that Declan's face had turned deathly pale.

"Oh no, how horrible!" Ann exclaimed. "The poor soul!"

"There's no one missing here except Alix. You say she's gone to bed, Declan?" Gavin asked.

"Yes. Well, I took her to her cabin. I didn't exactly put her to bed," he replied.

I'll bet, Fiona thought.

187

"Gosh, I hope nothing has happened to her," said Cassie with a worried frown.

"She *was* very drunk. Perhaps we should check on her."

"I think we should mention it to a crew member and let them check," Richard suggested. "They'll have a key to her room."

He went in search of one as the others headed out on deck, their previous high spirits deflated. What a horrible ending to a lovely Christmas Day!

They stood on deck with the other passengers, all eyes scanning the water. They were all thinking how awful it would be, to be lost in that immense sea.

They watched as the ship did a U-turn and the rescue operation went into action. The dark sea was lit up by searchlights and smoke flares as the crew lowered lifeboats into the water to look for the unfortunate passenger.

A short time later CSO Allen and his deputy approached Richard to say that they had searched Alix's cabin and that she was not there.

"We don't want to alarm you but it looks like she had an accident and may possibly be the person who went overboard," he informed them.

They were all shocked.

Fiona again noticed the pallor on Declan's face and that he was perspiring profusely.

"What kind of accident? How do you know?" Bunny asked.

"I can't say more at the moment," he said.

Fiona had a sinking feeling that it *was* Alix overboard and she wondered if Declan had had something to do with it. Surely not even *he* would stoop to something like that?

"We will do everything we can to find her," CSO Allen

assured them. "If any of you can shed any light on this incident, please don't hesitate to contact me."

"You don't think it was foul play?" Bunny pressed.

"We can't say at the moment," he replied.

Gavin looked at Fiona and was alarmed at the look in her eyes.

"I'm feeling faint," she said, reaching out to him.

"Is it okay if I take my wife to our cabin?" he asked. "She's pregnant."

"Please feel free to go," CSO Allen replied.

"Would you mind if we also go to our suite?" Bunny asked. "We can keep a lookout from the veranda there."

"Of course, Mrs McElroy," he replied sympathetically. "We'll keep you informed if we locate your friend."

"I do hope it's not Alix who went overboard," Cassie cried, wringing her hands.

Fiona noticed that Declan said nothing.


The first report that they might have an MOB – the abbreviation for Man Overboard – had been from a passenger in the cabin directly above Alix who hadn't been feeling well at dinner and had returned to his cabin for his medication. He'd heard voices arguing outside and, when he went to check, saw what he thought was a towel floating in the water. He thought nothing of it but when he mentioned it to his wife on his return she had insisted he notify one of the crew.

The alarm was raised.

Then, when Richard had reported that Alix had left the dinner table and returned to her cabin, Security had gone to check up on her and found the bloodstained veranda but no sign of Alix.

CSO Allen was pretty sure that she was his MOB. He reported all this to the Captain.

The search went on all night. Eventually the passengers left the deck one by one. They were all pretty sure that the passenger overboard was gone. Another cruise ship and some smaller ships in the vicinity had come to help in the search but there was no sign of any body.

Cassie was worried. Declan was acting very strangely. She'd seen how upset he was over Alix. Back in their cabin, she tried to talk to him, to reassure him, but he would not discuss it.

"Please, darling, talk to me," she pleaded. "I know you're worried as you were the last one to see her but you were only helping her by taking her to her cabin. You couldn't have known what would happen. Nobody could blame you."

He didn't respond.

"Come to bed," she begged, patting the bed beside her. "Let me hold you."

Declan refused and turned away from her.

He spent the night on the veranda, watching the search. She went to bed at two-thirty knowing there was nothing they could do. When she woke at seven he had left the cabin. The ship was still not moving so she supposed it meant Alix had not been found. She dressed quickly and made her way to the Buffet, hoping to find Declan there. There was no sign of him but Fiona was there having coffee. Cassie grabbed one for herself and sat down beside her.

"Any news on Alix?" she asked.

"I'm afraid not. Once daybreak came they brought in helicopters but there's still no sign of her. I guess she's gone." She looked at Cassie sadly.

"How awful! Poor Alix. I hope she didn't suffer too much."

"Cassie, I have to talk to you . . ." Fiona faltered, not knowing how to begin. "I spoke to Alix yesterday . . ." she took a deep breath.

"What is it, Fiona?" There was fear in Cassie's voice.

"I'm really sorry, Cassie, but well . . . I don't know how to tell you this . . ."

"Please, Fiona, just tell me, whatever it is."

"Well, I found out that she and Declan were having an affair. She booked on this cruise when a colleague told her he was going to be on it."

Cassie stared at her for a long while, not quite able to believe what Fiona was saying. Then she put her head in her hands and let out a long moan.

"I'm really sorry." Fiona reached out and put her hands on Cassie's shoulders. "I didn't want to tell you yesterday and spoil your Christmas night but I was going to tell you, I swear."

"It's okay. I believe you."

Cassie looked up. Her face was ashen and she had a strange look in her eyes.

"Declan has been acting so weird lately," she said, her voice breaking. "Before we came away I suspected he might have been having an affair – it's happened before – but then he booked this cruise as a second honeymoon and everything was wonderful for a while." She started sobbing gently. "Looks like I was right all along. I've been such a fool . . ." Then a thought struck her and she stopped crying and looked at Fiona, panic-stricken. "You don't think he had anything to do with Alix going overboard, do you?" she asked, her voice trembling.

"I don't know . . ."

"Oh my God! This can't be happening." Cassie dropped her head into her hands and started sobbing once more.

"Cassie, I'm afraid I have no choice but to disclose what I know to CSO Allen. You understand?" Fiona's voice was shaking.

"Of course. How could I have been so stupid? He's been so on edge and tense these last few days and to think it was because his mistress was on board!" Cassie was distraught.

"What will you do?"

"First I'll go find him and hammer the truth out of him," Cassie replied, her voice a little stronger. "Then we'll see."

"I'm so sorry," Fiona said once again. "You have my number. Call me any time. I'm here for you."

They parted with a hug.

After the helicopters failed in their search, the Captain had acknowledged that there was little chance of finding Aix. Finally, ten hours after it had begun, he reluctantly resigned himself to the fact that there was nothing more he could do and he gave the order to abandon the search and head for St Thomas.

They would arrive later than planned which meant that his staff would be busy re-arranging tours. He made the decision to leave the island two hours later than scheduled that evening to facilitate the tours. For now, it was full speed ahead to make up for lost time. This was his second MOB. The first had been a suicide. But, with the blood on the veranda, he had a feeling this one wasn't. That would be another headache.

Shortly after the engines started up, he made an announcement over the tannoy. He said that, despite their best efforts, the person who had fallen overboard had not been located and the search had to be abandoned. It had delayed their itinerary which meant that they would arrive later than scheduled at St Thomas. However, they would also leave the island two hours later than planned so as to maximise their time there. He thanked them for their help and understanding.

"Do you think it could have been suicide?" Richard asked Gavin over breakfast.

"No, I don't. Fiona and I think it might be more sinister than that."

"What do you mean?" Bunny exclaimed, appalled. "Do you know something we don't?"

"Well, they did say there had been some kind of accident. We've asked for a meeting with CSO Allen at ten. We'll talk to him first. We may learn more then."

Bunny was dying to know what Gavin thought but knew he would not divulge anything till he was ready. My goodness, what a sad mess!

# Chapter 17

Cassie found Declan on the upper deck, staring out to sea. He looked wretched and appeared to have aged overnight.

"We have to talk," she said to him. "About Alix."

"What do you want to know?" he asked.

"Everything. Where you met her. How long you've been having an affair and most importantly what happened last night."

Declan broke down in tears. "Fiona told you?"

"Yes, but I'm stupid. I should have guessed."

He admitted it – hesitantly at first then it all came rushing out. "My main thing was to keep you from finding out. She was blackmailing me."

Cassie looked at him with disgust. "How could you? And what happened last night? Did you have anything to do with it?"

"It was an accident, Cass, I swear. I took her back to her cabin and we started arguing on her veranda. She wouldn't leave me alone. Then she attacked me and in the struggle she fell and banged her head. She got up, dazed, lost her balance and fell over the rail. It all happened so fast." He put his head in his hands.

"Why didn't you call for help?"

"I panicked. How would it look? Everyone would think I'd killed her," he said, anguished. "I was trying to shield you."

"God, what a horrible death!" Cassie shuddered. "You probably did kill her by not raising the alarm."

"Don't say that," he whispered hoarsely. "I'm so sorry. Please understand." He started crying again.

"It's a bit late for that," she said. "You have to go find CSO Allen and tell him everything. And I'm going with you to ensure that you tell the truth."

He looked at her bleakly and, seeing the look of revulsion in her eyes, realised that he'd lost her anyway.

When Chief Security Officer Allen heard what Declan had to say he summoned the Captain.

Declan squirmed under their barely disguised disgust. He repeated his story.

"You know you could be considered responsible for her death?" the Captain said.

"It was an accident. She was very drunk."

"Yes, but if you'd raised the alarm we might have saved her."

Declan was tempted to tell them that she was already dead when she went into the sea but that would be an admission that he had lied. He stayed quiet.

"As we have no police on board we will need to report this to the American authorities who have jurisdiction of the ship," CSO Allen informed him. "They will want to question you on your return to Fort Lauderdale. In the meantime, we will need to take your fingerprints and hold your passport until the authorities there have spoken to you. Can you come with me, please?"

Sheepishly Declan followed him and his deputy from the room, leaving Cassie with the Captain.

"I am so sorry for what you are going through," the Captain said sympathetically. "Your husband is a fool. Can I help you in any way?"

"Well, yes. Perhaps you could find me another cabin if that's possible. I need to be alone to come to terms with this."

"Consider it done. Do you have a cellphone number?"

Cassie gave it to him.

"I shall contact you as soon as I arrange it. By the way, I have that invitation inviting you to dine at my table tonight ready to go to you. Do you want your husband included on it?"

"No. I'd prefer not. Our marriage is over. He has betrayed me once too often." To her horror, Cassie felt tears spring to her eyes. The Captain handed her a snow-white handkerchief and she gratefully accepted it and wiped her eyes.

"I look forward to your company tonight and that of the McElroys. I shall let you know when your cabin is ready," he said gently as he patted her shoulder.

When he had finished fingerprinting Declan, CSO Allen met with Gavin and Fiona and was particularly interested in what they had to say. They seemed like a level-headed young couple. Fiona told him of her conversation with Alix the previous afternoon and that Alix had confided she'd been having an affair with Declan. She also mentioned that he'd been gone a very long time from the table and seemed strange when he returned.

"And it was you who told Mrs Jordan this morning that her husband had been involved with Alix Lynch?"

"Yes," Fiona replied, wringing her hands. "I was going to tell her yesterday but I didn't want to spoil her Christmas evening. If I had done so maybe none of this would have happened."

Gavin took her hand in his and squeezed it tightly.

"Now, now, Mrs McElroy, you can't blame yourself for any of this," CSO Allen assured her. "You couldn't have known what would happen."

"*Hmmm* . . . very interesting," CSO Allen murmured to himself after they'd left.

He then questioned the bar staff and discovered that Alix had been drinking in various bars since noon the previous day. The waiter at her dinner table also reported that she'd been very drunk at dinner. He sighed. There was no doubt alcohol had played a part in her demise. How often had he seen stupid accidents like this happen because of alcohol? However, something about this case wasn't right. He was convinced that Declan wasn't telling the whole truth. There was something that didn't ring true about his story and it seemed the young McElroys were of the same opinion. He'd got the impression that they suspected Declan had a part to play in the demise of Alix Lynch.

He met with the Captain and conveyed his uneasiness about the whole incident.

"That rail on the veranda is quite high, as you know. I

don't see how she could have accidentally fallen over it. If, as Mr Jordan says, he was right there when she fell over, why did he not grab her? He knew she was drunk and dazed after banging her head." He looked perplexed as did the Captain.

"I agree with you. Please put all that in your report. I take it you've sealed off her cabin?"

"Of course."

"Well, there's nothing more we can do now except keep an eye on Mr Jordan. Do you think he's a suicide risk?"

"I doubt it – his type always think they can wangle out of anything," CSO Allen remarked bitterly.

"Well, let's get that report back to Fort Lauderdale as soon as possible and see what they make of it."

"Aye aye, Captain."

The talk on board all morning was of the unfortunate accident that had befallen Alix. Nina sought Ann out at breakfast to offer her sympathy. Tony sat grim-lipped and scowling as Nina asked what had happened. Seeing this, Ann suggested to Nina that they take their coffee out on deck. When she'd filled Nina in on the little she knew, she agreed to go with her to the talk on Antigua which was about to start. She hoped it would take her mind off last night's tragic events.

Tony was relieved to get her out of his hair as it left him free to meet with Jess for a couple of hours. She was there waiting for him on their veranda. It amazed him that no one had yet discovered this secret hideaway.

He found her sitting up sideways on the sun-lounger, fully dressed and very subdued. She was very upset at what had happened to Alix.

199

"What a horrible way to die," she said with a shiver.

"I wonder if we'll ever know what happened?" mused Tony. He was also suspicious of Declan whom he did not like at all.

"We never know when our end will come, do we?" Jess observed sadly.

"That's true – which is why we must live in the present and make the most of every moment."

It was obvious that she was distraught and in need of comfort and he came and sat on the bed beside her. He put his arms around her and stroked her head as he would a child's. She felt safe and comforted but couldn't stop the tears rolling down her cheeks.

"There, there, Jess. Don't cry," he murmured. "I'm here. I'll take care of you forever."

Jess was taken aback and pulled away from him. What did he mean by that?

"Tony, you have a wife and family to think about. They need you."

"Of course," he said, and she allowed him to put his arm about her again and comfort her.

He was so crazy about her that she was the only thing he cared about. For the first time in his life he was truly in love. She occupied his thoughts every moment of every day. It was the most exhilarating feeling in the world. He was determined that he would win her over. Until then, he would have to hide his feelings. He was terrified that it would scare her away.

Sarah meanwhile was sunbathing on the pool deck with the two young American college footballers she'd met after the salsa competition. Their names were Todd and Hank and they were travelling with their parents. They were handsome and enthusiastic and explained to her that their ambition was to become professional footballers.

They were cock-a-hoop when they heard she was from Dublin.

"Hey, we played in Dublin last year," Todd told her. "Great city."

"We play for Notre Dame." Hank grinned at her.

They were great fun and Sarah basked in their attention.

"I want the first dance at the disco tonight," Todd insisted.

"And I want the last!" Hank slapped his pal on the shoulder.

Sarah laughed.

"Now, now, boys, no fighting please!" She looked at them sexily. They were like puppy-dogs looking for a pat on the head and she lapped it up.

Jack Kenny could go to hell. Who did he think he was, ignoring her all the time? He was too big for his boots anyway. These guys appreciated her.


After leaving the Captain, Cassie had called Fiona but it went to voice message. Then Fiona had called her back after talking to CSO Allen.

Fiona listened in shock to what Declan had admitted and what had transpired at the meeting with Security and the Captain.

"So what are you going to do now?" she asked Cassie.

"I really don't know. I'm so confused. I just can't believe what Declan did. I don't think I can ever forgive him. The Captain has said he'll find me another cabin. He's been so kind. He's invited me to dine at his table tonight. I told him

I don't want Declan there. To be honest, right now I don't ever want to see him again."

"I understand. We also got an invite from him in our cabin just now, along with Bunny and Richard. How nice of him!"

As she hung up, Cassie's phone rang again. It was the Captain.

"If you'll join me at Guest Relations, I'll show you to your new quarters," he said.

Cassie was shocked to find that he'd given her one of the best suites on board. One similar to Bunny's. "Oh no, this is much too grand," she told him.

"Nonsense. You've had a terrible shock. You deserve a little TLC. My pleasure."

Tears sprang to her eyes again at his kindness. He handed her another pristine handkerchief.

"I don't have an endless supply of these, you know," he laughed. "No more crying."

She laughed through her tears with him. She said she would move in right away.

She went back to the cabin she'd shared with Declan and packed her stuff.

As she was leaving Declan walked in.

"Where are you going?" he asked, looking at her luggage.

"I'm moving to another cabin," she informed him.

"Please, Cassie," he pleaded. "Please don't leave me now. I need you. I love only you."

"No, you don't. You only love yourself, Declan. I can't forgive you. I have one question and please don't lie to me. Alix was not the only one, was she?"

Numbly he shook his head.

"How many women were there?" Her gaze never left his face. "It doesn't make any difference now but I'm curious. I'd like to know."

"Lots," he whispered.

"As soon as I get back to Ireland I'm filing for divorce. I can't take your lies and empty promises any more."

With that she turned on her heel and walked out of his life.

The mood on board was very sombre in the light of Alix's disappearance. Rumours continued to fly and, when it became known that Declan had been arguing with her in the apartment, people gave him a wide berth. Word had somehow got out that he had been having an affair with Alix, which made them all the more suspicious.

Declan tried to brave the curious looks but it was difficult. It irked him that the Irish Mafia were rallying round Cassie who was now seen as a victim. If only he could have made them see that Alix was a psychopath intent on destroying his marriage maybe they'd have understood. His marriage was doomed anyway, he realised, when he saw the way Cassie had looked at him. Now she'd walked out on him. He took to his cabin and emptied the mini-bar.

In the end Alix had won.

When the ship docked in St Thomas just before noon the passengers were amazed to see five other cruise ships anchored there. All were anxious to get off, in an effort to put the shocking events of the night before behind them. Most headed for the beautiful beaches for which St Thomas is famous. Richard, Gavin and Tony had booked to play golf with Declan and were greatly relieved when he cried off. It would have been a very awkward foursome indeed after the events of the previous evening.

Much as he loved golf, Tony would have preferred to spend the day with Jess but she'd arranged to spend the day with Sarah and Fiona who had persuaded Cassie to also join them. They planned to head out to Coki beach which was supposedly the most beautiful beach on the island.

As she lay in the sun and swam in the warm turquoise sea, Cassie felt herself relax a little and the tension seeped from her body. She was grateful that she'd agreed to come. She was trying to come to terms with the fact that her life with Declan was over and that she should move on. But how did one even begin to go about that? He had been her whole life and she felt lost. The knowledge that all the time he'd been cheating on her was very hard to bear. She felt a physical pain just thinking about it and tried to put it out of her mind but she couldn't. She didn't think she'd ever get over it.

Jack had read about the amazing SkyRide on the island and was mad keen to go. After much persuasion, Emily and Tarquin agreed to join him. It took them up seven hundred feet above the island. There was a Ferris wheel there but Emily, who was afraid of heights, absolutely refused to get on it. Jack and Tarquin went ahead and felt as if they were on top of the world. Emily couldn't even bear to look up at it. It made her feel ill.

They had asked Ann earlier if she'd like to go with them but she declined. Instead she joined Nina on a tour of the island and then went shopping in the duty-free mall.

Bunny spent the day on board and had booked several spa treatments. It was very relaxing. The majority of the other passengers had gone ashore and she had the ship almost to herself. It was a good  feeling. She'd been to the island before and so was quite happy to wave the others off.

# Chapter 18

The atmosphere on board had lightened considerably by that evening.

The Captain's invitation to dinner included a pre-dinner drinks reception which was held in a private room in his quarters. Bunny was in her element and brought out as much bling as one could for a semi-formal evening. How she wished it had been a formal one when she could have wowed them all with her new diamonds! Cassie wore a simple blue silk dress and a piece of her own jewellery. She also brought along the piece the Captain had admired at his cocktail party. In another bag she put her business card along with a box of white handkerchiefs she'd bought in St Thomas and a small thank-you card.

His eyes shone when he opened the bag and found the necklace. "You are too kind," he said, kissing her hand.

She blushed prettily.

When he opened the second bag he laughed out loud. "You won't be needing these, will you?" he remarked, pointing at the handkerchiefs.

"I hope not," she replied without much conviction.

They were ten. His other guests were a Director of the cruise-line and his wife, and the Chief Engineer and his wife who usually travelled with him. After the aperitifs, the Captain led them to his table which was in the centre of the dining room. They were aware of the envious glances of the other passengers as it was quite a coup to be invited to dine at the Captain's table and only a handful of passengers ever got to experience it.

They had a wonderful evening and the Captain was charming to them all but Fiona and Bunny could see that he was extra-attentive to Cassie.

While their parents and brother were enjoying the hospitality of the Captain, Sarah and Jess were having drinks in the outdoor bar on Deck 15 with Sarah's new friends Todd and Hank. The two guys were more than happy to have another glamorous blonde join them.

Tony had been annoyed when Jess said she would not be joining him for dinner. She thought it best as she would feel awkward sitting at the same table as Ann, especially as Tony increasingly made no effort to conceal his interest in her. Right now the young footballers were a welcome distraction. Sarah seemed to have calmed down quite a bit. About time, Jess thought. She guessed those Italians thieves had given her younger sister a jolt. She was actually quite enjoying Sarah's company, which was a first.

They went in to dinner and Jess waved to Ann and Tony as she passed their table. He was miserable and overcome with jealousy when he saw Jess laughing and having fun with the young people. He was infatuated with her and could think of little else.

Ann wondered why he was so quiet but he just waved his hand dismissively when she asked him. She gave up and chatted to the other people who had joined them at their table. It was nice to meet new people and hear their stories. She enjoyed their company but Tony appeared disinterested.

"Methinks Cassie has bewitched the Captain," Gavin remarked when they were back in their cabin.

"He's just being kind after what she's been through," Fiona told him.

"Kind my foot! He has the hots for her," Gavin insisted.

"Well, she is beautiful. I don't blame him."

"I'd like nothing better than for her to shove it to Declan, after the way that bastard betrayed her," he said fiercely.

"I suppose you're right. Not to mention poor Alix. When I think of her lost in that big sea . . ." Fiona shuddered at the thought.

When the Captain's dinner was over, he had insisted on escorting Cassie personally to her suite.

"You've been very kind to me," she said when they reached it, her voice catching with emotion.

"Uh-oh, I feel another handkerchief going astray!"

"No way," she replied. "Seriously, I don't know how to thank you."

"How about inviting me in for a nightcap?" he suggested. "I want to make sure your suite is comfortable . . . and I promise I'll be an utter gentleman." He held his hands up in front of him.

Cassie laughed. "I'll keep you to that."

He poured them both a brandy and they went out on the veranda. She stood looking up at the full moon lighting the sky and making a path in the water behind them.

"This is so beautiful," she murmured. "You're a lucky man to have this all the time."

"I suppose but it gets lonely too. Constantly on the move. Sometimes I wish I was a normal man working in an office nine-to-five and coming home every evening to a loving wife and kids." He sounded wistful.

"That's not you. You'd go crazy within a week."

He sighed. "Perhaps you're right."

"Is it not possible to do like your Chief Engineer and have your wife travel with you?"

"Not many women would want to live that life."

"I don't know. I can think of worst things."

"Could you live that life?" he asked, turning to look into her eyes.

"With the right man, and if I loved him, then yes."

"You're a very special woman," he said, brushing her cheek lightly with his finger.

"I think maybe we should go in, Captain," she said, embarrassed.

"Do you think you could drop the 'Captain' and call me Dimitri?"

"Yes, Dimitri," she smiled.

"Thank you, Cassie." He raised his glass to her.

They went inside and she curled up in an armchair. "I take it someone is driving this ship?" she asked.

"We don't drive, we steer," he corrected her, "and yes, my Staff Captain is on the bridge taking care of things."

"Oh good!"

"Will you be okay?" he asked her, his voice full of concern.

"I don't know. I'm still reeling from finding out that my husband has been cheating on me with multiple women. Beside the hurt, I just can't believe that I never guessed. How was I so blind and stupid?"

He heard the quiver in her voice and longed to comfort her. She was such a lovely woman.

"You weren't stupid. Serial cheaters are very clever at covering their tracks. You can't blame yourself."

"I'm so confused at the moment. It's exhausting me."

"Forgive me, you must be very tired," he said, standing up. "It's time for me to go."

"Thank you for everything," Cassie said as she showed him out. "And you *have* been an utter gentleman!"

She made herself a cup of camomile tea and went back out on the veranda. The beauty of the scene took her breath away as the wash from the ship cut a path through the moonlit water. She suddenly felt the urge to capture the scene on canvas. How strange! She had brought her painting gear with her but had not done anything since the cruise started. Painting had always calmed her soul and so she went and got the paints out and started painting the tranquil scene.

She painted through the night. She couldn't have slept anyway. It was the best work she'd ever done. When she had finished, she put away the paints and lay on the veranda watching the sun rise. She felt empty, as if a numbness had enveloped her. She'd heard this was how people felt when a loved one died – like the brain can't assimilate the pain. Her love for Declan had died. He had made her feel worthless and unlovable. To think he had been cheating and lying for so long with all those women and she'd been too blind and in love to see it! She wondered if she had ever really known him at all. Had she been in love with an illusion? She couldn't think straight any more.

She was grateful to Dimitri who had made her feel worthwhile tonight. It was a good feeling and one – she now realised – she hadn't had for a long time. She knew her life was about to change irrevocably and she was scared. She had to be strong. She found it hard to feel sympathy for Declan. He had brought all this on himself.

Cassie's phone rang at seven the following morning. She was nervous answering it as she suspected it might be Declan and she did not want to talk to him.

It wasn't. It was Dimitri.

"Cassie, I thought you should know. We sent the report of the MOB to the Police Authority in Fort Lauderdale and they are sending three officers down to Antigua today to investigate. They want to interview your husband and they may want to talk with you too."

"Does this mean they think he is responsible for Alix's death?" she asked nervously.

"Between you and me, that may be the case. It's unlikely that they would fly down here otherwise."

"Oh God!"

"I'm sorry. I know this is an ordeal for you."

"I'm fine," Cassie said with more courage than she felt.

"You'll need to stay on board in case they do want to interview you."

"That's okay. Let me know if they need me."

"I'll call as soon as I hear anything."

"Thank you, Dimitri."

Declan did not take the news quite so calmly.

"What is this about?" he demanded of CSO Allen. "I told you it was an accident!"

"I know, Mr Jordan, but there are obviously aspects of the case that the police are not happy with. I'm sorry but you cannot leave the ship in case they need to speak to you."

"Bloody hell! This is like a witch-hunt. Do I have access to an attorney?"

"I'm afraid not. We're in the middle of the Caribbean. They will be doing an investigation of Miss Lynch's cabin. If they are satisfied, they may not want to talk to you at all. I'll keep you informed."

Declan cursed again.

What an unpleasant individual, the Security Officer thought.

Fiona called Cassie to see how she was doing and was shocked when she heard the news.

"I'll come and stay with you," she offered.

"No, no, there's absolutely no need. You're going out with Bunny and Richard to that spa, aren't you?"

"Yes, but I can cancel."

"Please don't. I stayed up all night painting as I couldn't sleep anyway so I'm exhausted. I'll try and catch some shut-eye now. I'll be fine."

"Well, you know where I am if you need me. Just call my cellphone and I can be back in thirty minutes."

"You're so good but honestly, I'm fine. Have a nice time."

As they came into St John's, the capital of Antigua, they could see the massive *Harmony of the Seas* was in port. Everyone gazed in awe at the sheer size of it.

"Oh no!" Gavin moaned. "This means that there will be at least another seven or eight thousand people on the island today."

They docked thirty minutes later and at eight-thirty the passengers started to disembark. Some were going on tours but most were heading north from St John's to the beautiful beaches where they would snorkel and jet-ski and just laze on the powdery beaches. Sarah and the two American boys were amongst them. She was looking forward to a fun day. She'd had her morning dose of coke and was feeling high as she stepped off the gangway to be greeted by a steel band playing reggae music. She couldn't resist dancing to it and Todd and Hank joined her.

Jack passed by with Emily and Tarquin.

"Sarah certainly looks like she's having a good time," remarked Tarquin.

"She's a fabulous dancer," Emily said enviously. "Isn't she, Jack?"

"*Huh!*" was his only reply.

"Don't tell me you're jealous?" She looked at him curiously.

"Don't be ridiculous," he snapped, walking away.

"I think he is," she whispered to Tarquin. "He fancies her, you know."

The three investigators from Fort Lauderdale arrived on board at 10 a.m. After a briefing from CSO Allen they were shown to Alix's cabin. They quickly set to work and when they were finished they met up with the Chief and the Captain.

"There's no doubt about it. We found hair samples in the blood on the table and the floor. From the amount of blood on the floor it looks like she must have incurred a serious injury. But we are certain that she could not have fallen accidentally over that height of rail, even if drunk or dazed. She must have been pushed."

"Just as I thought," CSO Allen said solemnly.

"We have dusted the veranda for finger and footprints and have taken away evidence which we'll need to analyse. And now we'd like to interview this guy who was with her."

The Deputy SO went to collect Declan. Under interrogation he was aggressive and uncooperative. He didn't do himself any favours. But these were very experienced investigators and they knew he was lying. They were determined to get the truth of what had happened to Alix on that fateful Christmas night.

"You claim she fell over the railing, Mr Jordan?" the one who was playing bad-cop asked incredulously. "We know that can't have happened."

He asked Declan to go over his story time and time again, all the while taking notes. He wouldn't let up. They grilled him for three hours.

"There is no way Miss Lynch, who must have been badly injured, could have fallen overboard accidentally," said the bad-cop. "Now stop wasting our time and tell us what really happened!"

"Come now, Mr Jordan," the good-cop said kindly. "We know it was an accident. We've no doubt you didn't mean for it to happen, but you did push her over the rail, didn't you?"

These guys were good. Eventually Declan cracked and told them the truth.

They nodded at each other, satisfied to have made progress. They knew it might not be the whole truth but it was enough to arrest him on.

"Mr Jordan, we are arresting you as a suspect in the death of Miss Alix Lynch. You will accompany us back to Fort Lauderdale this evening and you will appear in court there tomorrow to be indicted."

"*You can't do this!*" Declan shrieked.

"We most certainly can," the chief police investigator replied. "We will accompany you to your cabin now and expect your full cooperation. We suggest you find yourself good legal representation. You're going to need it."

When Declan had been taken out CSO Allen asked the Chief Police Investigator what would happen to him.

"At the moment we have no body but there's evidence of foul play and he is involved. Most likely he'll be indicted tomorrow on suspicion of murder. When the body is recovered then an autopsy will tell us whether she was alive or dead on entering the water."

"What then?"

"If she was alive, then he'll be charged with murder. If not, it will be manslaughter. Either way I guess he'll be going away for a long time."

"I can't see him garnering much sympathy with a jury," CSO Allen commented.

"No. He's an obnoxious man. I can't see that happening either," the Chief said with a grimace.

The Captain made his way to Cassie's suite where she was sunning herself on the veranda. Serious as his quest was, he couldn't help admiring her toned body as she slipped on a cover-up.

She went pale when he told her that Declan had been arrested.

"So they think he had something to do with her death?" she asked, shaking her head in disbelief.

"I'm afraid he has confessed to throwing her overboard, Cassie. But he claims she was already dead at that point, after hitting her head against the table on the veranda. They're taking him back to Fort Lauderdale this evening."

"Will he be charged with murder?" asked Cassie fearfully.

"That depends. A good lawyer might be able to get it reduced to manslaughter."

"How could he have done this?" Cassie couldn't get her head round it.

"Do you want to see him before he goes?" the Captain asked.

"I don't know. I'll have to think about it." She buried her head in her hands.

He saw she was shaking. "I understand. Will you be okay or shall I send someone to stay with you?"

"No, I'll be fine. I'd like to be alone now if you don't mind."

When he left she collapsed in a flood of tears. She had been married for all those years to a monster. How had that happened? How had she not seen it? She lay on the bed until her tears were spent. She would have to call her father and Julie at some point but she couldn't face them quite yet.

All the tragic events seemed to have released another dimension to her creativity and she knew she was painting her best work ever. She also needed this time to come to terms with what had happened. Once again she immersed herself in painting the beautiful scene from her veranda. She was happy she managed to catch the exact iridescent turquoise and green of the shimmering Caribbean sea. For a little while she escaped the reality of what was happening. It was cathartic.

Cassie called her father first. He was shocked when he heard what had occurred.

"I'll come out there right away," he said, his voice shaking with anger at what Declan had done.

"No, no, Dad. Don't do anything yet. I need time to think."

"Are you sure? You're all alone in a strange place. You need my support."

"I'm fine. I have made some good friends here. They're Irish and they're taking care of me."

"If you're sure, Princess. You know I'd drop everything immediately."

"Honestly, Dad, I'll be fine. I'll let you know if I need you."

She hung up quickly, afraid she might break down in tears. When she had composed herself, she called Julie. Her friend was equally shocked and called Declan all the names under the sun.

"You'll divorce the bastard of course," she said.

"Yes. But right now I'm just devastated and not able to think that far ahead."

"That low-down rat! I hope you'll now move on and find someone worthy of you, Cassie!"

"I doubt I'll ever be able to trust a man again," Cassie said sadly.

She decided she had to see Declan again and get the truth about what happened from him. She called the Captain to tell him so. She was shaking as she went to confront her husband. The policemen kindly left them alone.

"Did you kill Alix?" Cassie asked him bluntly.

"It was an accident, honestly, Cass." His eyes pleaded with her to believe him.

"Please tell me what happened exactly," she said coldly.

"She attacked me and as I tried to defend myself she slipped and fell and gashed her head off the edge of the table. She was very drunk, as you know."

"And?" Cassie prompted him.

"And . . ." he took a deep breath, "when I checked she had stopped breathing."

"Dear God!" Cassie exclaimed, clutching at her throat. "And what did you do then?"

"What could I do?" Declan cried, jumping up. "She was dead. People would think I killed her!"

"So you threw her overboard?" she said, her voice low.

"I had no choice."

"Of course you had a choice!" she cried. "You should have called for help. How could you be sure she was dead?"

"I *was* sure she was dead!" he cried, his voice rising.

"You're despicable!" she said, her hands visibly shaking. "You've broken my heart and I will never forgive you, Declan. You deserve everything they throw at you!"

Without another word, she turned and walked away.

Sarah and the boys wandered around St John's, which was cute and quaint, before taking a taxi to Dickenson Bay which was the most popular beach on the island. She recognised many passengers from the ship enjoying the magnificent beach and facilities. As they walked past the fabulous Sandals Hotel Resort she vowed to come back and stay there one day.

They were just about to set their towels down in the powdery sand when she spotted Tarquin and Emily nearby.

"Hi there!" she called out.

She and the boys went over to the others and put their stuff down near them. She introduced Todd and Hank.

"Isn't this glorious?" Emily exclaimed. "It's like all those perfect postcards you see of tropical islands."

"It's paradise all right," Sarah agreed.

Jack had gone down to the water's edge and when he returned and saw Sarah with her friends he was annoyed. She was busy taking selfies of herself and the boys. She was wearing the white bikini again.

"C'mon, boys, last into the water is a rotten egg!" she called out, flying down the sand to the water – the two boys in hot pursuit.

She and the boys had a wonderful time and swam out to a platform in the sea where they met some other young people. Then they played beach volleyball and jet-skied before going to lunch in a beach-side café where they drank the best rum punches on earth. Tarquin and Emily joined them but Jack refused.

Emily was having a wonderful time. Sarah was such fun. Emily admired her greatly and wished she could be more like her.

Jack wandered off on his own, feeling disgruntled, unable to take all this jollity. Emily and Tarquin seemed really close and, watching them together, Sarah thought that they were perfect for each other. She was happy for Tarki. They all had a wonderful time and were sorry when the time came to go back to the ship.

# Chapter 19

Tony had told Ann that he would be playing golf so she agreed to take a tour of the island with Nina. In fact he had no intention of playing golf but it was as good an excuse as any. He desperately wanted to see Jess and, when Ann had left on her tour, he went in search of her. To his immense relief she said she had no plans and he told her that he had a special treat for her. She didn't want to encourage him any more but he was good company and when he told her what he'd planned she couldn't resist it. After all, his wife had fucked off again without him and she was alone for the day. Why not?

Tony had gone online and found a beautiful luxury hotel on the south of the island where you could book in for the day. Once the coast was clear they left the ship and took a taxi to Rendezvous Bay on the south-west of the island which he'd read was much more secluded. He'd chosen it because they would be unlikely to bump into other passengers from the *Liberté*.

It was idyllic and Jess was mightily impressed. The hotel was fabulous and the beautiful pool had a waterfall and a pool-bar. After Tony had paid at reception they settled on two of the luxurious sun-loungers and Jess slipped off her mini-dress. Today she was wearing a stunning turquoise bikini with fringing – every bit as revealing as the previous ones she'd worn. Tony was overcome with excitement as he looked at her.

"I hope this is not too revealing," she said with a frown. She'd noticed most of the other women around the pool were wearing one-piece bathing suits and not itsy-bitsy bikinis.

"It's perfect. You look beautiful." He felt proud to be with her as he saw the lustful looks of the men and the envious glances of the other women sunning themselves around the pool.

When she dived in a perfect arc into the pool all eyes were on her. Tony dived in after her and lifted her, swinging her around as she laughed gaily. They swam up to the pool-bar where he ordered two rum punches. They sat up on two stools and as they sipped them he put his arm casually around her.

"This was a wonderful idea," she said, turning to him. "Thank you."

Feeling her body so close to his, he thought he would burst with joy.

They frolicked in the pool and she was more tactile than usual, her inhibitions loosened perhaps by the alcohol. She loved the waterfall and kept dragging him in, laughing as the water cascaded down over them both. After another rum punch, they dried off in the sun and then went for lunch on the shaded patio. They enjoyed the delicious seafood –

lobster, shrimp and scallops baked in a creamy sauce – and Tony ordered a bottle of champagne to wash it down. He was blissfully happy and Jess appeared to be happy too.

The hotel was situated on a cliff overlooking a small private cove which was not quite deserted but had only a handful of people. Most of the residents favoured the pool. They took the lift down to the beach where there was a tiki bar dispensing exotic cocktails. There were luxurious sun-loungers here too and snorkelling equipment available. First they went snorkelling and again the marine life was stunning. Tony was delighted to see how much Jess was enjoying herself. This had been a wonderful idea of his.

After the snorkelling, they took the two sun-loungers farthest away from the other people there and the barman brought them two more rum punches. Jess had seen two other women going topless so, without asking him this time, she slipped off her top and sat sipping her drink. Again the sight of her amazing breasts excited him and he couldn't take his eyes off them. He longed to kiss and caress them. He looked up and saw that she was watching him.

"You like what you see?" she asked, bending towards him so that her breasts were almost touching him. She was enjoying herself and feeling a little tipsy.

He moaned. "I love it. You're driving me crazy, you know."

"I can see that," she said mockingly, her eyes going to his crotch. She laughed a low sexy laugh and he knew she was turned on by his desire.

They lay contented side by side and Tony oiled her back once more. This time she moaned with pleasure when he stroked the sides of her breasts sensually. He knew she wanted him too and he kept stroking her, enjoying her

223

pleasure. When he stopped she looked at him and suddenly sat up.

"C'mon, let's go for a swim," she suggested, much to his surprise.

She ran down the beach, her naked breasts swaying as she went, and dived into the clear turquoise sea. He went awkwardly after her, his erection slowing him down. He saw that she was swimming around the headland away from the beach. He followed her and found she had stopped swimming. They were in a tiny deserted cove and she was standing in the shallow water, the sun glistening on her magnificent body. She turned to face him, jumping over a wave, laughing, and he just couldn't resist it. He reached for her and softly caressed her breast. She threw back her head and moaned, putting her hands on his shoulders. He played with her nipples and then bent down and kissed them before sucking on them. They tasted spicy and filled his mouth. She moaned with pleasure and before he realised it she had opened the ties of her bikini bottom and pressed her naked body against his, wrapping her legs around his waist.

He gasped as he entered her, luxuriating in her wetness. He had never made love to such a beautiful woman before and certainly not naked in the water. Their desire and passion carried them to a climax at exactly the same moment. He thought he'd died and gone to heaven.

She clung to him as they came down from their reverie.

"That's the nicest thing that's ever happened to me," he whispered, his voice breaking. He was overcome with emotion. "You know I've fallen in love with you, Jess."

She felt panicked as she tied her bikini bottom back on. He didn't really mean that, did he? What on earth had she done? She found herself blushing. The sex had been amazing but she should never have let it happen. She knew she was to blame. She had led him on. Those rum punches and the champagne at lunch had made her lose the run of herself. She was fond of him and enjoyed his company but that was as far as it went. And now he was saying he loved her. She could never let this happen again. She was quiet in the taxi on the way back to the town. When Tony had paid off the driver he reached down and kissed her.

"Thank you for a wonderful, magical day," he whispered before they parted to make their way separately back to the ship. He would never forget it as long as he lived.

It had been a miserable day for Jack. Everyone had seemed to be having a great time except for him. Eventually he couldn't take any more of Sarah prancing around with her score of admirers at her beck and call. She'd managed to pick up some more on the beach and had Emily take photos of her with them all. She'd asked Tarquin to stand in for them but not Jack. She had totally ignored him all day and he wasn't used to that. She was getting under his skin.

Pissed off, he had decided to go back to the ship earlier than the others.

Then, as he got out of the taxi in St John's he spotted his father and Jess exiting another taxi. They stood close together and he was shocked when he saw his father reach down and kiss her on the lips. Jack was rooted to the spot as he saw them go their separate ways. He wouldn't have believed it if he hadn't seen it with his own eyes. His father had said he was playing golf today. Obviously scored a hole-in-one, Jack thought bitterly. My God! What should he do? His mother would be devastated if she knew about this. He knew things were not going well between them at the moment. Now he knew the reason why. Those bitches of McElroy girls, he thought savagely – kicking the ground and hurting his toe.

Sarah had thoroughly enjoyed the day, though her proximity to Jack had been a thorn in her side. She still fancied him and wished he'd lighten up and stop ignoring her. As she and her friends passed by the *Harmony of the Seas* they stopped to look up at it. There were some people standing on a veranda and she gave a cry as she recognised Enzo and Sofia, the Italians who'd done a flit. CSO Allen had reported only this morning to her father that they were at a loss as to where the thieves might have gone from Nassau. Now she knew. Clever dicks.

"I don't believe it!" she exclaimed, grabbing Todd's arm.

"What is it?"

"It's the Italians – the thieves – they're on that ship!" she cried, pointing.

"Good God, are you sure?"

"Absolutely."

"They cleaned our parents out too," Hank said. "Sarah, we have to get back and tell Security that we've seen them."

Sarah nodded. They raced back to the *Liberté* where she asked to see CSO Allen.

"Are you absolutely sure?" he asked her.

"Yes, definitely. It's them," she insisted.

He was elated. What luck! Just when the police investigators from Fort Lauderdale were on board. He contacted the Captain who immediately called the Captain of *Harmony of the Seas.* Two of the investigators hotfooted it over there while the third remained with Declan. It looked like he would be having company en route back to Fort Lauderdale.

The McElroys had spent the day at the Hermitage Bay Hotel quite close to St John's. Bunny and Richard had stayed there before and insisted on booking Gavin and Fiona in for the day too as a special 'congratulations on making us grandparents' present. Fiona had to laugh. The hotel was very luxurious and didn't normally take day bookings but as usual Bunny pulled strings and so they spent the day in 'Paradise' as Fiona called it.

There was a beautiful Garden Spa set amongst the oleander and frangipani trees and Bunny had insisted they avail of whatever treatments they cared for. Such luxury.

Fiona felt totally relaxed as they made their way back to the ship.

She was shocked when she got back to find that Declan had been arrested and was being taken back to Fort Lauderdale by the police. She immediately called Cassie who asked her to call to the suite.

Fiona went straight there and hugged Cassie who wept in her arms.

Then Cassie pulled herself together and anger took over. She said she couldn't believe that her husband could be so evil.

"He's been a liar and a cheat since the day I met him and now he may even be a murderer!" she cried.

"What will you do?"

"What can I do? I'll start divorce proceedings once I get back home. I'm thinking of flying home from St Lucia."

"Please stay on, Cassie. The weather at home is dreadful. Four inches of snow yesterday, I hear. Why not stay on here with us? You have enough friends on board and we'll take care of you."

"You're very kind. I don't know. I'll think about it. Dad's in Switzerland so I don't have much to go home to. The Captain has tried to persuade me that it would be better to stay on and rest up after all the drama."

"He's right," Fiona agreed. "I do hope you'll consider it."

The McElroys had planned to dine en famille that night in the speciality restaurant, Maxim's, but Fiona offered to stay with Cassie.

"No, no, you go dine with your family. Actually Dimitri . . . er . . . the Captain has offered to join me for dinner here tonight."

Fiona raised her eyebrows. "Really?"

"Don't read anything into it. I know the whole ship is talking about Declan and I couldn't bear being stared at and the scrutiny I'd face in the restaurant."

"I hadn't thought of that. It is very thoughtful of the Captain. He does fancy you, you know."

"He's just being kind. Believe me, that would be the last thing on my mind. Don't worry!"

Fiona gave her a hug. "Please call me if you need me. Okay?"

"To rescue me, you mean?" And she laughed for the first time that day.

Cassie was right. The whole ship was agog with the news that Declan had been charged in connection with Alix's death. She was right to keep a low profile. Then the news broke that the Italian thieves had been apprehended on the *Harmony of the Seas*.

Sarah was the heroine of the hour. It was she who had brought the thieves to justice. She basked in the glory but the best moment was when Jack approached her and congratulated her.

"Not just a pretty face then," he couldn't resist adding.

"Much, much more than that," she answered smartly.

He laughed. She was something else.

Strangely, despite his remark, she felt flattered. "I'm well able for you, Jack Kenny," she murmured when he'd sauntered away.

Her family were over the moon that the thieves had been caught. They'd pulled the same stunt on another ship since the *Liberté* and had planned the same for the *Harmony of the Seas*. It transpired that they had planned to disembark in Barbados and go to ground. Sarah was certainly the star of the night and, when the Captain came to thank her, Bunny glowed with pride.

"That's my girl," she said proudly, all past sins forgiven.

The Captain informed them that the police had recovered all the stolen goods that had been taken and they would be returned to them in Fort Lauderdale.

Jack was relieved that Jess was not at their table that night. However, Nina had joined them with her husband Paul, who as usual said not a word. Tony looked distracted and sat lost in his own thoughts and didn't contribute to the conversation. Tarquin and Emily were wrapped up in each other so it was up to Jack to help his mother out. He was furious with his father and before dessert was served he asked Tony if he could have a word in private.

"Sure, son," Tony said magnanimously. "Let's go up on deck for a few minutes."

On deck, Jack turned to face his father.

"Dad, I saw you today with Jess."

Tony faltered, his face going pale. "What? Where?"

"Getting out of a taxi. I saw you kissing her. Dad, what's going on?"

Tony was breathing heavily as he leant his hands on the rail. "Well, you may as well know it now. I'm in love with Jess. Truly in love. I want to spend the rest of my life with her."

Jack was stunned. "Does she love you?"

"She hasn't said so but I know she does."

"Oh Dad, don't be foolish! You're way too old for her."

"Jess doesn't think I'm too old and she makes me feel young again." Tony gave a little smile as he thought of her.

Jack realised that his father was serious. "What about Mum?" he demanded.

Tony sighed. "Your mother and I have grown apart. That happens in marriages. I can't help my feelings. I honestly love Jess."

Jack could see that his father meant every word. What a catastrophe! This would kill his mother. What could he do about it?

"Well, now you know. I was going to wait till after the holiday to tell your mother. I'd appreciate it if you'd say nothing to her till then. No point in spoiling the trip for her. Now we'd best get back inside."

Jack's head was reeling as he took his seat again. How could his father be so blasé? He looked at his mother sitting there, quite unaware that her whole world was about to come crashing down. He wished he could do something to save that happening. What a mess! The saying 'no fool like an old fool' flitted through his mind.

When the Captain arrived at Cassie's suite he spotted her paintings drying against the wall and was amazed at how good they were.

"You are seriously talented," he told her. "Jewellery first and now painting. Wow!"

She smiled. "Painting is my escape – it soothes my soul," she confessed.

Although the dinner was delicious Cassie barely ate anything. She had no appetite for it.

Afterwards she curled up in her favourite armchair again as the Captain poured two brandies. The alcohol warmed her somewhat. She'd felt cold inside since this whole debacle. They chatted companionably, he wanting to take her mind off her troubles. They were both comfortable with each other. He told her about his life and the two loves he'd had and she shared her life with him too. She told him about Declan's infidelities and he longed to comfort her but knew it would be inappropriate. He was pleased when she told him she'd decided to stay on the cruise.

"Everyone's been so kind," she said emotionally, as she felt herself tearing up. The last thing she wanted was to cry again in front of him. "I'm sorry but I'm very tired. I haven't had much sleep since all of this . . ." She waved her hand wearily.

"I understand. Forgive me. I'll leave you now," he said, rising to his feet. "I am happy you're going to stay on and, if you need anything, you know where to find me."

"Thank you, Dimitri."

As she drifted off to sleep she thought how nice it was

to have someone who listened to what she had to say and who found it interesting. That hadn't happened in a long while.

The following day was a sea-day and followed the usual pattern; gym, exercise classes, games at the pool, Zumba, a wine-tasting session, another cooking demonstration, a talk on St Lucia where they would dock the following day, a lecture on astronomy and a behind-the-scenes tour of the ship.

Ann was interested in many of these but when she mentioned them to Tony at breakfast he said, "Count me out. I just want to chill. Why don't you go with your friend Nina?"

You could have knocked Ann down with a feather. "I thought you didn't like Nina?"

"I don't. But I don't have to suffer her, do I? And you seem to enjoy her company. So go ahead."

She was gobsmacked but kept going. "There's a full-day tour in St Lucia tomorrow that I would also love to go on. Are you interested?" She didn't mention that Nina was the one who had suggested it.

"You know I can't stand those guided tours – being herded around like sheep. But you go if you'd like."

She didn't know what had got into him but went off happily to meet Nina and give her the good news.

There was method in Tony's madness. He'd belatedly realised that if he endorsed her friendship with that awful woman then he'd be free to spend his days with Jess. Why hadn't he thought of that before?

He was very concerned about the conversation he'd had with Jack last night. Would he tell his mother? He hoped not as he could just imagine the tears and recriminations that would follow. He prayed Jack would keep his trap shut. He wouldn't tell Jess that Jack knew about them either. He wasn't sure how she would take it.

He made his way up to their secret veranda and his heart dropped when he saw it was empty. He settled down to wait for her but, when after an hour she hadn't arrived, he began to panic. She hadn't been in the Buffet that morning which was unusual. He hoped she wasn't sick or anything. When she still hadn't arrived by eleven he went in search of her.

He searched high and low but there was no sign of her. He spied Sarah at the pool doing Zumba but no Jess. He was getting worried now. He hoped nothing was wrong.

The truth was that Jess wanted to avoid Tony at all costs. She felt bad about what had happened in Antigua and knew it was all her fault. She had been flattered by his attention and the way he desired her had boosted her confidence but she had not expected or wanted him to fall in love with her. Tony had said he loved her. She wished he hadn't said that. He surely must have realised that she was just having fun. A holiday flirtation.

She knew what she'd done was wrong and unfair to Ann but she couldn't undo it. She didn't know how she could get herself out of this. All she could do was avoid him like the plague which is why she asked her mother if she could spend the day in her suite.

Bunny was surprised. "Of course, darling," she agreed, wondering what Jess was up to. She had been off by herself every day so far and now suddenly she wanted to spend the day with them. Strange!

When Jess arrived for breakfast Bunny could tell that something had happened but her daughter didn't explain, despite probing.

Jess didn't give anything away. What Bunny would say if she ever found out about Tony didn't bear thinking about.

The *Strictly* lesson was on again that afternoon. Today it was the cha-cha. Todd and Hank both wanted to dance with Sarah and they tossed a coin to decide. Todd won and gleefully took Sarah onto the floor. He was a good dancer but not a patch on Jack. For the final Galina took him as her partner but he only came second.

That was when they announced that the winners from each day would take to the stage for the grand finale as part of the New Year Gala Show in the Theatre.

"You're joking me!" Sarah exclaimed nervously.

Jack, who was standing beside her, made a face and turned to her. "That's a bit mean. They could at least have told us before we started taking part."

"Then no one would have got up on the floor at all," she replied.

"I suppose," he agreed with her.

He had given the matter of his father some thought. It was the need to protect his mother – not his father – that decided him to wait until the cruise was over to say anything. No point in ruining the remainder of the trip for her.

Cassie had spent the morning on the veranda of her suite, painting. Just before lunch the Captain called to say that Alix's body had been picked up by a fishing trawler and taken to St Thomas. It would be taken to Fort Lauderdale where an autopsy would be carried out to determine the cause of death. Then her body would be flown back to

England for burial. He had notified her brother who she had named as her next of kin on her booking form.

Cassie stayed on the veranda, staring at the sea where Alix had foundered. Had she still been alive then? Whatever she had done in the past she hadn't deserved this horrible death.

When Fiona came to have lunch with her she found a very despondent Cassie. "What's going to happen to Declan now?" she asked her.

"I've no idea. The Captain says he'll contact the authorities this afternoon and he'll let me know what they say."

Fiona was worried about her friend's dark mood and stayed the afternoon with her. She relaxed on the sun-lounger while Cassie continued painting. They spoke little and Fiona could see that the act of painting had a soothing effect on Cassie. Fiona, who didn't know a lot about art, could still see that the painting was really very good.

Fiona was still worried about her as she prepared to leave. "Cassie, you can't stay hiding away here forever. It's not good for you. Come to dinner with us tonight and brave the curious hordes. When they've seen you once they'll forget all about it. You've done nothing wrong. You're a victim too."

Reluctantly Cassie agreed to go.

Fiona had just left when the Captain phoned to say they had got word that Declan had been up in court and charged with the suspected murder of Alix Lynch. He'd hired himself a good lawyer who had got him out on bail but his passport had been confiscated in case he should abscond.

"They will decide after the autopsy on her body whether to charge him with murder or manslaughter. They'll keep us posted," the Captain informed her.

She received the news with a sinking heart and told him she was going to dinner with the McElroys that evening.

Cassie discovered Fiona was right. After the initial few minutes people stopped looking at her and got on with their business. She was grateful for the wonderful Irish friends she'd made. They were so supportive. They would see her through. As for Dimitri, his kindness to her since that awful night had overwhelmed her. He had hinted that he was more than fond of her but she'd let him know that she wasn't remotely ready for a new relationship yet.

"Let me tell you, I am a very patient man. I have waited this long to find the right woman so I can wait some more until she's ready," he replied with a twinkle in his eye.

Cassie laughed. "Don't hold your breath!"

"Where's Jess?" Gavin asked as they took their seats in the restaurant.

"She's having dinner in the suite," Richard replied.

"Oh!" Gavin said, surprised. "What's up with her?"

"God knows!" Bunny sighed. "She spent the whole day there. I think she's avoiding someone but she wouldn't say." She turned to her daughter-in-law. "I was hoping you might have a word with her, Fiona. She'll tell *you*. I'm worried about her. She's been such a loner on this cruise and she's become secretive. I've no idea where she's been spending her time and now suddenly she's hanging around us and she appears distracted."

"You worry too much," Richard admonished her. "She's a big girl."

"I know my own daughter and something is up," Bunny insisted.

"Leave her be. She needs time to recover from her marriage breakdown."

"Don't say that!" Bunny cried. "I still have great hopes that she'll go back to Philip."

Richard didn't answer. He didn't think that was on the cards. His eldest daughter was glowing lately and he suspected it was because of a man.

Jack sat with Galina, Emily and Tarquin as they watched Sarah jiving. Todd was no match for her. *She needs a real partner*, Jack decided.

"Why do you never ask Sarah to dance?" Emily asked him.

"I've wondered about that too," Galina said. "You're so perfect together and she likes you very much."

Just then Sarah collapsed beside them, panting. "God! Jiving can be hard work."

"Not if you've got the right partner," Jack remarked.

"Oh, and I suppose you're the right partner?" She looked at him, her eyebrows raised.

At that moment the DJ put on a salsa track and before he could stop himself Jack had grabbed her hand and propelled her onto the floor. She was shocked but the music took over and she started to match his steps. It helped that it was the number they'd danced together at *Strictly*.

They were perfectly synchronised as they twirled, shimmied and gyrated around each other. The whole floor cleared as the other dancers watched in admiration. Jack and Sarah didn't even notice, so caught up in the music were they. As the dance was ending he suddenly lifted her in the air and then swung her round so she ended up with her back across his knee, her head towards the ground and one leg extended to the ceiling. They'd never done that move before but she trusted him implicitly. His face was inches from hers as the music ended and they were both breathing heavily. She felt that jolt of electricity again as he looked deep into her eyes. She saw that he felt it too and was elated.

Finally, aware of the crowd cheering and clapping, he lifted her up and they made their way back to their table.

"*Wow!* That was fantastic!" Emily said.

"You two are made for each other," Galina said softly. "I knew it from the first moment I saw you dance together."

There was nothing Jack could say. She was right and he felt it. He looked at Sarah. Her face was flushed and her lips parted seductively.

"Truce?" she asked, holding out her hand.

"Truce," he replied, taking it.

Galina slipped away quietly and Jack asked Sarah for the last dance which was a slow one. He held her close and she felt like she was melting into him. When the disco was over they both looked at each other expectantly but neither of them would make the first move. Jack thought that he might very well have his heart broken again but he had to risk it.

"What have you planned for tomorrow?" he asked her.

"Just the usual. Take a taxi to a beach somewhere."

"Why not come with me?" he suggested. "I want to go horseback riding along the beach and also do some other adventure stuff.

"Great. I'd like that." She smiled and it took his breath away.

"Nine o'clock at the gangway?"

"See you then."

They parted, both of them nervous and excited and anticipating the morrow.

The following morning they docked on the beautiful island of St Lucia. It was the perfect Caribbean island with something for everyone.

Ann disembarked with Nina at eight-thirty and Tony stayed on in the Buffet, anxiously waiting for Jess to come to breakfast. He hoped they would have another beautiful day together and make love as before. He couldn't wait.

Bunny and Richard had hired a car for the day. Bunny was surprised when Jess said she'd like to join them. Something was definitely up with that girl.

Gavin and Fiona and Cassie were joining them too and luckily the car was a people-carrier so they had room for everybody. They were doing a tour of the island, stopping off at Dasheene restaurant in Soufrière for lunch. Bunny and Richard had eaten there before and promised them they were in for a treat.

And they certainly were. They all agreed it was wonderful. The restaurant was open-air, on a cliff with fantastic views of the Pitons, the two mountains that rose like cones majestically from the sea. It was awesome and the food was delicious.

They started with conch fritters which had them all licking their fingers. The fish that followed must have jumped from the sea to the plate, as Cassie remarked, it was so fresh. They had a wonderful day and all of them agreed they would like to return to this beautiful island.

Cassie was relaxed for the first time since that dreadful night and was grateful to her good friends for including her in this trip.

Fiona noticed that Jess was very quiet and often had a faraway look in her eyes. She waited for a chance to talk to her alone and it came when they went for a walk after lunch on Anse des Pitons beach.

"What's up, Jess? What's bothering you?"

"How do you know something is bothering me?"

"I know you and your mother is convinced that there's something wrong too."

"Oh, God!" Jess cried. "Please don't tell her! Promise me?"

"Tell her what?"

"Promise me?"

"Okay, I promise," Fiona assured her.

"I've done something awful," Jess admitted. "I had sex with Tony."

Fiona stopped dead in her tracks. "Tony? Tony who?"

"Tony Kenny, Ann's husband." Jess could barely look at Fiona. She felt so embarrassed.

"Oh my God! How did that happen?"

Jess told her the whole sorry story.

"I feel terrible about it and Mummy would have a fit if she found out."

"Then we have to make sure she doesn't. And he says he's fallen in love with you?"

Jess nodded her head and let out a long sigh. "I didn't mean for that to happen. I suppose I desperately needed to feel attractive and sexy after Philip's betrayal and Tony was so attentive and obviously fancied me and I suppose I was flattered. I know I should have gone for a single man, not Tony whose wife and kids I know and like. I feel terrible about that . . ." She put her hands to her face. "Oh God! I don't know how I can face any of them. I feel such a bitch."

"The main thing is to keep out of *his* way at all costs," Fiona advised.

"What do you think I've been doing yesterday and today. I never want to see him again."

"That will be awkward on the ship."

"I know," Jess said miserably.

"C'mon. It could be worse. I don't know what I'll tell Bunny. She asked me to talk to you." Fiona shook her head.

"You'll think of something," Jess replied hopefully.

Later Bunny asked Fiona if she'd had a chance to talk to Jess.

"Yes, she's fine. I think the reality of her marriage break-up is beginning to hit her now."

"Thank God for that," Bunny said, relief in her voice. "Maybe she'll reconsider now and see sense and go back to Philip."

Fiona wished her luck with that!

# Chapter 20

Jack met Sarah at nine as planned, ready to disembark. He thought she looked good enough to eat when he saw her in her tiny white shorts and top. He spied the sexy white bikini peeping out from her top and wondered how he'd survive the day without jumping on her.

"I thought we might go zip-lining first. It's through the rainforest and it sounds exciting. Are you on?"

"Great. I've never done that. Where are Emily and Tarquin?"

"They're doing their own thing. I think they're in love so I suppose they want to be alone."

"I'm happy for them. This is certainly the island for lovers."

He looked at her with raised eyebrows which made her blush. She was surprised to see that he had hired a driver for the day.

"Isn't this a bit extravagant?" she asked.

"Well, I want us to have a really great day," he confessed.

"A day we'll always remember."

Sarah was flattered that he'd done this for her. They drove up over Castries and could see the ship down in the harbour. They asked the driver to take a photo of them with the ship in the background and collapsed in fits of laughter when they saw he'd only taken them from the waist down. Then down to Soufriere where the scenery was just amazing.

The Zip-line Centre was in the rainforest and the guides there were fun and entertaining. They even took their phones and took photos of them whizzing down through the trees, picking fruit as they went. The views were quite spectacular and it was a thrilling experience. After a drink the driver took them north to the Riding Centre where they saddled up and followed a forest trail down to the beautiful pristine Cas en Bas beach. The beach was secluded and they galloped along the length of it and back again, exhilarated with the sheer joy of it. Jack could barely keep up with Sarah and marvelled at her horsemanship.

"You're pretty good," he said admiringly.

"I should hope so. I've been riding since I could walk."

"Oh. I suppose you had your own ponies and were in the Pony Club?"

She heard the slight criticism in his voice and was hurt by it. "Truce, we said. Right?"

"Sorry," he replied sheepishly.

"It's not my fault that my parents were wealthy."

"I know. I'm sorry." He smiled at her. "Now race you through the water."

"Hang on a second." Sarah jumped off the horse and stripped off her top and shorts. Jack couldn't take his eyes off her. She was so sexy in that bikini.

Their guide suggested that they take off the saddles so they could go deep in the water. Sarah quickly undid hers and handed it to him then hopped back on her horse. Jack was slower and needed help. He too had stripped to his bathing trunks. She waited patiently till he was ready and then they set off at a gallop along the water's edge. Up and down they went, Sarah always a little ahead. Then they rode deep into the water to cool the horses off. The horses loved it and Sarah handed her phone to the guides and asked them to take photos. Then the guides took the horses from them and they both slipped into the warm silky turquoise water.

"That is the best thing I've ever done," Jack admitted.

"Me too. Thank you so much for arranging it."

They swam out to sea for a bit and he saw she was as strong a swimmer as he was.

Swimming back in he asked her, "Is there anything you don't excel at?"

"Maybe," she laughed, "but I'm not going to tell you what. That you'll have to find out for yourself."

"I doubt you're bad at anything but I'll enjoy trying to find out," he said as he watched her stand up and shake the water from her long blonde hair. She looked as beautiful as any Bond Girl that ever emerged from the sea.

After a barbecue on the beach which was included in the package they rode back to the riding stables to meet up with their driver.

"The day's not over yet," Jack announced as they walked to the car.

"And already it's one I won't ever forget," she replied quietly.

He reached out and stroked her cheek and she moaned

softly. "Later," he whispered, pulling her close and then releasing her.

The rest of the day was equally wonderful. Sarah had always wanted to scuba dive but, after seeing a man die once in Turkey when she was a child, it had always frightened her. However, snuba – which was their next adventure – was a cross between snorkelling and scuba diving and was quite safe, as Jack assured her. It was thrilling and the electric colours of the fish in the sea mesmerised her. She'd never seen anything like it.

When they'd given back the equipment they lazed in the crystal-clear water, coming closer together until at last they kissed. Sarah knew she would never forget that moment as long as she lived. Nor would Jack. They both wanted this magical day to go on and on . . . but they had to get back to the ship.

"Do you think we could elope here?" he asked her jokingly on the way back.

Sarah laughed. "Maybe not but we definitely should come back some day."

"That's a promise."

They held each other close on the drive back and both knew that something special was happening.

After such a wonderful day they did not want to part and Jack asked Sarah to have dinner with him in the open-air La Brasserie restaurant where they would dine under the stars. They had cocktails first in the outdoor Montmartre bar and Sarah took out her phone to post her photos on Facebook and Instagram.

But when she started checking her texts Jack got upset.

"Sarah, could you please put that phone away?" he asked gently. "And let's enjoy the beautiful sunset together."

She could see his point. She often got annoyed when she was out with friends and they spent the whole time texting other friends.

"You're right. I'm sorry." She put the phone away.

He kissed her tenderly then and they sat together holding hands as they watched the golden sunset.

"This has been a beautiful day. I mean it, Sarah, it's been the best day ever."

"For me too," she whispered, leaning in to him.

He took her head in his hands and kissed her. She was so happy she thought she'd explode.

Afterwards Sarah couldn't remember what they'd eaten, so entranced was she. They left the restaurant and went straight to her cabin without having to say a word. Once inside the door they fell on each other, neither of them able to wait another second. As they came together they both understood the expression 'the earth moved'. They'd both had sex before but nothing that could compare to this.

Sarah lost count of the number of times they made love and as they drifted into sleep Jack murmured, "So this is what all those love songs are about. I never understood before."

"Me neither," she whispered softly. She was smiling.

The next day they docked in Barbados in the early morning. The ship would leave at six and start to make its way north again with a stop in St Maarten before heading on to Nassau.

Bunny had often stayed in the famed Sandy Bay Hotel on the west of the island. The Irish owners were friends of hers and she arranged for the whole family to spend the day there. Cassie was also included.

"You're one of the family now," Bunny told her when she said she didn't want to intrude on their family day.

Cassie was touched by this and happily agreed to go along.

Indeed, it was true. They had all become very fond of her.

The evening before, when Sarah had mentioned to Jack that her parents were taking all the family to Sandy Lane, he'd been very disappointed.

"There's a great music festival in Bridgetown tomorrow. I was hoping to go and that you'd come with me. Do you have to go to Sandy Bay?"

"Of course not, if you'd rather I come with you."

"Are you sure your parents won't mind?" He looked worried.

"I'm sure they'll understand."

He hugged her tight, happy that she wanted to be with him.

Bunny was surprised when Sarah asked if she could spend the day with Jack.

"This is new," she said to Richard. "Before now she would have *told* me not asked. I suppose I can't blame them. They don't want to be with us fuddy-duddies."

"I guess our little girl is all grown up and spreading her wings at last," replied Richard.

After the ship had docked Tony went down to the Buffet for a coffee, knowing Jess was always there first thing in the morning. He was very put out when she informed him she would be spending the day with her family at Sandy Bay.

"I miss you, Jess," he pleaded with her, praying she'd

change her mind. "I've hardly seen you since Antigua. I'd hoped we'd spend the day ashore together and maybe find a private resort and cove like we did there."

"Tony, it's too dangerous. We have to be more careful. People are getting suspicious. It's better this way."

"I don't care. I love you. They'll know soon enough."

Jess was firm. "No, Tony. I told my parents I'd go with them and they'd be very disappointed if I cancelled. I'm already committed."

"Please, Jess, please?" he begged her, desperation in his voice.

"I'm sorry. Goodbye, Tony."

She didn't look back as she walked away.

She was breaking his heart.

Angry with Jess now and at a loose end, he suggested to Ann when she came up for breakfast an hour later that they should have a family day together on Barbados.

"I'm sorry but Jack is going to some music thing with Sarah and Emily has plans to go with Tarquin. As for me, I've booked and paid for a full-day tour of the island for myself."

"With your friend Nina, I suppose," he remarked snidely.

"No, actually. She's staying with Paul today. I'm going alone."

He couldn't believe his ears. Ann always needed someone to hold her hand. "What about me?" he asked plaintively.

"It's all booked out, I'm afraid. I was lucky to get on it. Somebody cried off and I took their place."

He looked at her in astonishment.

She knew he expected her to cancel but she stuck to her guns.

"I'm really looking forward to it," she declared, smiling.

"But what will I do?" he asked petulantly. "Can't you cancel?"

"You told me you wanted to chill today. I'm sorry but I'm already committed."

He blew up at this. Two women in the space of an hour telling him they were already committed. Didn't he matter to them at all?

Ann ignored his tantrum and calmly walked off.

He was speechless. She'd never done that before. Usually it ended up with her crying but there were no tears today. What was happening? Was he losing his grip? Feeling very sorry for himself he went to the bar and ordered a whiskey. It was only 9 a.m. He had a feeling that it would not be a good day.

Ann strode gleefully along towards the tour bus. Tony's face when she'd walked out had been priceless. She felt a sense of power that she had never felt before. 'Timid Ann' was gone forever and it was all thanks to Nina.

She'd come to know her new friend very well on their day trips and it was on one of these that Nina had opened up about her first marriage.

"When I saw the way Tony was treating you, it brought back the horrors of my first marriage," she confided. "He was a bully just like Tony and he undermined my confidence to such an extent that I couldn't even leave the house. I wanted to kill myself." She looked into the distance and Ann saw the sadness in her eyes. "I tried it once and that was when my only friend suggested I try therapy. It took me three years to find the courage to leave. He almost killed me the night I told him I was leaving but I survived, determined not to let anyone bully me ever again."

She looked at Ann. "You have to stop letting Tony get away with this. You have to reclaim yourself."

Ann had done a lot of thinking after that.

Now, as she drove around Barbados, she felt strong and confident. Nina was right. She had let Tony get away with undermining her all these years. Well, those days were over. She'd found a new sense of self-worth. It was funny. He'd always claimed he wanted her to be more assertive and, now that she was, he wasn't liking it.

She enjoyed the trip but found Barbados to be the least attractive island they'd visited. They started the tour in Bridgetown which Ann found very touristy and the hustlers on every corner bothered her. The fact that *Harmony of the Seas* was in port too didn't help. The streets were crowded and she couldn't wait to get away from there. The island was pretty enough but it seemed to have been taken over by the English. She was happy when they arrived back at the ship.

She headed straight to the Buffet for afternoon tea where she had arranged to meet Nina.

"I half-expected to see Tony here. When I told him this morning that I was going on the tour alone he was shocked. He was obviously at a loose end and wanted me to cancel and spend the day with him. When I said I couldn't he threw a tantrum."

"But you stuck to your guns and went anyway. Good girl!" Nina said gleefully.

"Now that I've become more assertive – thanks to you – he doesn't like it," Ann said. "Although that's what he's always been pushing me to do." She shook her head in bewilderment.

"Damned if you do and damned if you don't," Nina declared.

"I've been thinking a lot about things you've said and I've accepted that my marriage is in trouble."

"Is it worth fighting for?"

"It used to be. I'm not sure it is any more," Ann confessed. "Sometimes I long to be free. Living alone somewhere in a little cottage by the sea."

"Alone isn't all it's cracked up to be," Nina said with feeling.

"I suppose. The grass is always greener, isn't it?" Ann gave a little laugh. "I had hoped this cruise would bring us together but it's actually had the opposite effect. He doesn't want to go anywhere with me. I don't even know what he does with his days." Her eyes were troubled.

"Could it be something to do with that young girl, Jess, do you think?" asked Nina.

Ann looked surprised. "Why do you say that?"

"He pays her a lot of attention and I noticed she flirts back with him."

"Tony has an obsession with staying young. He's probably flattered that a young one pays him any attention."

"I don't know," Nina said thoughtfully, "I'd keep an eye on them if I were you."

Ann thought about what she'd said afterwards. Nina was very wise. Maybe there was some truth in what she said.

What Tony had done that day was foolhardy. He'd been furious with both Ann and Jess and, after knocking back two whiskies in quick succession when Ann had left for her tour, he decided that if Jess wouldn't come to him he'd go to her. He disembarked and took a taxi to the Sandy Lane

Hotel. It was a hotel after all so he had a perfect right to be there.

Bunny and Richard were at the pool when they saw Tony standing at the hotel door, scrutinising the place.

"What's he doing here?" Bunny whispered to Richard.

"No idea. Looks like he's looking for someone."

He spotted them and made his way over.

"Lovely place here," he greeted them.

"Yes, we love it," Bunny replied coolly. "Where's Ann?"

"Oh, she's off on a tour. You know her." He laughed but it sounded false to Bunny's ears. "Where are the others?"

"Who do you mean?" Richard asked.

"Oh Gavin, Fiona and eh . . . Jess."

Bunny caught on straight away. Even Richard, who wasn't always switched on to nuances, realised it was Jess he was looking for.

"They're on the beach."

"I'll just go and say hello then," he said, leaving in a hurry.

"I wonder if that's who she's been trying to avoid," Bunny murmured, nodding. "I can't imagine what he's doing here."

"He's obviously fascinated with Jess but I can't imagine she'd get involved with him."

"Of course not," Richard assured her. "Jess has more sense than that and so has he, I'm sure."

"I hope you're right. If not, what can we do about it?" Bunny fretted.

"Not a damn thing. But don't worry. I'm sure it's not that."

Tony found Jess having a drink at the beach bar. She was with a very handsome tanned young man. They were laughing together and Tony felt his stomach lurch with jealousy.

Then Jess spotted him. Her face froze.

"Hi, Jess," he said, going up to her. "Aren't you going to introduce me to your new friend?"

"Will you excuse me for a moment, Mark?" she said to the young man who looked amused.

Jess pulled Tony aside and he could see that she was very angry.

"How dare you follow me here?" she demanded through clenched teeth.

"This *is* a hotel," he replied. "And who is that guy you're laughing with?"

"That is actually none of your business but he happens to be the son of one of the owners and I've known him since I was a child. We grew up together." Jess was beyond furious.

Tony suddenly felt ridiculous. He knew it was stupid to have come here. "I'm sorry, Jess. I just couldn't bear to be away from you."

"Well, you better get used to it. Now go away!" she cried angrily. "I'm going back to my friend. What must he be thinking? I'll never forgive you for this, Tony."

With his head down he left her and walked off along the beach. He was too embarrassed to go back by the pool and have to explain things to Bunny and Richard.

Jess left the beach shortly afterwards with Mark. She was very upset with Tony. How could he have embarrassed her like that?

As she passed the pool her mother called her over.

"What did Tony want with you?" Bunny asked suspiciously.

Jess could see that even her father was curious.

"Nothing. He happened to be passing and remembered me saying we'd be here," she replied, as nonchalantly as she could.

"Oh yeah?" said Bunny, with arched eyebrows. It was obvious she didn't believe that for a minute.

Jess wanted to cry with fury. What a stupid stunt for Tony to pull. There would be hell to pay now. Her mother wouldn't let this go.

"I've had enough sun. Mark is going to show me round," said Jess, before hurrying off.

"Dear oh dear!" Bunny exclaimed as she lay back on her sun-lounger. "Children! Who'd have them?"

# Chapter 21

Tarquin and Emily had taken a taxi to a beach outside Bridgetown. It was nice to be alone for the day. They swam and lay in the sun and Tarquin thought how perfect it all was.

After lunch they were sitting relaxing and talking when suddenly the young couple who'd been sitting close to them and who were now in swimming, started yelling and gesticulating from the sea. Tarquin looked to where they'd been sitting and saw a long-haired guy with dreadlocks making off with their belongings. Tarquin gave chase along with the man, who had dashed from the water, but the thief had a bike and made his getaway through a housing project across from the beach. They had no hope of catching him. It turned out the couple were American passengers on the *Liberté* and the thief had got away with their bags which contained cash, credit cards and their ship's pass.

"Dear God, what can we do?" cried the man. "We've lost everything."

Tarquin and Emily offered them money and the four of them took a taxi together back to Bridgetown where they reported the theft to the police.

"Y'all know how many times a day this happens on this island?" the policeman asked. "At least fifty. Sorry for your trouble but we ain't gonna get it back."

Tarquin and Emily invited the dejected couple for a drink and then they all went back on board, disillusioned and vowing never to visit Barbados again.

Tony wasn't the only one who was having a bad day.

Meanwhile Sarah and Jack were having another great day together. The music festival was great but it could have been awful and they'd still have enjoyed it. They loved the Caribbean vibe and Jack said he would definitely get into reggae when he got back home. Sarah was thinking how much more fun this was than being at Sandy Lane. They danced to the steel bands and after lunch Sarah took out her stash of cocaine.

"What are you doing, Sarah?" Jack looked at her in horror.

"Just a little line," she replied, as she made two lines on the mirror she carried everywhere. "You first." She offered him a rolled-up note.

When he didn't reply she looked up.

His eyes were like ice.

"Are you serious? You're not stupid enough to do this stuff?"

"It's only a little coke – "

"Only coke? Have you any idea what this does to people's lives?" He grasped her wrist so hard it hurt. "I had two friends who died from this stuff. I don't want a third."

"I'm sorry, I didn't think it was any harm. Everyone does it."

"It is a killer," Jack said vehemently. "Don't you know it's addictive and leads to other harder drugs? How long have you been taking it?"

Sarah had tears in her eyes. "Just this week since the cruise began. It was Carlo one of the Italians who gave it to me first."

"That bastard! This is worse than the thieving he did."

Sarah started to cry and he felt sorry for being so harsh with her. He put his hand out for the package. "Please promise me, Sarah, that you will never touch this stuff again."

Terrified of losing him, she readily promised. "I'm sorry, Jack, I didn't think it was any harm." She couldn't stop the tears falling.

"Now you know," he said gently as he hugged her. He hated to see her cry.

They left to go straight back to the ship and Sarah clung on to him tightly as they walked in. She never wanted him to look coldly at her again. Not ever.

Jack and Sarah met in the Montmartre bar for a cocktail before dinner.

"I have something important I want to talk to you about," said Jack, holding her hand. "I don't know how to start . . . or how you'll take it . . . but my father and Jess are having an affair."

Sarah looked at him open-mouthed. "Are you serious? What makes you say that?"

"I saw them kissing getting out of a taxi in Antigua. Then last night I tackled Dad. He says they're in love." Jack's face was grim.

"Oh my God! I can't believe it!" Sarah cried, shocked at what he was saying. "What about your mother?"

"She doesn't know yet. He says they've grown apart. He's going to divorce her."

"Oh my God!" Sarah put her face in her hands. "I wondered about Jess lately. She's been so secretive. I don't know where she spends her days."

"With my father presumably," Jack said bitterly. "He says she makes him feel young."

"Oh dear! Mummy will have a fit. She'll kill Jess if she finds out."

"Not as big a fit as my mother will have. I don't know what to do. I feel I should tell her but I don't want to ruin this cruise for her." He was biting at a nail.

"It's not really up to you, is it?" Sarah took his hand in hers. "Surely it's your father's responsibility."

"He wants to wait till we get back to Florida. It will ruin that part of the holiday for sure."

"Can I do anything?" Sarah asked.

"You're close to Jess, aren't you?"

"Not really. Though things have improved since we came on this cruise."

"Maybe you could talk to her and find out if she is serious about Dad?"

"I could try but, knowing Jess, it might not do any good. She's very strong-willed."

"Do your best," said Jack. "Now, let's forget about them and enjoy our second date together."

The next day was New Year's Eve and that night would be a formal night with a cocktail party and gourmet dinner, with a fireworks display and party at midnight to celebrate the New Year. It was a sea-day again and there was the usual round of activities to be enjoyed. Jack and Sarah were inseparable, much to the disappointment of Hank and Todd. However, they took it good-humouredly and joined them at the pool for the games and dancing, along with Tarquin and Emily.

"Where's Jess?" Hank asked Sarah.

"Good question," she replied, wondering where the hell her sister was.

She badly wanted to ask her about Tony. She had scoured the ship looking for her but there was no sign of her anywhere. She even tried her cabin, afraid she might find her there with Tony, but there was no reply to her knock.

Gavin joined them at the pool while Fiona was at Pilates but he could throw no light on the subject either. It was beginning to bug Sarah.

Her parents had asked them all to meet up for lunch in the main restaurant and were surprised when Sarah asked if she could bring Jack.

"That little girl seems to have matured a lot on this cruise," Richard commented to Bunny as they got ready to go to lunch.

"About time!" Bunny remarked but in fact she was smiling. "Actually, I agree with you. She's drinking much less lately, thank goodness."

"I wonder if it's Jack's influence? I wasn't aware they were particularly close, were you?"

"No. But you can't keep up with kids these days," Bunny sighed.

"Where's Jess?" Sarah asked when she arrived at the table. Everyone else was there except her sister.

"I have no idea," Bunny replied irritably. "She's been acting very weirdly lately. I don't know what's got – " She broke off, seeing the look exchanged between Jack and Sarah. "Do you know something I don't, Sarah?" she asked archly.

"No . . . no . . . I just wondered," Sarah mumbled.

But Bunny wasn't fooled. Something was going on, she was sure of it. She'd have to get to the bottom of it.

Just then Jess came in, looking flustered. She was wearing dark glasses and a large hat with her hair hidden under it. She looked like she was trying to go incognito.

"Sorry I'm late," she apologised, taking her seat.

"Take off that ridiculous hat and glasses, Jess," Bunny said sharply. "Where have you been? We were just saying that we never see you around the ship."

"I was tired so I slept in," Jess answered, blushing.

"I knocked on your cabin door but you didn't answer," Sarah said, taken aback.

"Why were you looking for me?" Jess asked.

Bunny ears pricked up.

"Oh, no reason." Sarah replied, looking uncomfortable.

Bunny did not believe that for a moment. Something was definitely up with Jess.

"Thanks, Sis," Jess muttered as she took up her menu.

She was surprised to see Jack at the table and it was obvious that he and Sarah had something going on. She caught Jack looking at her strangely and wondered if he guessed about her relationship with his father. She sincerely hoped not.

They were leaving the restaurant after lunch when Sarah caught up with Jess.

"Jess, I want to talk to you. In private."

"What about?" Jess asked, on the defensive.

"I think you know."

Jess sighed. The cat was obviously out of the bag. Now there would be hell to pay. They went to her cabin where she took wine out of the mini-bar and poured them one each.

"I guess I'm going to need this," she said grimacing.

"I know about you and Tony," Sarah told her.

"How? Fiona promised she wouldn't say anything."

"It wasn't her. How does *she* know?"

"I told her," Jess sighed, taking a big slug of her wine.

"It was Jack. He saw you kissing in Antigua and tackled his father about it. Tony admitted you were in love. Please tell me that's not true?" She stared at her sister.

Jess buried her face in her hands. "Oh God! This gets worse. No, of course I'm not in love with him! I had sex with him once but I thought it was just a bit of fun – you know – a holiday fling – Friends with Benefits."

"You had sex with Tony?" Sarah exclaimed, a horrified look on her face.

"Yes. Unfortunately, now he says he's in love with me. I didn't mean for that to happen or to hurt anyone. I don't know what to do." She looked at her sister with eyes pleading for understanding.

"Oh my God! You're serious? I still can't believe you had sex with him!"

"I'm afraid so. Does Mummy know?"

"No, but I'm sure she suspects something. She says you've become very secretive."

"Of course I have. Can you imagine her reaction if she finds out? You won't tell her?" Jess asked nervously.

"No, I won't. But what about Ann? Jack is worried about her. What happens if *she* finds out?"

"Jack wouldn't say anything to her, would he?"

"He won't. Not till the cruise is over anyway. He doesn't want to ruin it for his mother."

"God, I feel such a bitch," Jess admitted. "I know how I felt when Philip cheated on me. I wouldn't wish that on anyone. Tony says they've grown apart and he wants to divorce her."

Sara was genuinely worried. "Golly, Jess, you've got yourself in a right pickle this time."

"I know. But it was exciting. I didn't think for a minute that he'd fall in love with me."

"You can't play with people's lives just for a bit of excitement."

"I know that now," Jess said shakily. "My self-confidence was at zero after Philip and I was flattered by Tony's attention. I mean he *is* good-looking and I *am* fond of him. Not to mention the sex which was amazing."

"T.M.I!" Sarah squealed. This was way too much information. She didn't want to hear what her boyfriend's father was getting up to with her sister. "Don't you think you should let him know that you're not in love with him?"

"I have tried to tell him but he doesn't want to know. I'll have to do it more firmly – but gently. He'll be awfully upset."

"I can imagine. Meanwhile I think you should be more visible on board so as to quell Mummy's suspicions. She knows there's something up."

"Yes, I'll do that. Thanks, Sis." Jess gave her a hug.

They finished the wine and Jess promised to join her at the pool once she'd told Tony about their talk.

As she suspected, she found Tony on their veranda.

"Where have you been? I've been frantic  I looked everywhere for you. I've been so worried, my darling "

"Tony, I have to talk to you," Jess said, visibly upset. "Seriously. Sarah told me that Jack saw us kissing and I know he spoke to you about it. Why didn't you tell me?"

He was annoyed to hear Jack had relayed their conversation to Sarah. "I didn't want to upset you," he confessed.

"Tony, you should have told me. This is terrible. Now my family know. I have to think of them and Ann too."

He felt bad. He could see she was upset. "I'm sorry, my darling," he apologised.

She stayed standing over him.

"Aren't you going to lie down?" he asked.

"No. We need to cool it for a bit. I think it's best if I join the others at the pool. Now Jack and Sarah know about us we can't afford for anyone else to find out – especially not Ann or Bunny. We have to be more careful or there will be hell to pay."

"Maybe I should tell Ann today," he suggested. "Do you want me to do that?"

"Good God, no! That's the last thing I want. Don't even consider it. Promise me you won't say a word," Jess pleaded. She was afraid of the outcome if he did.

Reluctantly he agreed. "Okay, I promise."

Meanwhile Sarah met up with Jack and told him what Jess had said. "I think your father's got the wrong end of the stick. Jess is fond of him and enjoys his attention but for her it's only a flirtation."

"Why am I not surprised? It was the sex, I suppose?" he asked, his voice bitter.

"I'm afraid so. 'Friends with Benefits' is what she called it."

"My father is a fool. A bloody old fool," Jack said disgustedly.

Gavin and Fiona went to the Trivia Quiz with Bunny and Richard. Ann and Tony joined them as usual. Jess opted to go to the *Strictly* class so as to avoid Tony. She knew she'd have to level with him at some stage but she wasn't ready for a showdown just yet. He was very disappointed when she didn't show up.

The *Strictly* class today was the rumba.

"This dance is the most sensual dance of all," the choreographer explained. "It tells a story of love and passion between a strong male lover and a coy teasing woman."

"*Oooooooh!*" said the crowd.

"Now take you partners, please."

"This is our dance," Jack murmured, leading her on to the floor.

The steps were difficult and many people couldn't manage them so dropped out before the lesson was over. Neither Jack nor Sarah were eligible to win the day's competition as they'd both won before and would already dance in the final. However, when the finalists were chosen the choreographer asked them if they wouldn't mind dancing it again together, even though they could not win. The three finalists danced with three of the professionals but it was Jack and Sarah who were by far the best. Their dance was sensual and the chemistry between them palpable.

"This is the sexiest dance I've ever seen," one passenger remarked aloud.

"That's exactly what the rumba is all about," the choreographer declared.

The Gala Show would be in two days' time. There would be a dress rehearsal for the finalists beforehand and they would then compete for the trophy in the theatre that night.

The choreographer then approached Sarah and Jack and asked if they would consider dancing the rumba together at the Gala Show also. As an exhibition dance.

"Oh, I don't know – " Sarah began.

"It would be great for us as it means the Cruise Director would consider keeping on these lessons when he sees what we've achieved with you two," the dancer said.

"We'll do it," Jack agreed, squeezing Sarah's waist. "Don't worry, love. You'll be with me."

"Okay." She would have followed him to the ends of the earth if he'd asked her.

The dancers were thrilled and they all went for a drink together.

The success of the Irish didn't stop on the dance-floor. The *IrishEast/West* team were now joint-leaders of the Trivia Quiz and they all retired to La Montmartre bar for a drink. Sarah and Jack went there with Jess after the dancing and they all could see how excited they were that they'd been asked to dance the rumba at the Gala Show.

"Wait till you see them dancing together. They're sensational!" Jess exclaimed exuberantly. "You would think they were professionals."

Bunny was pleased to see Sarah happy but there was still Jess. She saw how she avoided Tony while he looked at her with puppy-dog eyes. The poor fool was obviously infatuated with her. Bunny sighed. That was all she needed now. A scandal.

"Jess, could you come to the suite, please?" Bunny said to her as they were leaving. "I'd like to talk to you in private."

"Now?"

"Yes, *now*," Bunny said in a steely voice.

Sarah and Fiona both looked at Jess nervously as she meekly followed her mother. No doubt about it, Bunny had found out about Tony and Jess was in for the third degree.

"Do you have something to tell me?" Bunny asked as soon as they entered the suite where her father was reading.

He looked up from his book, wondering what this was all about.

Jess figured her mother would know soon enough so she might as well come clean.

"I'm afraid I have a confession to make," she said quietly. "I . . . eh . . . did something very foolish."

She kept her head down and eyes fixed on the floor. She didn't want to see the disgust in her parents' eyes when they heard what she had to say.

"I had a bit of a fling with Tony Kenny and now it turns out he thinks he's in love with me. I thought you should know."

They were both so shocked that they said nothing for a moment.

Bunny clutched at her throat.

"*I knew it!*" she shrieked. "I knew that guy was up to no good! So that's who you've been with all this time."

Jess looked up and quaked at the anger in her mother's eyes.

"Jess, how could you have had anything to do with that man?" her father asked.

"Honestly, Jess!" Bunny exclaimed. "What were you thinking? Of all people – Tony Kenny!"

"I know, I know, you're right. It was incredibly stupid. I was an idiot. It just happened."

"Does Ann know?" Bunny asked.

"Not yet. He wants to tell her but that's the last thing I want."

"Foolish man," Richard remarked. "If it was just a fling maybe they'll get over it."

"Unfortunately, Tony says he wants to divorce her and marry me."

"You're not serious?" Bunny couldn't believe her ears. "Please don't tell me you're in love with him?"

"Of course not. It was just a bit of fun to me."

"Poor Ann. I bet she won't see it like that." Bunny shook her head in disbelief.

"You've got to get this sorted out, Jess," her father advised. "Try and persuade him to see sense."

"I just can't believe you'd do such a stupid thing. Tony! Of all people!" Bunny reiterated incredulously. "Maybe I should talk to him," she suggested.

"No, Mummy, please. I'll sort it," Jess cried, wringing her hands.

"Well, do it quick!" Bunny ordered. "Or I'll step in. Now go and get ready for the New Year's Eve Gala. We're late already."

Jess shuffled out of the suite, feeling mortified. The hurt look in her father's eyes was more than she could bear. He'd always been so proud of her.

Now that Sarah was getting her act together, Jess was going off the rails, Bunny thought to herself.

But she had a plan.

CSO Allen received the result of Alix's autopsy late that

afternoon and he called on Cassie to tell her. She invited him into the suite, apprehensive of what he might say.

"The Captain apologises that he can't come to give you the news himself but he's otherwise occupied at the moment," he told her.

"Please, take a seat." She motioned him to the chair and sat down opposite him, bracing herself for whatever he had to tell her.

"We've received the autopsy result on Miss Lynch and it appears there was no water found in her lungs, so it looks like your husband may have been telling the truth. She was actually deceased when she entered the water. She died from the wound to her head."

Cassie put her hands to her face. "So he threw her overboard when she was dead?"

"It appears so."

"What happens now?"

"It looks like your husband will be charged with manslaughter but not murder."

"So he'll have to go to prison?" She looked searchingly at him.

"That depends on how good a lawyer he gets to defend him. They only have his word on what actually happened that night. A jury will decide on whether to believe him or not." He saw how Cassie's face paled. "I'm so sorry, Mrs Jordan," he said gently.

She tried to pull herself together. "Can I get you something? A coffee or a drink?"

"No, thank you," he replied, standing up. "I'd better get back to work. The Captain sends his regards."

"Thank you for coming personally to give me this news," she said as she showed him out.

She went out on the veranda, hugging her arms around herself for comfort. She wondered what would happen to Declan and what had really happened that night.

# Chapter 22

Another Formal Night and the photographers were again out in force as before. There was a cocktail party before dinner where they all met up.

Sarah and Fiona both approached Jess as soon as she arrived and she told them that her parents knew about Tony.

"How did they take it?" Sarah asked, glad that it was not her in her sister's shoes.

"Okay, considering," Jess replied, making a face. "Mummy wants to sort him out but I told her I would take care of it."

"Good luck with that," Sarah said. "Rather you than me."

"As long as it's over, Jess," Fiona chimed in. "And just pray that Ann doesn't find out."

Fiona was glad that it was out in the open now. She hated keeping things from Gavin but she'd promised Jess. Now she rejoined him and told him about the affair.

"Jess? And Tony? You can't be serious?" He was as shocked as his parents had been.

"The affairs of the heart are very complicated," she mused. "I guess Jess just needed to feel attractive and desirable and Tony made her feel like that."

"When did you get to be so wise?" he asked, pulling her close and kissing the top of her head.

Jess looked dazzling, despite her problems. She was wearing a long sea-green silk gown that was the exact colour of her eyes. It was cut dangerously low in the back which showed off her golden tan. Bunny determined to keep an eagle eye on her as she saw the Staff Captain and young officers flock around her. But no sign of Tony. Just as well.

Cassie had been invited to dine at the Captain's table that evening. She was reluctant to go.

"I'll feel sad tonight, remembering all the New Year's Eves I spent with Declan and wondering where he is at midnight," she said to Fiona.

"All the more reason to go to the Captain's table," Fiona pointed out. "It will keep your mind off that."

"I suppose," Cassie said, not very enthusiastically.

"We'll meet up with you for the midnight celebrations," Fiona promised.

"You're a wonderful friend. I don't know how I would have coped with all this if you hadn't been there." There were tears in Cassie's eyes as she spoke.

They all left to go to dinner and passed the photographers on their way to the restaurant. They stopped to have their photos taken, this time against a backdrop of the ship, and none of them could help but think of the last time they'd stood there for the photographers. It was Christmas night when Alix had posed with Declan. Six hours later she was dead and he was now awaiting trial in connection with it. How lives had changed that night!

The Captain posed with each of the couples and then with Jess alone.

"What a handsome couple they make!" Bunny whispered to Richard as Jess and the Captain smiled for the camera. "Oh, if only . . ." She smiled, envisaging years of free cruises in the future.

"Don't bet on it, my dear," Richard said sagely, knowing his wife's flights of fancy. "I gather the Captain is carrying a torch for Cassie."

The Staff Captain asked Jess if she'd mind having a photo taken with him. She smilingly agreed and Bunny thought what a stunningly beautiful couple they made. After all, he'd be a Captain someday too.

By now other passengers had gathered around and the Captain patiently posed with all of them, laughing and joking as he did so.

Tony was beyond himself with anxiety and regret. He was seated facing the McElroys' table with a clear view of Jess. She looked sensational. Beside himself with jealousy, he watched her laughing with the handsome man seated next to her. Why was she doing this to him? He'd made a fool of himself in Sandy Bay and he desperately needed to talk to her but couldn't get near her. Bunny's chilly reception at the Sandy Bay pool was still fresh in his mind.

It didn't even bother him that they'd been seated at the same table as Nina, so obsessed was he with Jess. He couldn't take his eyes off her.

Nina raised her eyebrows at Ann who was beginning to think that there was definitely something in Nina's suspicions. She didn't know what had happened in Barbados yesterday but Tony had been in a vile humour since and she'd bet any money it had something to do with Jess. When she'd asked him where he'd gone there, he'd told her to mind her own business.

She decided to just ignore him and settled down to enjoy the food and Nina's company. He'd notched up quite a few whiskies before dinner and now he was steadily knocking back glass after glass of wine while barely eating anything.

"I notice she hasn't glanced his way even once," Nina murmured.

"I noticed that too," Ann replied. "He's making a fool of himself. I doubt she'd be interested in him."

"Men can be so stupid," her friend agreed.

Towards the end of this stupendous meal the lights were dimmed and music starting playing. Then all the waiters paraded around the dining-room holding blazing Baked Alaskas alight. Ann and the young ones were jubilant, clapping their hands as the beaming waiters passed their tables one by one. Nina and Bunny, who'd seen this ritual on every cruise they'd ever been on, smiled at the amazement on the faces of the newbies – as first-time cruisers were known.

Even before the Baked Alaskas were served, Tony announced that he was off to bed. He was very drunk so Ann offered to go with him. He rudely brushed her hand away and told her he didn't need her.

Nina took Paul to bed also. He was still not one hundred per cent recovered from his cold. She promised to join Ann on deck once she had him settled.

Jack and Emily came over to Ann's table when dinner

was over. Jack had been aware of Tony's behaviour throughout the meal.

"You look happy, Mum," Emily said.

"Why wouldn't I be? Celebrating New Year's Eve in this beautiful setting."

"Why is Dad behaving like a moron?" Jack asked angrily. "Does it not upset you?"

"Not in the least," Ann replied, much to everyone's surprise.

"Gosh, Mum, this cruise has done wonders for you," Jack commented. "You've come into your own at last."

"I have, haven't I?" Ann beamed at them. "It's all thanks to my wonderful new friend Nina."

"Does she not drive you mad talking?" Jack asked.

"No, not at all. We get on great together. I enjoy listening to her. She's had a very sad life. I'll tell you all about it sometime. She's also very lonely. We've been good for each other."

"Dad still doesn't like her, does he?" Emily asked.

"Who cares?" Ann replied, shocking them once more. "C'mon, let's go and watch the fireworks. Your father's gone to bed."

"Is he not staying to ring in the New Year with you?" Emily asked.

"No," Ann replied, her lips pressed firmly together. "He was very drunk."

They went on deck where a calypso band was playing in the balmy evening. The atmosphere was magical and everyone was in great form.

Nina arrived back and then the five McElroys joined them.

Jess was relieved and started to relax when there was no

sign of Tony. God knows what kind of a scene he'd cause.

Sarah, Jack, Hank and Todd and their girlfriends all danced together to the music and eventually all the others joined in. Cassie arrived with the Captain and Fiona was delighted to see she was a little tipsy and seemed to be enjoying herself.

Party favours were handed out and they all donned hats and blew poppers and, as it got close to midnight, there were streamers around everyone's neck as they gaily sipped the champagne the waiters were handing out. Finally they were counting down the old year and welcoming the new with cheers and laughter. Everyone kissed and 'Auld Lang Syne' rang out across the Caribbean Sea.

Fiona was standing beside a woman she didn't know when the fireworks started. As the first flashes lit up the sky she saw the woman clamp her hands over her ears, a terrified look on her face.

"Are you okay?" Fiona asked her, concerned.

The woman looked at her wildly and suddenly bolted from the party, her hands still over her ears.

"Gavin, quick," Fiona cried, grabbing his hand.

Bewildered, he ran with her, dropping his glass as he went. The woman had been running towards the back of the ship and they followed. They arrived there to find her climbing up on the rail, seemingly trying to get into a lifeboat. Dashing across the deck at speed, Fiona cried out, *"No, stop, please!"*

The woman turned just as Gavin lunged and caught her. She fell to the deck with him, wailing with a sound that Fiona knew she would never forget.

*"They're coming to get me! They're going to kill me!"*

Fiona held her in her arms, trying to soothe her. "You're

okay, you're safe, you're okay. It's only the fireworks."

The woman looked at her with wild eyes. "Did you hear the guns? They're trying to kill me." She clamped her hands over her ears again, looking around wildly as more fireworks burst in the sky.

"Nobody's trying to kill you. It's only the fireworks, honestly!" Fiona said, still holding the shaking figure.

At that moment some people erupted onto the deck, the woman's husband and the Captain among them. Someone who had seen Gavin and Fiona run had alerted them, sensing something was wrong.

The man took his wife in his arms. "You're okay, honey. It's me. I'm here. You're safe."

She looked at him wildly. "They're trying to kill me!" she cried.

"No, no, they're not. You're safe now." He cradled her until she quieted.

"I think we should take her to the infirmary," the Captain suggested, already on his radio.

Within minutes the medics arrived and escorted them there, the woman still holding her ears.

"Good God! What was that all about?" Gavin asked, dusting himself down.

"I've no idea," Fiona replied, still shaken.

Word had spread like wildfire back at the party that someone had tried to jump but that Gavin and Fiona had saved her. They arrived back to applause.

But Fiona could only feel sad for the poor demented woman

There was an air of gaiety about the rest of the night – early morning actually – that comes when a tragedy has been averted. The adrenalin was running high as they partied into the wee small hours.

The husband of the poor woman returned and approached Gavin and Fiona.

"I can't thank you enough for saving my wife's life. Thank goodness you were here."

"How is she? Is she okay?" Fiona asked.

"Yes, she's sleeping now, in the infirmary. They gave her a sedative."

"What happened?" Gavin asked.

"She's on heavy medication for depression and she's been having delusions. The fireworks must have set her off."

"I'm so sorry," said Fiona. "I do hope she'll be okay."

"Thank you. We're flying home from St Maarten tomorrow. She really needs hospitalisation. Thank you both, yet again, for your quick thinking."

"I'm just happy we were able to help," Gavin said as Fiona nodded her agreement.

The man clasped their hands warmly as he bade them goodbye.


"Do you mind if I sleep with you tonight, Emily?" Ann asked her daughter. "I just can't face your father after his behaviour."

"Of course, Mum," Emily replied. "Just let me know when you're ready to go."

A short time later Emily came to her, blushing like mad. "Actually, Mum, Tarquin has asked me if I'd like to . . . er . . . spend the night in his place. Just to sleep, you understand. Nothing more. Is that okay?"

"Of course, dear."

Emily hugged her, still blushing.

"And Emily . . . If you decide to do more than sleep . . . please be careful."

Emily blushed a deeper shade of red but when she saw Ann was smiling she hugged her again and handed her the cabin key.

"Thanks, Mum. I'll remember," she said, scurrying off to give Tarquin the good news.

My little girl is becoming a woman, Ann thought to herself as she headed to Emily's bed.

There were a lot of sore heads the following morning but nobody complained. All the talk was of the events of the previous night.

CSO Allen contacted the Florida Police for news of Declan.

"No news 'cept that he wants to meet with his wife when you get back to Fort Lauderdale."

"I'll tell her but I don't think that's going to happen," CSO Allen informed him.

"How's she holdin' up?"

"Okay. Keeps herself to herself."

"I hear she's a nice lady. Any more excitement down your way?"

"Well, we did have a lady try to jump overboard last night but another passenger saved her. Delusional, poor thing. Thought the fireworks were people coming to kill her."

The police sergeant chuckled. "Quite an excitin' cruise you're havin'."

"I can do without this kind of excitement," was the reply.

"Better keep an eye on that lady or I'll be sendin' more

of my men down to you."

"I sure will," CSO Allen said firmly.

The ship docked in St Maarten that morning. It was an island that was half-French half-Dutch. Most people had left the ship early as they would be leaving St Maarten at four-thirty that afternoon to head for Nassau. Tony woke with a dreadful hangover. He was very annoyed when he saw Ann hadn't slept in the bed last night. However, he had bigger worries than that. He had to find Jess and talk to her. He called and got her message machine then scoured the whole ship looking for her. She was nowhere to be seen.

The last thing Jess wanted to do was see Tony so she had taken breakfast with her parents in the suite. Bunny was in great form and never mentioned her indiscretion with Tony. It seemed her mother had forgiven her as she invited her to join them on a trip to the French part of the island. Bunny had booked lunch in the world famous Bistrot Caraibes restaurant in Grand Case which was renowned for its lobster thermidor. She suggested that they visit the market in Marigot first and also the very exclusive shopping area there. Jess was more than happy to go along, pleased that her mother was no longer angry with her.

Fiona and Gavin decided to go to Orient Beach because they read it was the best place to snorkel. They were pleased when Cassie agreed to join them.

Nina had booked a driver so she and Ann could take a tour of the island. Paul was due to go too but didn't feel up to it. The youngsters wanted to go to Maho Beach where the planes came in to land just metres above your head on the beach. They'd all seen the *YouTube* video of it and wanted to experience it for themselves. The Americans joined them and they shared a taxi out together.

Jack and Sarah found Maho Beach just as exciting as they'd expected. It was literally only yards from the airport runway and it was nerve-racking seeing the planes flying in so low that you could almost touch their landing gear. Every time a plane was coming in they all cheered and waved. It was fun.

The frozen cocktails in the Sunset Grill right on the beach were delicious but Sarah and Jack only had one each. The last *Strictly* class was later and they wanted to practise their rumba after it. Jack had a great new idea that he wanted to add to it. He was excited about it and Sarah wondered what it could be.

Tony found himself almost all alone on the ship and felt that everyone had deserted him. He didn't blame Jess – he knew he had overstepped the mark in Barbados and she was upset that Jack knew about them – but he couldn't understand Ann's behaviour. It was unacceptable. She was his wife for God's sake!

He had no interest in going ashore. He would be looking out for Jess all the time. He wondered where she was. He needed to talk to her and longed to hold her in his arms once more.

Jess enjoyed the market and bought some lovely souvenirs. She was surprised when her mother still made no mention of Tony. She'd thought she'd be paying for that indiscretion for some time but seemingly not. Bunny seemed in very high spirits and Jess actually heard her humming to herself at one point. They went shopping in the very expensive

French quarter and Jess was even more surprised when her mother insisted on buying her a beautiful bikini that she was admiring. Something was up.

She soon found out. They arrived at the Bistrot Caraibes which was simply beautiful with its white décor and delicate furniture. They were waiting to be seated when Jess heard her name called. She turned around and had to grasp her mother's arm when she saw her husband Philip walk in. He was carrying a bouquet of yellow roses – her favourites.

"Philip!" she gasped. "What are you doing here?"

"I came to tell you that I can't live without you and that I love you and want you back. Please, Jess, forgive me? I'll never hurt you again."

She was shocked when he started to cry. She had never seen him cry before.

"Please, Jess. Just give me one more chance?"

She could see that he really meant what he said and she was touched.

"But how did you –" She broke off as she saw Bunny beaming from ear to ear. "Mummy, you didn't?"

"Of course I did. I know you so well and I know this is right for you. Now I've ordered a private table for you two so you can talk undisturbed. You can join us whenever you feel ready."

Philip took her hand and they followed the maître d' into an alcove draped with white voile. It was very romantic.

"I missed you so much, Jess," Philip said when they were seated. "You wouldn't believe how much."

"I missed you too." She realised it was true.

The sommelier arrived with a bottle of Dom Perignon

champagne, courtesy of Bunny, as they started talking in an effort to mend their marriage.

Jess found out that Bunny had called him and told him to get his ass over there. He didn't wait for a second invitation and flew out immediately, although he hadn't been sure she would even consider taking him back.

She smiled at this. She would never have thought Philip capable of such decisiveness. She reached out and took his hand. She had to tell him about Tony. It was difficult but she got through it.

"Look, I'm not one to judge you after what I did," he said. "Let's put it all behind us and start afresh. And I want you to know that I'm willing to try for a baby. If it's what you want, then it's what I want too."

Jess couldn't believe her ears. She felt tears threatening to fall. Suddenly she felt hope that they could make this work again. She knew he loved her. What more could she ask?

After the lobster, which was as good as it was reputed to be, they went to join her parents. Bunny clapped her hands in delight when she realised that her ruse had worked.

"You know you took a huge gamble asking Philip to come all this way here," Richard chided her later. He'd known nothing of what his wife was up to.

"Well, it paid off, didn't it? And you know my motto – always trust your instinct."

Philip told Jess that he would fly to Fort Lauderdale and wait for her there. It had all worked out exactly as Bunny had planned.

When it was time to go back to the ship, Richard went to get the car and Jess had to go to the bathroom.

"Bunny, how can I ever thank you?" said Philip.

"Just make my daughter happy and please . . . no more wandering."

"Believe me, I've learned my lesson there. Now, I have a big favour to ask you."

Philip leaned in close to her and said something in a low voice.

"Brilliant!" Bunny exclaimed, smiling happily.

Just then Jess came back and they left. They dropped Philip off at his hotel and he clung to Jess as they said goodbye.

"I love you," he mouthed to her as they drove off.

She stayed watching out the back window until he was out of sight.

# Chapter 23

By three o'clock people started drifting back on board and Tony stood at the rail watching for Jess. Finally, he spotted her walking along the pier with Bunny and Richard. He ran down to the Buffet, guessing that's where she'd head first for a coffee. And he was right.

He waited till she was sitting down, then he approached her and sat down opposite her.

"Jess, I have to talk with you. I beg you to meet with me. I want to explain." He took her hand in his.

"There's nothing to explain," she said sadly.

He looked absolutely wretched and she felt a little sorry for him.

"Please, just give me ten minutes. I'm begging you."

She relented. She supposed she owed him that. "Okay, I'll meet you on our veranda in thirty minutes."

"Thank you, thank you so much." He lifted her hand and kissed it.

Neither of them saw Ann watching from the coffee

station. She shook her head, a rueful smile on her lips. There was no mistaking the passion in Tony's gestures. So it was true then. Here was the proof. They had a thing going on. Jess was the reason her husband had been behaving like he had. She took her coffee to the other side of the Buffet as she pondered what she should do. The old 'Timid Ann' would have turned a blind eye. Not now.

When she saw Jess leave the Buffet she marched over to her husband. He was sitting with a dazed look on his face.

"You look happy," Ann greeted him.

"I am, I am," he replied, smiling.

And I'm just about to wipe that smile off your face, Ann thought, feeling more than justified.

"Do you want to tell me what that was all about?" she asked, sitting down opposite him.

"What?"

"You and Jess. I know you've been having an affair. So tell me about it," she ordered.

She had taken him by surprise. No point in denying it.

"What's there to say? We're in love."

She gasped. "You're in love? How can you be in love when you only know her a little over a week?"

"I know her enough. I feel like a new man. She makes me feel young again."

"Has she told you she loves you?"

"Well, no. But I know she does."

Ann laughed. "You poor deluded man! How long do you think this is going to last?" She looked at him with pity.

"Let's face it, Ann, our marriage is on the rocks."

"Well, it certainly is now. I want a divorce. I want to be free of you."

He looked at her in shock. He didn't recognise this

woman. His Ann would never have challenged him like this. He was the one who'd always called the shots.

"Well, I'll see you round," she said, getting up and walking away, head held high.

Nina would be proud of me, she thought.


He was waiting for Jess with apprehension. He would ask her outright if she loved him and if she would marry him. Her face looked serious when she arrived and she appeared withdrawn. He felt as if there was a barrier between them. She sat down on the sun-lounger but made no attempt to take off her top and shorts. He was aching for her to strip off so he could drink in her wonderful body and then maybe they'd go to her cabin and make love.

"Tony, we have to talk," she started.

"Yes, I know. Ann knows about us and she wants a divorce."

Jess let out a low moan. "Oh no!" she wailed. "What have you done?"

"Nothing. I promised I wouldn't tell her and I didn't. She figured it out for herself when she saw us together this morning."

"I don't believe it!" She moaned again, burying her face in her hands.

"What's the matter, my darling? It's good that she found out. Now we can come out in the open with our love. We can be married and we'll have a wonderful life together." He took her hands away from her face and was frightened by the look in her eyes. "Isn't that what you want?"

"Of course not!" she gasped. "Where did you get that idea? How could you imagine I love you? I don't. I never said I did."

He recoiled as if she'd slapped him. "What do you mean you don't love me? After we made fantastic love together that day in the water? You know we have a connection."

"It was sex, Tony, pure and simple sex. It was fun but that's all it was. It didn't mean anything."

"Sex?"

"Yes. We were both in need of it and it was great – I'll hand you that – but it was nothing more."

"Jess, you don't mean that! Please tell me you love me!"

"No, Tony, I don't. I'm truly sorry. I'd better go. I'll try and find Ann and explain to her."

With that she was gone.

He sat in a daze. He couldn't believe he'd heard right. Did she really say it was "just sex"? That it didn't mean anything? How had he got it so wrong? Then reality hit him. He had been willing to give up everything for this woman but all she had wanted was a romp in the hay or in the sea, as it turned out. Dear God, what a fool he'd made of himself. He'd even been willing to give her the baby she wanted so badly.

He sat there for over an hour, trying to make sense of it, and eventually had to accept that it was over. She wasn't his and never would be.

Suddenly he couldn't wait to get away from this place where he'd been so happy lying beside her all those days. His life was over. He understood for the first time in his life the term 'heartbreak'. His heart felt like it was breaking.

There was an envelope waiting for Fiona and Gavin in their stateroom when they got back. On opening it they were touched to find a thank-you card from the husband of the woman they'd saved. In it was a gift voucher for $500 for the cruise-line. He had left no address but Fiona checked at Guest Relations and they gave it to her so that she could write and thank him. They both agreed it was a very nice gesture, though unnecessary.

The last *Strictly* class was for the tango and it was fun and very dramatic. Sarah and Jack enjoyed it immensely and danced together. They were not eligible to win of course. The choreographer, Tim, came up to them after the finalist was chosen.

"You know, you two would have won every single dance this week. Luckily you're only eligible to dance one dance each or the other passengers would not be a happy bunch."

They laughed.

"And if you two ever want a job with us, just let us know."

"We're going to practise our rumba now," Jack said, "and there's a move I'd like to put in at the end if that's okay with you?"

"Sure, go ahead. What is it?"

"Well, you know the movie *Dirty Dancing?*"

"My favourite movie of all time!" Tim exclaimed.

"Uh-oh, I think I know what's coming," said Galina, who had joined them. "Does Sarah know what you have in mind?" she asked Jack, grinning.

"Not yet."

Sarah looked mystified. She'd never seen that movie.

"Okay," the choreographer said. "Galina and I have done that move often. We'll show you."

With that, they faced each other on the floor and Galina took a run at him and he lifted her high in the air above his head like a bird.

Sarah gulped. "You're not serious? You want me to do that? I can't. I'll probably fall and break my neck."

"Don't worry, I'll lift you, you won't fall, trust me," Jack said confidently.

The dancers gave them some tips and nervously Sarah agreed to try. It was clumsy at first but, true to his word, Jack lifted her and she didn't fall. They tried again and again and eventually it was almost perfect. Sarah grew in confidence with each try.

"Amazing!" Tim said. "You'll knock their socks off."

They were thrilled with this high praise and, elated, they joined Emily and Tarquin who had stayed on to watch.

"That was just fantastic!" Emily hugged them breathlessly.

"Yes, amazing," Tarquin agreed.

Sarah was bubbling with excitement. "I was really scared. I honestly didn't think I could nail it," she admitted.

"But you did – perfectly – like I knew you would." Jack was grinning as he pulled her close.

They headed off for a shower as Emily and Tarquin went for a smoothie.

"Sarah's fantastic, isn't she?" Emily remarked as they sat down. "I wish I was like her."

"I like you as you are," he replied gallantly.

She swatted him playfully. "Beside the fact that she looks fabulous and is a fantastic dancer, she has great spirit. She wouldn't let anybody push her around the way I do." She sighed.

"I agree you should stand up for yourself more, come out from under your parents' wings."

"I'm afraid I take after my mother," she said ruefully.

"Maybe Sarah could give you some tips."

"You think?"

"Why not talk to her?" he suggested.

"I will!" she said with determination. It really was time she became more forceful.

Bunny had invited the family to dinner in the suite. Cassie and Jack were also invited so they were eight.

Raphael opened the champagne which was on ice and there were lovely appetizers of smoked salmon and shrimp to go with it.

"I think you'll all be surprised by the good news Richard and I would like to share with you all," Bunny announced dramatically.

They all looked at her, wondering what was coming now.

Jess knew and blushed deeply.

"Today, Jess's husband, Philip, met her in St Maarten to ask her to give their marriage a second chance and happily she has agreed to try again!"

For a second you could have heard a pin drop and then suddenly they were all around her, kissing and congratulating her.

"Well, surprised is an understatement," Gavin exclaimed. "Astonishment describes it better. I'm really happy for you, Sis."

He hugged Jess again as Fiona smiled happily on.

"He flew all the way from London to ask you that?" Sarah asked, shocked.

"Yes," Jess replied shyly.

"He must love you very much," Cassie said, smiling at her.

"I believe he does so I'm willing to give him a second chance. We all make mistakes that we regret, especially when we end up hurting others." She looked directly at Jack as she said this. He gave a little smile.

Jess took him aside after the brouhaha had died down. "Jack, I'm truly sorry for what I did. And especially sorry that your mother got hurt. I didn't want that."

"Look, Jess, my father's a big boy. He knew what he was doing. And to tell you the truth, I think it's the best thing for my mother that they divorce."

Jess reached over and kissed him on the cheek. "Thank you, Jack. Now I don't feel quite so bad."

"You were right about Jess," Ann had told Nina when they met for dinner in the restaurant. "I saw them together in the Buffet and I just knew. I walked over and confronted him. You'd have been very proud of me," she smiled. "Definitely AA! Anyway, he admitted they've been having an affair and says they're in love and he wants to marry her." She threw her eyes to heaven.

Nina was shocked. "He actually admitted it?"

"Yes. That's when I said *I* wanted a divorce."

"You said what?" Nina cried. She couldn't believe her ears. "What did he say to that?" she asked, open-mouthed.

"I don't think he could quite believe it."

"I'll bet," Nina chuckled. "You did well, girl!"

They high-fived each other as Emily joined them with Tarquin.

Their last sea-day dawned bright and sunny and everyone was determined to make the very best of it. The weather was glorious so most people spent the day by the pool relaxing although there were the usual many activities organised.

Tony tackled Jess again at breakfast. "Please, Jess –"

"Tony, it's over. Accept it and leave me alone. I'm sorry if you thought it was more than it was but it wasn't. So please, let's stop it now."

He looked at her dejectedly. "Is there nothing I can do?"

"No. That's it." She got up and picked up her coffee cup. "I'm sorry if this has affected your marriage but really that's not my responsibility – it's yours."

With that she was gone and he knew it was over. Jack was right. He was an old fool.

Jess went looking for Ann and came face-to-face with her in the boutique which was having a promotion. She took her courage in her hands and approached the older woman.

"Ann, I just want to say that I'm sorry about what happened. I didn't ever mean to hurt you."

Ann looked at her coolly. "No, you were just playing with my husband. I get that."

Jess winced with embarrassment. "I –"

Ann cut her off. "Actually, I should be thanking you. You did me a favour. I've asked him for a divorce."

Jess wished the ground would open up and swallow her. "Yes, I know that. I'm so sorry."

Ann softened. Jess was young and had just come through her own marriage break-up. She'd recognised the sadness in her eyes the first night she'd met her. She had probably been flattered by her idiot husband's attention and taken comfort from it.

"I don't blame you, my dear. Tony is a big boy. He's the one who cheated on me. I guess if it wasn't you it would have been someone else."

Jess had not expected this. She felt worse than ever now.

Ann had a big heart. In fact, she was worth ten of her husband.

"Thank you," Jess whispered, tears in her eyes. "I hope you have a good life."

"You too, my dear," Ann said kindly before walking away.

Jess was still upset when she met with her parents and Gavin for lunch in the main restaurant. Sarah was having lunch with Jack and the dancers in the Buffet.

Bunny saw instantly that something was wrong. "What is it, Jess? You look like it's the end of the world. What's up?"

"I spoke to Ann today. She was very kind to me. I didn't expect that."

"That was very generous of her."

"Yes. I apologised to her. She told me I did her a favour. It was she who said she wanted a divorce."

"I'll have to talk to her. She's well rid of him, if you ask me."

Their food arrived but Jess had lost her appetite and only picked at it. She felt deeply ashamed of what she'd done. Ann had been so gracious.

She spent the afternoon at the Spa having treatments and tried to put the whole Tony fiasco behind her.

Ann located her husband in the Louvre Bar after lunch. He had obviously been drinking for quite a while.

"Tony, we need to talk about Orlando. I want to take the kids there as we'd planned but I think it's best if you make other arrangements."

He waved his hand in the air. "Whatever you say. I'll

probably just fly home once we hit Fort Lauderdale. I don't care any more."

"Thank you. That makes it easier for everyone."

"Whatever." Tony waved his hand in the air again as he signalled the barman for another whiskey.

Ann tried to find some sympathy for him but couldn't. He'd always been so much in control but now he looked like a broken man. Funny how a little slip of a girl like Jess could bring him down like this. She would never have imagined it – not in her wildest dreams.

Bunny made a point of looking for Ann and found her having afternoon tea in the Buffet with Nina.

"Ann, I'm so sorry about what's happened. Jess told me how gracious you were about it and we're very upset. Her behaviour was inexcusable."

"Yes, it was but I don't have any bad feelings towards her or you or Richard. You've always been kind to me."

"Thank you for that," said Bunny, relieved. "We'd like to invite you for drinks tomorrow evening in the suite and you too, Nina, and your husband." She smiled at Ann's friend. "Sarah and Jack will join us along with Gavin and Fiona but I can assure you Jess will not be there." She looked embarrassed. "Is six-thirty okay?"

"Thank you, Bunny, that would be lovely." Ann looked at Nina. "Can you come?"

"I'd love to," Nina replied.

"Great. Richard will be pleased."

"And Bunny, please don't keep Jess away on my account. I hold nothing against her."

"You're too good," Bunny replied emotionally. Ann had gone up even higher in her estimation. "Don't forget we have the Trivia Final at five. We must pull out all the stops today."

"See you at five."

The two women watched her go.

"That was nice of her," Ann said to Nina.

"It can't have been easy for her, knowing what her daughter did to you."

"It was Tony who betrayed me and none of us are responsible for what our adult children do."

"I suppose that's true."

# Chapter 24

Emily found Sarah at the pool and asked if she could have a word with her.

"Sure. Is something the matter?" Sarah asked, frowning.

"No, not at all. I just need some advice."

"About Tarki?"

Emily laughed. "No. About me. I admire you so much and I wish I was more like you. I wish I had your courage."

"Don't be silly. You're much brainier than I am."

"Brains aren't everything. You've got the looks and you're so outgoing. I'm like a timid mouse," Emily admitted. "I feel invisible sometimes. I know I look frumpy. But what I really want is to be less of a pushover. I need to be able to be more firm with people – to stick to my guns when something is important to me."

Sarah could see that Emily was serious and genuinely wanted her help.

"You've come to the right person," Sarah said confidently.

"I'll take you in hand. Leave it with me. I need to think about it."

They met up for the final of the Trivia Quiz at five. Ann suspected Tony might not turn up and asked Tarquin to be on standby. They were all quite pleased when there was no sign of him as Tarquin was more of an asset than Tony had ever been. He made all the difference and they were thrilled when *Ireland East/West* won by one point. The prize was a magnum of champagne which they took back to Bunny's suite to celebrate.

As they waited for the dress-rehearsal to start, Sarah became very nervous. Although she'd promised Jack she wouldn't take any more cocaine she just had to snort a line to calm her nerves. She was wearing the same outfit she'd worn the day she'd won the salsa dance and was very moved when Jack presented her with a flower for her hair.

The prize for the winner of the final would be the Mirrorball Trophy and also a Mediterranean cruise for two in the summer. Sarah was sure Jack would win. He thought she would.

"Actually we both win because it's a cruise for two," he laughed. "Whichever of us wins will take the other."

Sarah's heart soared when she heard this. He obviously intended to continue their relationship back in Ireland. She wasn't just a holiday fling to him. He was much much more than that to her.

The five finalists took to the stage for the first time and the rehearsal went well with just a few mistakes.

Sarah had been worried about what to wear for the exhibition rumba that she would dance with Jack. She had nothing remotely suitable. Then Galina brought out a fabulous costume which was just perfect and pretty revealing.

"How do you expect me to remember a step when you look so sexy?" Jack whispered to her when he saw her in it. "I swear I want to take it off you right now."

"Let's get the dance over with and then you can do that," she murmured back.

Jack had wanted to dance to the music 'Stuck on You' by Lionel Richie rather than the modern Bruno Mars song that they'd danced to at the rumba lesson. The choreographer agreed that it was actually perfect for the rumba and added to the sensuality. Sarah loved it and was surprised that Jack loved eighties music as much as she did. Another thing they had in common.

When they'd finished dancing the rumba all the dancers and even the musicians applauded loudly. The jump at the end went perfectly.

"I hope that doesn't mean that I'll mess up at the real thing. You know what they say 'Bad dress rehearsal, great show' and vice versa."

Jack was surprised that she was such a bag of nerves. They went back to her cabin where he quickly did as he'd threatened and stripped the dress off her. Then they made love which he hoped would calm her down.

The Gala Show was due to begin at seven. This one was a particularly spectacular one with trapeze artists, gymnasts and the fabulous dancers and singers. As breathtaking as before.

Sarah was so nervous she thought she might throw up. She went into the bathroom and in the toilet laid out a line of coke. She had to do something to calm her nerves.

At that moment, Cassie came into the bathroom to freshen her lipstick. She heard the clicking sound coming from the cubicle. Then she heard the snorting.

She knew what that meant and wondered who was stupid enough to be taking cocaine. She was shocked when she saw Sarah emerging.

"Oh . . . Cassie . . . hello," Sarah greeted her, obviously taken aback. "I didn't hear anyone come in." She had a small mirror in her hand which she quickly hid out of sight but not before Cassie had seen it. "I'm so nervous about the competition."

"I'm sure you'll be fine," Cassie replied. "Good luck."

She left wondering what she should do about what she'd witnessed. She liked Sarah but she owed it to Fiona to alert her to what Sarah was doing. It was so dangerous. Uneasily, she took her seat in the theatre once again.

It was time for the *Strictly* dance final. There was a big screen to the right of the stage and it sprang to life. It was a recording from the BBC show *Strictly Come Dancing*. The judges Len, Darcy, Bruno and Craig appeared, wishing the contestants good luck.

"Just go out there and enjoy yourself," Len advised. All the dancers taking part in that TV show then wished them luck too.

The contestants were watching on a small screen backstage and were delighted with this message. And then it was Showtime.

There were three judges on the stage, Maja being the chief judge. The first dancer was a girl dancing the cha-cha. The judges awarded her twenty-five points out of thirty.

Jack was next. Ann gripped Emily's hand, praying that he wouldn't make a mistake. She needn't have worried. He was superb and Ann looked proudly on as he lit up the stage. She wondered where he'd got his talent from – not from her or Tony, that was for sure. She felt sorry for Jack that his father wasn't there to see him but that wasn't her problem. The crowd went wild when he finished and she watched proudly as the three judges gave him twenty-nine out of thirty for his samba. The next dancer only earned twenty-four points for her tango and the rumba dancer twenty-three for his.

Then it was Sarah's turn. She was still nervous, despite the coke, and terrified she'd screw up in front of all these people.

Jack held her close and whispered, "Go kill 'em, girl!" and next moment her partner propelled her on stage where she was blinded by the lights. She could see Jack standing in the wings, encouraging her, and her professional partner squeezed her hand.

"You'll be fine," he murmured and then the music started and she was away. She danced like she'd never danced before, completely caught up in the moment and the salsa beat. When she finished the crowd were on their feet cheering and clapping like mad. She looked to Jack in the wings. He was beaming and gave her two thumbs up. Then it was up to the judges. Her heart was in her mouth as they gave their scores. She couldn't take it in and then the crowd were cheering and hollering once more.

Jack ran on to the stage. "You won, you won!" he cried, swirling her round. Only then did she see her score – a perfect thirty.

"*Oh my God!*" she gasped as the Cruise Director came

out and handed her the trophy and an envelope containing the vouchers for a Mediterranean Cruise.

Bunny and the rest of her family were ecstatic and cheered loudly.

Sarah had to then rush off to go and change for their exhibition rumba.

The music started and then the spotlight caught Jack and Sarah in its glare. The audience were spellbound as they watched them dance the sensual passionate rumba. It was as good as anything any of them had seen on the TV shows *Strictly Come Dancing* and *Dancing With The Stars*. Afterwards complete strangers came up to them to congratulate them.

They went back to her cabin to change and he held her close. "You were spectacular," he said before kissing her.

Her face was flushed and her eyes alight and his heart skipped a beat. She was so incredibly beautiful. He knew then that she was the girl he would marry.

There was a great atmosphere at dinner that night as they celebrated Sarah's win and their rumba. Cassie wanted to alert Fiona about what she'd seen but didn't want to spoil the night for Sarah. Let her enjoy her moment of glory. She figured it could wait till the next day.

"So where's Dad?" Emily asked Ann.

"No idea," she replied.

Jack and Emily exchanged worried glances. Bunny raised her eyebrows. She barely recognised Ann as the downtrodden woman she'd first met. It appeared that Nina was the catalyst for this change in her. She was surprised to find that Nina was also much more pleasant than previously. They seemed to have benefited each other.

"You seem very happy, Ann," Fiona remarked.

"Why wouldn't I be? My son made me very proud this evening," she replied, smiling, "And Sarah too of course."

"Yes, we're very proud of them too," Bunny said.

Both she and Richard liked Jack a lot and felt he was a good influence on their daughter. She had changed for the better, Bunny acknowledged. No more smart-assed remarks or back-answers from her, thank God.

Both Jack and Sarah were on a high after the show. Emily was also thrilled for her brother and Sarah. Ann was happy to see both her son and daughter so obviously happy. She called for champagne to celebrate their victory.

After they had toasted the dancers Nina raised her glass to Ann.

"And here's to AA and a bright future!" she said.

The others looked at her, puzzled. Ann smiled. Only she knew it meant 'Assertive Ann' and not Alcoholics Anonymous!

After dinner Ann told Jack and Emily that she wanted to have a word with them in private. "Let's go up on deck where it's quiet," she suggested.

Jack suspected what was coming but Emily was in the dark and looked apprehensive. Something was going on with her parents and she guessed she was about to find out what it was.

"Is it about Dad?" she asked when they were seated.

"Yes, I'm afraid so. I'm sorry to have to tell you that he and I are going to divorce. This has nothing to do with either of you. We both love you and that won't change."

Emily burst into tears. "Why? What's happened?"

"He tells me he's been having an affair and that he's in

love," Ann said, trying to speak without rancour.

"He's a fool!" Jack exclaimed vehemently. "Jess is not serious. She's only playing with him." He smashed his fist into his other hand.

"Jess?" Emily gasped, her eyes widening with disbelief.

Ann was shocked at what Jack had said. "You knew about it?" she asked him.

"Yes. I saw them together and I tackled Dad about it. I was going to tell you, Mum, once this cruise was over as I didn't want to spoil the holiday for you." He looked miserable. "He's an idiot. He thinks she loves him but she doesn't. She told Sarah it was only a flirtation."

"*I hate him, I hate him!*" Emily burst out. "How could he do this to us?"

Ann put her arm around her daughter. "It's okay, Emily. It's for the best. It happens all the time."

"I can't believe he asked you for a divorce," Jack remarked angrily.

"He didn't. *I* asked him for a divorce."

Jack and Emily looked at her with open mouths.

"You asked *him* for a divorce?" Jack cried. "Why?"

"Well, I've taken stock of my life on this trip and I realise that I'm tired of being undermined and bullied by your father. Then when I discovered that he loves someone else it somehow seemed the right time."

"You're not upset about it?" Emily asked, her mother's revelations shocking her so much that she stopped crying.

"Not at all. Who wants to be with a man who loves someone else? So I asked him for a divorce."

"Mum, you're something else!" Jack exclaimed in amazement. "I never would have thought you'd have the courage to do that."

"Oh, I've changed a lot, son, believe me. I value myself now even if your father doesn't."

At that moment Jack was prouder of her than he'd ever been and he knew she'd be okay. He got up and hugged her.

Even Emily, shocked as she was, felt the new strength in her mother and was happy for her.

"So what did Nina mean when she toasted you as AA?" Jack wanted to know.

When Ann told them they laughed and left happily, arm in arm, to rejoin the others in the Montmartre bar.

"Do you mind if I move into your cabin, Emily?" Ann asked.

"Course not, Mum. It's all yours."

Ann suspected that she was glad of an excuse to spend the night with Tarquin.

"What happens when we reach Florida?" Jack asked. "Will we still be spending the week in Orlando?"

"Yes, indeed. I've been so looking forward to that but I'm afraid it won't be the family holiday we'd planned. Your father will be flying home from Fort Lauderdale."

"Mum, would you mind if Sarah joined us?" Jack asked. "I'd really love if she could."

"Not at all. That would be great. And what about Tarquin, Emily?"

Emily blushed. "Well, he did say that he could stay on for a few days if I wanted him to."

"Excellent. Ask him to join us too," Ann suggested. "I'll have to contact the hotel about rooms."

Bruno was on duty in the Montmartre when they got there.

"I got some good stuff here tonight," he whispered to Sarah when she went to the bar for a straw.

"Shush," she told him nervously, afraid someone might hear. "I'm not sure I want it any more."

Bruno was disappointed. This cruise had not been as lucrative as he'd have liked, especially since the Italians had left.

"It's good stuff," he assured her, hoping to persuade her to buy. She was tempted, he saw.

"I don't know. I'll think about it," she replied.

He wondered why she was reluctant to take it. Probably her fearsome Amazon of a mother had put a stop to it.

Sarah and Jack left the bar at midnight and headed to the Disco where they boogied the night away. He told her what Ann had revealed.

"So what happens to your father now?" Sarah asked.

"Do I look like I care?"

At the disco the crowd called for Jack and Sarah to reprise their rumba and they obliged to rapturous applause once more. Sarah felt like her feet would never touch the ground again. She was on top of the world.

# Chapter 25

The following morning the ship docked in Nassau, the capital of the Bahamas. Another beautiful sunny day and they all determined to make the most of this beautiful island. Most passengers had booked a visit to Paradise Island and the McElroys were heading there too. They were going to the Atlantis which was home to the world's largest open-air marine habitat and Aquaventure Waterpark with its thrilling water slides.

Richard and Gavin had booked to play golf while Bunny, Fiona and Cassie took a day-pass to the luxurious Cove Atlantis hotel. The men would join them there for lunch after their golf round.

Jess had declined invitations from Sarah and her mother to join them. She had decided to spend the day on the beach. She just wanted a quiet day alone. It was not to be. They all left the ship together and when Jess came through the Border Control doors she was flabbergasted to see Philip standing there, grinning from ear to ear.

"Philip! What are you doing here?" she cried, for the second time in three days.

"I couldn't wait till Fort Lauderdale to see you. I hope you don't mind."

She went into his arms. "Of course not! I can't believe you did this."

"I told you I couldn't live without you."

The others stood around smiling, all of them surprised except for Bunny who had orchestrated the whole thing.

When he finally let Jess go the others crowded around him, the men clapping him on the back and the girls hugging him.

"And that's not all," Bunny declared. "Philip asked me to try and book him on to the ship for the last two days of our cruise, which I did. So we'll have the whole family together for the rest of our time here."

Jess shook her head disbelievingly. Her mother had to be the greatest manipulator of all time but she wasn't complaining. It felt good to have Philip's arm around her again. She realised that she still loved him and, if he had come all this way for her, it must mean that he loved her too and wanted to make it work. She was willing to give it another try.

The Captain had arranged for a crew member to meet Philip and check him in and, once that was done, they left the ship to spent the day together on the island. Jess was delighted that Philip would be joining the cruise but a little apprehensive of what would happen if he and Tony were to meet.

Emily and Tarquin had left the ship a little earlier than the McElroys as they were anxious to visit the Marine Habitat, but they joined Jack and Sarah afterwards at the Waterpark. The slides were simply amazing and they had great fun.

Emily, who was afraid of heights, decided she could not possibly go on the Drop, a slide that dropped you in utter darkness before twisting and turning into the Current.

"C'mon, you said you wanted to be more outgoing and less timid. Now's your chance to start," Sarah cajoled her.

"Oh no, I couldn't!" Emily protested but the three others eventually persuaded her.

"We can ride together," Tarquin said, so reluctantly she agreed.

She hung on to him for dear life and kept her eyes closed the whole time but she did admit afterwards that it had been thrilling.

"Great stuff!" Sarah and Jack said, high-fiving her.

Sarah had become very fond of Jack's little sister.

They went for a drink then and when they were seated in the Café, Sarah turned to Emily.

"I've been thinking about what you said about feeling frumpy and invisible and I have a plan. It starts with a visit to the beauty salon on board this evening. I think a new hairstyle will do wonders for your confidence."

"Great idea," Jack agreed, thinking that was just what his sister needed.

Emily happily agreed.

They were saving the most daring slide for last. It was the Leap of Faith which was an almost vertical sixty-foot drop into a clear acrylic tunnel through a shark-filled lagoon.

Jack and Sarah decided to go for a cocktail before mentioning the slide to Emily. Unused to drinking alcohol she was a little tiddly by the time they suggested it.

"No way!" she squealed. "Look how high it is!"

Eventually she gave in and climbed up to the top of the tower. Once there she had second thoughts but Sarah convinced her that she'd be okay. Tarquin went first and when he'd finished he stood waving her down. Rigid with nerves, she let go and suddenly she was experiencing the most fantastic rush of adrenalin as she whooshed down the steep slide. Once she saw the tunnel she was tempted to close her eyes because of the sharks but she stayed brave and before she knew it she was out in the pool and Tarquin was kissing her. Jack and Sarah followed soon after and they all hugged her, delighted with her performance. She was laughing and crying as she looked up to where she'd come from. She would never have believed it possible that she could have done that. She felt proud of herself.

After lunch Cassie asked Fiona to go for a walk along the beach.

"Fiona, I don't know how to say this – there's no easy way . . ."

"What is it, Cassie?" Fiona asked alarmed.

"I was in the bathroom yesterday and Sarah was there and . . . I hate to be the one to tell you this . . . she was taking cocaine."

Fiona had stopped dead and put her hand up to her heart. "Are you sure, Cassie? Could you have been mistaken?" she asked hopefully.

"I'm afraid not. I heard her and I saw the mirror with a spot of cocaine on it. She tried to hide it. I'm sorry but it's true."

"Dear God," Fiona cried, sinking to the sand. "How is

it possible? I never thought she'd do anything like that. Gavin will go ballistic."

"Do you have to tell him?"

"Oh yes. This is too serious. We have to stop her but first I think I'll speak to Sarah. Lord, are our problems never going to end?"

"This cruise has certainly given us all our share," Cassie agreed, her eyes sad.

Ann and Nina as usual took a day tour of the island, ending up on Paradise Island. Ann had not seen any sign of Tony that morning for which she was grateful. She'd left the ship early for the tour and she guessed he was still sleeping.

Tony woke up just before noon to find the ship practically deserted. He sat having a coffee, wondering where everyone was and how this trip that had started out so promising had turned into such a disaster: his children were not speaking to him, his wife was seeking a divorce, people were avoiding him and worst of all the woman he loved wanted nothing more to do with him. Disaster was putting it mildly!

He needed to escape the ship where so much had gone wrong so he disembarked and made his way down to the town centre. He stopped at a bar and ordered a rum and Coke. No doubt about it, the rum here was terrific. He ordered another.

He got talking to the barman who told him about the John Watling Distillery which offered free tours and tastings of their famous rum. Hailing a taxi, he made his way to the Buena Vista Estate where it was located. He was greeted with the best Piña Colada he'd ever tasted and after a tour of the place went to the bar where he sampled their three rums and some cocktails. Having forgotten to eat, he soon was quite drunk. The barmaid was very pretty and friendly and he found himself pouring his heart out to her. She was very sympathetic. He purchased a bottle of their rum before he left.

Checking his watch, he saw that it was later than he'd thought. He left looking around for a taxi but there was none about. He started to walk in the direction of the ship but being drunk he was disorientated and got completely lost. Eventually he found himself on the outskirts of town where he found a taxi and ordered the driver to drive as fast as he could to the port.

Everyone was on deck watching the last sail-away and admiring the beauty of the island and sea when Emily cried out.

"Oh, look! Somebody is late!" She pointed to the quay where a car had screeched to a halt. They all looked to where she was pointing and saw the man scrambling out of the car and running while shouting at the ship with his fist raised.

"The fool!" Gavin exclaimed.

"Oh my God, no!" Jack cried, putting his hands to his head as he recognised the figure standing on the quay, gesticulating towards the ship. "I don't believe it! It's Dad."

Ann looked horrified as she too realised it was Tony. "Can't we do something?" she cried.

"*Will someone call the Captain and get him to turn back?*" Emily shouted.

"Don't be ridiculous!" a man standing beside them who had overheard exclaimed. "That won't happen."

"Yes. We've seen it happen before on other cruises," his

wife agreed. "There's no way the Captain will turn around."

"If people are stupid enough to miss the sailing they deserve what they get," her husband declared.

"Idiot!" said Jack.

"*But it's Dad!*" Emily cried, panic-stricken.

Ann put her arm around her daughter's shoulders.

"How could he do this? What will happen to him?" Emily wailed.

"He'll make his way to Key West or Fort Lauderdale and meet the ship there," Tarquin said, hoping to reassure her.

"You think?"

"Of course," Jack assured her. "He'll be fine."

"This really seals the mess he's made of this trip," Jack said angrily to Sarah when they were alone. "I'll never forgive him."

He and Ann had gone straight to Guest Relations to report that Tony had missed the ship. They knew and had already made arrangements for him to get back to Fort Lauderdale. Ann heaved a sigh of relief. They had also notified Immigration of the problem. They would get back to Ann as soon as everything was arranged.

When Jess heard the news she heaved a sigh of relief. At least she wouldn't have to worry about Philip running into him any more. Thank God for that!

The sail-away party was a muted affair for the Irish contingent in the light of Tony's mishap.

Sarah took Emily to the beauty salon with instructions for her to have a complete change. "Give her layers and blonde highlights," she ordered the hairstylist.

"Aren't they very expensive?" Emily asked.

"All taken care of," replied Sarah. "Jack and I are paying for it."

Emily was very touched.

Fiona saw Sarah come back on deck and took the opportunity to pull her to one side. "Sarah, I need to talk to you privately. Will you come up to the Montmartre bar with me?"

"Sure." She saw the frown on Fiona's face. "Is everything okay?" she asked nervously.

"I'll tell you when we're sitting down."

Now Sarah was really worried. Once they sat down Fiona ordered a juice and Sarah said she'd like a Mai Tai. She had a feeling from the look on Fiona's face that she would need it.

"What is it?" she asked when the waiter had brought their drinks.

"I have reason to believe that you're using cocaine. Is that true?"

Sarah went white and her hand started to shake so much that she spilt her drink.

"Who told you? Cassie?"

"So it *is* true. Oh Sarah, how could you? What possessed you to do that?"

"I only took a little, to calm my nerves before the Gala Show."

Fiona didn't believe her. "Sarah! The truth! When did you start?"

Sarah stammered and began crying. "Only on this cruise. I swear. The Italians gave it to me." She was snivelling now, her nose running.

Fiona handed her a handkerchief and she blew her nose.

"Those bastards!" Fiona exclaimed. "It wasn't enough that they robbed us, they had to introduce you to drugs!"

"Cocaine is not really a drug. Lots of people do it."

Fiona got angry with her. "For God's sake, Sarah, grow up! Of course it's a drug. Don't you remember that Irish model who died from it?"

Sarah looked at the ground miserably.

"Do you have any more?" Fiona asked.

"Yes, back in my room."

"C'mon, let's go. I'm taking it from you," said Fiona, standing up.

"Can I finish my drink first?"

"No, you can't. Come along."

She had no choice but to follow Fiona who strode away ahead of her.

In the cabin she handed the packet of coke to Fiona, feeling embarrassed.

"Is that it? Do you have any more?"

"No, that's it, I swear," Sarah protested.

Fiona believed her.

"I don't know how I'm going to tell Gavin. He'll go ballistic."

"Please don't tell him. He'll kill me!" Sarah started to cry again.

"I can't keep this to myself, Sarah. I'm sorry. It's much too serious. But I won't tell him till after dinner."

Sarah was sobbing now. She was sure Gavin would tell her mother and she was terrified of Bunny's reaction. What she was most afraid of was that Jack would discover that she hadn't kept her promise to him.

"C'mon!" Fiona hugged her. "I'm sure if you promise

never to touch it again, they'll forgive you."

Sarah wasn't too sure.

Ann's phone rang as she was getting ready for Bunny's drinks party. It was Tony and he sounded drunk.

"Where are you?" she asked.

"I'm still here in bloody Nassau," he replied.

No apology, nothing.

"What will you do?"

"I'll have to stay here overnight. They can't get me on a ship to Key West tonight but they'll get me on one to Fort Lauderdale tomorrow night. The Harbour Master here organised it. I'll be in Fort Lauderdale around the same time as you. You may have to bring my passport to me though. I'll call you from there."

"Tony, why did you do this?" Ann asked downheartedly.

He softened then and for the first time seemed to show remorse. "I'm sorry, Ann . . . I'm sorry for everything."

She heard his voice was close to breaking.

"Keep in touch," she said. "At least you'll get to Fort Lauderdale."

# Chapter 26

Bunny pulled out all the stops for her last drinks party in the suite that evening. Her guest list had grown and she was happy as she looked around at them all. It was wonderful to have Philip there.

Ann arrived and the first person she met was Jess. Bunny, on seeing this, moved over to them in case she was needed to keep the peace. It wasn't necessary and Ann went up even more in her estimation when she heard what she was saying to Jess.

"I'm pleased that you and your husband are back together again, Jess. Please try hard to make it work. He seems like a good man."

"Thank you, Ann, I will," Jess said humbly. She hadn't been sure she would be so forgiving but she had forgiven Philip. That was a start. However, there was no way she would be able to communicate with the ex-housekeeper. That was a step too far.

"I don't know how you do it," Bunny remarked to Ann

when Jess had moved away. "You're very gracious."

"Life's too short to hold grudges. You have to let go of them if you want to move on. And I do," was Ann's reply.

"How true!" said Bunny. "I admire you for that and I'm sorry that Tony missed the sailing. What's going to happen to him?"

Gavin joined them as Ann was telling her what Tony had said.

"Well, he'll miss Key West, that's for sure," Ann said. "But they'll have him back in Fort Lauderdale for the morning we arrive."

"What possessed him to miss the ship?" Gavin asked.

"God knows," Ann replied with a sigh. "He didn't say."

"You've really had a bummer of a cruise," Bunny said sympathetically to Ann.

"I've actually enjoyed most of it despite all the problems," Ann admitted. "I've made some good friends and it's great to see the kids happy too."

"You're amazing. You always look on the bright side," Bunny complimented her.

Bunny had invited the Captain and it was obvious that his admiration for Cassie hadn't waned as he never left her side for a minute. He had invited her to dine with him in his quarters that evening.

"Where are Sarah and Emily?" Bunny asked Jack. Both he and Tarquin seemed a little lost without the girls.

"Beauty Salon," Jack replied, wondering what was taking them so long.

Sarah had gone to the salon to see how things were going and was thrilled when she saw Emily's new hairstyle.

Emily's eyes were alight as she tossed her head this way and that.

"I love it," she exclaimed, beaming.

"*Wow!* Great job!" Sarah said to the hair-stylist.

Gone was Emily's limp straight hair and in its place was a trendy, choppy, layered bob which suited her perfectly. The mousy brown was now a honey blonde with brighter blonde highlights. There was even a strand of pink in her new fringe.

"The colour is sensational!" Sarah exclaimed.

"Isn't it?" Emily said, admiring it in the mirror. "I feel like a different person."

"I can't wait for the others to see it but first we're going to my cabin."

There, Sarah took out her make-up kit and did Emily's make-up. She then went through her wardrobe and picked out one of her favourite short dresses.

Emily put it on and it fitted her perfectly.

"Luckily, we're the same size," said Sarah, "though it's not as short on you as I'm much taller."

"Thank goodness," Emily giggled. "My mother and Jack would have a fit if it was any shorter."

She'd had time to think about her father while she was having her hair done and was beginning to think like Jack – that Tony had brought all this on himself. He had been utterly horrible to her mother on this cruise.

When Emily entered the suite with Sarah she caused all talk to stop.

"Emily, dear, is that really you? I hardly recognise you!" Bunny exclaimed, going forward to welcome her.

"Goodness, Emily," Ann cried, shock on her face.

"What have you done?"

"Don't you like it?" Emily asked nervously.

"I love it! You look wonderful," Ann exclaimed, hugging her.

Emily saw them all smiling at her. She didn't feel invisible any longer.

Jack hugged her and stood back to take it all in. "*Wow! Behold my sexy sister!*"

Emily blushed. "It's all Sarah's doing. She gave the orders," she admitted shyly. "And thank you for helping pay for it."

Jack put his arm around Sarah. "Thank you. You've done a fantastic job," he said, kissing her.

The reaction that mattered the most to Emily was the look in Tarquin's eyes. It was a look that she hadn't seen before.

"You look absolutely beautiful," he whispered, putting his arm possessively around her.

She felt beautiful.

Emily was the belle of the ball as they all admired her new look. She wondered why she hadn't done this before. She knew why – she'd never had anyone like Sarah to help her before. And Sarah had promised to help her shop for new trendy clothes in Orlando.

Ann took Sarah aside to thank her for what she had done for Emily. "It's not just the new look but she told me how you encouraged her to take the water-slides and she's so excited about doing that."

"She's still finding her feet but I think she's turned a corner," Sarah confided in her.

"I partly blame myself for her timidity. It wasn't good for her to see how passive I was. I'm hoping that now I've found courage, Emily will blossom."

"I don't doubt it," Sarah assured her.

"Could I ask a favour? I think it's time I had a makeover too and, when I see what you did for Emily, who better to ask?"

"I'd be delighted to help. We'll have to wait until we get to Orlando though. We won't have time tomorrow as the ship sails late from Key West."

"That's fine. I guess I can survive for a few more days like this," Ann replied, delighted she'd taken this step.

They all headed off in different directions for dinner. The youngsters headed off to dinner with their American friends in the main restaurant while Fiona and Gavin had arranged to meet their French friends Michel and Marisa in the Italian one. Bunny and Richard left for dinner in the private suites restaurant while Philip took Jess to the Brasserie where they dined under the stars.

"How do you feel about taking a second honeymoon once we finish this cruise?" he asked.

"Really?" Jess asked delightedly.

"Makes sense. We're in this part of the world now so why not make the most of it?"

"That would be fabulous. I must say I've got very fond of the climate here," she admitted.

"How about Cuba? Now is the time to go before the Americans go in."

Jess clapped her hands with delight. "I've always longed to see Cuba," she said, her eyes alight.

"Cuba it is," he said, smiling lovingly at her. "And it's great for diving too."

That night they made love for the first time in a long

while. Both of them were apprehensive – afraid that his betrayal and her one moment of madness with Tony might get in the way – but it didn't. Their lovemaking was more tender and loving than it had ever been. Jess had never found him more patient or anxious to please her and when she'd climaxed for the third time, she thought ruefully that perhaps she had the housekeeper to thank for that.

Cassie left Bunny's party to dine with the Captain in his private quarters.

There were two other couples and his Staff Captain and Chief Security Officer there too. They were all very friendly and good company and Cassie had a lovely time. The Captain escorted her back to her suite.

"Would you like to come in for a nightcap?" she asked.

"Do I have to be a perfect gentleman?" he asked.

"I'm afraid so," she laughed.

"Okay, I promise," he said with a downcast face.

Once again she curled up in the armchair as he poured them two brandies. He sat down in the other armchair.

"I hope we can keep in touch," he said sincerely. "I think you know how I feel about you."

"I have a fair idea," she replied, "and I enjoy your company very much – but you do realise that I'm still married and not ready to get into another relationship just yet?"

"As I told you, I'm a very patient man and I'll wait as long as it takes."

She smiled gently. "Let's keep in touch."

"Let's do that." He paused. "Cassie, I know this cruise has been very difficult for you. I'd like to make it up to you and when you're ready I'd like to invite you to come on another cruise on the *Liberté*, as my guest."

"That's very kind of you. I just might take you up on that."

He left then but not before reaching forward to kiss her on the cheek. To his surprise, she put her arms around him and hugged him. It gave him some hope that she had some feelings for him and that he would see her again.

The following day they docked in Key West, the southernmost point of Florida. Another glorious day to be enjoyed and sadly their last, for tonight they would start the last leg of their cruise back to Fort Lauderdale.

The Captain announced that they would not be leaving that evening until 8 p.m so that they could enjoy the sunset which was more spectacular here than anywhere else. They were all looking forward to that.

As always the youngsters headed for the beach to jet-ski and para-sail. To Jack's amazement, Emily agreed to do both.

"I can't believe you're willing to do this," he confessed.

"Me neither," she giggled. "I guess, after coming down that water slide in Atlantis, I figure I can do just about anything. It was the scariest moment of my life."

"I'm really proud of you, Sis," he said, giving her a big hug.

It was worth the fear to hear him say that.

Richard and Bunny said they were going to Ernest Hemingway's house. It was somewhere both of them were keen to visit as they were big fans of his. Gavin and Fiona were spending the day with Cassie and they were all keen to see it too. It was here that Hemingway had written *To*

*Have and Have Not* and *For Whom the Bell Tolls* and his house was now a museum.

The first thing that greeted them were the many cats that roamed the place. They were amazed to see that these cats, which were descended from Hemingway's cats, all had six and seven toes. They looked weird. The museum was very interesting and they found it hard to believe that he'd written these books on the old typewriter and sitting on the hard chair that were preserved just as he'd left them.

"Can you even begin to imagine," Cassie remarked, "how so many wonderful books were written like that? No Google, no spell-check, no cut and paste. I don't know how they did it."

"Unbelievable," Fiona agreed. "It must have been a labour of love."

They walked down Duval Street and, even though it was the middle of the afternoon, it was hopping. Every bar, she noticed, had a sign over the door saying *Ernest Hemingway Drank Here*.

"He was a big drinker," Richard explained. "It's the same story in Cuba and Madrid and there's actually a bar in Madrid that says *Ernest Hemingway did NOT drink here*," he told them, laughing.

Richard was very knowledgeable and told them many more stories about the great writer. Bunny was proud of him.

They strolled through the historic old town, admiring the unique architecture. The houses were of wood with large porches and dated back to the 18th century. They browsed some of the quaint little shops and then stopped for lunch. After lunch they split up because Richard and Bunny wanted to visit the West Martello Tower which they'd heard was very interesting.

The others headed off on a kayaking eco-tour through the mangroves and they all agreed to meet up later when Jess and Philip would join them.

Jess and Philip decided to go scuba diving. They had both done it in Sardinia and the diving here was said to be great. They had a wonderful morning on the coral reef and in the afternoon explored the old town.

Jess had heard that Key West was a fun place but that was an understatement. It was also the gay capital of Florida if not the whole USA and she thought it was good to see so many gay men and women having the freedom to be themselves without fear of discrimination. She was all for gay rights.

She was also fascinated by the glamorous transvestites on Duval Street who urged them to visit their clubs. "Maybe later," she replied, laughing.

They all met up as planned at a bar the Captain had recommended called Schooner Wharf. It was jam-packed and the atmosphere both inside and out was electric. There they ordered margaritas and also conch fritters – the local delicacy – which were delicious. There was a guy on a guitar who was very good and very funny and they sat in the sun, enjoying the music and the margaritas. Then they made their way down to Mallory Square which was crowded with holidaymakers enjoying the craft stalls and street performers. This was where everyone gathered every evening to watch the sunset. There were sail-boats offering to take people out to sail across the path of the sunset. Philip bought two tickets for himself and Jess.

They saw Sarah and the other young ones who had met up

along the way with Ann and Nina. It was a happy group that settled down to watch the magnificent sunset. They cheered loudly with everyone else as the sun sank into the sea. They saw the boat that Jess was in pass over the sun at exactly that moment. Richard started to sing 'Red Sails in the Sunset' and an elderly couple beside him joined in. It was all very jolly.

In the boat, Jess lay her head on Philip's shoulder and felt happier than she'd felt in a long time. The sails of the boats appeared red as they passed in front of the setting sun. It was magical and very romantic.

They got back on board in plenty of time and the sail-away party was tinged with sadness as it was their last. Afterwards they went for dinner.

They had been asked to pack and leave their luggage outside their cabin doors to be collected, not later than ten-thirty. Immigration Officers would come on board at seven the next morning and after that disembarkation would commence.

After dinner Ann went to the cabin she'd shared with Tony and packed for both of them. She wondered where he was and if he'd make it to Fort Lauderdale by tomorrow.

Just then her phone rang. It was Tony.

"Where are you?" she asked.

"I'm on the *Bahamian Princess* on my way to Fort Lauderdale. I should be there around the same time as you. They say you'll have to bring me my passport. Guest Relations will let you know and give you instructions."

He sounded very subdued.

"Okay. I'll call you in the morning once I know. At least you're on your way."

The young people rocked on, getting the very best out of

the last hours of their cruise. The more sensible adults, knowing they had an early-morning call, said goodnight and retired early. They all arranged to meet up the following morning but exchanged phone numbers and email addresses in case they missed each other. They promised to keep in touch and to meet up back in Ireland. The McElroys wished Ann the best of luck and were pleased to hear that she had agreed to visit Nina in Florida later in the year.

"Who knows? We may even take another cruise. I've got a taste for it now," Ann declared.

But first she had to go home and start the ball rolling on her divorce. She was not looking forward to that.

After dinner the Captain called Cassie to say goodbye.

"I was just about to call you," she said. "I have something I'd like to give you."

"Does that mean I can say goodbye in person?" he asked.

"Yes. I know you'll be an absolute gentleman," she said laughingly.

"*Ab-so-lute-ly!*" he laughed back. "Actually, I have a little memento for you too."

He was at the door of her suite in two minutes. He came in and handed her a gift-wrapped box. She opened it and saw it was a model of the *Liberté* – perfectly, exquisitely done.

"It's beautiful," she told him, turning it around in her hand, admiring it. "Thank you, Dimitri." She reached forward and kissed his cheek.

"It's so you won't forget me," he admitted shyly.

"I'll never do that. And this is for you, to thank you for being a friend in need."

She reached behind the sofa. It was one of her paintings. The one of the view they'd both stood admiring on her veranda.

"Oh my goodness!" he exclaimed. "It's beautiful." He saw there was an inscription on the back – *To my dear friend, Dimitri. Remember me, Cassie.*

"As if I could ever forget!" he whispered. "Thank you so very much. It's the nicest gift anyone has ever given me. I'll keep it with me always."

He was getting emotional and so was she.

"I think we'd better say goodnight," she murmured. "Till we meet again." Cassie held out her hand and he took it and pressed it to his lips, holding it there.

"Till then. And I pray it won't be too long, my beautiful friend."

With that he was gone and Cassie let out a long sigh. Who knew what the future held for them? Only time would tell.

# Chapter 27

Everyone had been given a Zone number to facilitate immigration and disembarkation. Suite passengers were Zone 1 which meant they were the first to be called.

As Fiona and Gavin were waiting in their cabin to be called, Fiona brought up the subject that she had been dreading for two days now.

"Gavin, I have something to tell you," she said nervously, a frown on her face.

"Yes?" He looked at her apprehensively.

"I don't know how to say it . . . but I found out that Sarah has been using cocaine."

He was incredulous. "Please tell me that you're not serious?"

"I am," she replied, biting her lip. "Cassie found out and told me and I tackled Sarah. She admitted it and I took what she had left of it and threw it overboard."

Gavin's face was grim. "When did all this happen?"

"Cassie told me in Nassau and –"

"That's two days ago!" he said, raising his voice. "And you didn't think to tell me till now?"

Fiona had never seen him so angry. "I didn't want to spoil the rest of the cruise," she tried to explain.

"I don't believe this. My wife finds out my kid sister is taking drugs and doesn't bother to inform me!"

He was standing now, pacing back and forth, hitting his fist into his hand.

"Didn't you think I had a right to know?" He glared at her.

"I'm sorry," she said, tears coming to her eyes. Gavin had never spoken so harshly to her before. "I sorted it," she whispered, her voice breaking.

"Well, I'll sort that young lady out right now," he fumed before marching out of the cabin, banging the door.

Fiona started to cry. She felt miserable. He was right, she should have told him.

She called Cassie but there was no reply. Of course, Fiona realised, she was in Immigration right now. She sat on the bed, dreading to think what was happening in Sarah's cabin.

Gavin banged on Sarah's door and she opened it quickly, thinking something was wrong. She took one look at Gavin's face and knew she was in trouble. Fiona must have told him.

"Please let me explain –" she started, but he cut her off.

"How could you be so stupid?"

She started crying.

"What made you take that stuff? How long have you been doing it?" He took her by the shoulders and shook her.

"I only started on this cruise," she confessed between sniffles. "The Italians gave it to me."

"*Those bastards!*" he yelled. "Are you still taking it?"

"No, no, I swear. Fiona took what I had left. I could have bought more but I didn't. I swear I'm telling the truth."

He believed her. He dropped his hands from her shoulders and slumped.

"Sarah, please promise me you will never touch that stuff again." He put his hands on her shoulders once more. But this time it wasn't in anger – he was pleading with her.

"I promise. Honestly, I swear I'll never touch any kind of drug again. Believe me, Gavin. I'm so sorry." She was crying softly now. "You won't tell Mummy?"

"I should, but I don't want to be responsible for what she might do to you."

Sarah threw herself into Gavin's arms and he patted her on the back.

"Stop crying now. As long as you mean what you say, it's okay. If I ever catch you taking any kind of drug again, I'll certainly be telling the parents."

"Thank you," she murmured, hugging him tight. "I promise."

"Now tell me where you could have bought more of this cocaine?" he demanded.

"From Bruno, the barman in the Montmartre bar. The Italians got it from him and I bought it twice from him too."

"Right. He won't be the barman there for much longer," Gavin said grimly.

He looked at his little sister. "And I'm very angry at Fiona for not telling me sooner."

"Please don't be. I begged her not to tell you at all but she wouldn't agree. She made me stop. She just didn't want to spoil the last few days of the cruise. It's not her fault."

Gavin had calmed down. He had to admit that she was probably right.

Gavin went straight to Guest Relations and asked to speak with the Captain urgently. They called the Captain who asked him to come to the Purser's office. The Captain was very disturbed when Gavin informed him that Bruno, one of his barmen, had peddled drugs to both Sarah and the Italians.

The Captain was shocked. Looking grim, he called CSO Allen and told him what Gavin had said. Nodding, he instructed the Security Officer to detain the barman.

"Thank you for coming to me," he said to Gavin. "We will not tolerate this. I'll make sure that he's barred from all cruise-lines in the future. We cannot expose our passengers, especially the young, to this. It will be a matter for the police now of course."

When CSO Allen called the police sergeant, the same one he'd dealt with previously, the man chuckled.

"You are sure makin' me earn my salary. Any chance you could move to the Mediterranean?"

"No way. We aim to keep you on your toes," CSO Allen assured him, but he was laughing too.

Fiona was relieved when she saw that Gavin's anger had evaporated.

"I'm sorry for yelling at you. I was just so shocked at what you told me."

She put her arms around him and he hugged her tight.

"You're forgiven but you're right, I should have told you." She vowed that she'd never keep a secret from him again.

As for Sarah – she couldn't believe what a lucky escape she'd had. Gavin could have told her mother what she'd done. And Jack might have found out that she'd broken her promise to him. But the promise she'd made to Gavin was one that she'd keep. She'd never go near drugs again. She'd learnt her lesson.

The Purser had arranged with Immigration for Ann and her kids to go through first the following morning. They would release Tony's passport to her and she would take it over to Immigration on the *Bahamian Princess*. Jack insisted on going with her and an upset Emily went along too. They were not actually allowed on board but the Deputy Chief of Security met her and assured her that they would take care of it. He said Tony would likely be last to go through Immigration as he was not actually a registered passenger.

She called Tony to give him this news. They agreed to meet up later in the Hyatt Regency where they had arranged to pick up the rental car to take them to Orlando.

"I'll call you when I've disembarked," he told her. "And Ann . . . thank you for everything."

She felt sad when she'd hung up. She had no idea what Tony planned to do but neither she nor the kids wanted him to come to Orlando with them.

After Bunny and Richard were finished with Immigration they met with up with Gavin, Fiona, Jess, Philip and Sarah to say goodbye. Cassie was there too along with Jack and Tarquin. Sarah and Tarquin had arranged meet up with the

Kennys later. Bunny and Richard were going to stay with friends on the Gulf Coast and hugged Sarah with instructions for her to behave and not give Ann any trouble.

Jess and Philip were catching an afternoon flight to Cuba.

"I'm sure you'll have a wonderful time," Bunny cried. "Cuba is one of my favourite places in the world."

"I'll take you there again if we decide to buy a house in Florida," Richard promised her.

Jess kissed them both and they were relieved to see that her marriage was back on track. Philip seemed more relaxed than they remembered and it augured well for them.

"I can never thank you enough, Bunny, for what you've done," he whispered in her ear as they embraced.

Just then Fiona and Gavin's Zone was called and they hurriedly said their goodbyes to his parents and Cassie, wishing them all a safe onward journey.

With a flurry of goodbyes Bunny and Richard disembarked and picked up their rental car before making their way across Florida.

"Such drama!" Bunny exclaimed as she finally sank into the comfort of the Cadillac they'd rented. "I thought cruises were meant to be relaxing."

"Only if you don't bring your offspring," Richard remarked, laughing.

"Or make new friends. We seem to attract problems like a magnet," Bunny declared. "Let's hope the next week is a little more relaxed."

They enjoyed the drive across to Sarasota. They'd always loved Florida and had considered buying a property there.

Here it was the 3$^{rd}$ of January with sunny blue skies and twenty-eight degrees. She had called her friends back in Dublin from Fort Lauderdale to be told that it was snowing there and bitterly cold. This was the life for her.

They drove across Alligator Alley and Bunny had fun counting the alligators lazing on the banks of the river. She gave up after 103! She was looking forward to this break. The cruise had been more nerve-racking than any other she'd taken. All that drama of the robbery and the Declan fiasco and the worry over her two girls. Once again she thanked God for Gavin and his level-headed wife, Fiona. She'd become very fond of her on this cruise and understood why Gavin loved her so much. And now she, Bunny, was going to be a grandmother. She couldn't wait. She'd be the most glamorous granny in Dublin!

She was really looking forward to the week in Sarasota and relaxing with her old friends. She needed to unwind. She'd had enough drama on this cruise to last her a lifetime.

Gavin and Fiona were happy to be getting away on their own too. They were both a little subdued after their biggest row to date.

"I enjoyed the cruise but I'm kind of happy it's over," he admitted.

"Me too. It was time to leave."

They were heading to Orlando to visit Fiona's sister, Ciara, who was due her baby in three weeks. Her parents were staying with Ciara and Fiona was very excited as she still hadn't told Ciara or her parents that they were coming. She was also bursting to tell them the news of her own pregnancy.

As they drove north they discussed the cruise. A postmortem, as Fiona liked to call it.

"One thing you can say, it was never boring," she remarked.

"You can say that again!"

"I spoke to Cassie briefly before we left."

"How is she? I only got a chance to say a quick goodbye."

"She's fine. She's decided to go and see Declan today. She's not looking forward to it but she feels it will be closure."

"Good luck to her with that one. What's happening with him?"

"I gather he's still awaiting trial in Fort Lauderdale which will take some time. She'll know more after she meets him, I suppose. I don't think she cares too much to be honest."

"Dead right," Gavin said. "What a bastard!"

"She's engaged a solicitor to start divorce proceedings. He says that after what Declan did it should be an open and shut case."

"Naturally."

"The Captain called to say goodbye to her last night and gave her a beautiful hand-painted model of the *Liberté*."

"I told you he had the hots for her," Gavin laughed.

"I think it's more than that. She's very fond of him but it's too soon for her. He says he'll wait for her till she's ready for a relationship."

"That *is* serious. Another relationship begun on the *Liberté*," Gavin observed.

"Along with Sarah and Jack, Emily and Tarquin."

"They should rename it *The Love Boat*!" Fiona laughed.

"Not to mention Jess and Tony . . . *aaagh!*" Gavin pretended to throw up. "Thank goodness that didn't go anywhere."

"Yes, but Jess and Philip reunited on the cruise too. That's another one. Of course, two divorces have come out of it too. Cassie and Declan and Tony and Ann." Fiona sighed.

"And that's only among the Irish on board. I doubt any other nationality had as much melodrama as we had."

"Let's change the subject," Fiona suggested. She really didn't want to talk about those creeps Tony and Declan any more.

She hoped Ann would be okay. She knew Cassie would.

Tony met up with Ann in the Hyatt and was met with a very cool reception. He looked awful. She was gratified to see that he also looked ashamed and embarrassed. As well he should!

"I can't tell you how sorry I am for everything," he murmured. "Can you find it in your heart to forgive me, Ann?"

"No, Tony, I can't. And it's not just because of your sordid little affair. It's because of the twenty-two years you bullied me and sapped my confidence. Well, I've got it back now and I don't intend to be bullied ever again." Her voice was firm and strong and he saw she meant every word.

"Ann, please . . . please, give me another chance. I'll make it up to you, I swear."

She shook her head. "I'm sorry, Tony, but it's too late for that. I'm my own person now and intend to stay that way. I've learnt a lot these past two weeks."

"Don't do this!" he pleaded.

"You did it, Tony. Now, about Orlando. I'm sure you realise that the kids and I don't want you there. What are your plans?"

He put his head in his hands and for a brief moment she felt sorry for him but she said nothing and waited to hear his reply.

"Can I talk to the kids? I'd like to hear it from them."

"If they'll talk to you. They're angry and hurt. It will take time for them to come around."

"At least let me try."

Ann called Jack's phone and told him what Tony wanted.

"Put him on," said Jack tersely.

She didn't hear what Jack said but it only took less than a minute. Tony sighed as he handed the phone back to her. He looked very dejected.

"What about Emily? Can I talk to her?"

Ann spoke into the phone. "Jack says she crying so much she can't talk."

Tony dropped his head into his hands and groaned.

"I guess I've blown it with you all. I'll fly home as soon as I can get a flight but I worry about you driving to Orlando. They drive on the right here. Maybe Jack should drive?"

"That would cost a fortune in insurance," she told him. "Don't worry about me. I can do it. I'll be fine."

He was taken aback. He didn't recognise this determined woman. "Well, I guess that's that. I better go."

He stood up and looked at her sadly, hoping for a reprieve. She met his look calmly.

"Here are your flight details," she said, taking his return boarding pass out of her bag. "You'll need these to change your flight."

"Oh, thanks." He hadn't even thought of that.

"Goodbye, Tony," she said and then she walked away.

He looked after her as if in a daze. What had he done? Why had he destroyed his life?

Ann called Jack and arranged to meet up. He told her that Sarah and Tarquin had arrived from the ship. They were all relieved that Tony had not insisted on coming with them. It would have made it very awkward.

"Do you want me to drive?" Jack offered when they reached the Car Rental office.

"Your father suggested that but, as I told him, the insurance would be very expensive. Don't worry! It's automatic transmission and I have GPS. What could be easier?"

Jack shook his head in amazement at the change in his mother.

They were in high spirits as they headed to Orlando, Ann firmly at the wheel. She had no problem driving and as the kids belted out songs she hummed along with them. Then they started singing Adele's songs and Sarah was surprised to find that Ann knew every word of them and sang along.

"How do you know these?" she asked Ann.

"Oh, I love Adele. I play her all the time when I'm doing housework or baking."

Sarah looked at Jack with raised eyebrows. He grinned back. Sarah wasn't the only one surprised. His mother never ceased to surprise him these days.

Cassie entered the hotel Declan was staying in with some trepidation. She dreaded coming face to face with him but it was something she knew she had to do. He was waiting in the lobby for her. He'd lost weight and looked gaunt and dishevelled. The old smooth, suave look was gone.

"Cassie, we need to talk. I need money for my legal team. I need you to transfer funds over here."

This is how he greets me? No 'How are you – are you okay? – I'm sorry – thanks for coming,' she thought. Selfish to the end.

"How much do you need?" she asked him.

"A hundred thousand dollars," he replied.

She gasped. "Do you have that much in your account?"

"Of course not, but you have," Declan retorted.

She couldn't believe it. The sheer brazenness of him took her breath away. Did he really expect her to cough up that kind of money?

"You're not getting a penny of my money. You got yourself in this mess, you can get yourself out of it," she told him calmly.

He raised his voice, almost shouting now. "*How could you do this to me? I need funds for my legal team here. I need your money!*"

She was aware that people had turned to look at them and was relieved when she saw a security man come closer. Declan looked like he might hit her. She let him rant on.

When he'd finished, she said calmly, "I'll transfer whatever money you have in your account. Let me know where to send it."

"*I don't believe this!*" he shrieked.

"We're done, Declan," Cassie said, getting to her feet. She was shaking with fury. Did he really expect her to pay his legal fees? She was beginning to wonder if she'd ever really known him. He was like a stranger to her now.

Calm and dignified, she walked out of the hotel, her

head held high.

Closure! She had it.

Ann's phone rang as she was unpacking in the hotel. It was Tony. He sounded very subdued.

"I'm just checking that you arrived in Orlando okay. I was worried about you driving."

"Yes, we're here. Everything went great. Where are you?"

"I'm at Miami airport. I'm boarding soon for Orlando and home from there."

"You had no trouble changing your flight?"

"No. The Aer Lingus staff were very helpful."

She sighed. "Have a good flight," she said.

"Thanks, Ann . . . and . . . I'm sorry for everything."

With that he hung up and Ann felt a sadness that surprised her.

# Chapter 28

Tony arrived back in Ireland the following morning. It was an overnight flight but while all around him slept he couldn't sleep a wink. All he could think of was what a fool he'd made of himself. His life was a shambles and, if Ann was serious about this divorce, then financially he'd be ruined. He would have to sell the house and as she was a director of the company that would cost him big-time too.

When he landed in Dublin he called his older brother, Alan, who was a barrister in Dublin. He was surprised to hear Tony was back in Ireland already.

"I thought you were staying on in Florida for a week," said Alan.

"Yeah, well, there's been a few problems."

"Are Ann and the kids with you?"

"No."

Alan straight away realised that something was wrong. "Look, come straight here to my house for lunch. I'll ask Trish to join us." Trish was their older sister who was a school principal there.

Tony knew it would be an inquisition and was not looking forward to it but the sooner he got this over with the better. He knew the shit was about to hit the fan.

"What do you mean Ann wants a divorce?" Trish stood with arms akimbo as she listened to what Tony had to say.

"Could I have a whiskey, Alan?" he asked, feeling like a schoolboy facing the headmistress.

"At eleven-thirty in the morning?" Trish demanded, eyebrows raised.

"I've a feeling we'll all need one shortly," Alan remarked, pouring a large whiskey for Tony. "Why does she want a divorce?"

"Well, I had a brief fling with a younger woman on the cruise and Ann found out about it."

"You can't be serious! Even *you* are not that stupid!" Trish exclaimed.

Tony had taken a few large gulps of the whiskey and found his courage returning. "Who are you to judge me?" he cried. "You, who have never had a moment's passion in your whole life!"

Trish looked affronted. "A whiskey please, Alan," she requested.

"Now, now, let's all calm down," Alan said, pouring a whiskey for her and one for himself. "Now start at the beginning," he ordered Tony.

Tony told them about Jess and what had transpired.

"I'm not surprised Ann wants a divorce," Trish commented.

"It's not just about Jess. Ann says I've bullied her and sapped her self-confidence for twenty-two years."

"Well, we all knew that," Trish remarked snidely.

"Just like you've done to your poor namby-pamby husband," Tony shot back at her.

"Now, now, let's stop this mud-slinging," Alan, ever the lawyer, intervened. "We're here to help Tony," he admonished his sister. She had the grace to look abashed.

"Okay, Tony, go on," she said, somewhat chastened.

"I've tried to reason with Ann but she won't listen. I don't recognise my own wife. She's completely changed. She says she's her own person now and she wants to be free," he told them, his voice anguished,

"Ah-ha! The worm has turned," Trish muttered.

Alan threw her a warning look.

"Do you love Ann? Do you want to stay married to her?" Alan asked.

"Of course. I just don't recognise her any more. She's become a real ball-breaker. I quite admire her, actually."

"Where is she now?" Trish wanted to know.

"In Orlando with the kids and it looks like they're having a great time without me." Tony looked downcast.

"Look, I know Ann," Trish said gently. "I don't think she'll give up on your marriage quite so easily. You'll just have to woo her back."

Tony was grateful for this little consolation. "You're right. I guess I'll have to change. Treat her better. I don't blame her. She's had to put up with a lot."

"You can say that again!" Trish couldn't resist adding.

"Right, that calls for another drink," Alan declared, pouring three more whiskies.

Ann made sure the week in Orlando was fun for all of them. They saw it all – all the parks, the shops and other attractions that the city had to offer. They were exhausted but happy every evening when they fell into bed.

Sarah was as good as her word and did a complete make-over on Ann who looked at least ten years younger with her new look. She loved it. She had never looked better and she was feeling on top of the world.

Sarah also took her and Emily shopping for clothes.

"Boy, can that girl shop!" Ann said to Jack over dinner that night.

"She could shop for Ireland," Emily giggled.

They were both extremely grateful to Sarah for their new looks and both had become very fond of her.

"You're quite a hit with my mother and sister," Jack teased her after they'd made love that night.

"That's good," she replied, smiling.

"You minx! You have us all wrapped around your little finger."

"Something I've wanted to ask you," she said as she lay beside him. "Why were you so horrid to me when we first met?"

He hesitated a few moments before answering. "Honestly? I thought you were one of those spoilt little rich girls that I've come across before. You know the type think they can have anyone and anything their little hearts desire."

"I have to admit I was like that once but I've changed. I'm not that kind of girl any more."

"I can see that. I think I'm good for you."

"You are."

"Then I guess I'll have to stick around," he murmured, caressing her head.

Tony woke with a feeling of apprehension in his stomach

and then he remembered that it was his birthday. The empty place in the bed beside him mocked him as he realised that he had in fact lost his best friend. What had he been thinking? How could he have imagined that Jess loved him. He was a fool and now he was paying for his mistakes.

The past few days since he'd got home had been very tough. The house felt empty without Ann and the kids. Without her it wasn't a home. He wondered was she even thinking of him today. Probably not. He was so unfocused at work that people were beginning to notice. His whole life was out of kilter.

Aside from that there were all the niggling domestic things that he suddenly had to do. When he went to wash his clothes on his return from Florida he did not know how to work the washing machine. He had to call his sister, Trish.

"I do not believe this!" she'd exclaimed. "You don't even know how to turn on the washing machine? Where have you been all your life?"

"I had a wife to do it for me," he'd snapped.

"Well, you don't now so you'd better learn fast," was her retort.

She tried to talk him through it but her supercilious manner annoyed him and he was short with her.

"Look, Tony, I suggest you look up the manual of the machine, if you can find it."

He banged down the phone on her. He did find the manual – Ann had everything filed away carefully so that was easy. He also had to read up on how to use the microwave but the oven and cooker were beyond him. As a result he ate cold or takeaway food all week. He hadn't realised just how many home comforts Ann had provided. He was lost without her.

He was feeling sorry for himself as he sat over a meagre breakfast of cornflakes and thought of the slap-up fry Ann always cooked for him on his birthday. Then the phone rang.

"Hello, Tony, it's Ann. I'm just calling to wish you a Happy Birthday."

Hearing her voice from so far away got to him and he broke down. Ann was shocked as she listened to him crying into the phone.

"Tony, are you okay? What's wrong?"

"Everything," he sobbed. "I should be there with you having a great birthday as you'd planned. I miss you so much, Ann. This house is empty without you. I know I did a terrible thing and I've treated you badly all these years but I'll make it up to you if you'll give me a chance. I promise. Please, Ann. I love you. Come home to me."

She listened, her heart breaking. She knew he meant what he was saying. She'd never heard him so humble. But it was too little, too late.

Ann knew that she didn't love him any more. And more to the point, she loved herself now. She had found an inner strength and self-respect. She would never give that up.

"I'm sorry, Tony, I really am, but it's too late. I can't do that. Goodbye."

She hung up the phone, feeling sad. That part of her life was over. It was time to move on.

Fiona and Gavin had arrived at Ciara's house to discover that she had been rushed to the hospital in labour.

"But the baby's not due for another three weeks," Gavin said.

"Babies come when they're ready," Fional told him, smiling. "I can see you have a lot to learn before June. Better get cracking."

They drove to the hospital just in time for the birth of Fiona's goddaughter-to-be. She was very happy that she'd made it in time. Ciara arranged to have the christening while they were there. It was a wonderful happy time – made all the more happy by Fiona's good news that she was also pregnant.

It was the perfect ending to their holiday.


Bunny and Richard didn't quite have the relaxing holiday that they'd envisaged. They arrived safely in Sarasota and were made feel very welcome by their friends there. Frank and Helen were old friends who spent summers in Dublin and winters in Florida. They lived in a private gated community that included membership of the golf club and country club and the house was like something you'd see in the movies. It was enormous with a large swimming pool under a screened lanai with a huge barbecue and seating for twenty people. Beyond was a garden that ran down to the water's edge where Frank's boat was moored.

That first evening Helen had arranged a welcome drinks party for them and had invited some neighbours and the Irish ex-pats that she had become friends with in the area. They were all tanned and healthy-looking and extolled the joys of winters in Florida.

In typical Irish style all the men gathered together around the bar while the women sat chatting around the pool.

"Isn't it time you retired, Richard?" Frank asked him. "You could be enjoying this lifestyle all winter away from grey Irish skies."

"I must say it has its attractions," Richard replied.

"My biggest regret is that I didn't do it much sooner," one of the other men confided.

"Gavin will keep the business going so what have you to lose?" Frank asked.

"The golf courses here are fantastic," another man said.

"Not to mention the cost of living. It's way cheaper to live here," Frank tried to persuade him.

"Yeah, I see your point," Richard conceded.

"Bunny would love it here. The women have a great social life, don't they, guys?" Frank asked the others.

"You bet!" they all agreed.

"None of us are getting any younger and now is the time to buy," advised Frank. "Prices are rising steadily."

"*Mmm . . .*" Richard said. They'd certainly given him food for thought. He knew Bunny was anxious for him to retire and she'd love the all-year-round sunshine. "I'll think about it," he told them.

At the same time the women were extolling the virtues of the area and Bunny decided that she absolutely had to persuade Richard to buy here. God knows their money was not earning anything sitting in a bank in Ireland.

By the end of the evening Richard had invitations to play golf for the whole seven days they planned to stay there. He was in his element. It didn't take long for Bunny to persuade him. He agreed to retire and told her to go look for a house.

At eight-thirty the following morning Bunny called the estate agent. She was a woman on a mission. She saw six houses the first day and the sixth one was IT. She fell in love with it the moment she laid eyes on it. It reminded her of the

Taj Mahal with its white marble facade and Doric columns. It was perfect. They signed the papers the next day and transferred the money from Ireland. Within five days they were the proud owners of a magnificent Florida home.

They had been due to fly back to Ireland on Sunday with Gavin and Fiona.

"Where's Bunny?" Fiona asked when they met Richard at the airport in Orlando.

"She's staying on. We just bought a house in Sarasota."

"You what?" Gavin cried.

"You heard. And not only that but I'm handing over the business to you. It's time I retired."

Gavin was flabbergasted. This was the last thing he'd expected. "Well, that's a shocker!"

"Congratulations!" Fiona said. "I think you're doing the right thing."

"I think so too. Bunny persuaded me. Your mother is a veritable virago when she puts her mind to something, Gavin!"

"She certainly is," he agreed.

Jess and Philip both agreed that this second honeymoon in Cuba was much better than their first had been. He was tender and caring and couldn't seem to get enough of her. The sex was better than it had ever been and she began to wonder if he was taking Viagra.

They both fell in love with Cuba and especially loved Havana where they stayed for five nights. It was vibrant and colourful and the music and dance were infectious, but mostly it was the smiling, friendly Cubans that stole their hearts.

They then moved out to the beach resort of Varadero

where they went scuba diving on the days they didn't spend lying on the beach or doing water-sports. It was idyllic.

They spent a magical night in the Tropicana outdoor cabaret extravaganza which was ten times better than the Moulin Rouge or Crazy Horse of Paris – and the girls more beautiful and exotic.

She called Bunny from the hotel the next day and was shocked and delighted to hear they'd bought a house in Sarasota and that her dad was retiring.

"How did you get Daddy to agree to retire?"

"After two weeks at sea and then the relaxing life here, he began to see that there was more to life than work," said Bunny smiling. "It was what I had in mind when I booked this holiday."

Jess couldn't but admire her mother's scheming mind. She certainly knew how to manipulate her husband. Women who could do that always seemed to get what they wanted. Jess took note. She remembered her mother saying once that it was better for a woman if her husband was a teeny bit more in love with her than she with him. Her mother was something else!

"And how are things with you two?" Bunny asked her and Jess could imagine the arched eyebrows as her mother said it.

"Great," Jess replied and Bunny was relieved to hear the happiness in her voice.

"And Mummy . . . thank you for bringing Philip to me."

"You don't have to thank me," Bunny replied, feeling justified. "Just remember – mothers *do* know best."

# Chapter 29

Ann and her charges made their way to Orlando airport where there was a last flurry of shopping for souvenirs to take back home. Tony had called to say he would pick them up at Dublin airport.

"No, no, we can take the train," Ann protested.

"No, I want to come," he insisted. "I'm so looking forward to seeing you."

"Tony, I'd prefer to take the train. If you could meet us at the station in Galway, that would be better. We're due in there at noon," Ann insisted.

Tony heard the steeliness in her voice and immediately pulled back.

"Of course, my dear, whatever you want. I'll meet you at the station."

"Then we'll have to discuss where we go from here. Which one of us will move out," she said, to clarify that things would not be going back to the way they had been.

Sarah was in a quandary. She had a business-class ticket but the Kennys were in economy. She went to the Aer Lingus desk to see if she could change her ticket to economy.

"I'm sorry, Miss, but we're fully booked. We have no available seat in economy for you."

Sarah was in a panic. She desperately wanted to be with Jack on the flight home. She needed to spend every available moment with him. The agent took pity on her when she explained the problem.

"Is there anyone in your party who would be willing to swap with you?" he asked.

"Maybe," she said, hoping that Ann would be willing to do it.

When Ann saw the state Sarah was in she quickly agreed to change. She'd never flown business-class before and it was an eye-opener. She relaxed in the wide comfortable seat sipping the champagne the nice stewardess offered her. Then she enjoyed the superb meal they offered and chose a current movie to watch before reclining her seat flat which allowed her to sleep the rest of the trip. She figured Sarah must really love Jack to have given up this luxury for the more cramped economy cabin.

Back in economy Sarah sat with her head on Jack's shoulder, their arms wrapped around each other. It would be back to reality for them both once they hit the ground. For the moment they treasured every minute they had left.

Tarquin and Emily were also feeling the pain of parting. Although their relationship was more slow-burning than Jack and Sarah's, it was none the less deep and genuine. Emily knew that she and Tarquin were destined for each other. He felt the same way but they had plenty of time. All of their lives in fact. They were both committed to their studies and determined to get good degrees. After that they would decide their future path.

Too soon for Sarah, they landed at Dublin Airport and it was time to say goodbye to Jack. They hugged and kissed and Sarah wanted to hang on to him forever.

"Remember every moment of every day that I love you," Jack whispered as he released her.

"I will and I'll be loving you too," she whispered back, trying to withhold the tears.

"I'll call you and we'll see each other soon," he promised, releasing her.

Just then Richard appeared and she was grateful to have him there. He hugged her, sensing how upset she was.

"How are you getting home, Tarquin?" Richard asked.

"I'll take a taxi," Tarquin replied.

"Nonsense! I'll drop you off."

"Are you sure, sir?"

"Absolutely! No trouble."

Then it was time for Emily to say goodbye to Tarquin.

He kissed her gently on the cheek then whispered in her ear.

"Thank you for everything. It's been wonderful. I'll call you this evening."

To everyone's surprise, the normally bashful Emily threw her arms around him and kissed him on the lips. "Thank you," she said, tears coming to her eyes.

Then it was goodbyes all round as they left, Sarah looking back at Jack until he was out of sight. She didn't know how she would survive until she saw him again.

Tony was waiting for them at Galway train station. Ann

could tell he was very nervous. Emily gave him a hug while Jack nodded coolly but made no effort to do any more. Ann was grateful that he didn't try to kiss or embrace her. She greeted him and noticed that his hands were shaking as he took her case.

"You look different," he observed as they headed for the car.

"Yes, doesn't she look marvellous?" asked Jack, who had overheard, his voice almost challenging his father to disagree.

"Yes indeed. You look wonderful, Ann," Tony said, his voice sincere.

"Thank you, Tony. I've had a bit of a conversion lately."

"You can say that again," Tony muttered under his breath. Luckily nobody else heard him as he piled the luggage into the car.

Tony had bought in ready-made meals from Marks and Spencer for lunch, for which Ann was grateful. After lunch Jack and Emily went out straight away to meet their friends. Tony offered to stay and help her unpack but she whooshed him back to work. She wasn't ready to have a serious talk just yet. When they had all left she busied herself unpacking and loading the washing machine. There was a lot of washing to be done.

Tony had offered to take them out to dinner that evening but after three weeks of restaurant food Ann was longing for a home-cooked meal and insisted they eat at home. Tony acquiesced without a murmur.

The first thing she did was call her sister, Rose, in Dublin, hoping that she would keep her mother for a while longer until she and Tony sorted things out. She knew her mother would be dead-set against a divorce and the last thing Ann needed was her interference.

To her amazement, Rose told her that her mother had decided to stay on in Dublin. "She's happy here. She takes the bus into the city every day – she's in there now and she loves that there's so much to do there, unlike the country."

Ann could hear that Rose was gloating.

"We'll have to build on a granny flat for her, of course, but she's agreed to sell her house in Galway to pay for it."

Ann realised that was the reason Rose was willing to take her mother in but she was too tired to object. She had enough on her plate at the moment. Maybe it was for the best.

She went shopping then as there was no food in the house and made a shepherd's pie for dinner which was heavenly after all the rich food they had been eating.

After dinner the kids went to their rooms and she and Tony were alone. Ann couldn't put it off any longer. It was time for the big talk.

She had lit a big fire in the den and they retired there.

"What would you like to drink?" Tony asked. "A cognac perhaps?"

"A glass of wine will be fine."

He handed her the glass and she noticed he'd poured a large whiskey for himself. He was obviously as nervous as she was.

"Can I say you are looking wonderful," Tony started. "That hairstyle really suits you. You look ten years younger."

"Thank you," she replied calmly. "I feel it."

"Maybe this can be a new start for us, Ann."

"It certainly is, Tony. I'm going to see a solicitor tomorrow about our divorce. We have a lot of decisions to make about our future."

"Will you not reconsider, Ann?" he begged, the whiskey in his glass threatening to spill due to his shaking hand.

"Tony, please let's not make this more difficult than it already is. Our marriage is over and I hope we can be civilized about it for the children's sake."

Devastated as he was, Tony couldn't help but admire the woman his wife had become. It was a shame that she had to get rid of him to achieve it.

Gavin was very busy in the office, readying himself to take over as head of the company. Richard was meeting with solicitors and accountants in preparation for stepping down. He would remain on the Board as a non-active director. He had every confidence in Gavin and was now eager to hand over as soon as possible. He could hardly believe how quickly things had happened. But as they all kept telling him – life was short and he wasn't getting any younger. He was ready to embrace this new phase of his life.

Fiona had invited Cassie along with Richard and Sarah to dinner on Saturday night. She was looking forward it.

On Friday afternoon she and Gavin went to the hospital for her first scan. They were both a little apprehensive in case things were not all right.

Gavin held Fiona's hand and watched the screen with bated breath as the sonographer started the scan. Soon they got their first glimpse of their baby. It was very emotional as the lady moved the device around Fiona's stomach explaining what everything was.

"Everything's fine – oh!"

"What is it?" Gavin and Fiona cried together, fearing something was wrong.

"There's more than one baby here," she beamed at them. "You're having twins."

"Oh my goodness," Fiona gulped, staring at the screen.

"Yes, see here," the sonographer pointed out. "This little one was hiding behind the other."

They gazed mesmerised as their babies moved around. They were elated.

"Two for the price of one!" Gavin exclaimed, squeezing Fiona's hand.

"Are you sure they're both okay?" Fiona asked nervously.

"They're perfect," the lady replied, smiling. "Congratulations!"

"I can hardly take it in," Fiona admitted as they left the hospital, the photo of their babies clutched tightly in her hand. "Let's not tell anyone yet. It will be our secret for a while – until I get as big as a house anyway."

"You heard what the lady said – you're amazingly small considering it's twins."

"That won't last long," Fiona smiled ruefully.

Fiona went shopping that evening and on Saturday morning set about preparing for her dinner party. She was really looking forward to seeing Cassie again. She had invited them for six-thirty.

Cassie was the first to arrive, armed with a bottle of wine and one of the paintings she'd done on the boat. "To remind you of our cruise," she said as she greeted Fiona with a kiss. "My but you're blooming!" she exclaimed, standing back to look at Fiona. "Pregnancy suits you."

"Thank you. And thanks for this lovely painting."

Fiona held it up for Gavin to see. It was of the Caribbean. "It's beautiful."

Gavin kissed Cassie and thanked her for the painting. "It's so realistic. I almost feel like I'm back there," he said, admiring it.

They ushered her in and she had just accepted a drink from Gavin when Richard and Sarah arrived.

They had a lovely evening and Richard gave them the news from Bunny about the house. "She will Skype us later."

"Bet you're glad you're not there for all the hoopla," Gavin said.

"You bet. But I'm dying to see how Bunny has furnished it."

"I'm sure it will be lovely," said Fiona. "She has such exquisite taste."

"So how is Jack getting on, Sarah?" Gavin asked.

"Great. He's coming up next weekend. I can't wait." Her eyes were aglow, a fact not lost on the others.

"Young love," Fiona nodded to Cassie.

"Ah, enjoy it while you can," Cassie replied, trying not to sound bitter. She remembered how much in love she'd been with Declan at that age.

"How is the Captain?" asked Gavin.

Cassie blushed. "He's fine. He's thinking of coming to Ireland later in the year."

"We must all get together then," Richard suggested.

"He'd like that," said Cassie, smiling.

"I have some good news," Sarah announced. "I've been signed by the top model agency in Dublin. They want me to start work straight away."

"What?" Gavin cried, looking at his father. "Did you

know about this?"

"She just told me on the way here. It was a surprise to me too."

"What about your college studies?" Fiona asked.

"I hate studying. I only went to college for the social scene and all of a sudden it bores me. It's so childish. I want to start earning my own money."

Gavin and his father were taken aback but Sarah seemed determined.

"After all, Mummy was a model and Jess did very well too. Why not me?"

"It's hard work," Gavin warned her.

She jutted out her chin. "So? I'm not afraid of hard work."

This was a Sarah none of them had seen before.

"Does Bunny know?"

"Not yet. I'm planning to tell her when she Skypes us. I think she'll be pleased. She wanted me to do modelling."

They hoped she was right or all hell would break loose.


Bunny Skyped them at ten.

There was great *oohing* and *aahing* as she walked around the house with her iPad, pointing out what she'd done.

"It's fabulous," Sarah squealed. "Just fabulous." She was delighted when she saw her huge bedroom.

"This is yours, Gavin and Fiona. You've got the biggest one, obviously," Bunny told them. "Plenty of room for a cot here too."

Gavin and Fiona exchanged amused glances. Enough room for two, they were both thinking.

"Well done, darling," said Richard, delighted with how

his wife had furnished the house. "You are a marvel. I can't wait to come out and see it all for myself."

"Yes, I've been a busy bee," Bunny admitted.

"So when can I come out?" Sarah wanted to know.

"For your Easter college break," said Bunny.

"Well, eh . . . that's the thing, Mummy . . . eh . . . I've decided to leave college. Topflite Models have signed me up so I'm going to give modelling a go."

For once Bunny was speechless. Sarah had taken the wind out of her sails.

Finally, she said, "Are you sure about this, Sarah? I thought you love being at Trinity."

"Not any more. I've grown up, Mummy. I want to start earning my own money. I start with them next Monday."

"Well, what can I say?" Bunny exclaimed. "If you're sure about this then go for it, girl."

While Gavin went to open a bottle of champagne to toast the new house, Bunny had a chat with Cassie. Then, after raising their champagne glasses to her, they signed off.

# Chapter 30

Jess was worried. She had missed her period and she had always been as regular as clockwork. She checked her dates over and over but there was no mistaking it – she was overdue. She hoped that it was all the travelling that had caused it but the second morning that she got out of bed and had to run to the bathroom to throw up, she feared the worst. She couldn't actually vomit but just retched for what seemed like forever. She'd been on the pill but she was lackadaisical about taking it and often forgot.

It wasn't that she didn't want a baby but she was terrified that Tony might be the father. She couldn't bring herself to tell Philip. On the flight back to London he had told her that he was thinking of moving his business to Dublin.

"I know it's always been your wish to move back there and now with Brexit it makes sense. Lots of companies are relocating. Why not Ireland?"

This was what Jess had always wanted and she was

grateful to Philip but the fear that she might be carrying another man's child left her unable to even think about that. What would happen if it was Tony's? How would Philip react? He'd leave her, for sure – just when they'd found each other again. She was devastated.

The first thing she did when she got home was to buy a pregnancy test – the one that told you how many weeks pregnant you were. It was positive and showed she was two to three weeks pregnant. That meant that either Tony or Philip could be the father. Would God be so cruel as to make it Tony's?

She called her mother.

"Whose baby is it?" Bunny asked fearfully.

"I don't know," Jess admitted. "It could be Philip's or it could be –"

"*Don't even say it!*" Bunny shrieked. "It couldn't possibly be his, could it?"

She was horrified. What a calamity that would be!

"I don't know," Jess replied wearily. "It's a possibility."

"My God! How did you get yourself in this mess?" Bunny cried. "What will you do? Will you get an abortion?"

Now it was Jess's turn to be horrified. "How could you even suggest such a thing?" she cried. "This is *my* baby, regardless of who the father is and I don't intend to kill it." Suddenly she felt an overwhelming bond with this little speck that was growing inside her.

"What will you tell Philip?"

"I'll tell him the truth, what else?" Jess replied.

She knew she had to do that and then it was up to him. She was terrified of what he might do. Either way she'd know soon enough.

"It will be okay," Bunny tried to reassure Jess. "After all, it could be his baby," she added hopefully. "And, Jess . . . I'm proud of you that you're keeping this baby regardless. You know your dad and I will support you."

Jess had tears in her eyes as she prepared to hang up. "Thanks, Mummy," she whispered. "And please, don't tell anyone else except Dad. I don't want them to know yet."

"Don't worry. Your secret is safe with us."

She sat waiting for Philip to come home from work.

"Philip, I have to talk to you," said Jess as he took her in his arms and kissed her.

He saw the look in her eyes and was afraid she had changed her mind about him. He became panicked when he saw she was crying.

"What is it, my darling?" he asked, taking her hands in his. "Have you changed you mind?"

"No. I'm pregnant, Philip," she said quietly.

The joy in his face made the next part even more difficult.

"Jess, that's —"

"Stop! I'm not finished," she said nervously. "I'm not sure it's your baby. It could be – but it could also be . . . you know . . ." she tailed off lamely.

"Did you love him?" he asked, his voice quiet.

"Not at all. I love you." The tears were sliding down her cheeks and he brushed them away gently.

"Then that's all that matters, isn't it?" he murmured. "I love you too and I'll pray that this baby is mine. If not, well, I'll love it because it's yours. Okay?"

She collapsed into his arms, relief flooding her body. "What did I do to deserve you?" she asked him.

Jess could not believe how he was taking this. She prayed like never before that this baby was his. She had to think positive. If it wasn't then she would have to let Tony know he had a child and she would be tied to him for the rest of her life. She called her mother to tell her how Philip had taken it.

"What a lucky girl you are to have such a wonderful husband," Bunny declared.

"I realise how lucky I am," Jess admitted humbly. "And I do love him very much."

Sadly, Ann's hopes of having a civilized divorce did not materialise. It took a lot of persuading by the kids and his family and his solicitor to get Tony to move out of the house. He would have insisted on staying but he was warned that he might lose the company if he did so.

Jack told Ann that he would be moving to Dublin after his final exams. His band had secured an agent who had got them a record deal and was lining up gigs for them. That meant that he and Sarah could move in together.

Emily also announced that she would like to transfer to Trinity College to finish her studies, so she would also be moving to Dublin. She admitted that Tarquin was the main reason for this.

What could Ann do? Her children were adults now and it was time for them to fly the nest. It was decided that they would put the house up for sale. Ann would buy a smaller place for herself once the divorce was through. She didn't need a big house any more. She would also benefit substantially from her share of the business which she would sell to Tony.

The future was looking bright for her.

# all at sea

She and Nina kept in touch by Skype and her friend was as supportive as ever. In early February Nina called to say that Paul had passed away. He'd come down with pneumonia after they'd got home and had not recovered.

"I miss him terribly even though we both did our own thing. The nights are the worst," she confided.

On the spur of the moment Ann invited her to come to Ireland for a visit.

"That would be wonderful," Nina replied. "What will Tony think of that?"

"Tony? Tony who?" Ann asked and they both convulsed with laughter.

"Girl, you're a tonic," Nina remarked when she'd stopped laughing. "I'd love to come. How does September suit you?"

"Perfect! It's the best time and I'll take you around and show you the real Ireland."

"You've lifted my spirits no end," Nina confessed. "And now I have that trip to look forward to. Thank you, Ann, I'm very grateful."

"I'm the one who should be thanking you. You changed my life," Ann replied.

And indeed her life had changed. She was taking much more interest in her appearance now and had her hair done every week. She also visited the beauty salon regularly and had updated her wardrobe. She signed up for golf lessons and a bridge course for beginners and was thinking of enrolling in a French course at the University.

When Tony heard this he became apoplectic. He complained to his sister Trish about it but got little sympathy from her.

"That woman has taken care of you – and God knows

369

that can't have been easy – for twenty-two years, gave you two lovely children, raised them, helped you with the business and pandered to your every need. Then you repay her by having an affair with a floosie –"

"Jess wasn't a floo –"

"Shut up, Tony! I'm surprised Ann didn't divorce you years ago. You're finally getting what you deserve."

As always, he banged the phone down on her. Imagine being married to that ball-breaker. He should have treasured Ann. He could have been married for twenty-two years to someone like his sister!

Cassie was happy with her life. She had a great support team around her: her father first and foremost, then Julie and Fiona and of course Dimitri. She'd introduced Julie to Fiona and they'd become firm friends. The three girls met often for brunch at the weekend.

Cassie had no idea what was happening with Declan. She refused to answer his calls and had deleted him from her Facebook page. She did receive some emails from him but she deleted them without even reading them. He was her past. She was now living in the present.

Dimitri called every Sunday night and they sometimes stayed talking for the best part of an hour. She could tell he was lonely but was surprised when he mentioned he was considering retiring. He was only forty-two years old but the years on the sea had taken their toll.

One Sunday night she answered the phone, expecting it to be Dimitri.

It wasn't – it was Declan.

"Don't hang up, Cassie. This is important."

She heard the urgency in his voice and waited to hear

what he had to say.

"I want to know what's happening with our divorce?"

"Well, it's in the pipeline," she answered him cagily, wondering where this was going. "I'm waiting for a court date."

"Is there any chance you could hurry it up?"

She was taken aback. "Why?"

"I've met someone else, my attorney actually, and want to get married as soon as possible."

Cassie could hardly believe her ears. Was there no end to this man's base behaviour? She felt like laughing.

"Trust me, Declan, I want a divorce even more than you do but your new lady friend will have to wait. Please give her my sympathies."

She hung up on him and then did start to laugh. What neck! And what a lucky escape she'd had.

When Dimitri called a short time later she told him about Declan's call. He was equally astounded at her soon-to-be ex-husband's nerve.

The following day she called her father and Fiona and Julie. They were all equally shocked by Declan's audacity.

Cassie was now determined to get rid of this snake-in-the-grass as soon as possible. It couldn't happen quickly enough for her. She asked her father if he would be able to pull strings.

Thankfully he was and two weeks later Cassie had her day in court. Her father accompanied her and she left court skipping – much like Nicole Kidman after her divorce from Tom Cruise – waving her decree nisi in her hands. Free at last!

Philip was as loving and supportive as ever but Jess couldn't relax. It was eating her up not knowing whether the baby was his or Tony's. She had found out online that there was a new non-invasive DNA Paternity test which could determine the paternity of her baby once she was eight weeks pregnant. She felt she had to know. When she told Philip about it he insisted that they take the test. He felt quite sure the baby was his. Jess waited anxiously as the weeks passed and tried to hide her worry from him. He accompanied her to the clinic where blood samples were taken from both of them. The results would take ten days. It was an agonising ten days for Jess. He understood her concern and told her time and time again that it didn't matter to him. But it mattered to Jess.

He stayed home with her on the tenth day and they were sitting together watching TV when the call came. Jess saw the name of the clinic on her phone but her hands started to shake and she almost dropped it.

Her mouth was so dry she could barely talk. Philip held her other hand tightly as she waited to hear the result.

"Are you sure? Absolutely sure?" he heard her ask.

She started to cry and his heart sank but then he saw that she was smiling through the tears.

"Thank you. Thank you so much," she said to the voice delivering the news.

She turned to Philip, her face radiant with happiness. "It's yours! The baby is yours!" she cried exultantly before she collapsed into his arms.

He swung her round then as they laughed and cried together. Tears of joy and relief. Such relief for Jess. Now she could at last move on and enjoy her pregnancy.

She called Bunny right away and gave her the good news. It was only 5 a.m. in Sarasota but Bunny didn't mind. She was delighted and also much relieved.

"Another grandchild! How blessed am I?" she cried. "I'm so happy for you, sweetie, and how it's all turned out. Give Philip a big hug from me."

# Chapter 31

When Bunny heard that Captain Dimitri was coming to Dublin for a visit, she proposed that they throw a party for him.

A week later when Ann called her to say that Nina was coming to Ireland for a holiday and would be here the same week as the Captain, it seemed like an omen. The perfect opportunity to get everyone together again for a Cruise Reunion Party. It would be almost nine months since that trip which had changed so many of their lives.

Life had certainly changed for Gavin and Fiona. She had a wonderful pregnancy, mainly due to the fact that she was so fit and lived a healthy lifestyle. She gained some weight but it was all baby weight and she felt as good as she ever had.

She and Gavin had prepared the nursery with two of everything for the new arrivals. The babies arrived, a boy and a girl, with very little fuss, two weeks before they were due. Nothing mattered to Fiona – not their sex, nor how they looked – as long as they were healthy. And they were both healthy and beautiful and Fiona fell in love with them the first moment she held them. Other mothers had told her how she would feel but nothing prepared her for the indescribable love she felt for these two perfect little beings.

She was thrilled that her sister, Ciara, had made it home in time from Orlando for their birth. Fiona found it hard to believe that her goddaughter, Aisling, who was now a bouncing six-month-old, was once little bigger than the twins. Her daughter, Aifric, was a quiet and delicate little girl whereas Oran, her son, was strong and robust, always pumping his fists and legs and constantly hungry. His lusty cries could be heard all over the house when it was time for a feed.

Fiona was very excited about meeting everyone again at the Cruise Reunion. She told Bunny she would be bringing the twins with her. To be honest, she couldn't bear to be away from them for five seconds.

Jess was one of those women who bloom in pregnancy and she was very excited about the imminent birth of her child. Philip joined in her excitement as they counted down the weeks.

True to his word, he had relocated the business to Dublin. The nine months had flown as they sold their house in London and bought a lovely Georgian house by the sea in Killiney. Jess was delighted to be back in her native Dublin and happy that her baby would be born here. The Irish way of life seemed to suit Philip and he was more relaxed and happy than he'd ever been in London. So was she.

Their marriage had gone from strength to strength and this baby had cemented it further. Jess was so glad that she'd faced the music and put their minds at rest about the paternity. She couldn't have survived the nine months not knowing. Now they could welcome their baby together with joy. She had never been happier.

Philip was over the moon about becoming a father and was already talking about having another one next year. He treated Jess like a princess and still felt stricken when he thought how close he'd come to losing her.

He thanked God that everything had worked out for them. He was a very lucky man.

Sarah and Jess had become much closer since Jess moved to Dublin. Sarah was shocked when she heard that her sister was pregnant. She worried that Tony might be the father and was relieved, when they met for lunch one day, and Jess told her that Philip was indeed the father.

"Can I ask you something?" Sarah lowered her voice. "Were you not afraid the baby was Tony's?"

"Terrified," Jess replied, throwing her eyes to heaven. "I was shitting bricks until I had the paternity test that confirmed Philip was the father."

"I'm so glad he is," Sarah observed, mightily relieved. She knew Jack had been worried that Jess's baby might be his half-brother. Now she could let him know that wasn't the case.

Jack had passed his finals and, as planned, he moved to Dublin with his band – and also to be with Sarah. He had decided to give music a year. If the band hadn't made it by then he would look for a job in engineering. He knew the band was good and they were already attracting lots of followers who turned up to every gig. The band was also causing quite a stir in music circles and as their popularity grew so the gigs increased. They had been booked to play on the *Graham Norton Show* in October and he was very excited about that. He and Sarah were still madly in love and had moved in together to a small apartment in Baggot Street that she had found for them.

Her modelling career had taken off like a rocket and she was now the latest 'IT' girl in Dublin. She was very much in demand and her photo could be seen in every newspaper and magazine. She was getting invitations to every opening, party and function in Dublin and further afield. She knew they wanted her – not for herself – but for the publicity she would garner. It was a very fickle world. She turned most of them down, preferring to spend her evenings with Jack, and typically, the more she shunned them the more desirable she became.

Jack thought this was funny. "It's the Greta Garbo syndrome," he explained. "The more she said she wanted to be alone, the more they wanted her."

Sarah was surprised that he knew who Greta Garbo was. He never ceased to surprise her.

The good thing was that the more in demand she became, the more money she could command. Initially, she and Jack joined a dance club which they enjoyed but as both their careers took off there was less and less time to go.

Sarah went as often as she could to his gigs and tried not to feel jealous at the women who were obviously there just for Jack.

"Hey, you don't have to worry about any of those groupies," he'd assured her. "I love you. We have to trust each other. You're also in a job where you're meeting guys who fancy you all the time. It goes with the territory. But as long as we love each other and stay honest with each other, that's all that matters. Nobody else will ever come between us."

She loved him then. Their life was perfect.

Ann had never been happier. She had her divorce no thanks to Tony who had fought her every step of the way. She was now quite a wealthy woman. The house had sold very quickly for a very good price and Ann decided to move to Dublin. Her mother and siblings were there and now Jack and Emily too. It made sense. She would miss her beloved Galway but she could always go back to visit. It meant she didn't have to worry about running into Tony whenever she went out for a drink with her friends. She'd heard he was drinking heavily and she didn't want to have anything to do with him. It was better this way.

She decided to rent for a year to make sure she would settle there but within a month she knew she'd made the right decision.

Emily and Tarquin had both gone to Munich to work for the summer and Emily would move in with her when she got back but would probably spend a couple of nights a week at Tarquin's apartment. Emily had gained in confidence and was excited about going to Trinity. They were both still concentrating on their studies. She and Tarquin were very much in love and Ann was delighted to see them so happy.

Ann continued with her golf lessons and also her bridge in Dublin. She enrolled in a French course at the Alliance Francaise and was loving it. She also volunteered with Oxfam and was making friends at all these activities. Yes, life was good.

Nina arrived in early September and she and Ann set off on a tour of Ireland. Nina loved everything she saw and Ann was proud to show her what Ireland had to offer. They settled into the easy relationship that had started on the cruise and they arrived back the weekend before the Cruise Reunion. They were looking forward to seeing everyone again.

Ann knew Jess would be there and that her baby was due any day. She'd been very concerned when she'd heard Jess was pregnant, afraid it might be Tony's. The last thing her kids needed was a sibling born out of that mess. It was with relief that she learnt from Jack that Jess had taken a paternity test and that the baby was Philip's. She was happy for Jess. What a catastrophe for her if it had been Tony's! That would surely have destroyed her marriage.

Like Ann, Cassie's divorce had given her a new lease of life. Happy to be rid of her sleaze-bag husband, she had embraced her freedom with gusto. She kept busy and her jewellery line was booming thanks to an interview she did on morning TV. She'd also had another exhibition of her paintings and the ones she'd done on the cruise had sold like hot-cakes.

She and Fiona met up once a week and their friendship was stronger than ever. She enjoyed throwing a baby shower for Fiona and it was good to meet the other McElroy girls again.

When all the other guests had left, Cassie sat chatting with them.

"What about Declan?" Sarah, not known for her subtlety, had asked as they sipped champagne.

You could have heard a pin drop as everyone looked at Cassie.

"Well, as you probably heard, in March he called and

said he wanted a divorce from me in a hurry as he wanted to marry his attorney. Naturally I obliged and rushed it through."

"Did he? Marry her, I mean?" Jess asked.

"Yes, shortly afterwards. Unfortunately, it didn't help him."

They were all agog now. Only Fiona knew the story.

"What happened?" asked Bunny.

"She mustn't have been very good at her job," Cassie stated calmly. "Because she didn't get him acquitted. Declan is now serving fifteen years in jail for the manslaughter of Alix Lynch."

They all gasped in shock.

"Well, I never!" exclaimed Sarah.

"Justice is served," declared Bunny, smiling.

"To Justice!" Cassie raised her glass in a toast and they all joined in heartily.

And then there was Dimitri . . . He was a constant in her life and she now felt free to start a relationship with him. His phone calls had become more frequent and lasted longer and when he asked if he could come and visit her in September, she gladly agreed.

They made love the first night and it was like coming home for Cassie. He was gentle and loving and it didn't take long for her to fall in love with him. He had already told her that he was in love with her and wanted to marry her.

"Let's take it slowly," she'd laughed. "We have plenty of time. All our lives."

This is how things stood as they prepared for the Reunion party.

# Chapter 32

It was the best party any of them remembered. Bunny thought it was because they'd all got to know each other so well and had been through so much together on the cruise. Even so, there were a lot of happy endings.

The first to arrive at the party were Fiona and Gavin, carrying the twins in their little baby seats. Bunny and Richard, the very proud grandparents, gushed over them.

Next to arrive were Jess and Philip and Bunny thought that Jess had never looked more beautiful. She was literally blooming and it was wonderful to see the tenderness with which Philip watched over her. They were both very excited about the upcoming birth of their baby and it was obvious that they were in love.

Thank God for that, Bunny thought.

Jess made a beeline for the twins, admiring them as she tried to imagine what it would be like to hold her own baby in her arms.

Then Ann and Nina arrived to a warm welcome.

"Ann, how are you?" Bunny said, kissing her. They'd met regularly since Ann had moved to Dublin. "And Nina, so great to see you again. I hope you enjoyed your tour of Ireland."

"Thank you for inviting me," Nina replied, "and yes, it was wonderful. Ann was a great tour guide."

"I'm sure she was," Bunny said, smiling. "What a pity Emily and Tarquin couldn't be here today, Ann."

"Yes. They almost made it. They're still in Munich and will be home next Friday for the start of the college year."

"You know everyone here so go on in," Bunny suggested as the doorbell rang again. "We'll join you in a moment."

When Ann entered the living-room the first person she saw was Jess who spotted her and waved, then came to meet her.

"Hello, Ann. It's good to see you. I'm glad you could come," she said, shaking her hand. "And you too, Nina – how nice that you're here for it."

"Yes, it will be lovely to see everyone again," Nina replied.

Just then Philip appeared and put his arm around his wife's waist protectively.

"Let me introduce my husband, Philip," said Jess. "I don't think you've met him." The look on Jess's face when she spoke his name said it all.

He shook hands with them, smiling. He and Jess made a beautiful couple.

"Congratulations are in order, I believe," noted Ann. "You're going to have a baby soon."

"Yes, we're over the moon about it," Philip replied.

"I'm very happy for you both," Ann said, smiling. "You look wonderful, Jess."

"Thank you, Ann. You look great too. I love the hair."

"Thanks. And you look glowing. I don't know how you do it."

It was true. Jess looked sensational for a woman about to give birth.

"I looked like a hippo when I was pregnant with Jack and Emily," Ann confessed, looking rueful.

They all laughed at her description.

"Are you having a boy or a girl?" Nina asked.

"We don't know. We want it to be a surprise," Jess admitted.

"It doesn't matter what sex it is, as long as the baby is healthy," Philip told them.

Sarah and Jack burst into the room just then. There were hugs and noisy hellos as they greeted everyone.

"Hi, Sis, you look great," Sarah said, kissing her sister. "Not long now."

"No, thank God. I think it'll never come."

Sarah made a beeline for the twins and cooed over the them, making baby noises. She asked if she could lift Aifric who was her goddaughter.

"Go on, but I'm not going to let you spoil her," Fiona warned her.

Sarah lifted the baby gently out of her chair.

"Isn't she beautiful?" she said to Jack.

"Don't tell me you're getting broody?" he asked nervously.

"God no! Don't be daft! We've plenty of time for that."

Jack was relieved. He did want to have children someday, with Sarah, but not just yet. They had so much living to do before that.

The party was in full swing when suddenly Bunny clapped

her hands. They looked around.

"I give you Captain Dimitri of the *Liberté!*" Bunny announced dramatically, her arms outstretched.

"No, no, please! I *am* off-duty," Dimitri protested, grinning widely as he entered to loud applause.

He hadn't been expecting this. He'd thought he'd been invited to a family Sunday lunch.

Cassie was standing behind him, smiling happily as she gave little waves to her friends.

Richard introduced him to the Kennys and Nina, who he hadn't met before.

"You were all on my ship and I didn't meet you?" he said, sounding surprised. "Shame on me!"

"And this is my daughter, Sarah, and her boyfriend, Jack," Richard said proudly.

"Ah, I know you!" Dimitri admired the young beauty before him. "You won the dance competition. You are a wonderful dancer."

He took her hand and kissed it and she gave him a dazzling smile.

"And you too, Jack," he added. "I wish I could dance the rumba like you. It was very passionate. Now I see why." He winked as he nodded at Sarah.

"Thank you, Captain."

"Dimitri – please. I really am off duty. And you met on board my ship? I think I should rename it *The Love Boat* with all the romance that's happened there."

They found him utterly charming as he moved around the room and chatted to one and all, Cassie always by his side.

Finally, they came to Fiona and Gavin.

"Congratulations!" he exclaimed, kissing her and

shaking Gavin's hand. "I'm sorry I couldn't be here for their christening but Cassie told me all about it."

They greeted Cassie with a kiss. She'd had dinner with them the previous week and they both knew how excited she was to see Dimitri again. It was obvious now as she stood with his arm around her shoulder that they were very happy together.

"Now where are these babies? I want to meet them," he demanded.

Fiona pointed to the two chairs where the babies were sleeping peacefully, looking angelic.

"They're so tiny," Dimitri said in a hushed voice as he bent down to stroke their cheeks. "You must be very proud," he said enviously.

"We are," Fiona and Gavin replied in unison.

Like all Bunny's parties it was a great success and after a splendid lunch they all discussed how much their lives had changed in the six months.

"I think that cruise was a catalyst for all of us," Bunny acknowledged.

"For me too," Dimitri declared. "I met my future wife on that cruise." He grinned mischievously. "Will you tell them, Cassie?"

She blushed shyly. "Dimitri has asked me to marry him and I said yes."

There were cheers and clapping as Richard ordered the waiter to bring some champagne.

They toasted Cassie and Dimitri and wished them every happiness.

"The *Liberté* is sailing to Mexico next Christmas," Dimitri said, "and we're planning to get married there.

We'd love you all to join us on the cruise and celebrate our wedding with us – babies and all –" He nodded at Fiona and Jess.

"That would be wonderful – we'd really like you all to consider it," Cassie said, looking around at them all hopefully.

"Another Christmas cruise on the *Liberté*?" Bunny gasped. "Would we ever survive it?"

"We survived the last one," Richard reminded her.

The others all nodded vigorously. It was true.

"Why not?" Bunny succumbed. "Hands up who's interested?"

Every hand in the room went up.

"Well, I guess that's that! Mexico, here we come!"

## THE END

*Also by Poolbeg.com*

# The Birthday Girls

## Pauline Lawless

They'd met on their first day at school – four little girls
who were very different from each other but who somehow
became close friends. Their friendship has now lasted thirty-
five years. As their birthdays all fall in the same week they
long ago made a pact to spend each big decade birthday
together. So far they've managed it.

Now as their thirty-ninth birthday looms, Angel, a famous
Hollywood actress, announces that this will be her last
birthday. Terrified of aging, she absolutely refuses to turn
forty. So Lexi, the mother hen of the group and an artist,
invites them to Florida for a week-long celebration of this,
their last birthday together.

Brenda, mother to five grown-up children, flies in from
Dublin, eagerly looking forward to her first foreign holiday
ever. Mel, however, has to be prised away from New York
where she is a successful partner in a law firm – Mel is a
workaholic with no other friends or love in her life.
The four come together for the celebration but soon things
start to unravel and the week ends disastrously. Lexi is
distraught.

Can their friendship endure? Only time will tell.

ISBN 978184-223-5492

*Also by Poolbeg.com*

# *Meet*
## *and*
# *Delete*

## Pauline Lawless

"No more meeting crappy men in crappy pubs! Online dating is the modern way to meet Mr Right," declares Viv to her two friends and housemates. All three are in their mid-thirties and have been unlucky in love. "Out of every ten replies I'll probably get two perverts, two nerds, two frauds – usually married – and four genuine guys. Not a bad percentage really."

Claire is apprehensive about it and Megan downright sceptical but Viv, with her usual joie de vivre, takes to it with gusto. Many men and many dates later – from the boring to the bizarre – Viv thinks she has found her Mr Right. But does the course of true love ever run smooth?

Meanwhile she coerces a doubtful Claire into joining the dating site too. Add to this mix Claire's nasty sister Sarah who, bored with marriage, embraces online-dating with even more enthusiasm than Viv.
Not to mention Megan's thrice-married mother who's looking for a toy boy not a husband . . .

Is online dating the answer for all these women?
Read on and find out!

ISBN 978178-199-9998

e Book available

*Also by Poolbeg.com*

# If the Shoes Fit

## Pauline Lawless

'*Calling All Shoe Addicts*', said the advertisement that triggered a response in four very different women, each at a difficult time of her life.

**Niamh,** at 23, the mother of a five-year-old and twin girls aged four, is desperate to have a home of her own. She longs to escape the house of her vicious mother-in-law but her charming, irresponsible husband and the mountain of debts they have makes this seem ever more unlikely.

**Amber,** former air stewardess whose husband Dermot left her for a younger woman, has lost all her confidence and is drowning her sorrows with alcohol.

**Tessa,** beautiful former model, paid the price for living life in the fast lane when she almost died from a heart attack. Her reliable friend, George, persuaded her to come and live with him in Ireland. She now realises that she's made a dreadful mistake.

**Rosie,** recently widowed, can't come to terms with the loss of the man she loved so much. Life without him doesn't seem worth living.

All of them, needing a way out, find it with the Italian designer shoe company, '*If The Shoes Fit*'. This leads them to a new career, great friendships and a life-changing experience.

ISBN 978184-223-3887